The K Handshape

MAUREEN JENNINGS

A CHRISTINE MORRIS MYSTERY

The K Handshape

A Castle Street Mystery

THE DUNDURN GROUP
TORONTO

Editor: Barry Jowett
Copy-editor: Marja Appleford
Design: Jennifer Scott
Printer: Webcom

Library and Archives Canada Cataloguing in Publication

Jennings, Maureen
    The K handshape / Maureen Jennings.

(A Christine Morris mystery)
ISBN 978-1-55002-763-1

    I. Title. II. Series: Jennings, Maureen. Christine Morris mystery.

PS8569.E562K25 2008   C813'.54   C2007-904679-7

1   2   3   4   5   12   11   10   09   08

 Conseil des Arts
du Canada Canada Council
for the Arts Canada  ONTARIO ARTS COUNCIL
CONSEIL DES ARTS DE L'ONTARIO

We acknowledge the support of the **Canada Council for the Arts** and the **Ontario Arts Council** for our publishing program. We also acknowledge the financial support of the **Government of Canada** through the **Book Publishing Industry Development Program** and **The Association for the Export of Canadian Books**, and the **Government of Ontario** through the **Ontario Book Publishers Tax Credit program**, and the **Ontario Media Development Corporation**.

Care has been taken to trace the ownership of copyright material used in this book. The author and the publisher welcome any information enabling them to rectify any references or credits in subsequent editions.

J. Kirk Howard, President

Printed and bound in Canada.
Printed on recycled paper.

www.dundurn.com

Dundurn Press	Gazelle Book Services Limited	Dundurn Press
3 Church Street, Suite 500	White Cross Mills	2250 Military Road
Toronto, Ontario, Canada	High Town, Lancaster, England	Tonawanda, NY
M5E 1M2	LA1 4XS	U.S.A. 14150

For Iden as always

To make the sign for "to kill" make the K handshape and strike against the opposite hand in a sharp downward motion. (American Sign Language)

ACKNOWLEDGEMENTS

As usual there are many people to thank who shared their time and expertise with me during the course of my writing this book. At the Behavioural Science Centre, OPP Headquarters in Orillia: Acting Detective Superintendent, Director Behavioural Sciences Section, Angie Howe; Detective Staff Sergeant, Criminal Behavioural Analysis Services, Chris Loam; Detective Sergeant Criminal Profiling Unit, Ed Chafe. Ontario Provincial Police Constable Doug Thomson; Cadet Robert Brigden, Northern Constabulary, Outer Hebrides; Inspector Philip MacCrae. Thanks to the following people for letting me bend their ears in consultation on police matters: Kim Peters (Ret.) and Donald Adams, who will always find whatever I need. For matters regarding Deaf Culture, Linda Scott of the Canadian Hearing Society in Toronto and Michelle Tasch. A special thanks to Jane Hooey and her father, Bob (Buf) Hooey. To those who helped me get my facts straight on how casinos work, thanks. You know who you are but they mustn't. A special thanks to Dave Snake of The Gathering Place, Casino Rama, Orillia. My friend and wonderful architect, Mark Hall, took time to show me around the beautiful Elgin Bay Club, so I could make the living space of my character believable. To the authors of all the invaluable books on serial murderers, thanks. We didn't meet personally but your work assisted me enormously.

CHAPTER ONE

It was not yet six and the night darkness had hardly shifted, the reluctant concession to morning signified by faint strips of light in the east. Lake Couchiching, aptly called Lake of Strong Winds, was black and malevolent, white-capped waves slapping onto the sodden beaches. The park was deserted except for Leo and me and a man walking his dog by the bandshell.

As best I could in the murky light, I was inspecting the shoreline near the trees, while Leo had elected to search along the edges of the concrete pier. He was walking slowly, peering down into the choppy water.

"Christine! Here!"

I turned to see him drop to his knees and start to tug at something that had snagged underneath the pier. I ran to him, not quite able to identify the nature of the bundle but fearing the worst.

And it was.

Leo had hold of a body and he was struggling to maintain his grip as the waves kept shoving the whole thing back on the underlying rocks. I joined him and reached down to grab the jacket. Together we managed to drag the body to the surface but it was too waterlogged to bring up any further, even with the two of us. A white face floated into view, a young woman whose long dark hair was waving out in tendrils around her head. I didn't have to ask if it was Deidre. It was obvious from Leo's stricken expression that it was.

"Hold her," he cried.

Before I could stop him, he jumped into the water. It wasn't deep this close to shore, but Leo was a short man and he lost his footing. He went under, emerging almost immediately, spluttering and gasping as a wave struck him in the face.

"Pull when I lift," he shouted. Reaching underneath the body and with superhuman strength, he lifted her. I pulled at the same time and we managed to hoist her level to the pier. Suddenly, another pair of hands was helping — the man who had been walking his dog. With Leo pushing and the two of us pulling, we got her over the wooden lip and onto the concrete. Immediately, I rolled her onto her back, but it was obvious she had been dead for some time and any attempt at resuscitation would be useless. Her skin was blue-grey and ice cold, her eyes partially closed. In the meantime, Leo was trying to climb out of the water, no easy task as there was no good foothold. I think he might have walked on top of the water by sheer dint of will but I grabbed his hand and hauled him out.

"Oh God," he kept repeating, "oh my God." He crouched down and tried to bend the girl's head back, pulling down on her chin to open her mouth. I caught his arm.

"It's no use, Leo, she's gone."

The body was in fact already in a state of rigor and he couldn't move the head at all.

"Shall I send for an ambulance, miss?"

For the first time I paid attention to our helper, who had stepped back a few feet and who was watching me with frightened eyes. He was a stocky, fortyish man whose face was whipped scarlet from the wind.

"I know her," he said before I could answer. "She lives near me. I think her name's Deidre. She's deaf."

"I know who she is," barked out Leo. "You don't have to tell me." Frantically, he began to fish in his pocket. "We'd better phone 911 right away."

He took out his cellphone but his fingers were trembling too violently for him to dial and I wasn't sure it would have survived the dunking anyway. I used my own.

"Here, miss. Give him my coat," said our good Samaritan. "I've got a thick sweater on."

I'd grabbed my windjammer when I'd got the call from Leo but I hadn't expected we'd be facing winter conditions this early in November. I'd left my gloves behind and only had a light cotton baseball cap on my head. The man looked in better shape than I was, and gratefully, I accepted his offer. He removed his parka. It was shabby but down-filled and felt warm from his body. Leo, the man I'd hitherto experienced as in control and commanding to the point of aggravation, was as unresisting as a child. Quickly, I unbuttoned his sodden coat, erstwhile a good cashmere, and got it off him. Underneath he was wearing only his flannel pajama top. I got that off too and started to rub his chest as vigorously as I could around his heart. I was afraid he was going to go into hypothermic shock at any moment.

He shoved my hands away.

"I'm all right. Give me the coat."

I held out the parka and he managed to put it on and pulled the hood over his head.

"Why don't you take my gloves as well," said our helper, and without a word, knowing the necessity, Leo put them on.

He'd hardly taken his eyes off the body, and suddenly, he pointed. "What's in her pockets?"

Deidre had been wearing a black leather jacket. I could see both pockets were bulging.

"Stones. They're stuffed with stones."

Before I could stop him, Leo started to scrabble at the pockets, unloading them as if it would make any difference now.

He yelled up at me. "She wouldn't have killed herself. She wouldn't."

Suddenly, he stopped and jerked back almost as if he had received a blow.

"Christine, look!"

It hadn't been obvious at first because the jacket collar was up high on her neck, but Leo, in his desperation, had tugged it down. I could see that a red-striped scarf was around her throat, biting deep into the skin.

"My God," he whispered. He fell to his knees.

At that moment, we heard the wail of a siren, and an ambulance, lights flashing, came racing down the street that led to the park.

I turned to our bystander, who was standing a few feet away, staring transfixed at the body.

I shifted so I could block his view. "Would you mind going over to the bench, sir?"

He complied without protest. He'd tied his dog to a lamppost and she jumped up at him happily, oblivious to the drama that was unfolding.

The ambulance had turned in at the gate and was headed toward us. I waved my arms for them to stop and they jerked to a halt in front of me. The driver, a young freckle-faced lad, rolled down his window.

"What's happened?"

"I don't know yet." I fished in my inside pocket, glad for my ID. "I'm a police officer, Detective Sergeant Christine Morris, OPP. We have what looks like a homicide."

The other paramedic was female, blonde hair spilling out from under her wool toque. Both of them were just kids, and they looked apprehensive. Orillia is still small-town Ontario and I doubted if equivocal death was an everyday occurrence.

"I'm going to have you take the man over there to hospital. He's already going into hypothermic shock."

And who wouldn't be if you'd just found the murdered body of your own daughter?

CHAPTER TWO

The female paramedic jumped out of the ambulance. "I'd better check on the woman."

I flung out my arm. "She doesn't need your help, believe me. She's long gone. She has to stay here."

The girl looked doubtful as if it went against her training, but the guy called out. "Leave it, Cathy. Let's get this man to the hospital."

They wheeled out the stretcher. I thought Leo would give me a hard time about leaving but he wasn't functioning properly and he knew it. He let them help him onto the stretcher and put an oxygen mask over his nose.

"I'll call you as soon as I can," I said. He raised his hand in acknowledgement and closed his eyes.

I gave the paramedics his name, got theirs, and they drove away. Strictly speaking, I should just wait for the police to arrive. I was a police officer but not front line anymore. However, there was no way I could act like a civilian because I wasn't. I went over to the body. Deidre was bareheaded and without gloves, although whether or not she'd had them previously and lost them, we'd have to find out. Her nails were painted a bright cherry red. She was wearing newish Nike running shoes and snug-fitting blue jeans. Unless there was a physical handicap I couldn't see, she looked trim and fit. The forensic team would have to tell us what had happened and whether or not she had been able to put up a fight. The scarf had been tied very tightly. I sighed. Seeing a murder victim was never pleasant, and it was especially hard when that victim had so much life snatched from them.

I heard a couple of soft yelps from the direction of the band shell behind me. The man who had helped us gave me a tentative wave when I turned to look at him, as if reminding me he was still there. He'd picked up his dog, a cute little papillon, and was holding it on his lap, stroking it as people do sometimes when they themselves are upset.

I went over to him. "Sorry to keep you waiting, sir, but I'm going to have to ask you to stay a bit longer. I'll need some information."

"Oh, I didn't see nothing. I was just walking Lily, here, when I heard a man shout. I came over to help. That's all I can tell you."

The poor guy was acting as if he was under arrest. I gave him what I hoped was a reassuring smile, although by now my facial muscles were frozen and not working too well.

"I do appreciate your help, sir. I just need your name and address for our records. Besides, I have to get your coat and gloves back to you."

"Yes, yes, of course. I'm sorry. My name, it is Sylvio Torres, like the baseball manager, but with an 's,' so no relation." A joke he'd told many times before. He waited for my smile. "I live at 72 Mississauga Street West. That's just a couple of blocks from the young lady. I've seen her when I've been walking Lily." He suddenly put his hand to his eyes, pushing down tears.

"What on earth's going to become of her poor child? I seen her too. She's deaf as a post like her mother. What a tragedy."

This was news to me. Leo had never even mentioned he had a granddaughter and I only knew about Deidre because he had a graduation picture of her on his desk. He was close-lipped in the office and, unlike a lot of us, didn't share his personal life at all.

Mr. Torres was shaking his head. "Dreadful to have that handicap but not reason to take your own life, don't you agree, ma'am?"

He obviously hadn't seen the scarf around Deidre's neck but I didn't want to reveal anything more for now.

"You were in the park when Dr. Forgach and I arrived. It's early to be walking your dog. Is that usual for you?"

I kept my voice casual, not wanting to alarm him any more than he was already. He blinked rapidly, holding his dog even tighter.

"No, not the usual. She had an upset tummy last night, a touch of the runs, so I thought I'd better get her out soon as possible. She hates it if she has an accident. Don't you, Lily?"

The dog answered by licking his chin. I put out my hand, fingers tucked in, for her to sniff.

"She's certainly a pretty one... Did you see anybody else in the park when you arrived? Any cars?"

"Nobody. I wasn't paying a lot of attention mind you but no, I'd say there wasn't anybody else here."

Screaming sirens shredded the air and I saw an OPP car speeding down the street, a fire truck following close behind it. The patrol car raced down to the pier and pulled up by the bollards at the end of the pier. Two uniformed officers got out. One of them I knew quite well. His name was Ed Chaffey. He was a big rangy guy, mature, nearing retirement, and he emanated an unflappable air of authority. I was glad it was he who'd got the call. The other officer was younger and I hadn't met him before. The fire truck also pulled up, with its lighthouse-sized beam swirling on the roof of the cab. Four firefighters suited up for action jumped down.

I turned to Mr. Torres. "I'm going to have you sit in the police car. It'll be warmer in there and we may be a while yet."

"What about Lily?"

The noise and lights were frightening the dog, who was trying to shrink into his lap.

"You can take her with you."

Daylight had seeped in as much as it was going to but a sleety rain had started up and the damp went to the bone.

Chaffey came over to me. "Hi, Christine. What have we got?"

"Let me deal with Mr. Torres here first. He helped us recover the body. I'm suggesting he sit in the cruiser to keep warm."

"Sure. Go with this officer, Constable Johnson, will you, sir."

They left and I led Chaffey over to the body. He took one look at her and called out to the firefighters who had hung back by the truck.

"Thanks, guys, we won't need you."

They climbed back into the fire truck and, silently now, drove off.

"Do we know who she is?" Ed asked.

"Her name is Deidre. Her father is Doctor Leo Forgach."

Ed whistled through his teeth. "Not the forensic shrink?"

"That's him. We both found her. He's in hypothermic shock and I've had him taken to the hospital."

Ed knelt down, gently moving aside the collar of Deidre's jacket.

"Some bastard wasn't leaving anything to chance, was he? Why the stones, do you think?"

"Keep her in the water, wash away evidence, delay the discovery of the body as long as possible. Any or all of the above."

"Anything in her pockets, other than stones, that is?"

"I didn't check. Thought I'd leave that to you."

"I'll let the forensic guys do it. At least we know who she is."

Ed straightened up and glanced around the park. In spite of the early hour, there was already a cluster of the curious gathering on the perimeter. The huge bronze memorial to Samuel de Champlain glistened in the rain. The explorer, cape blowing in the wind, perched high on his stone pedestal, looked out across the lake. Below him, magnificently muscled and half-naked, the savages eyed the bible the priest was showing them.

"Pity old Sam couldn't tell us anything about what happened," said Ed.

Over the next couple of hours, more cruisers arrived and the emergency response team leaped into action. Chaffey dispatched his uniformed officers to keep onlookers at bay and had yellow tape strung across the narrow strip of beach and the end of the pier. The path was gravel and my first glance had revealed no sign of tire marks, or footprints for that matter, although I thought the murderer must have driven around the bollards and onto the pier itself in order to drop Deidre in the water. I couldn't imagine him carrying a body in full view all the way to the end of the pier where we'd found her. Too visible, for one thing, and for another, a dead weight is incredibly heavy.

There was no way we could properly secure the crime scene because essentially it encompassed the entire park. All we could do was keep contamination to a minimum. The forensic team arrived, but as the body had been in the water there wasn't a lot they could do on the spot except take photographs of the area. Finally, the body was loaded into the van and taken off to the morgue.

"D'you feel like having a coffee?" Chaffey asked me. "You'll have to share my Thermos."

I was about to say, "And your bed too if that's what it takes," but I wouldn't want him to take it the wrong way. At this hour of the morning, in the rain, with damp clothes, no breakfast, I was a coffee slut.

We settled into the patrol car and he unscrewed the lid of the Thermos and poured me a cupful. It was sweet and I don't take sugar but I was past caring.

He helped himself to some, put the cup on the dashboard, and took out his notebook.

"All right. Start at the beginning. How the hell did you and the shrink get to be here at dawn, fishing the body of a murdered girl out of the pond?"

Chaffey was a good cop. He allowed me to tell my story with the minimum of interjections on his part. What follows is what I told him, although I left out the personal bits concerning my mother.

I was awakened by my phone. It was ten minutes past five, and as I had gone to bed late because I was working on some statement analysis requests, I was a tad grumpy when I answered. I thought it was my mother, Joan, calling from the Hebrides. She has a cavalier disregard for time zones and this wouldn't have been the first time she had phoned in the early hours of the morning. It turned out the caller was Leo Forgach. He's the resident forensic psychiatrist at the Behavioural Science Centre where I work, and frankly, he's not one of my favourite folks. He can be an irritable cuss when he's under pressure, which is often. When he wasn't taking everybody's head off for asking him a stupid question, he was all right, but he could never be called warm and fuzzy. I hardly recognized his voice over the phone; all that aloofness had vanished. He was almost frantic. He said that his daughter, Deidre, appeared to be missing. Her roommate had called to say that she hadn't come home that night. She herself had just woken up and discovered Deedee's bed hadn't been slept in. This was so totally out of character that both of them — Leo and the roommate, Nora — were alarmed. Apparently, Deidre had left about seven o'clock for her usual Tuesday evening jaunt to Casino Rama. She did this on a regular basis but never, ever stayed past midnight. He asked me to help.

Leo picked me up and we drove straight to the casino to see if for some reason she was still there. He recognized her car, which was parked in the lot. The driver's side front tire was flat. We checked inside the building just in case, but there was no sign of her. Leo pulled rank and got the security staff to help us, and the stamped receipt at one of the blackjack tables indicated she'd left at 10:33.

"What made you think you'd find her in the park?" Chaffey asked.

"Leo has a spare key to the car and he found a note on the passenger seat. It was handwritten and said ... let me get this as exact as I can ... it said, 'Okay. I'll meet you in Memorial Park at the monument. Eleven. Don't be late, I won't wait.'"

"Do you have the note?"

"No, I don't, sorry Ed. It must be in Leo's pocket. I didn't think to retrieve it."

"That's understandable. You had other things on your mind. There won't be any prints on it anyway."

I sipped some more of his coffee, trying to make it last. "I've never met Deidre, and at this point, I thought she might be shacking up with somebody and would show up bright-eyed and bushy-tailed back at home." I hesitated, feeling as if I was betraying a confidence. "He was particularly concerned because she did make a fairly serious suicide attempt when she was sixteen. She jumped off this same pier but was rescued by a pair of joggers."

"So he was afraid she might have done it properly this time?"

I nodded. "We got here as fast as we could and started to search the shore. When he found her and we got her out of the water, at first it seemed she was in fact a suicide. Then we saw the scarf. There's no way she could have strangled herself like that."

"We'll have to see what forensic tells us." Ed groaned. "I'm sorry for the girl and I'm sorry for him, but I'm also bloody sorry for myself. All traces are likely washed off; this is a public place with dozens of people going back and forth even at this time of year. And trying to get statements from witnesses at the casino will take us months. Do you know how many people go through those doors on a given day?"

"A lot, I'm sure. Even at five-thirty in the morning, there must have been a couple hundred players in there."

"Three thousand a day! Give or take."

He switched on the windshield wipers and stared out gloomily at the black wind-whipped lake.

"Poor bugger. Is he married?"

"Divorced. He also said that relations were strained between him and his daughter."

"Reason?"

"He didn't say."

Ed poured out the last of the coffee into my cup and I finished it off.

"I told Leo I'd phone him as soon as I could. The roommate should also be informed. She's probably worried sick."

Chaffey turned to look at me. "This is tricky, isn't it? You're absolutely the best person to do that job but you're not exactly on the case, are you?"

"I could be your consultant if you want to go through proper channels."

For the first time, he smiled. It looked good on him. "Done. You've got yourself a job, Christine Morris. The thrill of the chase is still in your blood, isn't it?"

I shrugged that off. He was partly right. I had inadvertently got involved and I knew I would have to follow that up as far as I could. I might not have a close friendship with Leo Forgach but I had a lot of respect for him. He was also one of us, one of the team, and as far as I was concerned, that counted for a lot.

CHAPTER THREE

The nurse on emergency said that Leo was under sedation and asleep. He was in no danger and she thought that he could be discharged by tomorrow. I left a message to say that I had called and gave her my personal cell number.

Ed decided to send Constable Johnson with me to speak to Deidre's roommate, Nora. First we had to drop off Mr. Torres, who was sitting quietly in the back of the police car, Lily asleep beside him.

I got in the back seat, not wanting him to feel awkward with the protective grid separating us.

"What do you think happened to her?" he asked.

"I don't know at this point. Did you know her well?"

"No, not at all. She live on my street, that's all I can say. I see her perhaps once or twice when I'm walking Lily."

"Do you live alone, Mr. Torres?"

I saw Johnson glance at me in the rear-view mirror. He could hear what I was saying and I had obviously slipped into a familiar mode of questioning. I couldn't really help it. You can get too suspicious when you're in homicide and can end up suspecting everybody, which isn't helpful. On the other hand, I didn't want to make the mistake of *not* asking questions that might help us later.

"Why do you ask?"

"You've had a shock. I wanted to make sure somebody was at home for you."

This was a bit of prevarication on my part. I was frankly "gathering," as we call it. Pulling in as much information as possible.

"I'll be fine," he said. "My mother is at home." He leaned forward and tapped on the screen. "Turn left at the next street," he said to Johnson. "I'm in that apartment building on the right. The one with the canopy."

"Thank you for your help, Mr. Torres. I'll get your things back to you as soon as I can."

"I hope the poor man recovers."

He slid out of the car and with Lily tucked underneath his arm he hurried away.

"Where now?" asked Johnson. He sported a moustache; perhaps he hoped it made him look older but it didn't. He had the sort of round face and fair skin that always seemed youthful. He was also unsure of himself, which added to the general impression of gaucheness.

I sighed, not relishing the task ahead. "Let's give the roommate the news. She's on Mary Street."

Lights were on in all rooms in the house, which was a small red-brick detached with a covered porch. There was a child's tricycle on the front lawn. With Johnson behind me, I went up the steps and rang the bell. The door was opened at once. A woman, twentyish, husky, whom I presumed to be the roommate, Nora, stood in the doorway. A skinny little blonde girl of about three, still in her PJs, thumb in mouth, was beside her, eyeing me curiously. I felt a clenching in my stomach. How do you tell a child that age her mother is dead? I didn't think I'd shown my feelings but I must have revealed something because Nora took a quick intake of breath.

"Have you found her?"

I nodded. "Do you mind if we come in? I'm Detective Sergeant Morris and this is Detective Constable Johnson."

"I'm Nora Cochrane. We can go into the kitchen. Joy is just finishing her breakfast." She tapped the child on the shoulder and when she looked up at her, Nora pointed to her own mouth in a gesture that was universally recognizable for food and pointed down the hall.

"You don't have to be careful about what you say. She won't hear you. She's deaf."

She took the child by the hand and stepped back so we could come in. The living room and dining room were open concept, with a plant-filled divider separating them from the hall and the stairs.

"Don't worry about your shoes," said Nora. "We're back here."

We followed her into the kitchen where she stowed Joy in a chair. She put a spoon in her hand and shoved a bowl of cereal closer to her. Then she turned to face us.

"Is Deedee dead?"

"I'm afraid so."

Nora bit her lip hard. She was a tough-looking young woman, mannish in her red plaid lumberjack shirt and spiky black hair. A tattoo of a skull and crossbones decorated one side of her neck and she had several studs, one in her nostril, another in her lip. The kind that always made me wince.

"I knew it. I knew something bad had happened. Dee would only ever not come home if she was dead or unconscious. What happened? Was she in an accident?"

"No, I'm sorry to have to tell you this but we are treating this as an equivocal death."

"What the fuck does that mean?"

"We found her body in the lake at Memorial Park. She appears to have been strangled."

Nora gaped at me. "That's fucking ridiculous! Who the hell would do that to Dee?"

"We don't know yet."

Seeming to sense the disturbance in the air, Joy suddenly made a guttural noise deep in her throat. She made some rapid hand signs which Nora responded to slowly and awkwardly, reinforcing her movements with words.

"Mommy at work. Joy finish brekkie now. There's a good girl. See Mommy tonight."

The child didn't look convinced but she went back to spooning her cornflakes into her mouth, her eyes steady on Nora.

Behind me, Constable Johnson shuffled his feet. I could sense his discomfort with the whole situation but he'd have to get used to it if he was going to make it as a police officer. Heartbreak came with the territory.

"Where's Leo Forgach?" Nora asked.

"He jumped into the water to help get Deidre's body out and he's currently at the hospital. He'll be all right. He's got a touch of hypothermia."

"Yeah? I'm surprised. Him and cold water are compatible."

Nora's shoulders were shaking and I would have tried to comfort her, but I had the feeling she was one of those people whose grief converts into anger in a second. I thought it was wiser to keep my distance for a while. She looked up at the clock on the wall.

"I'd better call work and say I won't be coming in. Somebody'll have to stay with the kid."

"Is there anybody else who can help out? I know this isn't easy for you."

She glared at me. "Don't give me that fucking cop speak. You don't have a fucking clue what I'm feeling."

Johnson made a scolding noise. "No need to carry on like that, miss. Detective Morris is only trying to help."

She flung him a look that would have shrivelled the soul of a stronger man.

"What isn't *easy*, as you put it, is that I'm the one who has to turn my life inside out now. The kid'll be dumped on my lap and I'm just the fucking babysitter, for God's sake. Well, let me tell you, I'll do it for today but that's all. He's going to have to find somebody else. I'm not going to lose my job for anybody."

The words were ugly and sounded abysmally selfish but I could feel her panic underneath. I tried again.

"Miss Cochrane, I wish I could have told you the news in a softer way but there is no blunting the truth. Deidre Forgach..."

She interrupted me. "Larsen. Her name was Larsen. She changed it years ago. She took her mother's name."

"Deidre Larsen was most likely murdered and at the moment we don't know who did it. We intend to find out. If you can answer some of my questions now, I would appreciate it."

Joy growled and made signs at me. Nora managed a smile. "She wants to know why we are going bam-bam. She's a sensitive little brat. She picks up feelings like a radio antenna."

She signed something back to the little girl. "I told her we were just discussing something and we're friends." Some of the tension in the room relaxed and Joy grinned at me.

"I'm going to have to get her dressed. I'll see if Mrs. Somerset can take her for now. She runs the daycare. It'll be better for her there." She beckoned to the child, who got out of the chair. Nora picked her up and held her close for a moment but Joy squirmed to be put down. "I'll be back in a minute," Nora said to us. "Help yourself to coffee if you want. It's on the stove."

The door closed behind her. Johnson exhaled ostentatiously. "Boy, why do dykes always have to prove they've got the biggest balls?"

I felt like snapping at him that dykes weren't the only ones but he was too easy a target. We were all upset.

CHAPTER FOUR

Joy was picked up by a babysitter who had been quickly apprised of the situation and whose shocked face immediately provoked a wail of anxiety in the child. Protesting, she was however carried off.

"She'll have to get used to it," said Nora. "Life's shitty for kids most of the time anyway."

While she'd been getting Joy ready, I'd had a chance to take in the setting, always helpful. The kitchen was bright even in this dreary morning light, with white cupboards and daffodil yellow walls. It was as tidy as you're going to get with a three-year-old around and there was lots of evidence that Joy was the centre of the universe, the fridge adorned with crayon pictures, stick figures doing the important things they do in a child's life. I could see through an arch, blocked off by a baby gate, into the main living area. It too was pleasant with good light, comfy-looking furniture, crammed bookcases.

Nora came back into the kitchen. In spite of her "I'm so tough" attitude, she looked really distressed and I thought her interactions with the child had been very affectionate.

"Do you want some coffee, cuz I do." she asked.

"Sure, thanks." I answered.

The constable shook his head. I would have dearly liked to have got rid of him but you're supposed to have a second person present if you are conducting any kind of official interview. It would have been better if he could have faded into the background, but his dislike of Nora was palpable and it hung in the air like a bad smell.

She busied herself making the coffee, not looking at us. "Have you got in touch with Deedee's mother yet? She might even tear herself away from saving the planet and come up here to take care of the kid. Not that Joy knows her, really, but she is family. She should do something."

"I expect Dr. Forgach will take care of that."

"Are you kidding? From all I've heard, you might as well ask Israel and Palestine to form a government. Those two don't talk. Period."

"I gather the family was not close," I said, choosing my words carefully. "Not close" in this case seemed to mean utter alienation. Nora got two mugs out of the cupboard, slamming the cupboard door as she did so.

"Deidre's mother, Mizz Larsen, is what you might call a career woman. She's an environmental lawyer in the Big Smoke. She travels all over the country suing people who cut down trees and shit like that. I'll give her this, she's not a hypocrite. She's always made it clear she's not going to be doting grannie, especially since Deedee deliberately produced a handicapped kid. I've been on the scene since the week after Joy was born, and in two plus years, I'd say Mizz Larsen has visited twice. No, I lie. She came last Christmas. That makes it three times." She poured out a dark aromatic mug of coffee and handed it to me. "Do you take milk?"

"Just black."

We were both acting as if Constable Johnson wasn't in the room. I wished he was a smoker and would go outside for a few minutes. To my delight, he obliged.

He touched the phone on his shoulder. "I'd better call Sergeant Chaffey and report in."

"The reception should be better outside," I said.

"Be right back."

He shambled awkwardly out of the room, aware that Nora was scrutinizing him with hostility.

"Give him another five years and he's going to have a butt the size of a barn door," she said, just loud enough for him to hear.

I let that go, wanting to take this opportunity to establish a better rapport with her. She was thawing toward me at least.

"Nora, I'm going to sound like a TV cop but I have to ask this question. Did Deidre have any enemies that you know of? Anybody she might have quarrelled with?"

She stared at me for a moment. "You saying you don't know?"

"Know what?"

"Two years ago, Dee was one of the most hated women in the Sunshine Town. You must have read about it. Big headlines. Even got down to T.O."

"It's not ringing any bells at the moment."

Nora went into the living room, opened a drawer in a desk by the window, and returned with a file folder. She dropped it on the table. "Here. Take a look at this stuff."

I opened the file, which was stuffed with newspaper clippings. The *Orillia Packet* had a front-page feature.

> An Orillia deaf woman admits she deliberately conceived a child who had a 90 percent chance of being hearing impaired.
>
> Deidre Larsen, 25, who is deaf, admitted to our reporter today that she deliberately conceived a child with a congenitally hearing-impaired man so that she would have a child who was deaf. "Why not? Deaf Culture is just as good as any other, if not better," said Larsen. "My daughter will be brought up to understand ASL. Or in our terms, sign language."
>
> Larsen's mother, a prominent Toronto lawyer, contracted measles while she was carrying Deidre and the girl was born profoundly deaf. She has attended deaf schools since she was two years old and graduated with a B.A. from Gallaudet University in the States, the only university in North America exclusively for the hearing impaired. "I have been asked many times if I am trying to make a point," said Larsen, speaking through an interpreter. "I suppose I would answer yes to that. Deaf people have undergone centuries of discrimination from the hearing world. We are not dumb; we are as capable of raising children as a hearing person is.

Better probably. We have our own culture which is
as good as any that the hearing world has. We are
no longer trying to merely fit in; we can stand alone.
Let the hearing world fit in to us."

When questioned about the child's father, Larsen
refused to elaborate. "A friend obliged but he is not
in any way involved with the child."

The child's name is Joy, and she seems a well-
cared-for, contented infant. She smiled and reached
out to this reporter, making her own strange noises.
Her mother communicates with her by signs.

Larsen lives with another woman, Nora Cochrane,
who shares child-rearing duties with her but who is
not herself deaf.

Just as I finished reading, Johnson returned. He carried a
waft of cigarette smoke with him. I saw Nora give him a look of
disdain.

"I'm needed back at the station, ma'am, if you don't mind."

"Why don't you go ahead then? Tell Sergeant Chaffey I'll contact
him as soon as I can."

To heck with procedures. I wasn't going to get anything out of
Ms. Cochrane while the constable was hanging around. I decided
to go semi-official.

"How will you get back, ma'am?"

"I'll figure it out, Constable, don't worry."

He flushed and I realized I'd sounded sarcastic. I hadn't meant
to be. I think Nora's attitude was rubbing off on me.

He left and the air lightened. I could swear Nora muttered under
her breath, "What a prick," although poor Johnson had done little
to deserve her contempt.

"Well? Do you remember the story now?" she demanded. I
thought she or Deedee must have enjoyed the notoriety because
there were a lot of other clippings, including letters to the editor.
Readers were weighing in at a disapproval ratio of four to one as
far as I could tell. All of the letters were angry, expressing disgust
at her action and pity for the child. Leo wasn't mentioned in any of
the articles and I wondered how he'd managed to avoid the press.

"I wasn't in the country when the story broke," I answered Nora. I was in fact in the Hebrides having my own life turned upside down but I didn't tell her that.

The story had been pushed off the front page by the news of a suicide bomb attack in Afghanistan which had taken the life of a United Nations soldier, but there were a few more letters and an analyst or two debating the welfare of a child whose parents couldn't hear them.

"You called her the most hated woman in Orillia?"

"That's right. You should have seen the hate mail. We had to move, change the phone number, you name it. We were getting so many calls. Vile, scary calls, I can tell you. Men and women. She must have had fifty or more emails. All along the same lines: how could you do that to your child, you will go to hell for this, blah blah blah. What really incensed people was the way that bitch wrote the article implied Dee and I were lezzie lovers, which we're not." For the first time, Nora grinned. "She isn't, I mean. I live here strictly as a friend. I get free rent and she gets my ears. So far it's worked out well. You saw Joy. She's a happy little kid."

"Who outed Deidre?"

Nora fiddled with her eyebrow ring. "She did it herself. Called the newspaper and asked if they wanted her story. She went after the publicity. I don't think she expected quite such a reaction but as she says somewhere in there, she was trying to make a point. She's what you might call a militant for Deaf Culture." Nora made wobble movements with her hand. "And I mean, militant."

"How did Deidre support herself?"

"She's a teacher at the OHHA. The Ontario Hard of Hearing Association. And she does interpreting when she's asked to. It's a bit hard to scrabble the money together but we manage. It's evening hours mostly and we work it out so that she's with Joy in the day and I'm here at night."

"Where do you work?"

"At the addiction counselling centre on Lachlie Street. I answer the phone. I don't counsel, although I could probably do a better job than most of them."

"Nora. We found a letter in Deidre's car. Somebody was arranging to meet her by the monument in Memorial Park. Any idea who that might be?"

"Last night?"

"It didn't say but that's where her body was found, not far from the Champlain Monument. Her car was in the casino parking lot with a flat tire, so at the moment we don't know how she got from the casino or where she was killed."

Nora picked up a spoon that was on the table. It was a child's short-handled silver spoon. "Dee's social life was the pits. She was a good-looking girl but except for the very occasional party with the Deaf, capital D, folks, she just wanted to be at home with Joy and working at her computer. She had a large network of Deaf folks who she was always writing to. Tuesday was her one night out. Come hell or high water she went to the casino. Forty dollars for the night, win or lose." She tapped the spoon on her hand. "She often won, the little bitch, and then we'd celebrate. She'd order in a pizza. Big fucking deal. The rest went to the savings fund for Joy's education."

Suddenly, she put her head in her hands and gulped a couple of times as if something was stuck in her throat. "Poor sod. Why'd anybody kill her? She was as good a mom as you can hope to get."

I reached out to touch her arm. She tolerated it for a moment then shook me off.

"Goddam all those self-righteous shits anyway. Let them all rot in hell." She jumped to her feet and went over to the cupboard, her back to me. I waited. She started to open one cupboard after another and then banging them shut. I didn't know what she was looking for when she swivelled around.

"I don't suppose you have a fag on you? I could have sworn I stashed a pack in here for emergencies."

"No, sorry. I don't smoke."

"Smart woman, it's a filthy habit." She took in a deep breath and exhaled slowly. Then another. "There you go, craving gone. I quit a month ago but this has thrown me for a loop and man, oh man, those cravings!" She came back to the table. "What else do you want to know?"

"Can you give the names of her closest friends? We'll need to talk to them."

"She only had two that you'd call close, that I know of. They work at the OHHA as well. One of them is Joy's godmother if I remember right. She's Jessica Manolo. The other is Hannah Silverstein. I've met them a few times but they make a point of coming over when I'm out. They don't approve of me."

Nora had a look on her face that said volumes. The dislike went both ways, it seemed.

I wrote down the names. "Did Deidre keep the hate mail she received?"

"Not here. That stuff's bad karma, man." Nora shuddered. "I think she took them to work but I'm not sure about that."

"What about the emails?"

"Ditto. She printed them off and took them with her."

"Could I just have a look at her bedroom?"

Nora flashed me a quick glance. "What for?'

"I'd just like to get a sense of her."

"Come on upstairs then." She waved her hand. "Dee was the tidy one here. I can keep it together in the common areas but I hope you don't want to see my room because it looks like a bomb dropped in it."

I smiled at her, liking her more. "No, just Deidre's will be fine."

We went upstairs. The room at the top of the landing was Joy's and was filled with colour. The Little Mermaid swam along one wall, meeting up with Shrek on the other.

Nora paused at the door. "I did the murals. Not bad eh?"

"They're great."

The next door was ajar but Nora stepped forward and closed it quick.

"My room."

She pointed to the door opposite. "That's Dee's room. She took the smallest."

As Nora had said, Deidre was a tidy person and the bedroom was neat, the bed made, no clothes lying around. The room was indeed small, big enough for a bureau and a single bed. Not too good if she did want to have a love life. A computer was on a table underneath the window. The tabletop was pristine, no papers visible.

"What's this?" I asked. There was a little box sitting at the end of the bed.

"That's a bed shaker," said Nora. "It connects to Joy's room. If she cries, that thing vibrates. Dee's got one under her pillow too. She was always worried about sleeping through the kid's bawling. So we've got so many flashing lights to signal the door, the phone, fire, the kid, you name it. It's freaky at times. I mean that's my job really but she used me more as a fail-safe than anything else. Sometimes when Joy was younger, she'd cry and Dee would be there before I was."

There was a framed photograph on the bureau and Nora picked it up to show me.

"This is her grad picture. She went to the deaf university in the States. I forget what it's called."

"Gallaudet?"

"Yeah. That's the one. This blonde girl on the end of the row is Jessica and the little fattie on the left is Hannah."

The photograph must have been taken about four years ago. Deidre looked so happy and proud, full of life. Quite a contrast to how I'd seen her. I handed the picture back to Nora.

"Yeah. Sad isn't it? And you didn't even know her. It seems all so stupid and pointless, doesn't it? What a waste."

I'd seen all I wanted for now. Forensics would probably come back and do a thorough search but that wasn't my job. We headed back downstairs.

"Nora, you said Deidre didn't have a boyfriend?"

"Nope. I mean she must have got somebody to screw with when she conceived Joy but like she said in the article it was an arrangement. I don't think the poor prick even knew about the kid. That's the impression she gave me anyway."

"She does seem to have been heading for an assignation of some kind. Did she seem in any way different lately? Nervous? Excited?"

"Not that I noticed. But then again, we weren't exactly bosom buddies. I liked her, she liked me, but that's about it. We gave each other lots of space. She never confided in me or anything like that. I mean, I can get by now with some basic sign language but it was hard to communicate. Who wants to have to write everything down? I sure don't."

She opened the front door.

"Thanks, Nora."

She stayed there as I walked down the steps. "Catch the bastard, will you?"

CHAPTER FIVE

In crises like this, time has a strange warp quality. When I left Deidre's house, it felt like most of the day had passed already but the Orillia morning rush hour was barely tapering off. I hailed a cab and went back to my own flat. When Leo called, I'd dressed hastily in my jogging pants and a sweater and I needed a change of clothes. I also hadn't even fed my two cats, Victoria — or Tory — and Bertie. Yes, I know that sounds sort of cutesy, but believe me, the names suit them. Tory is a dowager skinny Abyssinian who is often mistaken for a kitten but who is actually eighteen years of age and showing signs of senility. Bertie is a Siamese with a paunch who dotes on Tory, grooms her, always wants to be near her or me. She seems indifferent to him but yowls at me constantly. I'd inherited them from the previous owner of the house, Mrs. Harley, who'd moved back to the UK to be with her daughter.

Both cats were sitting at the window watching the passing parade and when I opened the door they were round my feet in an instant, Tory yowling, Bertie mewing at me in his hoarse Siamese voice. I obeyed, fed them some fresh canned food, popped some toast in the toaster for me, and phoned the OPP Centre so people could have the news about Leo. I keyed in Paula's extension first. She answered on the first ring.

"Chris. I was just about to get hold of you. Where are you?"

"At home. I'll be there shortly."

"Katherine just told us what happened. Leo called her from the hospital. What a shock. How are you doing?'

"I was just giving the bad news to her roommate. Deidre had a child, about two years old. It's going to be rough on her."

"Really? I didn't know Leo was a grandfather."

"Neither did I. But he is. She's a cute little kid."

"And Leo? How's he doing? Katherine didn't have many details except he was being checked out in the hospital."

"Did he say we found Deidre's body in the lake?"

"Yeah, we got all that. Any ideas?"

"Not really. We found a note in her car which suggested she had an assignation but no names or anything. Unfortunately, Leo jumped in the water to get her out and the note was in his pocket. Still is. I'm not sure if we'll get anything from it. There is another wrinkle which I got from the roommate."

I told her the story of Deidre conceiving a deaf child and what a ruckus this had caused.

"My God, I remember that! Frankly, I thought it was wicked. You'd think any mother wants her baby to have the best chance in life, not to deliberately inflict a handicap on them."

When Paula found out she was pregnant she had immediately stopped smoking. She was a two-pack-a-day woman and it was hell for her but she'd quit cold turkey the day the pregnancy results came back.

"You're not the only one with those views, Paula. According to her friend, Deidre received a lot of hate mail, post and email both."

"Leo never once let on, did he? And I never connected him to her at all."

"You'd have no reason to. She changed her name to Larsen. According to Leo, they've had a troubled relationship since Deidre was young."

"I can see it being hard for him to have a deaf child. You know what an opera buff he is. He's passionate about it. Still, you can't not love a child just because they aren't perfect."

I agreed with her, but in our line of work, we'd both had too much experience of situations where love for even a healthy child was in short supply. Paula handled her frustration by volunteering at a local women's shelter, helping women cope with the demands of maternity. I didn't have the same credentials, no kids, no live-in mate. I found my hope in being a godmother to Paula's daughter, Chelsea, and whenever I could, I walked dogs from the animal shelter. That has its own heartache, let me tell you, but dogs are more resilient than abused kids are.

Paula's phone beeped indicating another call was coming in.

"I'd better go. Short day today."

Damn, I'd forgotten she was leaving early for a doctor's appointment. She'd noticed a peculiar lump on her sternum and her doctor had ordered a biopsy this afternoon.

"Good luck, La. Call me as soon as you're finished."

"Will do. Don't worry about me."

We hung up and I drew in a deep breath. Paula Jackson had been my best friend and soul sister since we were teenagers and the thought of anything being seriously wrong with her was more than I could take in. Her husband was going with her to the appointment but I wondered if I should have insisted harder that I go with her. In my book, Craig was more likely to worry about himself than Paula.

I was just on my way out the door when the phone rang. It was the very man himself.

"Hi, Chris. Do you have a minute?"

"What's up?"

"Frankly, I'm scared. Paula's going on as if this is nothing but I saw her doctor's face when he felt that lump. He's worried. He thinks it's cancer, I know he does."

"Even if it is, Craig, these days it isn't necessarily a death sentence."

"Maybe not but it'll be ugly if she's got to go through that chemo shit."

"Let's not cross our bridges, shall we? Let's hear the diagnosis first."

"I suppose you're right, it's just that..."

His voice tailed off.

"Craig, I..."

I didn't have a chance to finish what I was going to say.

"Never mind." He slammed down the phone.

Drat! Craig and I had learned to tolerate each other over the years even though we'd never be best buddies but the old antagonism was never too far from the surface. I could have been kinder.

Before I could do penance by calling him back, my phone rang again. I picked up the cordless extension and walked over to my toast, which was rapidly drying out in the toaster.

"Christine, Leo Forgach here."

"Leo, how are you?" I tucked the phone under my chin and tried to spread some almond butter on my toast.

"I'm fine. I just needed to get into dry clothes. I'm actually at home now. I'm going into the office shortly."

"Is that wise? You've had a terrible shock."

He clicked his tongue. "Come off it. We're professionals. The best medicine for me is to start finding my daughter's killer."

There was truth to what he said. Helplessness and inactivity were the most difficult things to tolerate for most people, especially high-energy people like Leo. However, I wasn't sure what the procedures were for somebody in our unit to be in on a case involving their own daughter.

"Who's the scene officer?" he asked.

"Ed Chaffey."

"Good. He's competent. Hold on a minute, will you?"

I heard him rustling paper and took the chance to bite into my toast. Tory came over and yowled at me. I picked her up and placed her at her food bowl, which she seemed to have forgotten. Leo came back on the line.

"I spoke to Nora and she said she filled you in concerning Deidre's actions a couple of years ago?"

"You mean about the baby?"

"Precisely..." There was the sound of a breath intake and I realized he was dragging on a cigarette — another thing I didn't know about him. "I admit I was very upset when she told me she had deliberately conceived a child that would most likely be born deaf. Then when she went to the papers to proclaim it to the world, I was furious with her." Another drag on his cigarette. "It was all aimed at me, of course. She wanted to pretend it was some high-minded statement about Deaf Culture but it wasn't. I'm a psychiatrist. Day in and day out, I see these scenarios. Murderers, rapists, felons, all acting out some script from their childhoods."

That might be true but Deidre was hardly a rapist or a murderer and Leo's clinical tone was rubbing on my nerves.

"Speaking of mothers, have you contacted her mother yet?"

"I had to leave a message. She is in the Yukon saving the polar bears or the icebergs or some such thing. I don't know when she'll check in. It might be days."

I think he ate his cigarette at that point, his anger burning through the wires.

"Anyway, what I was going to say was that after the news broke, Deidre began to receive hate mail. Some of it was by post, some email. She mentioned it to me on one of our few visits. If she kept them, they might be worth taking a look at."

"I agree. Nora told me about them but according to her they aren't in the house. She did think Deidre had kept them."

"Let's find them."

Nora had referred to Leo's daughter as the most hated woman in Orillia. It was not out of the question that somebody still harboured that hatred and had finally acted on it.

Tory had wandered away from her breakfast and was heading for the litter box. I waited a minute to make sure she went in it. She occasionally misjudged and did her business on the kitchen floor.

"I'll see you in the office in about twenty minutes…" Leo stopped, and when he spoke again, his voice was husky. "Christine, I can't thank you enough for your help this morning. I appreciate it."

Before I could answer, he hung up. I replaced my phone and went to get my coat. The wind flung rain pellets at the window and I glanced out at the deserted street below. I had intentionally purchased a house that was within walking distance of the Centre. I certainly didn't get much exercise during the workday, so walking to and from kept me reasonably fit and staved off the inevitable fortyish rear-end spread. However, physically and emotionally I wasn't up to battling the elements today. The car it was.

CHAPTER SIX

I love my work but I have to say, I don't like the office itself. The Behavioural Science Department is a rabbit warren that even the rabbits would have trouble negotiating. Rumour has it that visitors have disappeared for days trying to find their way to the washroom and one woman is still missing. All of the walls are a grey felt, or what seems like felt, with no windows. Only the head of the department, Katherine MacIsaac, and Dr. Leo Forgach have natural light. The rest of us email weather reports to each other because once inside, you don't know.

I buzzed myself through the security door and hurried down the hall to see Paula. All of the offices were tiny and hers was currently filled to capacity because two of the other profilers were with her. She waved me in.

"Chris, we were just talking about what happened."

One of the guys stood up and gallantly offered me his chair. I accepted. Why fight the equality battle here? Ray Motomochi was Japanese and a thoroughly nice man with old-fashioned manners. He, Jamie Stephens, and I had become good buddies in the two years since I'd joined the unit. Ray was our specialist in geographic profiling and Jamie was brilliant at administering polygraphs, which we are called upon to do from time to time. They were both wearing the required office uniform, suits and ties, in which the men expressed mild rebellion and individuality by choosing variant coloured shirts and outlandish ties. Jamie was the acknowledged champion of colour clash. Today it was a pink shirt and an orange tie with green stripes. He made me think of candy floss.

"Leo just called me," I said. "He's checked himself out of the hospital and he's coming here. He's determined to go on working."

"Katherine won't let him be on this one," said Ray.

"Officially she won't, but if you want my opinion, she's not going to be able to stop him unofficially."

"I didn't even know he had a daughter," said Ray. "I've never heard him mention her once."

"He's got a son as well from a first marriage. The only reason I know is because my wife knows somebody who knows his ex. Poor sod, he must be gutted." Jamie's parents were English expats and his speech was often peppered with English expletives and colloquialisms. He turned to me. "You and he were the ones who found her?"

"That's right."

I briefly explained.

"Why'd he call you in particular, Chris?" Ray asked. "No offence, just curious."

"She's the only single in the department," Jamie answered for me. "Who else could drop everything at six in the morning and rush to his side?"

"Correction. It was actually twelve minutes past five and pitch-black out and being single has everything to do with it. Leo knew I'd be out of bed fresh as a daisy in a matter of moments, unlike my married colleagues, who are always otherwise engaged."

They groaned at my little lascivious innuendo. Well, why not? Men don't have a monopoly on these things.

I got a lot of good-natured flack from the rest of them about being unencumbered, although I doubted anybody would change places with me, except maybe Jamie who often seemed weighed down with family concerns.

"Tell them what the girl did, Chris," said Paula. Her tone was indignant. I knew that she had faced down many horrible situations with great objectivity but this one seemed to have got to her.

I filled in the two guys with what Nora had told me.

"I remember it," said Ray. "She was truly raked over the coals by the *Packet* and the *News*. She certainly was unpopular. When they published the usual letters to the editor hardly anybody supported Deidre."

"I'd think not," retorted Paula. "Hold on." Her phone had rung. "Yes, Katherine, yes, Chris is here too. I'll tell them."

She hung up. "Katherine wants to have a meeting in the boardroom at twelve-thirty. That okay with everybody?"

The guys nodded. Jamie stood up. "I've got a report to send off. Ta-ta." At the door he halted. "What are we going to do about condolences? Shall I ask Janice to order a wreath from all of us?"

We all agreed to that and the two of them gathered up their coffee mugs and left.

I looked over at Paula. She always paid attention to her appearance, careful makeup, good haircuts, but this morning she was haggard and drawn, no makeup visible.

"How's it going, kiddo?"

"Not great, but I'm trying not to think about it. It could be nothing. You know doctors these days, they're alarmists."

I got up and put my arms about her shoulders and dropped a kiss on the top of her head.

"You're going to be fine. Try not to worry."

"It's the waiting that's so hard. You know me, give me a job and bam, I'm there, but we won't know anything for a few days after the biopsy." She touched her thick hair, which was layered in a fashionable crisp curl. "Oh God, Chris, I don't want to lose my hair."

"Shh. You don't know that's what will happen. And even if it does, Canute himself couldn't stop those waves."

That elicited a wan smile, but I felt for her. Paula had been a gangly, plain sort of adolescent and her abundant curly hair was her best feature. She'd blossomed into an attractive woman but she still returned to that image of her adolescent self — nice hair, too bad about the face. Nowadays, she wore it short, with blonde highlights. She was always smartly dressed and her makeup was an art. Heads still swivelled in her direction when she was all gussied up.

I sat down again. "What do you need to take your mind off things?"

"Morphine?"

I laughed a little over-heartily.

"Oops, Chelsea fell over." One of her files had knocked over a framed photograph of her daughter and my godchild, Chelsea, the apple of our eyes. It was a photograph I myself had taken when Chelsea was three years old. She was such a ham even then and loved to pose for the camera. She had on her Halloween outfit, Mary the contrary one, with gingham dress and apron and unexpectedly, by Chelsea's choice, a diamond tiara. The effect was only slightly marred by the fact that it was a cold day and she had to wear her outfit over her snowsuit. The stuffed lamb I'd brought back for her from the Hebrides was tightly tucked under her arm.

Paula stood the picture up again on her desk and stared at it. She was struggling to hold back tears. "Oh Chris, how could I leave her? Even when she was in utero and I knew she was a girl, I was planning her wedding."

"My God, La, I don't believe it. How would you feel if the poor girl wants to be a nun? It's not likely they will be marrying in our lifetime."

Paula and the Jackson family were staunch Catholics and Chelsea went to Sunday school regularly. This was one of the few places where Craig and I were in agreement, with the difference being that he had no hesitation in openly deriding Paula's faith. I'd learned a long time ago to keep my feelings to myself.

She frowned. "That would be all right too, of course it would."

"Hmm, you can't do much with that black serge but you could choose a tasteful veil."

My feeble joke didn't work. Suddenly she turned and grabbed my arm. "Chris, you know I'm depending on you. If anything happens to me, I want you to look after Chelse. You're the only one I can totally trust. Craig can be a bit … er … well, he loves her but I'm not sure he understands girls."

I tried to make a flip comment but failed. I squeezed her hand. "I was planning to come over tonight. I can put her to bed if you like."

"Let's see. I might want to do that myself."

"Okay."

I waited, feeling awkward and helpless. If this lump proved to be benign, I'd buy a bushel basket of candles and light them, or whatever Catholics did when they wanted to express gratitude to the Almighty.

Paula squeezed back for a moment. "Thanks, Chris. I'd better get on with things, I haven't come close to reading all the reports on that double homicide case in Hamilton."

"You can sound it off me when you're ready."

"Will do."

I left her to it and made my way to my own office, which was at the end of the narrow hall next to Ray's and across from Leo's.

Ray had his door open and as I went by, he called out.

"Janice said to tell you, your ICIAF package has arrived."

I groaned to myself. I'd been expecting it but I wasn't ready. A word of explanation. More than two years ago, I had been hired by the Behavioural Science Department after a long stint on the front lines of the Toronto police force. However, to become a fully-fledged profiler and an associate of the International Criminal Investigative Analysis Fellowship, I had to do what we called understudying. Other professionals call it interning or apprenticeship, and what it meant was that as well as my regular work, I had to spend time observing what the associate profilers did. I'd spent time with the Horsemen (the RCMP to you); I'd been on two long stints with the NYPD hoping I'd run into Dennis Franz (I didn't); and I'd spent one month with the Miami Police and three weeks in Quantico, Virginia, the home of the FBI. Now I was expected to write the big test. The package that Janice had delivered contained a real case, names removed, which I had to study and write my own assessment on. As the culprit had already been convicted, unless there was an unlikely gross miscarriage of justice, the name I came up with had to be the right one. Three members of the board would interrogate me. Like any other important examination, this one generated a lot of nerves. I didn't want to fail.

I sat down at my desk. I'd Scotch-taped my favourite pictures to my wall and most of them were of Chelsea at various stages of her growth. There was also an old photo of me and Paula, which we'd taken in one of those booths where you sit on a stool and make faces in the mirror until the flash goes off and the machine spits out a picture. It was almost thirty years old, that snapshot. We had our cheeks pressed together, laughing at nothing except that we were squashed in that booth getting our pictures taken.

It was my turn to bite my lip. I thought about what Craig had said about the doctor's alarm and my quick response, "It isn't necessarily a death sentence."

I could not imagine life without Paula. I couldn't buy a pair of shoes without consulting her first. She was threaded through my life so tightly that if the thread was pulled out, I feared the whole thing would unravel.

I pulled the package toward me. Better stop thinking and get working.

CHAPTER SEVEN

Almost everything is on CD these days and this was no exception. I popped it in my computer and opened it up:

> *In September 1990, a woman's body was found along the bank of a river in Europe. She was on her back, nude, with a pair of stockings knotted around her neck. She was covered with a light layer of dirt and leaves. She was wearing a wedding ring. She had been strangled, beaten about the face and arms, indicating a struggle for her life. There was no sign of sexual assault.*

I leaned back in my chair. I was finding it difficult to concentrate. We get cases from all around the world. Mostly North America but they can come in from the UK, Australia, you name it. Most of them are developing their own profiling departments, but they like to consult with us if the case is a tough one. We rarely get to see the actual crime scene and there is a certain amount of emotional protection in that. I can see the photograph of the beaten body, but I don't have to inhale the particular smell of human blood or a corpse that's been lying in a basement for weeks. I don't see in real time the damage that has been perpetrated on what was once a live being. I can be, and I am expected to be, objective. But only a few hours ago, I had helped pull a young woman out of the lake who was the daughter of my colleague. I couldn't flick a switch and wipe those images out of my mind. I'd also had enough experience as a front-line police officer to know how devastating it is to the victim's family to not have the culprit brought to justice. Perhaps this would be an easy case, such as a genuine confession from the murderer. Unfortunately I doubted that. The murderer had attempted both to hide the body and to ensure that it would be very difficult to get any forensic evidence. Forget what you see on *CSI* shows, immersion in water is virtually fail-safe for wiping out prints or fibres or detectable DNA.

I was about to go back to the test case when there was a telltale vibration at my belt from my cellphone. No happy tunes for me; it would have driven everybody mad in the office if all the cellphones played tunes.

I checked the call display. A long-distance call. My heart gave a little skip; there was always a tinge of anxiety at the sight of an unexpected long-distance call coming in, and I'd probably go to my grave with that reflex intact. Would it be a call announcing my mother was in trouble again? Whew, it wasn't. Gordon Gillies, better known to all as Gill, my lovely guy, calling me from the Outer Hebrides.

"Allo a Christine, *matain mhav*. Gill here."

He always announced himself, which I found rather endearing. As if there was anybody else in my life who'd tell me good morning in Gaelic with that deep voice.

"Have I caught you in the middle of something?"

Usually we called each other on Sundays, cheaper rates and more likelihood we would make direct contact.

"Nothing that can't wait, what's up?"

My anxiety must have shot through the phone. "Oh everything's guid over here if you discount an absence of sun and ignore the gale force winds and the fact that my own troo love is on the other side of the ocean. We're all guid … including your mother. She says she'll be calling you soon."

I hadn't spoken to Joan in about three weeks now. It was her turn to call me. If you'd asked me two years ago if I would be in even that frequent contact with my mother, I'd have made scoffing noises, but our relationship has improved considerably since I'd discovered her secret past, not to mention meeting the man who had fathered me. But that's a complicated story that I won't go into at the moment.

"I'm going to call you properly on Sunday," he said, "but this is a professional call, if you will. I'd like your advice on a situation we have here."

"Wow. Ask away but better still maybe you can request for me to be seconded."

"I'd have to falsify the crime rate stats. Yes, Inspector, we doo indeed need Miss Christine Morris to help us with this utterly unprecedented rampage of deaths. This is the second one in ten years and we're most concerned."

"You guys must be overwhelmed, but seriously you're not telling me you have a murder? Not in the Hebrides!"

Gill and I had a running tease about the difference in the rate of serious crime in our respective countries. Even though it was becoming more and more of a struggle, the Lewishans were still ahead of the game and violent assault was virtually non-existent except around the docks sometimes when the foreign boats tied up. Drug-related problems were on the rise but the usual incidents of petty crime such as theft, smuggling in contraband, drunkenness, all the myriad transgressions that occur wherever humanity chooses to gather together, were still far below national averages.

"Not a murder but for us a rather nasty case. Use of a restricted drug, cannabis, but also an alleged sexual assault."

"Spell it out."

I heard him sigh. "It'll take too long and I get the feeling you're on your way out. I'd like to send you my report and you can have a look when you get the chance."

"Fax it to me and I'll get to it as soon as I can."

"Thanks, Chris. How's everything over there?"

I hesitated. I wanted to tell him what had happened but I also wanted to help and I had a feeling he'd withdraw his request if he knew what was going on.

"Not good, really, but I can't go into it now. What's it like in Stornoway?"

"Getting dark already, the wind is hitting gale force. I almost got blown off the road driving across the moor. And the poor sheep look so miserable I want to bring them home."

"Ha. I always knew that under that tough exterior there lies a heart softer than a mushy pea."

He laughed. "It's peas, not pea, you foreigner you."

The intercom clicked on and Janice's cheery voice said, "Meeting in five minutes. I repeat. Meeting for all staff in the boardroom in five minutes."

We all complained about the intercom announcements, which have a Big Brother quality to them, but they were effective in keeping us on time and on track. We were an independent, sauntering sort of lot, otherwise.

"I've got to go, Gill."

"We'll talk on Sunday then? My turn to call."

"Same time, same place."

"Bye then. I miss you, Chris."

"Me too."

We hung up and I sat for a minute with the cellphone in my hand as if I could hold onto him. I must admit when we had first become involved two years ago, I'd been okay with the long-distance arrangement. I'd been single for a large proportion of my child-bearing years and I liked my routines. A few weeks here and there together when I was essentially on holiday was no problem. However, I'd noticed lately I was thinking of him more and more when I was sitting with the cats, all by myself on Saturday night and Sunday morning and wishing it was him I was cuddling. I hadn't seen him since the summer, when I'd spent three weeks in Lewis. That was three months ago.

I had a photograph of him on my notice board, one I'd taken in the summer. He was sitting in the tiny — by our standards — blue and white police car. He hadn't known I was taking the picture but I'd liked the look of his profile, the thoughtfulness of his expression, even though when I showed him the photo, he laughed and said he'd only been wondering what to have for lunch. I smiled at him *in abstentia*.

Why couldn't I have made my life simple and fallen for a good upstanding Canadian guy who lived at least within driving distance?

Janice was our office den mother. She was quietly efficient, always positive, cheered us up when we needed it, and made the best coffee to boot. To everybody's dismay, she had declared she was retiring at the end of the month and was going on a world tour.

"I've always wanted to travel and I'm going now before I have to be pushed around in a wheelchair."

I was happy for her but, like all of us, secretly hoped she'd change her mind.

She'd put a Thermos pot of fresh coffee and a plate of sandwiches on the table in the corner. Ray and Jamie were already tucking in. David Wojeck, our newest team member, like me understudying, was at the end of the table, sipping his customary cup of hot water. He was a lanky, skinny guy, his appearance completely reflecting his ascetic habits: always a white shirt, dark tie, and navy suit and thinning hair that was never allowed to get longer than an inch all over. He drank no beverages except spring water, ate no snack food except raw veggies. Good for him, except that he had the mindset of a religious fanatic and was always trying to convert us to healthy living. It grated on the nerves, especially if they were as raw as mine were today.

When I came into the room he waved me over. "Chris, I heard what happened and I brought you a homeopathic remedy. It's the best thing in the world for shock."

He held out a little plastic tube.

"Put three pellets under the tongue and let them dissolve. You mustn't eat or drink for at least fifteen minutes before or after the remedy."

"Then I'll have to wait. I'm going into caffeine withdrawal already and I'm ready to eat paper if I have to."

He shook his head disapprovingly. "Carbs aren't what you need right now."

I wasn't in a tolerant frame of mind and in a minute I would probably have grabbed his rather prominent nose, held it until he opened his mouth, and jammed some bread into it. Katherine saved me from such ungraciousness by sweeping in, Janice behind her. The word *sweeping* might suggest imperiousness and self-importance but that isn't at all how I meant it or how she is. Katherine, never Kathy, or Kate, is tall, almost six feet, slim, and the most elegant woman I've ever met. She doesn't even have to work at it. She has Audrey Hepburn cheekbones, but not the nose, hazel eyes, and the kind of iron grey hair that black hair can transition into. She favours classic blazers and silk shirts. Sartorial good taste aside, she is smart and extremely hard-working. She almost single-handedly formed the Behavioural Science Department and put forensic profiling on the map of Canadian law enforcement.

She came directly to where I was sitting and put her hand on my shoulder. Another woman might have hugged me; Katherine wasn't that sort of boss, but there was no doubt about the warmth of her concern.

"Christine, how are you feeling?"

"I'm fine, thanks. Have you heard from Leo?"

"Yes, he's on his way." She shrugged. "He insisted and frankly I don't blame him. I'd be the same if it were my daughter who had been murdered."

"He can't work on the case surely?" asked David.

"No, of course not directly, but we'll keep him as involved as we can." She sat down at the head of the table. "Paula has a doctor's appointment and won't be here. Chris, I'll leave it to you to bring her up to speed." Her expression was neutral. I knew Paula had taken her into her confidence but she didn't want anybody else knowing just yet. Katherine wasn't revealing anything. She glanced around. "Everybody here?"

Janice had gone over to the table to check on supplies. She poured a cup of coffee for Katherine, put a couple of sandwiches on a plate, and brought them over to her. She waited to get the nod of approval from Katherine, and domestic duties done, departed for her own desk. Jamie and Ray, carrying their coffee cups and a stacked plate each, came to sit down.

"All right, folks, let's start. Now I myself never met Deidre, did anybody else?"

Nobody had. As I mentioned earlier, Leo kept his private life very private. The rest of us mingled quite a lot, summer barbeques, Christmas drinks, that sort of thing, and even if we hadn't met all of the family members, we knew about them, saw pictures, heard their stories. They all knew mine, at least an abbreviated version that I was myself just absorbing. About Joan and me, my newly discovered father, and my relationship with Gill.

"The case is in the hands of Ed Chaffey," continued Katherine. "We can't tread on any toes, but given the peculiar nature of the situation, with one of our own involved, I know Ed's going to ask us for assistance." She paused, her eyes meeting everybody's at the table. "And we will make it our top priority. I know you all have other cases you're working on but I am asking you to put them aside for the time being and concentrate entirely on this one. Does anybody have any objections?"

I'd expected David Wojeck to voice an objection as he always did for form's sake, but he was silent. Jamie, who was also section head, looked a bit worried because he was swamped with a major government overhaul of the entire centre, which meant endless frustrating meetings and turf wars.

Katherine nodded over at me. "Christine, why don't you tell us what happened this morning?"

I did, and I was just wrapping up with my talk with Nora when the door opened and Leo entered. He was back in his office gear, tweed jacket and brown turtleneck; his hair was brushed tidily back from his temples and he'd taken the trouble to shave. His face was so pale and drawn, my heart went out to him. There was a murmur of sympathetic noises from everybody else followed by an awkward silence as Leo took an empty chair.

"Leo, I know I am speaking for everybody here when I say how deeply sorry we all are about what has happened," said Katherine.

"Thank you." He dropped his head and pinched the bridge of his nose hard. We waited and he soon had himself back under control. "I quite understand the protocol about staff involvement in personal cases but I do have expertise concerning cases like this, so I hope you won't shut me out."

His voice threatened to get away from him at the end of that sentence and Katherine spoke quickly.

"We wouldn't dream of doing that, Leo. You are too valuable. As for involvement, I leave that up to you."

His shoulders sagged with relief, then he leaned down and picked up his briefcase.

"I brought along a photograph. It was taken three years ago at her university commencement. She's let her hair grow since then but it's a good likeness. I've made copies."

He handed them around. In the picture, Deidre was smiling, a mortarboard perched squarely on her head. Her hair was ear-length, wavy and dark brown like her father's. Her eyes were brown, also like his. I flashed back for a moment on the image of her face, all colour leached out, emerging from the water, her hair waving in tendrils around her head.

"She's very pretty," said Katherine.

Leo held the photograph for a moment and studied it. "Yes, she was. She takes ... took after her mother in that." He put the picture back on the table and pushed it slightly away from him. "Now, I am prepared to give you as many details as I can. I must admit we were not particularly close and there are some things that frankly I do not know but at least we can start."

He was getting into what we called victimology. We've learned that by knowing as much as we can about the victim of violent crime we can deduce a great deal about the perpetrator. Janice had provided us all with notepads and pens and we each grabbed one. I could tell everybody else was as relieved as I was to have something to do. Those of us who had sandwiches half-eaten tried to eat them as unobtrusively as possible. To tuck in hearty fashion seemed unfeeling.

Leo had made notes and he began to read from them.

"Physical traits: She was petite, five feet three inches. The last time I saw her in person, which was last Christmas, she was in good shape and very fit. She weighed perhaps about one hundred and ten pounds."

"The coroner will give us a precise weight," said David. Unnecessarily, I thought. Why direct Leo's thoughts in that direction?

"She has always been an athletic girl, strong," continued Leo with a frown. "She would not have been easily overpowered."

That was important to know.

"Next. Marital status. Single. She has a child who is now almost three years old." He paused and did the nose-pinching thing again. "She never admitted who the father was, so I cannot help you there. I have never met any boyfriend, or girlfriend for that matter. As far as I am aware, my daughter was heterosexual. Next. Personal lifestyle. She lives, er, lived, with a female roommate but as I say, to my knowledge she is not a lesbian. The roommate's name is Nora Cochrane. She works at the addiction counselling centre on Lachlie

Street. Deidre had a job teaching at the Ontario Hard of Hearing Association. We'll need to talk to her colleagues there."

It would be up to Katherine to assign somebody and it would also depend on what work Ed Chaffey was willing to share with us.

"She has no criminal convictions that I know of but you will have to check on that. She may have failed to mention any to me."

His voice was flat but I could sense the pain behind the words. He didn't have to tell us how estranged he had been from his daughter; it wasn't hard to see.

"Shall we do the usual credit check?" asked Jamie. He spoke hesitatingly and Leo flashed him a sharp glance.

"Of course. Why wouldn't we?"

For a moment he was the old Leo, full of impatience at what he considered stupid questions.

Jamie flushed. I knew he had only been trying to be tactful. This was his colleague after all. I interceded.

"Leo, you told me Deidre was profoundly deaf and that she had become militant about Deaf Culture. I think that's worth repeating."

It was my turn to get the edge of his tongue.

"I was coming to that, Christine! It might be the most important fact about her."

Now it was me reacting. He noticed and he winced.

"I'm sorry. I didn't mean to take that tone ... I, er..."

"That's all right."

There was another awkward silence. Jamie hid his discomfiture in his coffee cup. Leo continued working down his list.

"Map of travel prior to the offence. This is more your province, Ray. I received a call from Nora Cochrane at five-thirty this morning. They live on Mary Street. Deidre had left the house just after seven-thirty Tuesday evening, which apparently is her regular time. She has the routine of going to Casino Rama every Tuesday evening. She is usually home between eleven and eleven-thirty. On this occasion, Nora had fallen asleep and didn't know Deidre hadn't returned. When she realized what time it was, she telephoned me. It is utterly out of character for her to be out all night."

David raised a tentative finger to indicate a question. "Had her bed been slept in?"

"Good question. I don't know. We must ask Nora."

I said, "I did have a brief look at Deidre's room when I was there this morning. The bed was neatly made."

Leo inhaled and went on. "That, of course, doesn't prove anything really but it is worth knowing. So where was I? Right, I telephoned Christine..." he paused. "Frankly I needed some collegial support. She accompanied me to the casino, where we found Deidre's car. It had a flat tire."

Another finger raise from David. "I presume we will impound the car and see if the tire was intentionally damaged or not."

"I'm sure Ed Chaffey has that under control," said Katherine. "Go on, Leo."

"We were able to locate her customary table. They all keep a receipt of bets with the time stamped when the bet was placed. Her last bet was at 10:33."

"We'll get a subpoena to watch the CCTV," said Katherine.

"I have a key to her car." He gave a wry grin. "Father's privilege." He reached into his briefcase. "We found this note on the front passenger seat. Unfortunately, I put it in my pocket and it did not survive the dunking in the lake. Christine no doubt explained what that was all about. I'll give it to you, Ray. You are a miracle worker."

He handed the piece of paper to Ray, who took it by the corner. "It was written in pencil and that has survived, but I don't think I can pull up any prints from it."

"Read it to us, will you Ray," said Katherine.

"It's in block letters. 'Okay. I'll meet you at the monument at 11:00. Don't be late, I won't wait.'"

"That certainly puts her in the vicinity where you found her body. Assuming '11:00' refers to last night. Did the roommate say if Deidre was out at any other time?" Katherine asked.

I spoke up. "Just the opposite. Apparently, her only night out was Tuesday and occasionally on Saturdays."

"This could be a crucial piece of evidence so I suggest we come back to it." said Katherine. "Are you doing all right, Leo? Do you need a break? Cup of coffee?"

He looked as if he was going to refuse, then he nodded. "That would be appreciated, thanks. There are just a few more points, and rather important ones, but the coffee sounds good, and one of those roast beef sandwiches. I haven't had a chance to have breakfast."

Suddenly he put his head in his hands. I could see he was trembling. I was next to him and I put my hand on his; it was cold. Over his head I caught Katherine's eye.

"Why don't we all take ten minutes?" she said. Jamie was closest to the coffee pot and he poured a mug. David rolled his little tube of homeopathic pellets down the table.

"These will do you more good than coffee. Just put three under your tongue and let them dissolve."

Leo didn't respond, but at a signal from Katherine, the others got up and made their way to the door. I sat where I was, trying to send some warmth into Leo's icy fingers.

CHAPTER EIGHT

Tactfully, the group took a long ten minutes, and by the time they shuffled back in, Leo's colour had returned and his hands weren't as cold. He had gulped down some food and was tackling the coffee and that helped. Once everybody was in place he took up his list.

"Deidre's mother and I were divorced when she was four years old. Her name is Loretta Larsen. She is an environmental lawyer, which means she travels a lot, trying to raise awareness of the shitty job we're doing everywhere on earth. Global warming, endangered this, endangered that." He couldn't keep the sarcasm out of his voice. "Loretta had measles when Deidre was in utero and the child was born profoundly deaf with no hope of cure. This was as you can imagine a dreadful shock to both of us. Loretta is what you would call a Type A personality. She blamed herself. She had continued to work until late in the pregnancy and who knows where she contracted the measles. She had only ever wanted one child. That child had to be perfect and it turned out Deidre wasn't."

By now he was back to his dispassionate, professional voice, but you didn't have to be Dr. Phil to see behind the words. Giving birth to what was seen as a defective child had broken the marriage apart.

"I was very busy establishing myself as the pre-eminent forensic psychiatrist in the country and I will admit I was only too happy to escape into my work to avoid the increasing tensions at home. Deidre was a bright child but neither Loretta nor I knew what to do with her. I tried learning sign language but I didn't get very far and Loretta refused to do it at all, insisting that Deidre learn to read lips and to speak. Which she did and very well. Loretta wanted to send her away to a special school for the deaf, and after we had considered the options, I agreed it would be the best thing for her."

We'd all been scribbling notes and he waited for us to catch up.

"Deidre has essentially been in residential schools most of her life. She went to Gallaudet University in the States and that's where she became what I'd have to call militant. And I mean fiercely so. Deaf Culture is equal to and as good as the hearing culture is the mantra. She stopped reading lips and refused to use her voice other than to make noises. It's all sign language for them." He pinched his nose again. "You know the scene, I'm sure. Same scenario, different characters. 'We the blankety, blank, totally reject the oppression foisted upon us for decades by the blankety blank, and we insist on our rights and privileges the same as everybody else.' We can fill in the blanks, you can say black people, Native, labour, women. Personally I'm all for equality but I resent being held to ransom or threatened if I don't comply. One of Deidre's classmates heard she could have a cochlear implant that would restore her hearing loss almost completely and the girl was literally spat at in the cafeteria when she made the mistake of telling people what she was thinking. She was called a traitor, a defector to the hearing world." He looked around the table. "I'm sure you know what I'm talking about. Fanatics. Their teaching fell on fertile soil and when Deidre graduated she was into it. She wouldn't communicate with me except by sign language, which I didn't understand, so we didn't communicate." Another pause. He straightened his papers. "Then shortly after she graduated, she wrote to me and told me she was pregnant. She also said that the father was a deaf man and that she had deliberately worked the odds to have a deaf child. Which is what happened. Joy, her daughter, has the same affliction. I admit I was furious. It's one thing to stomp around demanding your rights; it's another to deliberately choose to inflict your handicap on your child. You're shutting them out from one of the most sublime experiences we godforsaken humans can have."

His voice was filled with both anger and anguish. Leo was notorious in the office for his dedication to operatic music. He listened to it on his headphones in his office, but sometimes the sounds would leak out, and if you went in to talk to him, you'd find him, expression rapt, swaying and waving his hands like a conductor in time to the music. He let slip one day that he was part of a music group that put on opera excerpts once a year. I could understand how it would have been so hard for him to have a child who would never be able to share that passion with him and then to have her deliberately engineer a deaf grandchild.

He went on.

"This was a rare instance when Loretta and I were in agreement. She wanted Deidre to have an abortion but she flatly refused. She wouldn't tell us the name of the father, who she actually referred to as the sperm donor, and as far as I know from Nora, there has been no man involved in Joy's life at all. Now, here comes the crunch. About six months after Joy was born, totally deaf as planned, the story hit the newspapers and media. I don't know how it got out but it caused quite a stir. Deidre received a lot of hate mail."

He paused to have a drink of coffee.

"You said you haven't seen her since Christmas?" asked Katherine.

"That's right. I dropped in on Christmas Day with my gifts as I've done each year since Joy was born. It wasn't a good meeting. We had a row, if you can call it that when one person is yelling words the other can't understand and the other is waving her hands about and screaming incomprehensible noises. I'm not even sure what I communicated to get Deidre so angry with me except that I would like to have a relationship with my only grandchild." He stopped again, lost momentarily in his painful memories. "Anyway that was that. She wouldn't answer my messages or my emails. Since then, I have been cut off completely."

"Where is Loretta now?" asked Jamie.

"In the Yukon. I have emailed her and I assume she will come back as soon as she can. Deidre, by the way, changed her name after she graduated. She took her mother's name of Larsen. I don't know if Dee was in touch with her mother or not. She and I do not communicate either." He fidgeted with his papers. "I should add I have another son from my first marriage. He lives in Barrie. His name is Sigmund." He grimaced. "He hasn't forgiven me for that one and calls himself Sig. To my knowledge his relationship with his half-sister is virtually non-existent."

He looked over at Katherine, who nodded. "Thank you, Leo. Now let's have a look at the letter again. Chris, would you say male or female?"

I had a brief study of the note. "It's hard to tell with this short piece but the writing is quite bold and sprawling; more significantly, the tone is peremptory, no softening words. It doesn't say, 'Please, don't be late,' which a woman might do. I'd go for a male."

"Anybody else?"

The others agreed with me, even David who often disagreed on principle.

"What else?"

"The writer is replying to a previous letter, presumably from Deidre. The 'okay' isn't a question; it's a statement. Otherwise it would follow after 'monument.' 'I'll meet you at the monument, okay?' She must have said something like: 'Can we meet on such and such a day?' The answer is 'Okay.' He suggests the location, no asking. He's calling the shots. '11:00' supports my first statement. Deidre has already suggested a time so he doesn't have to specify morning or evening or which day. He's responding. He also doesn't say which monument, which suggests they both know what he's referring to, which in turn definitely points to a previous acquaintance. And then the scold, 'Don't be late, I won't wait.' Lots of irritation in those lines."

"She was chronically late," interjected Leo. "I've not known her to be on time once. It was infuriating."

"That's important to know," I went on. "It reinforces the possibility that he knew her well enough to have experienced the problem."

"You say you found the note in the car," said Katherine.

Leo took up the story once more. "It was slightly crumpled up but quite dry. No envelope. It could have been sent through the mail, of course, and she didn't have the envelope with her, but I have the feeling it was left on the car. Would you agree, Chris?"

"I would. It's written in pencil and torn out of a pocket-sized notebook. That suggests to me a spur-of-the-moment thing."

"But if it was on her windshield, she'd hardly drive to the casino with it there, so it was placed on the car either before she left the house or while it was parked at the casino," said Ray. "Do you know where she usually parked her car?"

"She had street parking."

"Don't forget, Doctor Forgach said it was dry," interjected David. "And it had been raining most of Tuesday evening if I remember properly. Anybody know when it started?"

I took that up. "I do. I walk dogs for the Humane Society and I'd just got them back when it began to pour down. I'd say that was just before six o'clock. The afternoon was overcast but no rain. So either she took the note to her car after receiving it in the mail — we can ask Nora about that — or it was left on her windshield before it started raining, meaning she got it before six."

"Let's go over this so far," said Katherine. "Deidre has some sort of correspondence with a person she knows in which she proposes a meeting at 11:00 p.m. Given that we've been told Tuesday is her only night out, let's assume she suggests Tuesday and that she was intending to meet this person after she had been at the casino. We don't know if that communication happened by snail mail or email. Did she use text messaging, Leo?"

"I have no idea. Not to me she didn't. I did not search her, er, her body but I didn't see any sign of a cellphone or a purse. I gave her a cellphone when Joy was born so I would assume she had it with her. I can give you her number."

Katherine went on. "I'll pass that on to Ed Chaffey. Eleven o'clock at night is late for a get-together and the monument is hardly cosy. However, on a cold November night the park was likely to be deserted. Was the meeting arranged there for the purpose of secrecy?"

"Not necessarily," interjected David. "It could simply have been a place they were both familiar with and that was private, as opposed to secret."

"Point taken. Either way, does that then mean the writer of the note is her killer? And if he is, why is he?"

"I'd say the casino is a good place to start," said Ray. "We should have a look at the security tapes first and have Ed's guys check the buses and taxis. Perhaps she came back into town on the bus after she found she had a flat tire. Leo, do you know if she's a member of CAA?"

"Yes. I pay for it."

In spite of having been cut out of his daughter's life, Leo seemed to have been a good dad in the financial sense.

"We'll check to see if she did make a call but it doesn't seem like it," said Katherine. "Now we don't know if she communicated with her rendezvous via phone. 'I'm on my way, etc. etc.'"

"I'd guess not," I said. "If they were able to text message, why leave a note?"

"Good point. So she comes out of the casino, sees the flat — we'll know soon enough what caused that. She didn't call for help, which again reinforces our idea that the appointment was for eleven o'clock last night. She didn't have time. So let's say she got into town by bus or taxi or..."

"Somebody gave her a lift," David finished for her.

"Exactly. If she did take a bus, she could have easily walked to the park from the terminal for her meeting. In which case, though, she would certainly have got there way past eleven. And if the writer of the letter meant what he said, he would have left. Even if she took a taxi, she would have been pushing it." Katherine tapped her fingers on the table. "We don't even know at this point where the murder occurred. Out on the pier seems far too public. If she knew her assailant she might have been standing out there with him and say there was some kind of quarrel. The scarf was tied at the back which tells us that her assailant was behind her..."

"It was her own scarf," said Leo. "It was a birthday gift from her mother."

Katherine paused to take a drink of coffee. I could imagine what she was thinking. Maybe it was a mistake to have allowed Leo to be present. It was very hard to maintain objectivity.

"All right then. We can probably assume she was wearing the scarf. She might have been running away from her assailant. Regardless, there would have been a struggle."

I could see there was a quick, almost involuntary lowering of heads. Nobody wanted to dwell on what that meant. We were all conversant with the mechanics of strangulation, including Leo.

Katherine took a quick check of Leo and continued. "She is overcome, then she is lowered to the ground. It would take several minutes to gather the stones and fill her pockets, so once again there is a great risk here of being seen."

Jamie interjected. "I'd say she was killed somewhere else, possibly in a vehicle, and then brought to the pier, stones stuffed in her pockets, and she was simply dump... er, rolled over the side into the lake."

He was trying to be sensitive to Leo's feelings but it was impossible to completely soften the facts of what had happened. Leo was sitting quite still and his expression was impassive but I thought every word was hitting him like a blow. Katherine noticed it too.

"It's obvious we need more evidence. Forensics have promised to be as fast as they can be and Ed has all his men out doing house-to-house. He's going to ask for reinforcements from Barrie. When all that starts coming in, we should have a clearer picture. In the meantime, Leo, I think you should go home and get some rest. I promise I'll keep you informed every step of the way."

I expected him to protest but he didn't. He got unsteadily to his feet.

"I'll leave the note here for the forensic lab." He swallowed hard. "Thanks everybody. I, er," he stumbled over his words, "I want you to know I do appreciate your support."

Underneath the tetchiness, Dr. Leo Forgach was a very lonely man.

CHAPTER NINE

Leo picked up his briefcase and headed for the door. Then he turned back to Katherine.

"I wonder if you would mind if I borrowed Christine? I..." His voice tailed off. "I took a cab here and my car is still at the park... If she's willing, that is."

Katherine looked over at me, eyebrows raised. "All right with you, Christine? We can't do much more here at the moment."

"Sure."

"I'll meet you in the lobby," he said and shot away. It must have been hard for him to sit still as long as he had. His agitation demanded he move and move fast.

I got my outdoor things and hurried outside to the parking lot. Leo was pacing up and down. His dapper cashmere overcoat had been replaced by a scruffy blue raincoat and he was wearing a black wool toque, clothes that yesterday I would never have believed I'd see him in. I wished there was some way I could soothe his hurt, but there wasn't.

He waited impatiently for me to unlock the car.

"I'd like to go to the place Deidre worked. I should tell them what has happened. They won't know."

I let him into the car and got in myself.

"Geez, Leo, should you be the one to do that?"

"Why not? I know she has a couple of friends who also work there. They might be able to help us."

I groaned to myself, realizing what he was up to. I headed out of the lot and turned onto Memorial Drive.

"Leo, why did you ask for me to come with you?"

He refused to look at me but I could see him clenching his teeth. "Frankly because I need a witness and you're a woman. They'll open up to you whereas they might not with me."

I felt like shaking him, sympathy temporarily gone. I couldn't coddle him; it was doing him no favours. I pulled over to the side of the road and stopped the car. It was pelting down now and cars swished past, spraying the windshield so we were soon closed inside a cocoon of wet glass that we couldn't see out of.

"Look, Leo. You are in danger of compromising this investigation. When we catch the bastard who killed your daughter, we have to have a clean case. You cannot be directly involved."

This time he did look at me. His eyes were cold and hard.

"All I'm proposing doing is giving my daughter's friends the courtesy of telling them *myself* what has happened. Any parent would do the same."

"Cut it out, Leo! You can't pretend this is an ordinary situation. It's not. I repeat. You could compromise the case." I let that sit for a minute, then I turned on the wipers. "I'm going to take you to your apartment. I will go myself and talk to Deidre's friends and I promise I will come back and report to you."

He reached for the door handle. "I can get a taxi. You can't stop me from doing that."

"I can call Ed Chaffey and have you prevented from entering the premises. Please don't make me do that, Leo. It will be embarrassing for everybody, and I repeat, the absolute last thing we want is to contaminate the investigation."

He slumped back in the seat and sat like that with his eyes closed. The windows were completely fogged over. I waited him out.

"Very well. Do you know who the friends are?"

"Yes. Nora gave me two names."

"Who are they?"

"Why do you want to know?"

He blinked. "They were part of Deedee's life. It comforts me to have their names."

I could see how hard it was for him to reveal this much vulnerability.

"One of them is Jessica Manolo; the other is Hannah Silverstein."

He nodded. "I recognize the names. They graduated from university together ... I saw the class list — she didn't invite me."

I started the engine and headed for his condominium. As I was about to make a turn onto Barrie Road, he sat forward.

"I need to walk, Chris. Let me out here. I promise I won't interfere."

I had no alternative but to trust him and I thought he'd be all right. I let him out and proceeded on to Lachlie Street. I could see him in my rear-view mirror, a small man hunched up against the rain, moving slowly and stiffly as if he'd had the breath knocked out of him and wasn't sure he had regained use of his limbs.

Like a lot of smaller associations dotted around the city, the OHHA had taken over a Victorian-era mansion which had once housed an affluent family with numerous offspring and several servants. It was a large, well-proportioned, red-brick house with gables, chimneys, and gracious windows. There was a striped canopy from the front door to the street and two workmen, muffled up against the cold, were digging up the path with jackhammers. They didn't seem to notice my approach and I walked around them carefully to get to the door, only to read a sign that told me, somewhat redundantly, that work was in progress and to watch my step. I pushed open the heavy wooden door and went inside to what had once been the gracious foyer of the old house. An enormous crystal chandelier, which looked original, blazed down warm, welcome light on this grey day. The floor was marble and the walls were panelled in oak. There had to be some concession to the house's present-day function, however, and one chunk of the space had been sectioned off by glass panelling, and behind that was a desk where a young woman was sitting. She saw me and smiled. I could tell she said, "Can I help you?" but the noise of the jackhammer outside drowned out her words. I took my ID out of my purse and held it up to her and shouted.

"Detective Sergeant Morris, I'd like to speak to the supervisor, please."

She glanced at the card, looked a little alarmed, and held up one finger, indicating I should wait a moment while she punched in a code on the telephone. I noticed she was wearing a hearing aid, tucked behind her ear. She looked to be in her early twenties, pretty, with long fair hair and blue eyes. I wondered with some dread if she was one of the good friends that I would soon be delivering such bad news to.

The jackhammer stopped abruptly and at the same time a door behind the reception desk opened and a woman came out. She was middle-aged, with auburn hair, well-hennaed, and a full round figure. She came straight around the partition.

"Hello, I'm Mrs. Helen Scott. How can I help you?"

The jackhammers began again, making conversation impossible. I saw the girl fiddle with her hearing aid, no doubt switching it off against the din. She was watching us curiously.

The supervisor gesticulated to me to follow her and she led me to her office where she closed the door behind us and somewhat muted the noise.

"Sorry about the row, we've had to take up the old paving out front. It was collapsing."

She faced me directly when she spoke and enunciated distinctly. She took a seat behind the desk and I perched myself on one of the chairs in front. She didn't seem to be hard of hearing and as far as I could see she didn't have a hearing aid.

"I've come about Deidre Larsen. I'm afraid I have bad news…"

I told her what had happened. There isn't any way to soften the impact of news like that and she gasped and covered her mouth with her hands.

"I can't believe it. That is dreadful. Absolutely dreadful. She was a lovely young woman. Very capable and well-liked. Oh, I can hardly believe it."

Tears were spilling unheeded over her hands. There was a box of tissues on her desk and I got up and handed it to her. It took a while before she was sufficiently composed to continue.

"You will be required to give a statement later to the police, Mrs. Scott, but right now I am not here in a formal capacity, more as a representative of her father, Dr. Forgach. He wanted Deidre's friends to be told personally."

"Of course."

"I am interested in speaking to the two young women who I understand were Deidre's particular friends. Jessica Manolo and Hannah Silverstein."

"Of course. Jessica is the person on the reception desk." She checked her watch. "Hannah should be coming in shortly. I ... er, sorry, I'm having trouble getting my thoughts together. What would be the best way to go about this? Hannah is deaf and communicates through sign language. Jessica has some hearing, but I could act as interpreter."

"I would appreciate that. I will need to ask them questions."

She stood up and then leaned for a moment against her desk. "Oh dear, my legs are quite shaky. This has been a most dreadful shock."

I can't tell you how much I hated this part of my job. Helen Scott was a decent middle-class woman and nothing like this had ever entered her life before.

"Do you want to sit for a moment?"

"No, I'll be all right. I'll get Jessica."

She left and I went over to the window. The office was pleasantly furnished in light oak and one half of a deep bay window let in as much light as was on tap. Perhaps in its previous life it had been part of the drawing room, which had been rather crudely severed by a dividing wall. Outside, the two workmen were taking a smoke break, sitting on a concrete planter near the door. I considered sending them away so we could have some easier conversation, but I realized the noise wasn't going to make any difference to the young women. The door opened and Mrs. Scott ushered in the blonde girl. Behind her was a shorter, dark-haired girl who still had her outdoor clothes on.

"Hannah has just arrived."

She indicated the other two chairs in front of the desk and they both sat down. Hannah shoved back the hood of her raincoat. She wore glasses and they had misted over so she removed them and wiped them off on the edge of her sleeve. Mrs. Scott was looking quite distraught and the two young women stared at her, curiously. She pointed at me, made a sort of chopping gesture, one hand on the other, then made some rapid finger signs. At the same time she said out loud, "This is Sergeant Morris from the OPP. I'm afraid she has brought some very bad news."

It was a little like watching a game of charades. "Bad" was somebody taking a drink and turning it away. Mrs. Scott continued, making a sign that looked like somebody firing a gun, "Deidre has been killed."

She didn't need to say aloud the word *strangled*. It was the universal sign. Hands clasped around the throat.

CHAPTER TEN

It was a long time before the two women were ready to answer my questions. Jessica spoke in the flat guttural tones of the hard of hearing. She kept repeating "Who? Who killed her?" and all I could say was, "We don't know yet." She essentially took over the job of interpreting to Hannah, who was making odd panting noises and weeping into the scrap of tissue she had used for her glasses. I went over the details of finding Deidre, where she was, time of day, and so on. At this point there weren't any particular trenchant facts I needed to hold back. The autopsy wasn't done yet, so I couldn't say if she'd been sexually assaulted, which was a question Jessica asked. I also didn't say she had been strangled with her own scarf. Even though the possibility that either of these women had killed Deidre was remote, you never told interviewee's everything about the crime scene. Many a suspect has been nailed because he or she knew something no one else but the murderer would know.

The two friends huddled together, hands and fingers flying, communicating I knew not what to each other.

"Can I get you something to drink?" asked Mrs. Scott. "I can offer juice, water, or soft drink?"

I accepted the juice but the girls ignored her. There was a small cooler tucked in the corner of the room underneath a bookcase and Mrs. Scott took out a bottle of apple juice and handed it to me. Suddenly, she was crying. "It's such a funny little thing but Deidre liked apple juice best. I always kept some especially for her. Oh dear, dear me, what a tragedy."

Neither Jessica nor Hannah paid attention to her, didn't even seem to notice that she was weeping. Mrs. Scott finally wiped her eyes.

"You said you had some questions you wanted to ask the girls."

"Yes, I do."

She stamped hard on the floor to get their attention and they stopped and looked up at her.

"Ms. Morris wants to ask you some questions." She nodded at me. "Go ahead. Speak slowly, please."

"We found a note near Deidre's car that suggests she may have been meeting somebody in the park. Was she seeing anybody? Did she have a boyfriend?"

Mrs. Scott signed that for me. The girls glanced at each other quickly then shook their heads.

"Nobody," said Jessica. "She wasn't seeing anybody."

"How long have you known her?"

Jessica passed that on to Hannah, who held up six fingers, clenched her fists, and rotated them around each other.

"Six years," said Jessica. "Me the same."

Hannah made a sweeping sign, one hand on top of the other, then held up the first two fingers of her right hand rather like a girl scout's pledge.

"We were at university together," said Jessica.

"Do you know anybody who might want to harm her?"

"No. None at all. It must have been a stranger."

Hannah was gesticulating and making signs vigorously. This time, Mrs. Scott, who had been sitting quietly watching the goings-on, was the one who interpreted.

"Hannah is very concerned about Deidre's daughter. Who is going to tell her and who is looking after her?"

"At the moment, she is staying with the woman who sometimes babysits. I don't know who is going to tell her. Nora the live-in nanny, I presume."

"No." The sound came from Hannah. So she *could* read lips. Awkwardly, she said slowly. "She bad woman. Not her tell Joy."

She brought her hand high up on her chest and her face lit

up and went back to normal with disconcerting suddenness and I realized that was the sign for Joy.

"Why is Nora a bad woman?"

"Not deaf."

That made a large percentage of the population on the sin side.

Jessica tapped me on the arm to get my attention. "Hannah means that Nora is not suitable. Joy understands sign language, but Nora hardly does. She is also prone to take drugs. She is not suitable to tell our dear friend's daughter what has happened. We will do it."

Having met all three women, I must say my sympathies were with Hannah and Jessica, but I supposed technically Leo had the right to make that decision.

"I will pass this onto Deidre's father. How can I reach you?"

"I will be here until four," said Jessica.

Mrs. Scott jumped in. "Absolutely not. We can manage. You should take the rest of the day off and be with Hannah."

"Thank you. In that case, Ms. Morris, I can give you my cellphone number. You can text me."

I wrote it down. So far I hadn't got much further in the investigation, but then I wasn't supposed to be doing the serious interviewing. That was going to be up to the local squad. Nevertheless I wasn't going to pass up this opportunity.

"I would like to get the names any other friends in your circle that you think I can talk to. Phone numbers and or emails would be great, too."

Mrs. Scott fussed a little in her desk, finding paper and pens. I watched them as they wrote down the names. They both looked so young to me. Jessica in particular was a head turner. Even on this chilly day, she was flashing some smooth flesh between the top of her jeans and her T-shirt. Hannah wasn't quite as pretty but she too was dressed up-to the-minute in layered clothing and designer small-framed glasses.

The intercom on Mrs. Scott's desk flashed and she picked up the phone.

"Yes. Wait there, I'll be right out."

She hung up the receiver. "There are two staff members outside. They are supposed to run classes this afternoon. Do you want to talk to them as well?"

I hesitated. I was within the bounds of legitimacy by talking to Jessica and Hannah on Leo's behalf but further questioning should be done by Ed Chaffey's team. Also I was frankly a bit bummed out by being the bearer of such bad news.

"I don't think I will at this time, Mrs. Scott. There will be police officers coming later today to talk to everybody."

I reached for my purse and picked up my coat, which I had draped over the back of the chair. The two young women were both watching me intently, presumably to understand what I was saying. Hannah signed something to her friend and whatever she said back seemed to cause her great distress and she let out another wail. I raised my eyebrows questioningly at Mrs. Scott, who tapped Jessica on the arm and made some rapid signs to her.

"Has something upset Hannah?"

Jessica herself was visibly distressed. "She thinks that Ms. Morris should see the letters that Deidre received. They are in her locker."

Good, that could mean only one thing.

"She received many letters when the newspaper reported the story of Joy's conception ... most of them are very nasty. I wanted her to throw them away but she wouldn't. She kept all of them."

Hannah had been watching her friend's lips as she spoke and she interjected loudly. "Hearing people don't unnerstan. We have no need of them."

She made a gesture with her right hand, finger bent and stabbing in the air. I was getting to know what the sign for *no* was.

"Did you know about this?" I asked Mrs. Scott.

She shook her head. "I was aware Deidre had stirred up a lot of people. We were deluged with calls when the news broke about her and Joy, but I didn't know she'd been receiving hate letters." She pushed her fingers against her mouth as if she was trying to hold back a cry. "I suppose they're going to be all over us again now."

There was no comfort I could give her on that one because I didn't think such a story would go unnoticed. As I said, Orillia wasn't exactly a hot bed of crime.

"She kept the letters in her locker," said Jessica. "You should probably have a look at them. Whoever sent them was sick, if you ask me."

I took my cellphone out of my bag. "Will you excuse me just a minute?"

I stepped out into the hall, punching in Ed's number. A man and a woman were standing by the desk and they both regarded me anxiously. I held up my hand to stop their questions and turned my back, huddling into the cellphone like a lovesick teenager. Ed answered right away and I told him what had gone down so far.

"Sure, get the letters. I'm not going to have anybody free to come out there until much later anyway. We're doing a house-to-house around the park. Call me."

I clicked off and with a quick smile at the couple who were watching me, I went back into Mrs. Scott's office. She had a key ring in her hand. "I have the locker key here if you need it." She sorted through the bunch and held up one. All were numbered. "I'll show you where it is."

"We do it," said Hannah. She looked fierce and Mrs. Scott meekly handed over the key ring.

Deidre's friends were certainly protective.

CHAPTER ELEVEN

Jessica led the way back into the foyer. The couple standing outside jumped forward and there was a flurry of hand signs punctuated with soft noises. Mrs. Scott was right behind us and she drew the two people away. She had the unenviable task of communicating with them what had happened. Jessica, Hannah, and I all continued across the reception area and Jessica opened a door into a spacious room that must have once been the dining room. The ceilings were high and there were deep bay windows, which were pulling in as much of the light from the day as possible. They faced onto what must have once been a lawn, now a parking lot.

"This is a lovely room," I said, and it was.

Except for a cluttered long table in the centre, the furnishings were elegant and welcoming: a couple of rose-coloured brocade couches along the walls, some wingback chairs, also brocade, and a soft old rug that covered the wood floor. The fireplace with its ornate mahogany mantelpiece was still intact.

"Let's have some light, for Christ's sake," said Jessica. She flicked on the switch and a beautiful crystal chandelier lit up.

"Over here," said Hannah.

I had expected an ugly metal bank of lockers like you see in high schools but somebody had found an antique oak lawyer's cupboard and it blended in beautifully with the rest of the décor. It stood against the far wall opposite the windows.

Hannah opened one of the lockers; it was high and narrow. Maybe the lawyers had kept their robes in there. Both she and Jessica stopped abruptly because, like any other private cupboard, this one contained its owner's personal possessions. There were a pair of runners, a sweater on the hook, and a photograph of Joy on the door. The sight of these things made Hannah weep again. She leaned her head on Jessica's shoulder, who stroked her hair softly. She appeared to be the stronger of the two. Her eyes met mine.

"The letters are in the envelope."

On the shelf, there was also a textbook for the deaf, a DVD, and a paperback novel. I checked the title. *The Heart is a Lonely Hunter* by Carson McCullers. A novel I'd read years ago and considered to be one of the saddest books I'd ever read. Tucked underneath was manila envelope.

Handling it by the corner I took it out. "I think it would be simpler if I took this with me and looked it over in my office."

In my bag I had what I thought of as a forensic minikit. It contained a pair of sterile gloves, several clear plastic zip-locked bags, a pair of tweezers, and a receipt book.

I put the envelope in one of the plastic bags and labelled it.

"I'm going to make out the receipt for the envelope to you, Jessica. Is that okay with you?"

She shrugged. "I suppose so. I'm the executrix of her will. We're all each other's."

Hannah didn't seem to have understood what I was doing and she signed at Jessica. I wrote out the receipt and gave it to Jessica, who folded it carefully and put it in her pocket.

"Have you yourself seen the letters?" I asked.

"Pardon?"

I'd been looking down when I spoke. I repeated myself so she could see my mouth.

"Some of them. I thought they were hateful but Deidre treated them as a joke." Jessica paused. "She felt they … what's the word, they vindicated her actions."

"In having a deaf baby on purpose, you mean?"

Hannah had read that and she glared at me. She touched her fingertips to her forehead, dropped her hand, then flicked her thumb from under her chin. Her expression was clear. *Why not?*

I didn't see any point in beating around the bush on this next question because it might be central to the case.

"Do you know who fathered her child?"

I was speaking directly to Jessica now, although Hannah was in my line of vision. There had been no signing as yet but it appeared that Hannah understood what I'd said. I caught the quick lowering of her eyes. Jessica shook her head and made the sign to her friend, who also indicated a no then made a back-and-forth and fingers-to-mouth movement.

"She never told us."

"Did you suspect anybody? Was she dating anybody?"

Another vigorous denial from both of them.

"I would like the names of any males in your university class."

Jessica shrugged. "That was three years ago; I don't remember."

"Whatever you can recall would be helpful."

We were going to have to get the list from the university and follow up on it, but I wanted to see who these young women came up with. I'd bet a month's wages that Deidre had used somebody at the university. The dates fit and she had plenty of deaf colleagues to choose from.

Both of them were looking decidedly uneasy. I felt rather like an airport sniffer dog who is getting the scent.

Maybe Deidre had sworn them to secrecy. I don't think these days there are a lot of reasons why young women would protect the father's identity. Shame is one of them. Embarrassment over an unsuitable mate you don't want to admit to. You don't want him to know you're carrying his child. Women's power since the beginning of time. My mind did a quick hop over to my own mother and the secret of my paternity that she had kept for forty years. I brought myself quickly back to the current situation and took the piece of paper out of my bag where they had written down friend's names.

"Were any of these men at university with you?"

"No," said Jessica.

"I'll just jot down any others from Gallaudet that you can think of then ... or you know what, maybe you could each do that for me. Do you have more paper?"

The amount of suspicion my request engendered was more fitting for the McCarthy enquiry.

"Nobody from there would have harmed Deidre," said Jessica.

"That's not what I'm asking. I'd simply like the names of any male friends she may have hung out with."

Reluctantly, they went over to the table, got a piece of paper from a drawer, and sat down.

I took one of the empty chairs and waited.

Hannah handed me her paper first. She had written down five names.

"Were any of these guys from Canada?"

She didn't wait to have that interpreted. "No, all from the States."

Jessica had got six names. I pointed to the additional name and asked Hannah, "Do you remember him now?"

She pursed her lips then shook her head. "No, I don't. If he was there he wasn't our particular friend." Jessica saw which name I was pointing to and she looked as if she was going to contradict. She made some quick signs and Hannah answered in kind. Emphatically.

"My mistake," said Jessica and she crossed out what she had written. "He wasn't in our year. I was acquainted with him but Deidre wouldn't have known him."

I had registered the name. Zachary Taylor. It might not be significant but I had seen a flash of intense anger between the two young women when Hannah had seen his name. I'd have given anything to understand what they were signing to each other.

I put the papers in my briefcase and returned to the locker. The girls came over with me.

"Do you know what's on the DVD?" I asked.

Hannah took the novel off the shelf and showed it to Jessica.

She talked, for my benefit, I presumed. "Why on earth was Dee reading this crap? It's so yesterday. Poor little deaf and dumb guy. How pathetic."

Well, that dismissed an acclaimed book with one swoop but I didn't feel like discussing its literary merits right now. I'd actually been very affected by it.

I picked up the DVD and waved it in front of her. It was unlabelled. "Any idea what's on this?"

Jessica and Hannah were continuing to have an intense exchange, presumably still focused on *The Heart is a Lonely Hunter*. I got their attention and they both indicated they didn't know what the DVD was.

"It's probably for the class," said Jessica.

We'd have to find out who was in Deidre's class sooner or later but I plumped for later. Ed Chaffey could get a list from Mrs. Scott. However, DVDs had proven integral to many cases and I wasn't going to take the risk of leaving this one unexamined.

"Can I have a look at it?"

Jessica pursed her lips. For a pretty girl she could manage some sour expressions.

"Are you planning to learn sign language? You can't master it in a day, you know. We don't want to be the latest fad." She shrilled her voice and fluttered her hands wildly. "'Oh look at me I'm doing sign language!' Whoopee."

I don't like rude even though I was giving both of them a lot of slack considering the circumstances.

I turned and faced them, making sure Hannah could read my lips. "Your friend has been killed and I'm very sorry about that. Her father is my friend. I am here to find out who killed her. There will be other police officers here and they will ask you similar questions. We have no interest in patronizing you or demeaning Deaf Culture."

I waited for that to sink in and to make sure they had understood what I'd said. They obviously did. Jessica flushed.

"I'm sorry," she said. "It's just that ... some people don't understand how long it takes to become fluent in our language."

"Tell me about it. Everybody and their uncle has a Ph.D. in Forensic Science after watching *CSI* for one season." I mimicked her voice elevation. "'Oh officer, have you tried checking the teeth for DNA? You can learn a lot from that, you know.'"

That brought a small smile to her lips. She signed to Hannah, who also brought up a bit of a grin.

What I'd said was in fact true. The *CSI* franchise was the bane of our lives. Most jurors were familiar with the show and expected miracles from us, demanding, "Why is this test result taking so long to get?" or journalists, who should know better, asking the same question a week after a crime had been discovered. Because there is a three-month backlog of other equally serious cases, and besides, we do not, contrary to popular opinion, have to solve our cases within a forty-five-minute time span. On the other hand, the shows had brought a new interest in the science itself, which was a good thing. I'm told you can get a lot of dates if you fess up to being a profiler. Male, that is, not female. The opposite is true for us women.

"We can look at it on the computer," said Jessica, her tone conciliatory.

She cleared away some filing trays that had strayed to one of the chairs, inserted the disk, and switched it on for me. The computer screen came up an ominous black with a strip of light at the bottom. Didn't look good.

"Oh no. It still hasn't been fixed."

She pressed some keys to no avail, turned it off then on again, but nothing made a difference.

"I'm sorry. We desperately need a new computer but it isn't in the budget for this year."

Being computer savvy wasn't my strong suit so I couldn't offer much help. All three of us stared at the black screen for a few moments, as if it were a sullen animal who might change its mind and come to life. Nothing doing.

"Don't worry about it. I'll take the disc with me and watch it at the office," I said.

Jessica removed the disc while I wrote another receipt.

"Is there anything else you need to take?" she asked.

"Not right now. The other officers might decide differently."

"I'd like her instruction book then. We can't just drop her classes and I'd like to know where she'd got to."

I removed the book myself and leafed through it quickly. You never know, Deidre might have written something important in the margins. People do, sometimes unconsciously. The book was pristine. There was nothing except a slip of paper with a note, "Homework, cover units 9–12 by next class."

I handed it over to Jessica, who hugged it to her chest. Both girls started to cry again. I sat it out until finally they subsided.

"I'm so sorry. We're going to catch the person responsible."

I shouldn't have said it like that. I should have couched my words in a vaguer way. We're not encouraged to make statements that sound like promises because it's not always possible to find killers. Some of them do get away with it, unfortunately.

CHAPTER TWELVE

I left the two girls to the cold comfort of their memories and headed out of the building. The jackhammers were back to full blast and the air outside the door was filled with dust particles. One of the workers, a young square-faced guy, sort of attractive if you like macho, glanced up at me as I walked past but lost interest as he gauged my particulars with one swift look. *On the edge of forty, doesn't really care about being smart and sexy. Cross her off.* I was annoyed with myself that it even bothered me.

I climbed into the car and turned on the ignition, warming up the car while I made my calls. I phoned Leo first but got his voice mail.

"Leo, it's Chris. I'm on my way over."

I hoped he was asleep but I needed to talk to him. I checked my own phone for messages. Katherine's voice.

"Chris. Give me a call if you're still out or come by when you get back to the office."

The second message was from a man and at first I didn't realize who it was. He spoke hesitantly and quietly as if he was standing away from the receiver.

"Miss Morris. Sorry to bother you, it's Sylvio here. I'm the man who was in the park this morning, Sylvio Torres, like the baseball coach but with an 's.' I was calling because I wondered if I could have my coat and gloves back. I know you have a lot on your plate at the moment but I would appreciate it." A little deprecating laugh.

"It's my warmest jacket and Lily needs her usual walk tonight. I think winter has come early this year. I gave you my address but here it is again in case you lost it. 72 Mississauga Street West. I'm just around the corner from the young lady who died ... have you found out any more about what happened yet? Thank you so much. Er. That's Sylvio Torres." He repeated his phone number and hung up.

Damn. I'd forgotten all about his jacket. I'd better get it to him before Lily lost out on more walks. I keyed in the number of the Centre and Katherine's extension. She answered promptly.

"Katherine, it's Chris."

"Is Leo all right? You've been a long time."

I wasn't sure how Katherine would feel about my detour over to the OHHA. She could be a stickler for following protocol. On the other hand, she had to know what I'd found in Deidre's locker. I filled her in and I had anticipated correctly. Her frown came right through the phone at my ear.

"We mustn't trespass on Ed's turf, Chris. We've got to wait to be invited."

"I know but if I hadn't gone over there Leo would have and that would probably have been a disaster. This has sped things up a bit."

"Let's be careful."

I heard Janice's voice in the background come over the intercom.

"Oops, I've got to go, Chris. A managers' meeting. More goddamn shift and shuffle."

Katherine almost never swore.

"I hope that doesn't affect you."

She chuckled. "They know I'd go kicking and screaming and it isn't worth it to them. I'm here till I'm carried out quietly."

"Good."

I meant it. Our department was clicking along nicely now. Even though I'd only been there for two years, I felt really at home. I liked everybody, yes, even Alternative David, and I thought our respective skills and strengths balanced very well.

We hung up and I set off for Leo's apartment.

Orillia is a pretty town in an old-fashioned, country way. Stephen Leacock didn't call it the Sunshine Town for nothing, but today you wouldn't think that. The miserable weather had emptied the streets and dulled the colourful gables and storefronts. It was quieter at this time of year anyway but at the moment, the streets were virtually empty, only a few diehards, clutching umbrellas, scurrying along the rain-slicked sidewalks. Sometimes I think I suffer from seasonal affective disorder, or in layman's language, "winter blues." Grey chill wet Novembers days make me want to pull the covers over my head and not stir until spring. This was, although I hadn't really admitted it to Gill, one reason why I wasn't keen on relocating to the Hebrides. Only seven hours of daylight for five months a year did not appeal to me. I wrenched my thoughts away from that particular dismal path.

Leo lived at the end of Elgin Street, near the lake in a brand new condominium building. The land surrounding it was barren, landscaping not yet completed, but the building was elegant and inviting. A discreet sign out front said "The Elgin Bay."

As I turned into the parking lot, I heard the familiar rumble of a skateboard. There was a skate park adjoining the building, and unbelievably, a dedicated young lad was ignoring the rain and was out practising his flips and twists. I watched him for a moment as he caught air, twisted, and landed solidly again on the board. He was good. I hoped he made it to the Olympics.

I parked the car and called Leo's number again. This time he answered.

"Hi, it's Chris, I'm outside."

His greeting had sounded grim but his voice livened. "Come right up. Entrance code is 235. I'm on the fourth floor, first door on the right."

I walked into a foyer that was so spacious and airy I felt like moving into *it*, never mind one of the condos. The décor was a novel blend of North American Indian and Regency, taking the warm earth tones from one and the elegance of line from the other. I particularly liked the light fixtures of leaded glass. Everything said good taste but not in a pretentious way.

Leo was waiting outside his door. Rather to my surprise, he pulled me into his arms and gave me a hard and painfully awkward hug.

"Thanks, Chris. You've been a brick."

One of the doors in the hall opened and an elderly woman,

dressed for the outdoors, stepped out. She beamed at him, rather coyly, I thought.

"Good afternoon, Dr. Forgach. No work today? Lucky for you."

He let go of me at once. "Quite so, Mrs. Pagel."

Grabbing my arm, he hustled me past her and into his own apartment.

"Let me take your coat ... I've just made some fresh coffee, can I get you some?"

"Thanks, Leo. That would be great. Just black, please."

He stowed my coat in the hall closet.

"I mustn't forget to give that fellow his jacket back. Do you think it would be appropriate if I bought him a bottle of wine?"

"He'd probably appreciate that."

Leo disappeared into the galley kitchen. The apartment was spacious, the furnishings very contemporary, very masculine, in shiny chromes and dark brown leather. I walked over to the windows, which were floor to ceiling. He had a stunning view of the lake and even on this dreary day it was impressive. No civilizing boats or swimmers or Sea-Doos, just an expanse of slate grey water whipped into white caps by the wind which was soughing at the windows.

He came back into the living room carrying a tray with two mugs and a plate of cookies. He placed the tray on a white wooden cube of a coffee table.

"I hope the cookies aren't stale. I don't eat them really and I haven't had visitors since I don't know when."

I sipped the coffee; the best that could be said of it was that it was scalding hot. The cookie was so bad I almost spat it out. I put the remainder on the plate.

"So did you get to meet with her friends at the OHHA?" he asked.

"Yes, I did." I picked up my briefcase. "I got the letters and emails that were sent to Deidre after the news broke in the media about Joy. She'd kept them in her locker. Are you up to taking a look?"

He nodded. "Indeed, I am. The worst thing at the moment is sitting around in a state of helplessness. The more I feel as if we are making progress the easier it is."

I removed the manila envelope from the plastic bag. "I have an extra pair of sterile gloves if you need them."

Before we could get started, his phone rang. He checked the call display.

"It's Katherine." He picked up the receiver. "Hello. Yes … Yes…" he looked over at me. "She's sitting here in front of me. I'll put the phone on speaker."

He put the receiver on the table and Katherine's voice came through.

"I wanted to let you know right away that the coroner has done an autopsy. It's Dr. Machamer, bless her speedy little socks. I'm going to have Janice send her some chocolates. She gave us top priority." I could hear breathlessness in Katherine's voice and it was not particularly like her to natter on. "Are you all right with me reading this out to you, Leo?"

"Of course I am." His voice was impatient. "Please stop treating me as if I might have hysterics at any moment."

I could tell by the short silence how much Katherine was struggling to cut him some slack. She continued. "There was no water in the lungs. Death was from strangulation. The scarf around her neck broke her hyoid bone. She was dead when she was put in the water." We heard Katherine shuffling papers. Leo jumped in.

"What else? There's something else, isn't there? Was she sexually assaulted?"

"No! Nothing like that. Dr Machamer is certain there wasn't any molestation … but she did determine that Deidre was pregnant."

CHAPTER THIRTEEN

Leo had gone very still. Finally he said, "I see. How far advanced was the pregnancy?"

"Very recent apparently. It's quite possible Deidre might not have even known."

"I see," Leo repeated. "That could be a pivotal point, given her previous history."

"That's true. On the other hand, some women do know the moment they've conceived..." Katherine's voice tailed off and I was struck once more by how little I really knew about her. I might be going on how private and close to his chest Leo was but all any of us knew about Katherine was that she was single, a workaholic, and lived with an elderly mother in some tony section of town. Her comment, even coming disembodied over the speaker phone, had sounded quite personal.

"I've heard that claim." Leo didn't add, "and it's a pile of crap," but he didn't need to. It was obvious what he felt.

"Well, that's pretty much it," said Katherine. "Ed said they're getting a subpoena to study the security tape at the casino and it would be good if you watched it too, Leo. You might recognize somebody."

"Not necessarily. Better if it were one of Deidre's friends. I keep telling you, I know almost nothing about her current life."

"We might have trouble getting permission for civilians to look at that particular tape but let's take it a step at a time. Ed said he'll have it by tomorrow at the latest."

"I presume they're doing house-to-house?"

"That's all underway. They're starting in the area around the park."

"I'd better go now," said Katherine. "Can you tell Chris to pick up the phone for a minute?"

Leo handed the receiver to me and switched off the speaker phone. He walked over to the window and stood, arms folded around himself, looking out at the lake.

"Chris?"

"I'm here, Katherine."

"Are we off speaker phone?"

"Yes."

"How is he doing? He sounds completely on the verge."

"Not quite but close."

"Look, are you all right with sticking with him? I think he needs somebody with him right now."

"Will do."

"Keep me posted."

We hung up. I looked over at Leo, sunk into himself staring out onto the cold waters that had so reluctantly yielded up his daughter. He realized I had finished my conversation with Katherine and he turned, walked back to the sofa, and sat down, sighing like an old man.

"If she was, quote, recently pregnant, unquote, when would she have conceived?"

"Around the end of September."

"Did you ask her friends if she had a boyfriend?"

"I did, and according to them, she wasn't going with anybody."

"Were they lying?"

"I don't think so. I had the impression they were very protective of Deidre and might have closed ranks, but that could have been because they haven't had a chance to absorb what happened. Besides, Nora Cochrane says the same thing."

"Deidre refused to say how she was impregnated with Joy. God knows, she might have gone on the Internet. 'Wanted: a male to donate his sperm. Anybody with a congenital defect that will be sure to be passed on is preferred. Can be deaf, blind, crippled, mentally retarded, doesn't matter, because God knows, those groups have been discriminated against for decades.'" He slammed his fist on the table, rattling the coffee mugs. "'And we all know that we must make a statement to the world even if it is the innocent who suffer.'"

I put my hand on his arm. "I'm sorry, Leo."

He patted my hand, took a deep breath, and got to his feet. "Why don't I make us some lunch?"

I wasn't actually hungry but he clearly wanted something to do. He strode off to the galley kitchen, leaving me feeling as if I were bobbing in the wake of a powerboat.

While he was slamming around with plates and sorting through his pots and pans, I laid out the emails and letters on the dining room table, arranging them by order of date. Then I took out my notebook and began to jot down some of my observations. Leo came back carrying two plates with a sandwich on each.

"I thought I had a can of soup but I don't." He grimaced at me. "I'm a bachelor, what can I say? My lady love lives in the Big Smoke so I don't bother to cook for myself. I eat out or order in."

It was news to me that he even had a lady love, and frankly, I felt a twinge of relief. *She* could take care of him.

He put the plates on the cube table. Even from where I sat, I could see that the edges of the bread were curling up. A touch on the dry side.

"It's tuna, no mayonnaise, I'm out. Is that all right?"

"Sure."

He picked up his sandwich, took a bite, and put it back on the plate. "Can't eat just yet. I'll save it for later."

Out of politeness I began to nibble on my sandwich.

"You have a guy over the pond, don't you, Chris?"

I nodded, speech being a little difficult at the moment as the bread was sticking to the roof of my mouth. I took a swallow of the weak coffee to wash it down.

"Long-distance relationships are hard, aren't they? I wish Caroline would move here but she's committed to her job. She also has a teenage son who she feels needs her to stay."

"At least Toronto is only an hour or so away. Gill, the man I'm seeing, lives in the Hebrides."

"Toronto? I didn't mean Toronto. Caroline lives in New York. We met on a conference this spring. She's a psychologist. No, I could handle Toronto, but we only get to see each other every couple of months."

"Have you told her what has happened?"

"Not yet. She'll want to come up here and be with me, and to tell the truth, I'd prefer to be alone for a while. I'll call her in a couple of days."

It wasn't up to me to give him a lecture about maintaining good relationships but I knew how I'd feel if Gill took a few days to tell me about the most important event in his life. I wouldn't like it one bit.

"Besides," he continued. "Loretta, my ex, my second ex, should be here tomorrow and she'll be enough to deal with. It's only decent if I offer her to stay here. I have three bedrooms."

"Right." I could see how a new girlfriend and an ex-wife under the same roof might be a little tricky.

He leaned back against the sofa. He looked exhausted.

"We always tell the families that death was instantaneous, don't we? Unless they insist on the truth, which is usually much uglier. I've often wondered why they don't press us for more details. Now I know. My mind keeps sticking on her last moments. How afraid she must have been. You don't strangle somebody who's young and healthy in a few moments. She would have struggled against it, feeling consciousness slip away, she would have been wondering if this was it. If this was in fact the end of her life."

Abruptly, he got to his feet, walked over to a cabinet and picked up a framed picture. He brought it over to me and held it out. A younger Leo was standing to the side of a fair-haired woman, attractive, smartly dressed. She was holding a baby in her arms. They were both smiling down on the child, their faces full of love.

"Deidre was only about three or four weeks old when we had the picture taken. Would you believe we didn't know she was deaf? How could we? Her eyes weren't focussing yet but she'd do the usual things babies do at that age. Cry, burp, fill her diapers... Loretta thought I'd be squeamish changing diapers but I wasn't. I enjoyed making her comfortable. I liked getting her to sleep."

"When did you learn she couldn't hear?"

"We began to suspect something was wrong when she turned two months. She didn't seem to follow sounds. We tried holding one of her rattles out of sight and shaking and she didn't turn her head. We took her right away to a specialist at Toronto Sick Kids and the tests showed she was profoundly deaf."

He took the picture from me and returned it to the shelf. "Deidre was a good mother. At least as far as I know she was. She was certainly devoted, which as we both know isn't necessarily the same thing... Her last thoughts would probably have been about her daughter. Imagining those final moments is almost unbearable, and I can also feel in myself an overwhelming desire to find her killer and make him feel exactly the same thing. I'd like to press the life out of him slowly, so that he knows what it's like. Then I'd revive him and then do it again... And again."

CHAPTER FOURTEEN

W e finished our sandwiches in silence. Or rather, I should say, I half-finished my sandwich, and Leo took one bite of his and put it back on the plate.

"Are you ready to look at the letters?" I asked.

He nodded. "How many altogether?"

"Twenty-six responses all told: fifteen email printouts, eleven letters."

"Let's look at the emails first. They're not going to yield up any physical evidence but the letters might."

We moved over to the table.

All the emails had been sent within the first week after the news broke in the media in April. Four were supportive, "good for you" sort of messages, and all of those senders identified themselves as part of the Deaf Culture. There was a sweet one from a woman who said she knew how difficult it must have been for Deidre when she discovered her child was deaf, she herself was hard of hearing now, and she wished her well. She seemed to have completely missed the point that Deidre had engineered the child's deafness. The remaining ten responses all expressed disapproval ranging from relatively mild to strongly worded anger and disgust at what she had done. Half of those had come from women and three-quarters claimed they were writing from Christian convictions. Two were foul and used explicit sexual language but neither of these used their names.

"We can get Ray to follow up on those email addresses," I said.

Leo was looking more and more haggard. "Why didn't she tell me this was happening? We could have put blocks on her computer."

"That would have been difficult. They were all going to the work address."

"Did her supervisor know about this?"

"I'm not sure. She knew that Deidre had caused quite a stir, as she put it, and she did say there were a few phone calls, but Deidre's friend Jessica works the reception desk so she could have fielded things for her. She said she wanted Deidre to get rid of the letters but she refused."

I could see Leo's jaw clench. "Why would she wallow in shit like that?"

I had no answer to that and it wasn't really a question.

"Ready for the letters?"

"I suppose so."

We both put on the sterile gloves and I removed the letters from the plastic bag. There were eleven altogether, and according to the dates, as with the emails, five of them were written soon after the news broke. All had been mailed locally.

"These five I put together because they were sent within a week of the news story." Leo nodded. He knew what I was getting at. Typically people respond to the news quickly or the impulse fades. "The remaining six were mailed at regular intervals of a month apart, the most recent being October 11. I'd say they are all from the same person who also sent one in that first week. Whoever wrote them is persistent and that as we know can indicate obsession."

"Let's look at the first batch." He examined the envelopes. "All of them were mailed to the OHHA."

We went on.

Two actually had letterhead and full signatures; both expressed disapproval but were quite polite in tone. A third was supportive. "Go stick it to them, Dee," signed Mags on pretty beige paper with flowers along the edge.   *

"Anybody you know?" I asked Leo.

"No."

Of the remaining two in this initial bunch, one was typed with no signature, short and to the point. *WHY?* The last one was handwritten and had the c-word repeated in clumsy letters across the page.

"Obscene but typically unimaginative, wouldn't you say?" remarked Leo.

People in the news who were in any way controversial received this kind of thing all the time. They might be boring and unimaginative to us, but to the recipient, they were often disturbing. A psychic spit in the face.

Leo put this pile to one side. "So let's have a study of our obsessive."

I'd arranged the letters with the earlier one on the top. It was handwritten, no signature. The lettering was in block capitals, the paper, yellow lined notepaper. The post office stamp revealed it had been mailed three days after Deidre had appeared on television.

"Hold on."

Leo went back to the kitchen and returned with a calendar.

"The first one was mailed on April 12, which was a Monday, three days after the television interview, which was on a Friday, and six days after the newspaper article, which was Tuesday, April 6."

This could mean the sender had been watching TV rather than reading the newspaper, but it wasn't conclusive obviously and in itself mightn't mean anything. However, when trying to draw up a criminal profile, these small details could add up to something significant.

The message was on an entire sheet of paper but the writer had used only the top section, double-spaced and kept within the lines.

> HOW COULD YOU DO SUCH A SIN. YOU AND
> YOUR OFFSPRING DESERVE TO Đ BURN IN
> HELL. I HOPE YOU DO.

"Anything obvious you see right off the bat?" Leo asked.

"There's a slightly unusual construction in 'do such a sin.' A more likely usage would be 'commit such a sin.' There is no question mark. The 'd' is stroked out; they could have been going to say 'die.' The tone is religious: 'sin,' 'hell.' 'Offspring' also isn't typical. It's an old-fashioned word. 'Child' or 'daughter' would be more common."

Leo tapped the next envelope. "This was written a month later almost to the day. May 10, which was a Monday."

"They're spreading out on the page and the writing isn't as tidy. Could be getting more agitated."

> YOU ARE SCUM OF EARTH. WHY ARE YOU HERE. I HOPE YOU GO TO HELL WHERE YOU CAN NO LONGER TORMENT OTHERS.

"The message is different in this one," I continued. "Another religious reference but look at 'you can no longer torment others.' It suggests that Deidre's act has been weighing on the writer's mind, or that they see Joy as being the one who is tormented, presumably by being born deaf…"

"Next is June 14, also a Monday."

"This one is taking up most of the page and the letters are not keeping to the lines anymore."

"Increasing disturbance?"

"Could be."

> YOU DESERVE NO SYMPATHY ONLY PUN-ISHMENT FOR SIN. HEDE MY WORDS. GOD WILL SMITE YOU IN HIS JUSTICE. HE LOVES ONLY THE PURE AND THAT IS NOT YOU AS WE ALL KNOW.

"'Hede' is misspelt, although that could be deliberate. But it's an unusual word, old-fashioned, too. A more threatening tone. Notice the writer reverts to the plural in 'we.' Previously they've used 'I.' Could be a dissociation taking place, a withdrawal from committing to the first person 'I.'"

"Number four is stamped, July 12. Monday. There was nothing in August. Five is a Wednesday, September 15, which breaks the pattern. The last one, number six, is October 11. A Monday again."

I studied the letters. "Number four is back to being neat, all the writing kept between the lines."

GOD SEES EVERYTHING AND YOUR SINS
ARE HATEFUL TO HIM. YOU EXPECT TO BE
PUNISHED.

"What do you make of that last sentence? Is it a Freudian slip, do you think?" I asked Leo.

"Could be. Is the writer unconsciously revealing that *they* expect to be punished or are they projecting something onto Deidre?" He shook his head. "Something that may unfortunately be true about her. She was always getting into trouble when she was in school. Negative attention is better than no attention." He looked up at me. "I wasn't the best father in the world, Chris. I took it personally when she lashed out at me and I withdrew from her. By the time I'd faced the truth and tried to make it up to her, it was too late. She was too bitter."

"What about her mother?"

"Loretta was worse and I mean that in all objectivity. She would disappear for weeks, sometimes months at a time on one of her special missions, but on more than one occasion she had to come back because Deidre was in trouble. Usually she was very resentful but at least whatever it was the girl had done, it brought her mother home." He rubbed his hand through his hair. "When Dee went to university, she seemed to have outgrown all of that hellraising and she settled down and got some good marks. I wasn't really aware of how militant she had become until she moved back to Orillia. The pregnancy was a smack in the eye for both Loretta and me. There's no doubt she was getting back at us. Who knows if this second pregnancy was the same deal?" For a moment, he looked devastated. "It's a moot point now, isn't it?"

I wondered if all psychiatrists considered that everything people did was in reaction to something else. Perhaps Deidre had strong convictions all on her own but who was I to say? Leo could be right. It had been pointed out to me by a therapist I had some sessions with that some of my own decisions were made on an unconscious level as reactions to my mother, including to some extent joining the police force. According to him, I felt a compulsive need to establish order and punish the disorderly. Hey, that's one explanation but it sort of left out believing in justice and protection of the vulnerable from the bully boys.

"Christine...?"

I returned to the letters, trying to sink into them, trying to get a feeling for the psyche of the writer. Think of it as the language whisperer.

The fifth and sixth letter were similar in tone and content.

YOU ARE A SINFUL DAUGHTER OF EVE. YOU SHOULD NOT BRETHE THE SAME AIR AS YOUR BETTERS. YOU WILL NOT ESCAPE HIS JUST RETRIBUTION.

THINGS ARE GETTING WORSE. DO NOT TAUNT ME WHORE OF BABYLON. GOD SEES AND HIS VENGEANCE IS SWIFT.

"What'd you think? What are we dealing with?" Leo asked, a touch of impatience in his voice.

"The gender is ambiguous. On the whole, the tone sounds more like it's coming from a woman: 'you should not breath the same air as your betters,' for instance. That suggests an identification with the female, as does 'he loves only the pure and that is not you.' On the other hand, 'do not taunt me, whore of Babylon,' is more male-sounding..."

"You're hedging your bets," interrupted Leo. "Give me something definite."

Threat assessment isn't a science. I understood his frustration, but you can't scan the letter into the computer and get a readout on a graph. The letters were ambiguous, which in itself said something about the writer. We could be dealing with some poor repressed woman who has spent her life being self-righteously nasty to others in the name of God but who would faint at the first sight of blood, or we could have a man who was shifting from the fantasy life to the real and was working himself up to murder.

"What is definite, obviously, is the religious language. It is constant throughout. I'd say this person is middle-aged, deeply involved with the church, comes from a strict fundamentalist upbringing perhaps with physical punishment, certainly imbued with the credo of sexuality as wicked. I'd say, they're probably unmarried and live alone or with an elderly parent or older sibling with whom there is no communication but a deep tie of unconscious anger and dependency."

"I agree with you so far. I'm going for a woman. What else?"

"The language is fairly literate, although as I said, English might not be their first language. They have at least high school education. A dropout. People don't persist in writing hate letters unless they're disappointed in their own lives."

"The most recent letter says 'things are getting worse.' That could be a warning of increasing psychosis," muttered Leo.

"It could for sure. Other than that, there is no obvious and clear sign of escalation. The handwriting doesn't change significantly but the last letter is the worst in terms of the irregularity of the letters and the disregard for the lines."

"So there may have been a tipping point somewhere between letter five, mailed on September 15, and letter six, mailed one month later."

"According to the pattern of the other letters, the writer would have sent another letter pretty much to the day Deidre was killed. Except for the September one, they were all mailed on a Monday."

Leo clenched his fist and pounded once on the table. "Why, damn it? Why the hell are they so regular? Goddamnit Christine, how many times have I sat in meetings dealing with exactly this sort of question? What is the pattern here? It's felt so obvious before. We've all sat around feeling detached and superior. Oh yes, it's obviously the subvert, travels out of town on a regular basis. All the crimes occur on Saturday or Sunday within easy access of Highway 11. Fuck it. I don't see a fucking thing here."

I had never heard Leo swear before. He rubbed his knuckles into his eyes, so hard I winced.

"Another apology, Christine. I didn't mean that."

"About sitting around feeling superior and detached, you mean? Apology accepted. Nobody I know has that attitude, except David maybe, but that's about his pure lifestyle."

"God. He's insufferable. He can live on cucumbers and grass for all I care but don't force your views on other people."

"I'm with you on that one."

I know we were dissing Dave behind his back, but first I felt the same way as Leo and second, at the moment, frankly I was treating him the way I'd treat a nervous witness. Find something in common even if it is a common enemy.

"Maybe a Sunday is the only time our man has to work up his nasty letters?"

"I suppose so."

"We've got some pieces of the jigsaw. We'll find the right places to make the picture soon.

He looked as if he were about to snap my head off again, then he smiled. A small curl of the lips but still a smile. "You always come up with the nice soothing thing to say, don't you?"

That sounded vaguely insulting but I decided to let it go for now. I collected the letters and put them back in the plastic envelope.

"There was a DVD in Deidre's locker. The girls thought it was part of the workbook for the class she teaches, but it's not labelled so I brought it along just in case. Why don't we have a look at it?"

"Good idea. My computer's in my library." He picked up my plate. "All done with your sandwich?"

I thought even the pigeons would reject the crusts that I'd left but he was trying to make nice.

"It's back here," said Leo, and he led the way down the hall, first dumping the plates in the galley kitchen. "I've taken over the master bedroom as my library. I figured I spend more time reading and writing than I do in bed asleep so why not use the best room?"

He ushered me into a room at the end of the hall.

He'd used the word *library* and he wasn't being pretentious. The room was lined on three sides with floor-to-ceiling bookcases, all crammed with books. Like the living room this one faced out onto the lake and also had its own balcony. Unlike the living room, it wasn't austere or pristine but comfortably messy, books on the floor beside a large plush armchair, a desk also cluttered, a thick rug, even a fireplace. Bright flames dancing merrily around a log.

Leo saw where I was looking and he waved his hand. "It's fake, just switches on, but I like it. I grew up with a fireplace and a home doesn't feel like a home without one."

Classical music was playing softly from a sound system that even I, non-audiophile that I am, recognized as state of the art. He must have been in here when I arrived and I suspected this was where he spent most of his time.

He booted up his computer and inserted the DVD.

There was no audio or graphics but it was immediately obvious this was no workbook aid. It was a homemade DVD. The date running underneath said September 29. The background was very dark but a light was focused entirely on a pair of hands, long fingers, smooth, young skin. The subject was wearing a long-sleeved black top that disappeared into the background, making the hands seem disembodied. I'd guess male but they were somewhat androgynous.

The index finger of the right hand jabbed out at the camera, then there was a rapid movement of fingers.

"Deidre. They just spelled out her name," said Leo. "I learned that much."

There was a flurry of signs from the headless person, eloquent, fast, but it was impossible to determine what the emotion was. Happiness? Anger? I didn't know and there were no facial expressions to give clues. Then the hands halted for a moment. The jabbing finger again, pointed at the camera. *You.* Both hands outstretched, palms down then quickly inverted.

"That's the sign for *dead*," cried out Leo. "I remember having to learn it when her damn gerbil died."

The fingers of the right hand formed a *v* shape with the thumb in between.

"It's a *k*," said Leo.

The left hand was held straight and the right hand struck against it in a swift downward motion. You didn't need to understand sign language for that one. It was like seeing somebody pretend to fire a gun.

"*I will kill you.* The bastard's saying, *I will kill you*," cried Leo.

CHAPTER FIFTEEN

We were crammed into Mrs. Scott's small office. Leo had telephoned her immediately and asked if she would look at the DVD and interpret for him. He'd also asked if both Jessica and Hannah could be present. "What do I know? Maybe somebody who knows sign language can pick out idiosyncrasies of expression the way you pick out signature words when you're analyzing statements."

He had a point and I was intrigued to know if it would be the same.

Deidre's friends were still very upset, especially Hannah, who couldn't keep back her tears. I didn't know how helpful they were going to be and I felt badly that we'd had to drag them out from whatever sanctuary they'd found. Mrs. Scott signed to them, speaking out loud for our benefit as she did so.

"I want you to try to pull yourselves together. It is important for Deidre's sake that we co-operate with the police."

Hannah replied with a flurry of gestures that Mrs. Scott translated simultaneously: "Even if we find who killed her, it won't bring her back."

Mrs. Scott replied, "Hannah, I know that is true but we all know how full of spirit she was. If the tables were turned she would be doing everything she could to bring to justice anybody who had harmed either of you."

Jessica clenched her fist and made a gesture as if knocking on a table. "You're right," said Mrs. Scott.

"Tell them I particularly want to know if they recognize the person in the DVD. The hands are distinctive."

Jessica didn't wait for Mrs. Scott to interpret. She faced Leo.

"We will do our best."

"The least I would expect," he growled. He was not being at all friendly or sympathetic to these young women and I suspected he was holding it against them that they had been closer to his daughter than he was, that they were bonded in a world he couldn't or wouldn't enter.

Mrs. Scott switched on the computer and slipped in the DVD.

"I'll interpret, but Jessica, if you or Hannah want to interrupt, please do so."

I took out my notebook.

The disembodied hands appeared on the screen.

"Pause there for a minute," said Leo, pointing. "Do any of you recognize them?"

"I'm afraid I don't," said Mrs. Scott.

Both girls shook their heads but I thought I'd detected a quick tensing in Hannah.

"Go on."

Mrs. Scott began her simultaneous translation while I scribbled madly to keep up.

"Hello, Dee..."

"Hold it! Does he say Dee or Deidre?" I asked.

"Dee." She automatically made the sign. Forefinger raised, other fingers bent.

"Did you refer to her as Dee or Deidre?"

"I always called her Deidre but I believe her friends called her Dee. Is that right, Jessica?"

"Yes. Dee was her pet name."

Mrs. Scott looked at Leo hesitantly. "This person must know her quite well."

"Not necessarily. He, if it is a he, could be claiming familiarity as a form of contempt and intimidation. Isn't that so, Christine?"

It was indeed. I'd known rapists who'd abducted victims, found out their names, and used a diminutive to demonstrate power over them. A woman who was always called Susan became Susie; Ellen became Ell; Karen, Kar. All the victims reported how disturbing this had been to them.

Leo nodded his head for Mrs. Scott to continue.

"This is a message from the anonymous man himself." She stopped. "So it is a man!" she said, then continued translating. "I don't usually look at the newspapers or TV, as you know, but by chance I came across the story of you and a baby you had made sure to be deaf. Believe it or not, I was in the crapper at the time and the newspaper was the only thing handy. Fortunately before I wiped my ass on your picture, I saw who it was. I thought to myself, Uh-uh. I might not be an A student like you but I can add up to nine as good as any man. According to the paper, your kid was born in December about three years ago, which would make her conceived in April. Unless you had a virgin birth, which isn't likely. I had my doubts when you came on to me that time. I'm a modest guy. Why me, I says to myself? This chick is smart and cute as well. Very cute. She could have anybody, so why me?"

I glimpsed Jessica and Hannah grab each other's hands. So did Leo.

"Pause a minute please, Mrs. Scott. Jessica. You know who this is, don't you?"

This was not a good interviewing technique, and in other circumstances, Leo would have known better. Never ask a subject a question that you are also providing the answer to.

"No, I do not," said Jessica. "Neither of us know him."

I could see that Leo was on the verge of cracking and he lost it. He jumped to his feet, and standing only inches away from both young women, he screamed at them.

"You are a liar. I saw the look you gave each other. You do know who it is. You've got to tell me."

Jessica hid her face in her hands and Hannah shrank away into her chair. At least the sound of Leo's rage wasn't hitting her nerves but his face was so contorted, you didn't need to hear. I was afraid he'd start shaking one of them any minute and I got up and caught him by the arm.

"Leo. Cut it out. This isn't helping. Everybody's upset."

He stared into my face, his eyes red and wild. I stared back as calmly as I could, although my adrenaline had shot up and my heart was racing.

"Would you like to take a break for a few minutes?" I asked.

He stepped back, took a deep breath, and lifted his chin to the ceiling, eyes closed as if he were praying. Then his shoulders slumped and he returned to the chair.

Mrs. Scott, bless her heart, was no wimp. These were her charges and she wasn't going to allow them to be abused no matter what the excuse.

"Dr. Forgach, I quite understand your distress but you must promise me there will be no further outbursts like that. I shall not proceed unless you do."

Leo knew that he was on shaky ground by even being here under the circumstances. He bent his head and mumbled. "I apologize. It won't happen again."

Mrs. Scott's eyes met mine, soliciting an agreement from me as well. I wasn't sure what I could do about him other than clap him in handcuffs, which I rather felt like doing. Leo was notorious for losing his temper. At least he didn't discriminate. A lot of people, from clerical staff to politicians, had been at the receiving end of his anger. He tried it on me early on but I'm glad to say never again after that. I had developed a very thick skin against tantrums from a young age. I could give as good as I got and I didn't have to raise my voice. Ice will reduce a fire to a splutter. However, I took the precaution of shifting my chair slightly so my body was more between him and the two young women.

"Are we ready to go on?" Mrs. Scott asked.

We were.

"We left off at, 'This chick is so smart and so cute.' ... Now I thinks to myself, you went for me because you knew I wouldn't stick around. I told you I was working and saving to buy my own sleeper van. A rolling stone gathers no moss. I've got one, by the way. It's ten years old but does me fine. Even got the Scottish colours. But back to the point. You got me to ... er, copulate with you," Mrs. Scott translated awkwardly.

"What? What are you doing? Is that the word he uses?" Leo's voice was loud again.

"No. But I don't see why I have to repeat what he does say. I'm sure you get the picture."

"I do indeed."

Neither Jessica nor Hannah seemed fazed by the obscenity. I'd missed it completely and I have to admit I was rather curious about what the sign was in ASL. Probably the universal one.

Mrs. Scott hadn't stopped the tape and she had to speak quickly to catch up.

"Er ... I left as I intended. You didn't seem cut up about it and I took that to heart. But I see now you had what you wanted. A kid you could flaunt in front of your parents."

Mrs. Scott couldn't resist a quick glance over at Leo to see his reaction. Hannah scowled at him. His face was tight.

"You wanted to embarrass them worse than anybody I knew. Lose it, Dee. It's not worth it. When I got over my shock at reading the newspaper, I thought to myself, man, you have a kid, a daughter. I've always wanted to have my own family but who would have me? So it's happened. I think she looks like me. She's going to be a blondie. I'm making this DVD to send to you and I will follow soon. I'm going to park myself somewhere in Orillia. We must meet and talk. You can send a letter to PO General Delivery, Orillia, and I'll pick it up. Don't, er, don't the F-word with me, Dee. You are dead if you do. You know me. I will kill you if you screw with me again. Signing off, the Big Bad Bogeyman. Zed." Mrs. Scott added, "He uses the initial."

Suddenly a face came into view. A young man, a straggly goatee, long fair hair, light blue eyes. He screwed up his face and stuck out his tongue. Then his hand appeared. Yes, it seemed the universal symbol for "fuck you" had travelled to the deaf language.

"It's Zach," said Jessica.

I managed to warn Leo before he leapt out of his chair again. He reined himself in.

"Who is Zach?"

Mrs. Scott started to interpret but he stopped her. "She can understand me. They both can if they want to. I'll say it again. Who is Zach?"

Jessica's face was sullen. "He's a guy we were in school with."

This must be Zachary Taylor, who she'd scratched off the list of males they were at school with. I was right. He was more important than they wanted to admit.

"Was he involved with Deidre?"

"Not that I know of. He was a jerk, a loner. Like he said, nobody would go out with him but the whole campus wanted to date Deidre."

Hannah tugged on her friend's arm to get her attention and signed vigorously at her.

Jessica shook her head and Hannah turned to face Leo.

"He wasn't a jerk." She spoke with the guttural flat intonation of those who can't hear themselves. "He's a goo guy. He wouldn't ave urt Deedee."

Jessica interrupted her. "Hannah is jealous because she thought she was his special friend. She didn't know he had slept with Dee."

Hannah flinched at this betrayal.

"When did you last see him?" asked Leo.

"Not since graduation."

"Do you know where he lives?"

"Nowhere. He bought a camper van and he just travels from place to place. It is his moveable home."

"Did he ever show signs of violence? Did he have a temper?"

Hannah had been watching my face intently. "Never. He was kind." She made a sign in the air and raised her eyes. "He giant. Very tall. A gentle giant." She circled her own face with her right hand. "Not handsome at all. Bad skin but he is a kind man. He would not have hurt Deedee. He loved her."

"Why does he say, 'I will kill you' then?"

"It is a joke. Hearing people say it all the time."

True enough. I'd scolded Tory yesterday in just that way. "If you wake me again before dawn, I'll kill you." She purred back at me.

"Did my daughter say anything to either of you about him coming into town?" Leo was struggling to keep his temper under control but his voice sounded peremptory.

More head shaking. I could see how hurt they were at this being a secret. But a secret it must have been. Given the message on the DVD and Dee and Zach's previous relationship, it seemed most unlikely that she would have taken another lover. I could only suppose she hadn't lost the desire to get back at her parents as Zach had said.

Leo stood up. "I'd like to go back to the office, Chris. We need to inform Katherine. Mrs. Scott, Jessica, Hannah. Thank you for your co-operation. I do apologize again for my behaviour. It was unconscionable. If you can find it in you to forgive me, I would be grateful."

I had never seen him so humble and my heart went out to him. Mrs. Scott smiled. The girls didn't. I don't know how much Hannah had understood but they both stared at him with angry eyes. Forgiveness would be a long time coming.

CHAPTER SIXTEEN

W e hustled through the driving rain to the shelter of the canopy that went from the parking lot to the side staff entrance. A couple of people were outside shivering, having a cigarette. Janice was one of them. She was an addicted smoker, always trying to quit but never succeeding for more than six months at a time. When she saw me she looked guilty and waved her cigarette in the air.

"This is my last one. I'm going on the patch as of tomorrow."

Leo stopped. "Janice, can I bum one off you?"

"Sure." She looked surprised, but she shook out a cigarette, low tar, low nicotine, the smoker's illusory sop to conscience. He took it, lit up, drew in a deep lungful of tobacco, coughed a little, and exhaled.

"I quit years ago," he said to me, "but it suddenly looked appealing." He took another drag, coughed again, then stubbed it out in the ash bucket by the door. "Thank God it isn't. It tastes like sawdust shavings."

Janice laughed. "Hey, that's my best friend you're insulting." She stubbed out her own cigarette. "That's it. I'll come in with you. I'm perishing." We headed for the door and Janice keyed the security pad. We went inside, leaving the other sufferer to his addiction.

"There has been a report on the news channel," said Janice. "They did use Deidre's name but there haven't been any calls here, so at the moment nobody is connecting the two of you. However, a woman called Trudy phoned three times. She said she was your, er, wife and she had heard the news and wanted you to call her at once. Did you have your cellphone off?"

Leo winced. "Trudy still insists on identifying herself as my wife even though we've been divorced for twenty-five years. She's Catholic and won't recognize civil laws, only God's or the Pope's, which is the same thing in her mind."

I suppose he wasn't to know that Janice was a devout Roman Catholic and probably felt the same way. I noticed the glance she threw at him.

Leo took out his cellphone, snapped it open, and keyed in a number as we walked down to the elevator.

"Trudy? Leo ... Well, what would you expect? ... No, I'm not being rude, I'm under stress at the moment ... No, there's nothing you can do ... No. Loretta? Yes, she should be here tonight ... No, I don't know how she's taken it. Badly probably ... Trudy please, I can't go into that right now. Of course I intended to phone you, I just haven't had time ... No, I haven't told Sig yet. I tried but I couldn't reach him. Yes, I will as soon as I can ... I realize that, Trudy. It's you who aren't being sensitive..." She must have hung up because he swore and closed the phone. His mouth twisted as if he were tasting something sour. "Where there's a carcass there will Trudy be found."

The three of us stepped into the elevator, thrown into uncomfortable intimacy. Janice smelled of cigarette smoke.

"By the way, Christine, a fax came for you from the Hebrides. I put it on your desk."

Damn. I'd forgotten I'd promised Gill I'd take a look at his report on major crime in Lewis. I'd have to do it later.

Leo and I left Janice at her desk and went on to Katherine's office. She was on the phone but beckoned us in at once.

"Yes ... thanks, Ed. I'll pass that along and get back to you. Bye." She hung up. "Ed Chaffey says he can have the casino surveillance tape ready for us by tomorrow morning. They'd like us to go there to view it. Okay with you, Leo?"

I sat down in one of the chairs, but he walked over to the window and stood gazing out. The view from here wasn't like the one from his condo. The office looked out on to Memorial Drive and cars coming and going. Definitely not interesting or beautiful. Without turning around, he said. "Tell Katherine about the DVD, Chris."

I filled her in. "We should be able to get information on this Zach Taylor fellow from Gallaudet University, although from what I could gather off the tape, he's a bit of a gypsy. He has his own camper van and he uses a post office box here in Orillia."

"I'll pass all that on to Ed and he can check it out right away."

"Tell him it's likely to be an older model, blue and white."

Leo turned and looked at me quizzically.

"The colours of Scotland," I explained.

He came away from the window and took the other chair. "We think this man is the father of Deidre's child. Maybe even of the second conception." He swallowed hard, hurt by his own words. "We need to talk to Nora again and see if he was at the house or if Deidre let on she was seeing him. I'm guessing the letter we found by the car was from him. Maybe Dee was planning to tell him she was pregnant. It's not always welcome news. Perhaps they had an argument and he lost his temper."

Typically, men who lost their tempers struck out with fists or knives if they had them. To strangle somebody to death required a colder frame of mind. However, at this stage I wasn't going to argue. Leo needed something to fasten on to, and as a real flesh-and-blood person, the unknown Zach was a likely candidate. He was also choosing to ignore what both of Deidre's friends had said about Zach being a harmless sort of guy. On the other hand, crime history is jam-packed with witness statements about what a nice man the accused was. "Quiet" is how they are most often described.

"Chaffey should start asking if anybody at the casino saw a camper or a sleeper type van in the vicinity of the parking lot. Maybe he went there to pick her up after all."

Katherine made a note. "We've passed on her photograph to Ed and he's checking the bus drivers and taxi drivers who were working that shift."

Leo got to his feet. "I'm sorry, I just can't concentrate. I shouldn't be sitting here; I must talk to Nora before anything else. We've got to work out what to do with Joy." He looked over at Katherine and held up his hand in a stop gesture. "I know you'd like to play it by the book and shut me down but this is private territory. I have a right to make sure my granddaughter is taken care of."

His tone was belligerent and Katherine bit her lip. "Of course

I understand that but to be blunt, Leo, you're in no shape to be conducting an enquiry at the same time, which I know you will do when you get there."

"Christine can come with me then. She'll keep it legit."

A good bedside manner had never been Leo's strong suit and for a moment I bristled at his tone and the assumption that I was at his beck and call. He must have picked up on it because his eyes met mine and he softened his voice. "I would appreciate your company. You're stopping me from going insane."

Katherine took back the reins. "Well if it's all right with you, Chris, why don't you do that now? I'll hold a briefing tomorrow."

I gathered my things and followed Leo, who was already moving out of the office. Over his shoulder, he said, "I'm going to take the fire exit. I can't face talking to anybody right now. I'll meet you at the car."

I was about to say, "copy that," which was a running joke in the office. We were all going around doing the 24 "copy that" and the scary "trust me," which Jack Bauer always said before disaster struck. Needless to say this was no time for levity and I kept my mouth shut. I was quite capable of walking down two flights of stairs but I thought he needed a time out so I took the elevator and headed for the car. He must have run down because he was already waiting. He hadn't brought a hat or an umbrella and rain was dripping off his nose. His hair was soaked. The man was going to get pneumonia if he didn't watch it. I felt my gut twinge in pity. Dr. Leo Forgach was in the grip of a massive dose of grief, heavily laced with guilt.

In the trunk I had what I called my emergency box. First aid supplies; extra clothes; boots; gloves; flashlight; flare; yes, even a packet of energy bars that I kept forgetting to replace, so they were probably stale by now. Orillia wasn't exactly in wilderness country but in my job you never know when you'd get a call to go somewhere rough. If I didn't need them, somebody else might. I fished in the box and took out a clean towel and handed it to him.

"You're not going to be any good to anybody if you get ill. Dry off."

He managed a grin. "Copy that."

I started the car, turning the heater on full blast.

"How about if I drop off Mr. Torres's jacket on the way?"

I'd grabbed it as I left the condo.

Leo glanced out the window. "I'll wait in the car if you don't mind. I'm not ready for him either. I suspect he'll ask a lot of questions that I don't have the answer to. Will you give him my thanks? Tell him I'll be in touch in person at a later time."

"Of course."

He lapsed into silence and I concentrated on driving.

CHAPTER SEVENTEEN

On the way, I tried Paula's cellphone but she hadn't switched it on. I left a message. I wondered if, God forbid, she was still waiting at the hospital or if the silence meant bad news. Surely she wouldn't know anything just yet. At Leo's request, I played the only CD he approved of, a disc Gill had given me called *Celtic Reverie*. He leaned back and closed his eyes. The music soothed both of us.

I parked in front of the apartment building and left the engine running so Leo could go on listening. A woman in a motorized wheelchair was manoeuvring her way through the lobby and I jumped to hold open the door for her. She gave me a cheery smile of thanks.

"It's wet out there," I said.

"I'm dressed for it," she said. "If I don't get out, I go stir crazy."

There was a plastic canopy attached to the arms of the wheelchair so that it resembled a golf cart. Nevertheless she was still exposed to the elements, and the rain was relentless. I didn't envy her.

Mr. Torres was in apartment 1A, which turned out to be the superintendent's. It had a slot in the door rather like the kind that toilets in airplanes have, except this one said, "Off Duty." I rang the bell. No answer. I rang again. Maybe "Off Duty" meant Mr. Torres was out. I was about to leave when the door opened. A square-shaped, grey-haired woman in a black dress stood on the threshold. She looked at me impassively, not speaking.

"Hello, is Sylvio Torres in? I, er, I wanted to return his jacket."

"No speak English," she said. "Why his jacket?"

I presumed she meant, why did I have his jacket in my possession, but if she didn't speak English it was going to be too complicated to explain. I held it out to her.

"Tell him, Christine Morris returned it with thanks."

She didn't touch it. "Why jacket?" she asked again. She was frowning but I thought that might be a permanent expression. At that moment, I heard the excited yapping of a small dog and Sylvio Torres pushed open the lobby door. He was carrying a couple of plastic grocery bags and he had Lily on a leash. She danced excitedly at the sight of me as if we were old pals. She had on a fluorescent pink rain jacket and little pink boots. Very cute. Mr. Torres had found an extra raincoat for himself but he looked chilled. The one he'd lent us was probably warmer. He greeted me with a big smile but that followed after a quick flash of apprehension.

"Miss Morris. I didn't realize who it was for minute." He said something in another language, probably Portuguese, to the woman who I assumed was his mother. She answered back, gesticulating to him angrily. He retorted in kind, and she turned on her heel and stomped back into the apartment, actually slamming the door behind her.

"I do apologize for my mother, Miss Morris. She is from old country." He seemed to offer that as an explanation for the old lady's bad manners. "Ah, I see you have my coat."

I handed it to him. "Thank you so much for lending it to us. Dr. Forgach wanted you to know that he is most grateful and he would be in touch with you at a later time to thank you in person."

"I saw him sitting in a car just down the road."

He stared at me and an oddly sullen expression crossed his face as if Leo had slighted him personally by not coming to speak to him.

"Er, he's quite upset." I stopped, suddenly realizing that Torres might not know that Deidre was Leo's daughter. I didn't think I should be the one to tell him. I gave Lily a quick scratch on the head. "Thank you again, Mr. Torres. And as I said, if you have any more information, please get in touch with me at the Centre."

He frowned. "What more information would I have? I was just walking Lily."

"It's not only today that we're interested in. We have to find out all we can about Deidre's movements. Her habits, that sort of thing."

"Yes, yes, of course you must. I'll think about it."

I hesitated. It wasn't generally a good policy to reveal information about an investigation early on but what the hell, he might be helpful.

"We would particularly like to speak to the owner of a blue and white camper van, older model. Have you noticed anything like that in the area?"

He thought for a minute. "Blue and white? A camper van is the kind people sleep in, no?"

I nodded.

"Then I have seen a van like that. It was parked outside her house, oh, maybe a month ago, or more now. The reason I noticed it particularly was because it had got a ticket. You can't park on that street from midnight to 7:00 a.m. I wouldn't have thought twice about it but it was the parking ticket that got to me. I get so fed up with those parking guys who prowl these streets. They're always trying to fill their quotas even if you're only five minutes over. Vampires, that's what they are."

All my antennae started to twitch. "Did you see the driver of the camper?"

"Let me think. Yes, I did see a young man getting into the van as I was coming back with Lily. He was sort of scowling at the ticket. I can't say I blamed him."

I didn't want to scare Mr. Torres off because he seemed like a nervous guy to me so I held on to my excitement. This could be a significant lead. Casually, I pulled my notebook out of my pocket.

"Do you remember what he looked like? How tall was he?"

"Quite tall and he was fair with long hair. That's why I'd say, womanish."

He didn't elaborate on that and I let it ride. He himself was Mediterranean, dark-haired, lots of grey happening, but thick, cut short.

"You say he was tall. Was he taller than me, for instance?"

I'm five feet seven and I was looking down at Mr. Torres. Tall can mean anything to a short person.

"I don't remember exactly." He squeezed his eyes shut. "Yes, now that I bring him up in my mind, he was quite tall. Not like a basketball star, you understand, but tall."

"Can you remember the date, Mr. Torres?"

From inside the apartment, a shrill voice yelled something. Mother must have been standing right behind the door. He shuffled his feet in embarrassment.

"Sorry, I'd better go. Mama wants her milk..." His voice tailed off. I got the picture but she'd have to suffer a bit longer.

"It could be really important, Mr. Torres. Even the day of the week would be helpful.

"Ah, that I do know. It was a Sunday for sure. I'd taken Mama to mass but I was late getting up and Lily hadn't had her walk. So I decided to skip church and go later in the day."

Why did I have the feeling his mother wouldn't have liked that?

"And it was a month ago?"

"About that. It was still mild out. We were all remarking how mild it was for October."

There was another call from the other side of the door. Lily barked an answer.

He shifted uneasily. "Sorry, I must go."

"You've been very helpful. Thank you, Mr. Torres."

Opening the door cautiously as if something feral might leap out, he slipped inside, the little dog skipping ahead of him. At least she wasn't afraid of Mama.

I headed back to the car, taking out my cellphone as I did, and keyed in the Centre's phone number.

"Janice, put me through to Ray, will you?"

I got his voice mail and relayed the information I'd just got from Mr. Torres. "See if we can get hold of that parking ticket. It should give us the licence number of the van. But I'm betting from the description this is our guy. His name is Zachary Taylor and he is very much wanted for questioning."

Leo was fast asleep, his head back, mouth open, so I opened the car door carefully and slipped into my seat. Let him have a few more moments of oblivion.

Deidre's house was around the corner. A few cars were parked on the street but no camper van to make our lives easier. There was, however, a news van from the local TV station right outside the house. A sprightly young woman, sheltering underneath a large multi-coloured golf umbrella, was holding forth on the sidewalk. The two cameramen had covered the camera in plastic but they were getting wet. There was no way we could enter the house unobserved, but the last thing Leo needed right now was publicity. They weren't likely to recognize me but he was often on TV giving expert opinions on forensic matters. They might know him. I grabbed my umbrella, a functional black stubby from the back seat.

"Leo?"

He woke up instantly. "Leo, there's a news crew here. Take this and hold it close in. I'll try to shield you."

He cussed under his breath but took the umbrella. We got out of the car and headed for the house. The sprightly person turned and I heard her saying, "The dead woman lived in this house on this quiet, peaceful street…"

One of the crew flapped his hands at us to warn us to keep out of camera range but we kept walking, me in between Leo and the truck. At a signal from the producer, the young woman started to come towards us, her microphone held out like a wand in front of her.

"Excuse me, excuse me, do you mind if we have a word?"

I stopped and Leo kept going up to the door of the house. He rang the doorbell. I faced the reporter.

"Yes?"

"Are you related to Miss Lawson?"

"Her name was Larsen and no, I'm just a friend."

"And the gentleman?"

"Sorry, I can't talk right now."

Leo was inside and I swirled around, conscious of the camera zooming in on me, and walked to the door. It opened immediately and I went in. Nora was standing in the vestibule and she peered over my shoulder.

"Oh, no. The vultures have gathered already."

Leo was stashing the umbrella in a stand. "Where's Joy?

Nora closed the door and actually slipped the safety chain on. "She's in her bedroom watching one of her videos."

"How is she?"

"She's been asking for her mommy non-stop but I haven't said anything yet. What the hell am I going to say?"

Nora was a mess. Her pupils were dilated and there was the pungent smell of weed in the air. "I don't even sign that well," she continued. "I just know the basics, you know, what do you want for lunch, time for bed, that sort of thing. How the hell do I communicate to a kid that her mother has been murdered and won't be coming back?"

"You don't," said Leo, his voice sharp. "Children Joy's age don't understand death and if you say her mother has gone away, she'll be waiting for her and she'll think she's done something wrong to cause it." He glared at Nora, his face full of rage. "We probably need somebody who can do sign language properly. And somebody who isn't stoned out of her fucking mind at the moment."

A more vulnerable person or one more in her real mind would have been intimidated by such force but Nora wasn't. She yelled right back. "You can fuckingly well get somebody fucking else if you like but I'm the fucking nanny, don't forget. You hired me. What you fucking see is what you fucking get."

None of us had moved from the cramped space of the foyer and who knows where this scene would have escalated to but at that moment, there was an odd sort of grunting sound from the top of the stairs. We all turned and looked up to see Joy standing behind the baby gate, a stuffed toy clutched under her arm. She made her strange noise again, then made some signs with her free hand.

"She wants her mommy," said Nora unnecessarily.

CHAPTER EIGHTEEN

J oy remained at the top of the stairs, her face solemn and worried in the way that almost-three-years-olds can be.

Leo held out his hand. "Come on down, sweetheart. It's your granddad."

"She doesn't have a fucking clue what you're talking about," Nora spat out. "First off, in case you fucking don't remember, she can't hear, and second, she hasn't seen you since last Christmas for ten minutes and that was eleven months ago."

"Through no fault of mine," he retorted.

I was getting fed up with this row. I don't care if the little girl was deaf, she could pick up on the fury that was going back and forth between these two. I decided to step in.

"Listen, both of you. I understand how upset you are but get a grip. Nora, maybe she doesn't need to know everything at the moment. Can you tell her that her mommy can't come home right now and leave it at that?"

Nora seemed reluctant to give up the fight. I thought she was the kind of person who went to anger as a default line.

"She's got to be told sometime."

"True. But perhaps when everybody around her is a bit calmer."

"Christine is right," said Leo. "Why don't you do what she says, Nora? I'll go into the kitchen and get Joy some milk. Does she like cookies?"

"Dee didn't let her have them. She doesn't believe sugar is good for kids."

"Well, she's probably hungry and it's important her routine be maintained as much as possible. What were you going to feed her for supper?"

"Jesus, I don't know. Dee did dinners. I'm just the ears."

Joy was coming slowly down the stairs, one step at a time as she'd been taught. She made signs again at Nora, who this time responded. Even I could see how awkward her signs were, but the child understood her. Her lower lip protruded but she didn't cry. Nora signed again but spoke as well.

"Let's go into the kitchen, babe, and make some dinner. What would you like? Baked potato and chicken? That sounds easy."

Joy stood looking up at Leo and me. He held out his hand to shake, making a clumsy sign.

"Hello, Joy."

Like any other kid in the world, Joy had her own method of diffusing of tension and she thrust her toy, a stuffed green dinosaur, into the air. Her right fingers spelled something rapidly and she made some of her own guttural sounds.

"She says this is Horace. He's hungry."

I pointed at my mouth and rubbed my stomach. "Me too." Well, it wasn't American Sign Language but it was pretty universal. To my delight Joy moved closer, took me by the hand, and started for the kitchen.

"You've made a friend there," said Nora. "Lucky you. She's not usually that quick to go to strangers."

Frankly, I thought the poor kid had chosen me as the least threatening of the three of us. Nora had a cloud around her as tangible as black flies in spring and Leo was barely holding it together.

"Let's see what we can find for you and Horace, shall we?"

"She can't understand you," said Nora with too much satisfaction for my liking.

"If she can't, you can. If you've no objection, I'll just root around the kitchen and find her something to eat."

"Be my guest."

She swung off and stomped off up the stairs. I was afraid that Joy might be upset at the disappearance of the only familiar face but she wasn't. She tugged my hand again.

"I'll wait in the living room," said Leo. "I don't think she's used to me and she's a bit apprehensive."

I was glad he'd said that because I was about to suggest it myself.

Joy was "chatting" to me. To free her hand she had to tuck Horace under her armpit. She was making incomprehensible sounds at the same time. I smiled at her and nodded vigorously. I know from my experience with Chelsea that children don't always want a response other than an indication that you are listening. I let her lead me into the kitchen.

It was already dark outside and I snapped on the lights. Joy headed for her own chair, climbed on it, and sat down, looking at me expectantly. Now what? Nora had said potatoes and chicken but the child probably needed a snack before that was ready. I opened a cupboard that was next to the sink. A lucky guess. It was the cereal cupboard. I took out a box of organic cornflakes, held it up, and pointed. Joy grinned happily and nodded her head.

The door swung open and Nora came in. She had a child's sweater over her arm.

"I thought she might need this…" She halted. "Hey, she shouldn't be eating cereal at this time of day. Dee would never allow that."

Before I could stop her, she actually snatched the box out of my hand.

"It seems like a long time to wait for her dinner to cook."

"It's not any different from her regular hour. She'll be fine. *He* said we shouldn't change her routine and he's a fucking shrink, so he should know."

Nora was turning this into a power play and I could have slapped her. I didn't even know if she was telling the truth and Joy couldn't tell me. But she did. She gave a high-pitched squeal and pointed at the cereal box then at her mouth.

Nora shook her head and tapped her fingers on her watch. "She likes her own way," she said to me.

I turned my back so Joy couldn't see my face or lips. Nora's eyes glittered and she reeked of marijuana. She must have lit up a fresh toke while she was upstairs. It hadn't had its legendary mellowing effect, that's for sure. I moved in closer so that I was only a couple of inches away. She had her back to the cupboard and couldn't move.

"Nora, I'm going to overlook the fact that you're using a controlled substance and that, as a police officer, it is my duty to charge you. I won't do that. This child needs you, and she needs you to be present and friendly, as I am sure you usually are. Clear so far?"

Her eyes darted away from mine. "Good. I take it that's a yes. Now, at this time of the day, shortly before dinner, which isn't ready, what would she normally have for a snack?"

"Carrot sticks and maybe some hummus dip."

"Do we have some?"

"Yes."

"Let's give it to her then."

I stepped away so that Nora could move. Joy was playing with Horace, making him wave his arm at her. She used her other hand to sign back at him.

Nora went over to the fridge, the door covered with the mandatory child's drawings. She took out a carton of milk and a plastic baggie of carrot sticks.

"There's no hummus."

I went back to the table and sat opposite Joy. Suddenly she looked up at me and made a low sort of growling noise at the same time making a sign at me.

"What did she say?" I asked Nora.

"What do you think? What she's already said a dozen times. Where's Mommy?"

She signed back at the child, who promptly stuck her thumb in her mouth and pressed the dinosaur against her cheek. Nora clucked her tongue.

"Dee didn't like her to suck her thumb. She's too old for that."

At that moment the door opened and Leo came in.

"Is everything all right?"

"Fine," said Nora. But it wasn't. Leo scared Joy. He said he hadn't had anything to do with her so maybe it wasn't personal. Maybe it was just because he was strange and so tense. Whatever the reason, she slumped down in her chair, squealed the high-pitched cry again, and waved her hand frantically for him to go away. He backed away. "Never mind. I'll go. Christine, can I have a word with you outside?"

I followed him out into the dining room. Joy was letting go. Nora must have gone to comfort her because the sounds abruptly ceased and became whimpers.

Leo opened the front door and went out onto the porch. I followed him. He was shaking with agitation.

"Christine, I don't know what to do. She's my granddaughter and I scare the bejesus out of her. I don't want to leave her with that drugged-out harridan but I don't know what else to do. Staying here isn't helping the situation."

Given the hostility I'd witnessed between Leo and Nora I was inclined to agree with him.

"I think you should get Hannah and Jessica over here. They are familiar to her."

"I don't feel as if I can do that either. You saw them. They hate my guts. I'm the bad dad. The one who abandoned his daughter."

He took a few paces up and down the porch in a way I was now becoming familiar with. It was cold out here and I pressed my arms closer to my body.

"*She* rejected me, not the other way around. Oh it's true I didn't agree with what she did but I would have come around. You saw that child in there. She's my flesh and blood. I would have been here every day if Dee had wanted me to but she was too stubborn." He turned to face me, his eyes full of anguish. "And now it's too late. Oh God, Chris, what am I going to do?"

CHAPTER NINETEEN

It took me a while to get everything sorted. I sent Leo home in a taxi, then I got hold of Jessica, who agreed to come over right away. Things in the kitchen were looking better, as Nora had found some frozen lasagne that she heated up in the microwave. While Joy was eating, I took the opportunity to ask Nora if she knew Zachary Taylor.

"Never heard of him," she said curtly.

If he had visited Deidre, it obviously hadn't been when Nora was around.

Finally Joy finished, licking her plate clean with evident relish. Nora didn't scold her for that, thank goodness. I indicated I was leaving and she ran over to me and flung herself into my arms, wrapping herself around me like a baby monkey clings to its mother. That was tough. I don't have children of my own, won't now, and to date I'd felt that my relationship with my goddaughter, Chelsea, was satisfying the need-to-nurture drive without any of the downside that mothers have to put up with. It was funny about Joy, though. Something had clicked between us that I couldn't quite explain. Generally I get along well with kids, but this was different. Perhaps it was just the circumstances. My knowledge of her situation might have been communicated in some way. Whatever it was I felt a real pang of loss that I had to leave her.

"Tell her I'll be back," I said to Nora. It was a foolish thing to say, as I wasn't sure when I would see them again, but it popped out of my mouth. Joy insisted on accompanying me to the door and stood waving Horace's foot at me as I got into the car.

As police officers, dealing with situations that are sometimes unbelievably horrific, we are constantly reminded not to get subjectively involved with our cases. Everybody, not just the supervisors, tries to keep an eye out for each other, picking up on the telltale signs of stress. That was true when I was a front-line officer in Toronto a couple of years ago; it's still true now at the Centre. Officers who are in the detection of child pornography department, for instance, have a limit of about two years. After that, you have to move on to something easier to handle, like homicide or assault. You know when those crimes seem like piece of cake in comparison, you probably stayed too long. I've never done a stint in the pornography department. Don't want to and admire those who can stick it out.

But here I was, up to my neck in subjectivity, planning in my head when I could come back, how I could learn some basic sign language. Speaking of subjectivity, I was getting anxious about having no contact or information about Paula and decided to go to her house. She and Craig lived in a beautiful house right on the lake. They'd built it from scratch and the house was designed to make maximum use of the waterfront, with deep windows and a wraparound balcony that faced the water. Craig had inherited money from his parents, and as far as I could tell, didn't see any need to add to that income by working. He spent his time studying his portfolio, keeping fit, playing golf in the summer, and skiing in the winter. He was handsome, if you liked perennial boyish looks, vague blue eyes, and a soft mouth. I couldn't stand the guy, a feeling that was returned in kind. He and Paula had met when she went to give a talk at a drug addiction centre. Craig was a recovering cocaine head and presented himself as reformed and repentant, a combination some women find irresistible. I'd never have expected Paula to be taken in by easy manners with a hint of wickedness but she was. He pursued her ardently until he had her then lost interest almost as soon as they were married. He was jealous of our friendship and constantly tried to undermine me in her eyes. Thankfully not succeeding. I knew enough not to badmouth him to her but I was hard pressed not to at times. They'd been married for eight years and I suspected Paula was long over being in love with the guy but they had a child and she was loyal to a fault. Although I say it begrudgingly, Craig was a good father to Chelsea, attentive, playful, but firm when need be. Without those redeeming qualities I would have been happy never to be in the same vicinity as him. Oh, I should mention he hit on me at their wedding reception. Paula does not know this.

I had to ring the doorbell twice before he answered. He was in singlet and shorts and sweating.

"Hi, Chris. I'm just in the middle of my workout."

"I came to see how Paula is doing; I didn't hear from her."

He slapped his hand to his forehead. "Oh God, I forgot to call you. My cell was out of juice and I intended to call you the moment I got in but what with one thing and another it fell off my radar. So sorry."

"What happened? Where is she?"

He had made no attempt to ask me in and frankly that was fine with me but it was awkward standing on the doorstep.

"She's at the hospital. They decided to keep her in."

"Why's that?"

"During the prep for the biopsy, they discovered her heartbeat was irregular. They had a name for it — atrial fibrillation. Apparently it was up to 140 beats a minute."

"My god, that's high." He started to wipe his face with the towel he'd draped around his neck. He did look worried.

"I know. They were afraid she might have a stroke. They want to control the heartbeat and find out what's causing the problem, so there you have it. She has to stay in until they bring it under control." He frowned. "It's going to be tricky with Chelsea but her grandma has agreed to come up and stay. She'll want to see Paula anyway."

I tried not to be irritated that he'd phoned Mrs. Jackson and had supposedly forgotten to call me but I pushed the feeling away. He'd made his point.

"Did they say what was causing this?"

"They think it's a result of the rheumatic fever she had as a kid. Somehow, don't ask me why, it's been missed up to now. Maybe the stress of having this biopsy aggravated it."

Half-heartedly he stepped back from the door. "Do you want to come in? I'll be done in a minute. I find doing a good hour on the treadmill relieves stress."

"I think I'll whip over to the hospital. Where's Chelsea now?"

"With Suri. We'd already planned that she'd have a sleepover tonight to give Paula a bit of space... Oh Chris, maybe you could take her some clothes and toiletries. She wants her own PJs and a robe. She wasn't expecting to be kept in and they stuck her in one of those ugly hospital gowns. I myself won't be able to get there until tomorrow."

"Quite right. You've got to get rid of all that stress first."

He gave me a nasty look but didn't say anything. I think we were both afraid to let go of all controls given the circumstances.

"I'm going to finish my workout. You know where the bedroom is. Let yourself out."

He turned on his heels and trotted off in a miasma of sweat, disappearing down the stairs to the basement, where he had his state-of-the art gymnasium.

I shucked off my shoes and ran upstairs. Having grown up in a cramped post-war prefab in downtown Toronto, Paula had always wanted to design her own "Barbara Stanwyck" bedroom. The kind where there's a monstrously large and high bed, piled with fat white pillows, only scarlet silk lingerie is allowed, and the butler brings up morning coffee in a silver pot and hands over letters on a plate.

I too have always wanted to have letters brought to me on a plate; it sounds kind of delicious. Now what I get are mostly bills or begging letters and they arrive in the afternoon anyway so I have to fish them out of my letter box when I come home. The butler has long been pensioned off.

I went into the bedroom. What Paula did have was the space, white walls, and furnishings, a king-sized bed, currently unmade with the fat white pillows piled in a heap on the floor. There was a chaise lounge, complete with a turquoise angora throw for the days when the weather was inclement and you wanted to read your mail. Outside a long balcony ran the length of the room. Nobody had thought to collapse the sun umbrella and it flapped in the wind, dripping rain from the edges.

There was a walk-in closet off to the side and next to that an ensuite bathroom with Jacuzzi tub, two sinks, and a bidet. I checked out the closet first, which contained a dresser as well as a clothes rack. It seemed uncluttered, which wasn't how I remember Paula to be. Since Chelsea was born, she'd tried to be tidy, but she had a messy fallback she couldn't overcome. I found a carryall tucked in one corner and did a quick scout of the drawers for underwear and nightclothes. Even though Paula and I had been best friends since we were teens and had shared bathrooms and swapped clothes, I felt a bit squeamish going through her private things. The first two drawers I opened were empty, and with a bit of a shock, I realized why the closet appeared tidier than usual. There were none of Craig's clothes hanging up, only Paula's. Uh-oh. I went into the bathroom for a robe. There was a slinky red silk one hanging on a hook behind the door. I grinned. Barbara Stanwyck lives. I folded it and put it in the carryall. The marble countertops were bare of any "stuff" and I opened the medicine cabinet to see if I could find a toothbrush. There wasn't much in there. No razors, no manly deodorant, only a stick of Secret anti-perspirant. So Craig wasn't sleeping up here. It didn't necessarily mean anything, but Paula hadn't mentioned it. Usually we shared every minutia of our mutual lives, from buying new shoes to ideas about repainting the living room, changing the cat's food, and so on. I grimaced at my own reflection in the mirror. Paula had learned to keep details about her life with Craig close to her chest. He had probably moved his bedroom down to the basement where he could get up and relieve his stress on the equipment whenever he needed to. There was also a separate entrance into the basement where he could come and go as he pleased. Oops, that wasn't a very charitable thought, but then does the leopard change its spots?

I went back into the bedroom. There were a couple of books on the night table. One was a recent release by one of the pioneers in the study of serial killers that I'd recommended to Paula. Underneath that was a paperback novel that had recently won the Giller Prize. The bookmark indicated she hadn't finished it so I popped it in the bag.

I straightened up the bed and replaced the pillows. As I let myself out, I could hear the whirr of the treadmill and the thump thump of Craig pounding away.

CHAPTER TWENTY

Visiting hours were still happening and the parking lot was full. I circled a couple of times before somebody left and I dived into the spot. Grabbing the carryall I hurried into the lobby, which was a swirl of people, nurses in pastel uniforms lacing through them, the ubiquitous cleaner slowly sweeping his wet mop around the edges of the entry. I checked the directory and headed to the cardiology floor. There were about four or five nurses at the nursing station, all too busy with very important things to notice me. I hung over the counter for a few minutes then interrupted a couple who as far as I could tell were discussing the latest episode of *American Idol*. But I could have been mistaken; it may have been that they were deciding who should be voted off the floor and sent home.

"What room is Paula Jackson in?"

One of the nurses, a round-faced, irritable-looking wench, frowned at me. "When was she admitted?"

"This morning." I waved the gym bag. "I have her clothes."

"See you," said her friend and she drifted off to compare favourites with somebody else at the other end of the counter.

The nurse checked a list in front of her. "Room 522. Go down the hall and turn right. But I'm afraid you only have half an hour. We start clearing the visitors at eight forty-five. Our patients need their sleep, you know."

I checked my sarcastic retort that I'd never heard of such a novel idea. The nurse, whose name tag said Irma, wasn't really the problem. I was tired out of my mind and an awful lot had happened since five-thirty this morning when Leo had called me. Including this situation with my best friend. I walked quickly down the hall wishing I'd stopped to buy flowers or chocolates,which she liked.

Paula had the bed closest to the door in a room with another woman. The fellow sufferer's curtains were closed but I know she had a visitor because I could see trousered legs beneath the curtain. They weren't talking though. There was no sound at all except the hiss of the oxygen that Paula was hooked up to. She had her eyes closed. The signs of her stress were etched deep in her face. I touched her lightly on the foot.

"Hi, Paula."

She opened her eyes at once. She licked her lips. "Hi, Chris. I'm so thirsty. Can you give me some water?"

I ministered to her, helping her to sit up in bed, trying to avoid disturbing all the plastic tubing that she was connected to.

"How're you feeling?"

"Thirsty, drugged, worried, any of the above."

"Chugalug that water then; we'll take care of one of those, at least."

She drank deeply, then smacked her lips. "Well it's not a fine shiraz but it sure tastes good."

"I brought you your nightclothes and toiletries."

"Good girl, this gown is the pits."

"Where do you want them?"

"Leave the bag on the floor for now... Did you pick them out yourself?"

"What, the clothes you mean?"

"No, the flowers that you failed to bring. Yes, of course, the clothes."

"Yes, I did."

She grimaced at me. "So you noticed I am all by my lonesome?"

It was like Paula to get to the point. I was relieved that I didn't have to tiptoe around the elephant in the room that nobody was talking about.

"When did that happen?"

"Just a couple of weeks ago. Craig says he gets too restless. We've always had different sleep patterns. He's a night owl and you know me. I turn into Cinderella after ten o'clock. So he suggested he take the guest room in the basement." She lay back on the pillow and sighed wearily. "It's not what you think, Chris. It's a temporary thing. I've been so worried about this lump; I'd have kept him awake anyway."

I held my tongue. If your wife was facing the possibility of a life-threatening illness, wouldn't that be a good time to be sharing her bed, holding her? Comforting her, maybe?

"Craig said he'll come over tomorrow morning. Now, according to Nurse Ratched down the hall, they'll turf me out of here soon, so tell me everything. What are the doctors saying and so forth. And Chelsea is fine, by the way. She has her sleepover with Suri and your mother is coming up from Toronto tomorrow to stay at the house."

Paula smiled. "Is she? What a mom. I haven't talked to her yet. She'll be worried about me. But I'm worried about her. She hasn't really recovered from Dad's death yet."

None of us had. Al Jackson had been my surrogate father ever since I essentially invited myself into the family to get away from my own mother when I was fourteen. We'd all been devastated when he'd dropped dead of an aneurysm over a year ago. Al was the man I considered to be my real parent.

Paula leaned back against the pillow. "This isn't exactly how I expected to be spending my evening. Anyway, I'm doing just fine for now, so you can take off your whey face."

"Hey, no insults allowed to faithful retainer."

She grinned at me. "No insult, just true. When you're worried you go sort of…"

I grabbed her toe. "Shut up or I'll pull you out of bed and then what?"

"Okay. Okay. So what's been happening? Distract me, tell me about the dark side. It'll make a change from thinking about death all the time."

I told her the gist of what had happened so far and we chewed it over for a while. Like me, Paula was passionate about her work, and it was true, the longer we talked, the more she seemed like her old self.

"What about our innocent bystander, Mr., what's his name, Torres? Could he be in the frame?"

Her question wasn't as out of order as you might think. There have been a sufficient number of instances of the bad guy returning to the scene of the crime to warrant us police being wary. Whatever you do, don't come across a dead body if you can help it. And if you do, don't run away. That will bring even more suspicion down on you. Sorry, but it's the truth. We'd question Jesus himself raising Lazarus from the dead.

I shrugged. "My feeling is he's what he says he is."

"What about this Zach fellow? Is he the anonymous letter writer?"

"I don't know. All possibilities are open at the moment."

A disembodied voice came over the intercom.

"Visiting hours are now over. Will all non-personnel please leave the building."

Paula and I looked at each other.

"I think that means you," she said. "I would gladly leave but I don't know how to disconnect the oxygen."

The person who belonged to the legs we could see beneath the neighbour's curtain stood up and the curtain swayed as he eased himself out. An elderly grey-haired man appeared, smiled at us, and walked to the door.

"His wife had a heart attack," whispered Paula. "She's not really conscious but he told me he sits there just in case she regains consciousness and she needs him. He's been here since I arrived."

Neither of us had to spell out the contrast between his devotion and Craig's. It rested unspoken in the air. The intercom snapped on again.

"Last call. All visitors please leave the building. Visiting hours will resume tomorrow at one o'clock."

"Have you connected your phone?" I asked.

"Not yet. We were in a bit of a rush. Craig had a squash game he couldn't cancel. I'll have to do it tomorrow." She reached up and tapped me rather hard on the chin. "I'm going to be fine, Chris. This heart thing is from stress. I'm not as concerned about it as I am about the lump and I won't hear anything about that until next week. So go home, you look exhausted. Call me in the morning and tell me all the news. I might have more to tell you myself by then."

I bent over the bed and gave her a hug as best I could.

"Sleep tight."

She hung on to me for a long minute. "Will do. Thanks for coming, Chris."

"Cut the crap, 'thanks for coming.' We're long past the thanking each other stage. We're blood sisters. You don't thank your blood sister. You take her for granted."

That got a smile out of her. When we were fifteen we had pricked our respective thumbs and mingled our blood in a solemn oath that we'd concocted from some adventure book we were reading.

I held out my thumb and she pressed hers against mine.

"One is both and both are one."

"Too bad we're not the same size," I said. "I liked the look of that green suit you have in your closet."

"Get out of here. It's brand new. I haven't worn it yet. I was waiting for an occasion."

Nurse "I'm not nice" Irma popped her head into the room. "Time for visitors to leave now."

I gave Paula another quick hug and left her. Her skin looked as white as the pillow she was lying against. Why, oh why hadn't I noticed how skinny she'd got lately and how pale?

I left the hospital with the rest of the stragglers and went to my car.

The street lamps cast pools of watery lights on the slick sidewalk and the few people out of doors hurried, heads bent under their umbrellas, to the warmth of their homes. I was hit with an unexpected pang of loneliness. I wasn't hurrying home to anybody. Suddenly I missed Gill fiercely. So far our long-distance relationship had been manageable but this dreary night made me wish he was waiting for me at home in a brightly lit warm house, dinner prepared…Whoa. dinner prepared? Sounded like I wanted a mother, not a mate. I groaned to myself. I was under the impression I'd resolved that issue a lot time ago. Apparently not.

CHAPTER TWENTY-ONE

I was still in a deep sleep when I was awakened by the phone ringing. It was pitch black outside, which wasn't surprising as it was just five o'clock.

"Chris, it's your mother."

It was all I could do not to growl into the phone. Joan refused, wilfully in my opinion, to get a grip on time differences. She was in the Hebrides, which was five hours ahead of me, a nice comfortable ten o'clock in the morning.

"Chris?"

"Do you realize it's five in the morning?"

"Oh, is it? I thought it would be seven and I know you get up early. Shall I call back?"

"No, never mind."

"You sound grouchy but then you always were a bear with a sore head in the morning."

I bit back my reply, which would only have proved her point. I was trying to be a grown-up person with her, although she too frequently managed to send me back to feeling like a sulky teenager.

"So you're probably wondering why I'm calling?"

"It had crossed my mind. Is the island sinking into the sea or something?"

There was a little silence followed by a forced chuckle. Joan didn't like it if I got sarcastic.

"Your father and I have decided to get married and naturally we'd like you to be at the wedding. We're thinking of this Christmas."

I shoved myself into a sitting position. I should offer a brief explanation. Two years ago, I discovered that my biological father whom I'd never met or even knew about lived in the Isle of Lewis where my mother had grown up. They were teenage sweethearts. She left the island, came to Canada at the age of nineteen, and discovered she was pregnant with me. She herself was in a state of rebellion and decided not to tell Duncan MacKenzie, that's his name, about his daughter. Unfortunately, when I met Duncan two years ago, the initial feeling was a mutual antipathy. Time had softened that a little but I still thought he was old school bossy and patriarchal and he considered me disrespectful and arrogant, especially where Joan is concerned. In his favour, I must say I'd never seen her happier or better cared for. However, I'd asked her several times not to refer to him as my father. He was the sperm donor but he'd nothing to do with parenting me. Al Jackson had done that. She always managed to slip it in.

"Are you listening?" she asked her voice sharp. She could get shirty almost as fast as I could. What a great pair we were.

"Yes, I'm listening. When did you decide this? The last I knew you were thinking of doing the deed in the summer, if at all."

"Oh no. We definitely want to make everything legal. People are much more tolerant than they used to be but I know they still don't approve of us living together outside of wedlock, especially my brothers."

"You shouldn't give them that much power. Who cares what they think? It's your life."

I'd met my uncles and found them, shall we say, unprepossessing. Dour and rigid, in fact.

"You can say that because you don't live here. Lewis is a different world. Anyway, your fath... Duncan and I were talking about it last week and we thought, why wait? He noticed a special on a cruise around the Greek Islands and it seemed a good way to spend a honeymoon. Besides, there are hardly any tourists at this time of year, so he can leave the business for a while."

Duncan put on herding and trick exhibitions for the visitors with his brilliant border collies.

I pushed Tory away from my feet.

"I'm not sure I can come. We're in the middle of a case for one thing and for another..." I paused. I didn't want to break my promise to Paula until she gave me permission to tell. Also Joan was jealous of my relationship with the Jacksons and I knew she'd be quite offended if she thought I was choosing them over her even if it was a serious matter like cancer.

"I thought you'd want to see Gill, at least," said Joan, her voice reproachful.

"He's planning to come here."

"He won't if I tell him we're getting married... It's not as if this is any old trip, Christine. This will be the most special day of my life."

Ugh.

"Your sisters are very happy for us."

"Half-sisters."

Mairi and Lisa were Duncan's daughters by his first marriage. I liked them a lot and I was very glad to have found them, but I couldn't stand it when Joan began the guilt trip, using them as levers.

"We've talked about having Anna as a ring bearer but Mairi thinks she might be too young."

Another heavy silence, then in the background I heard Duncan shouting something.

"I've got to go," said Joan. "We're driving into Stornoway to look at dresses. I was thinking of wearing white but it will probably be cold so I'm going for a nice pale blue wool suit I saw in Saracen's."

White? It was typical of Joan that she'd even contemplated the idea.

"What do you think?"

"Hm. Pale blue sounds good."

I sensed she wanted to have a girly talk about the wedding preparations but I just couldn't do it.

"Duncan says you should travel with Thomas Cook. They have more leg room."

"Right. Well, I'll have to get back to you about this. I can't promise."

Her voice became huffy. "Don't leave it too long. We're having the reception at the Duke and I have to make out the guest list. The places are limited."

That was a nice, under-the-counter stab but I deserved it.

"Let me get my head around it. I haven't had much sleep."

Another silence. "You haven't even given me your good wishes, Chris. My own daughter and you didn't say, 'congratulations.'"

She slammed the phone down.

I leaned back against the headboard. Chalk that one up as a failure. We'd both been trying to relate to each other differently, but the old tracks ran deep and mutual disappointment often reasserted itself

I snapped off the bedside light and snuggled back under the covers. Too late. I was awake. Or half awake anyway. I rolled over to head for the bathroom, Tory and Bertie both doing their best to trip me up so I could go crashing to the floor, die, and not be able to feed them. I came back to the bed, picked up the phone, and called Joan. A very British voice prompt said, "This is the answer phone service. The party you are calling is not available at the moment. Please leave a message."

"Joan. I'll come. Sorry I was so grumpy. You're right, I'm not good in the morning. Congratulations to both of you. I'll call again as soon as I can."

I padded into the kitchen, plugged in the kettle to make coffee, and opened a fresh can of cat food for the monsters, which they both dived into, Bertie making his usual little gobbling noise.

"I'm just a walking can opener to you two, aren't I?"

They agreed but didn't bother to look up.

I'd just made my coffee when the phone rang again. I hurried over to answer it but it wasn't Joan. It was Gary, my downstairs tenant.

"I didn't wake you, did I, Chris? I could hear you moving about and I heard the coffee grinder so I knew you were up to stay." So much for my private life. I'd have to be more careful about making strange noises that I didn't want overheard.

I'd inherited Gary and his partner, Ahmed, when I bought the house and we'd become good pals over the last year. Gary in particular loved gardening and he kept the backyard lush with shrubs and flowers, something I could never do. Ahmed on occasion made us all delicious Egyptian dishes.

It was not quite a quarter to six.

"Is something the matter?" I asked. Gary sounded stressed.

"Yes, I'm afraid so. Terribly the matter. I haven't slept a wink all night. Would you mind if I come up and talk to you? I just don't know where to turn."

What could I say? I owed him lots.

"Of course, come up. I'll make coffee. Is it just you or Ahmed as well?"

"Just me." His voice was tight. "Ahmed and I are separating."

"Oh dear. That sounds like a call for double sugar."

My feeble joke fell flat. Gary was notorious for having a sweet tooth and all his friends teased him about it.

"I'll be right there," he said and he hung up.

Two minutes later he was at the door. He was fully dressed but unshaven, something very unusual for Gary, who was fastidious about his grooming. I gave him a hug and he clung to me for a few minutes then stepped back so he could wipe his eyes.

He dabbed at the lapels of my dressing gown with his handkerchief. "Sorry, I've got snot all over you."

"It'll wash out. Do you want some coffee?"

"Yes, please, double-double."

While I was fixing his order, he was hovering in the kitchen. "I do like your apartment, Chris. It's very cosy."

"Thanks. Have a seat. Do you want some toast?"

"Sure."

I handed him the mug of coffee and he held it in both his hands.

"So what's this about you two separating?"

I knew they had rows like any other couple because I'd heard them, but they weren't frequent. Ahmed was several years younger than Gary, shy where he was flamboyant, a devout Muslim to Gary's vocal atheism. However, they'd been together for a few years and, in spite of the obvious differences, seemed very committed to each other.

Gary looked up at me with red-rimmed eyes. "As you know, his father died in June and he went to Egypt for the funeral. He hasn't been the same since. His family said he had brought about the old man's death because … because he hadn't provided him with an heir. Apparently, while he was there, his mother was relentless, dragging women over to the house for him to choose a bride… He's never told them about us. They would have disinherited him totally."

"But you've lived together for years."

He managed a sip of the coffee. "They think we're just good friends. They know I'm a schoolteacher and they approve of that. They also know I have a grown son." He managed a small smile. "I suppose they can't conceive of a man, er, changing his mind as it were."

"Ahmed is giving into the pressure, I gather?"

"He is. Oh Chris, he wasn't home all night. He told me yesterday that he's met somebody else, a woman, and he plans to marry her and have children. Then his mother will be happy."

He put his head down on the table and burst into tears. I came over to him and put my hand on his shoulder. There wasn't much I could say.

CHAPTER TWENTY-TWO

Gary thought he'd be better off going to work, so after about an hour of non-stop talking and weeping, he went downstairs to clean up. I'd been hoping to have a look at the report Gill had sent me but I just had time to get take a shower and have some breakfast. Katherine had scheduled a meeting for eight-thirty.

Leo, a glass of water in front of him, was sitting next to David, who was in the process of shaking out some drops from a brown vial into the glass. Leo didn't seem to be paying attention, the way a fox before it is about to strike the rabbit will be motionless. Quickly, I slid into the chair next to him.

"How's it going, Leo?"

He looked at me, his eyes hot with anger. "Get him away from me, Christine, before I kill him."

He spoke quietly but David couldn't help but hear what he said. He stopped what he was doing.

"It's just rescue remedy. It has a calming effect."

I moved the glass to one side, away from Leo. "Thanks, David. Not now."

"I'm only trying to be helpful," he replied in a particularly whiny voice.

Leo turned to him. "What would really help me at the moment is if you got as far away from me as you could. I am not interested in your potions. I do not need your help. In fact, if truth be told, I feel ill if I am within five feet of you."

He wasn't shouting but the force of his rage could have taken the paint off the walls. David blushed deeply.

"Sorry, I'm sure."

He gathered his file folder on the table in front of him and stood up. Body stiff with embarrassment, he shuffled to the other side of the table and sat down, making sure he wasn't in Leo's sight line. I felt sorry for him. I wouldn't like to be at the receiving end of that kind of lacerating anger.

Jamie and Ray were hanging out by the ubiquitous coffee urn where Janice was plying them with carbohydrates. The unpleasantness of the scene made them fall silent and I for one was heartily glad when Katherine came in and took her place. It might have just been me looking at the world through jaundiced, sleep-deprived eyes, but she seemed tired and stressed out. Her white blouse leached the colour from her face.

"Sorry I'm late. Let's get started, shall we? I only have an hour." She saw Leo and nodded at him. "Welcome, Leo." No fuss. She knew he was a grown-up and trusted him to tell her if he couldn't take it.

"Just to let you all know, I had a message from Paula this morning. She is in the hospital, nothing too serious, but they discovered an irregular heartbeat and she has to be under observation for a few days. She thinks they'll keep her there until the weekend at least."

"How did they discover it? What sort of symptoms was she having?" asked David.

"I've no idea. That's all she said. Chris, do you know anything more?"

"Not really. It's called atrial fibrillation and definitely has to be monitored but we'll know more when they've done the CT scan, which should be today."

"I'll send her some flowers from the team," said Janice.

Ah Momma Janice, we're going to miss you.

"Sounds good. Righto, folks, let's get going." Katherine tapped her pen on the table to get attention. "I've also heard from Ed Chaffey. He says the casino has agreed that we can have a look at the surveillance tapes this morning. He'll meet us there himself at ten-thirty." She glanced over at Leo. "It would make the most sense if you looked at them, Leo. You might recognize somebody. I thought Chris could go with you, if that's all right?"

He actually managed a smile. "I think we're joined at the hip now and if she's willing to be my minder, it's all right with me."

I never thought I'd be spending so much time with Leo Forgach, but so be it. Our shared experience of finding his daughter's body had created a bond between us that certainly hadn't been there before.

"So everybody has had a chance to look at the DVD and listen to the audio translation? Good. Janice has made copies of all the letters and emails that Deidre received. Christine has some first impressions but we can all throw in our two cents' worth." Janice started to hand around the photocopies. "We'll come back to those in a minute. Ray, what have you got?"

"I got in touch with Gallaudet University yesterday. They were very co-operative and gave me an address for Zachary Taylor in a small town in B.C. I contacted the police there. Just one guy and he was able to check it out right away." He grinned. "I think he was glad of the activity. Quiet town, I gather. He said it was the address of a rooming house. He went over himself and talked to the landlady but she'd never heard of Taylor. One of the tenants said she thought he might have been there before her and had moved to the States. Dead end so far but we'll see if there's a paper trail from the university. He must have paid his fees with something. That will take a while to trace, however. As for the DVD itself, I've given it to Fingerprints, but they weren't that optimistic about pulling up anything clear. A lot of people have been handling it. Same with the letters."

Katherine said to me, "Any further thoughts, Chris? Is this a serious threat?"

"I have no idea. Deidre's friends were positive he was joking. He liked to play tough guy imitations. I guess the 'kill' sign is the deaf person's equivalent of doing a Bogart lisp. That said, I'd bet he's the one who impregnated Deidre for the second time, and I'm guessing she arranged a meeting to tell him just that."

"He mentions a post office box, so I presume she sent him a snail mail letter," said Jamie.

"Probably, but we've got to get her computer. She seems to have kept the emails that were sent to her after her public announcement but I'd like to know who she was writing to."

"I'll get a subpoena to seize," Katherine said, making a note on her pad. "Finding Zachary Taylor is top priority. I've passed along a description of him and possibly the camper van to Ed. He's going to put a notice in the papers and there should be some TV coverage today, so we might get some results in soon. He's alerted all OPP stations in the vicinity to be on the lookout and we've also sent a description to the border folks."

"What's happening with the casino search?" I asked.

Katherine rested her head in her hands for a moment. "That is one helluva job. There are god knows how many surveillance tapes. They're everywhere, including the toilets — what fun that's going to be. Thank goodness for the receipts on bets placed. At least we can get an accurate read on the time she stopped playing. Ed's got his guys checking with the buses and taxi companies to see if she left in one of those. However, talking to the visitors may take weeks even if we can find all of them. She may have gotten a lift with somebody."

"Yeah," said Jamie. "Who the hell's going to notice one woman in that crowd? Besides, the only thing on anybody's mind is whether they're going to win tonight."

Katherine raised her eyebrows. "Are you speaking from personal experience, Jamie?"

To my surprise and probably hers, he turned a deep red, the flush meeting his auburn hair.

"I've been up there a few times."

Jamie was a quiet guy, conscientious and punctilious. Not the personality you'd necessarily associate with gambling, but it wasn't illegal, very legal in fact with profits benefiting the government and local Native groups. I wondered why he seemed so embarrassed to admit he frequented the casino. Personally I had tried it once early on and hated it. I'd expected to see people having a good time, laughing and yukking it up, but the opposite was true. To my mind, the pounding music drowned out moans of despair and rage, the neon lights hid haggard faces streaked with tears. Come on. Casinos do big business by appearing to be jolly friendly giants handing out lots of money with a ho! ho! ho! whereas they're actually raking it in and the customers are enticed to lose their shirts, and everything else on their person. A pawn shop on the premises would do a roaring business.

Enough of my little rant.

Katherine moved on briskly. "Jamie has a point but we've got to pursue it. Thank the Lord it's Ed's job to organize that. We'll just sit here on our fannies and analyze the results. Much easier. There are posters with Deidre's picture up now in the entrance to the casino. They've agreed to have a second uniformed officer stationed in the lobby in case somebody's memory is jogged and wants to unload right away. The registered coach trips are being followed up on but that is a huge job."

"Do you think Zachary Taylor wrote the hate letters?" Ray asked looking at me.

"I'd say no, given his preferred mode of communication seems to have been ASL and the DVD, and the tone of his monologue is completely different."

Katherine started to gather together her papers. "That's probably as much as we've got for now. Jamie, I believe you've asked ViCLAS to come up with any stats on similar cases. We'll see if they have anything for us. Thanks everybody. Janice will let you know about the next meeting."

Leo shoved back his chair. "Let's get to it then. Chris, you all right to drive?"

"Sure."

His restless agitation was contagious and I got moving promptly. Following him out of the door was almost a déjà-vu experience. It seemed eons ago that we'd been in this room.

Outside it was still pelting down. What was this, forty days and forty nights? We scurried to the car. At least he had his own umbrella this time.

I waited until we turned off Memorial Drive and onto Highway 12. He hadn't said anything, just sat staring morosely out the rain-streaked window.

"Leo, I think David deserves an apology. He was only trying to help."

He shot a look at me and I could see a protest about to jump out of his mouth. Then he swallowed.

"I know. I was an almighty jerk... What shall I do to make amends?"

"Well you could always send him a case of spring water."

He actually laughed. "Good idea.

We drove on.

"Loretta arrived late last night. She wanted to go directly to Deidre's house and see Joy. She's not had a lot to do with her, especially lately, but more than I have. I'm glad we did. It was almost midnight and Nora was plonked in front of the TV. Joy wasn't in bed — she was on the couch asleep beside her. I thought Nora was stoned. Loretta read it right away and said she'd stay in the house rather than at my place so she could keep an eye on things. Nora didn't like that, it might curtail her smoking up, but I felt much better. Loretta knows some basic signs — are you hungry, what would you like, that sort of thing — but it's more than I have.

"Jessica and Hannah are going back there today and Loretta thinks they should ask Joy some questions. You know, about seeing any men come to the house. Nobody is ready to tell her that her mother is dead but she keeps asking where she is. I don't know who's going to do that. The friends, I suppose."

We were driving through the rural area that separated the city proper from the casino. The fields were grey and sodden, the trees almost stripped of their leaves already. Here and there, dispirited cows cropped at the grass.

"I think that's a good idea to ask her about her mom's friends. I never thought about it. I trust they'll do it tactfully."

A sign directed us to turn off the road and Casino Rama, locus of despair and greed and exploitation, loomed in front of us.

It was just past ten but the parking lot was already jammed. At least a half a dozen coaches were pulled up in the bus section and simultaneously disgorging their passengers. I was struck by how many of them were elderly, probably on a field trip from their retirement homes. The majority were women, and one coach let off passengers who were all Asian. We hurried along with the flow of people, all chattering excitedly as they pursued the impossible dream. Sudden wealth literally pouring out of the slots, although in fact, at this casino, I had discovered, the slot machines no longer poured out money, you got vouchers instead.

Ed Chaffey was standing beside a tall uniformed officer near one of the doors. I saw the posters on the wall, but as far as I could tell, absolutely none of the hundreds of people rushing through the doors were paying attention to it. Jamie was right about that. Ed waved and came over at once.

"My condolences, Leo. I'm so sorry."

Leo barely nodded but they shook hands.

"The manager is waiting for us. His name is Todd Torvill. We can go up the back stairs."

He led the way across the lobby, forcing his way against the stream with me and Leo trotting in his wake. Once we closed the fire door behind us, there was a blessed quiet from the many excited voices.

"I asked him to take out the tapes that were running from eight o'clock to eleven. We'll start there at least and expand if we have to."

What could I say? Police work involves utter tedium sometimes, but then somebody's got to do the dishes.

CHAPTER TWENTY-THREE

The security office room was at the top of the stairs. A uniformed security man was posted at the door and we all had to show our IDs, which he examined carefully. He was young, twentyish, with a shaved head, swelling biceps, and a "don't mess with me" air that was impressive. He'd calm rowdies in minutes in my opinion even if it meant cracking heads, which I guessed he'd do with impunity.

"Thank you, sir, thank you, ma'am."

He gave some kind of secret knock on the door, which was opened immediately, and another shaven-headed security guard stood on the threshold.

"They're clear. They're here to see Mr. Torvill."

He was being super polite, as was the other-side-of-the-door guy, but I could tell how it irked Ed. As far as he was concerned he had authority over the entire place, including security, but they were acting like a city state. Another man, much slighter of build, middle-aged, appeared at the door. He had a neatly trimmed moustache, a neat grey business suit, and a look of anxiety that seemed perpetual. He made me think of the White Rabbit in *Alice in Wonderland*.

Ed introduced himself and us and Torvill stepped back so we could enter the room. It was large and I don't think I have ever seen so many monitors in my life. Think of one of those television stores that have the TV sets along the wall, all playing at the same time. Multiply by one hundred. A dozen people on roller chairs were seated at various places in front of the different banks. They were reminiscent of air traffic controllers. Nobody was talking, all focused on their screens. At the far end of the room, two uniformed security men, knees locked, stood watching us incuriously.

A tall, tan-skinned Native man with a phone device in his ear was walking up and down behind the scanners.

"That's our floor manager, Ben Snake," said Torvill. "He's got a good memory for faces. I've asked him to meet with us."

He beckoned and the man headed toward us. Suddenly his eyes caught something on one of the monitors and he swivelled around, leaning forward to study it more closely.

"Zoom in," he said, and the controller enlarged the image with a tap on the keyboard. An older Asian man sitting at one of the slot machines came into view.

"He's not supposed to be here. He's a self-excluder," said Snake. He tapped out a code on the receiver pack at his waist. "Jerry! Aisle 3, slot 45. Male Asian, baseball cap. His name's Lee. Remove him. This is the second time this week. Talk to him."

"It happens all the time," said Torvill softly, with an apologetic shrug. "People get addicted, lose their shirts, and voluntarily sign a request to the casino to bar them from playing. We do it, but in spite of that, there's always somebody who tries to sneak in."

Even as we watched the monitor, two large security men were at Mr. Lee's elbows. He shrugged, put down his cards, and accompanied them out. No fight.

Snake handed his earpiece and receiver to one of the men on the roller seats, who got to his feet. Vigilance couldn't take a break.

Ed checked his watch. "Sorry, Leo, I'm going to have to go. You've got my cell number. Either you or Christine can call me as soon as you have anything."

He left and the guard at the door let him out promptly. Muscles and bald head aside, he was still a glorified concierge.

"Let's go into my office," said Torvill, shepherding us like a little flock. The three of us followed him through a side door, padded to keep out the din of the casino, into a small room that was disappointingly plain for the head office at a multi-million-dollar-earning casino. No thick burgundy carpet, no mahogany desk or leather chairs here. The furniture, what there was of it, was bland

and dull. It reminded me of an airport waiting area but maybe I was still influenced by the control tower feeling of the other room. Torvill performed the introductions and Ben looked for what seemed an unusually long time into my face, I presumed committing my features to memory. I didn't notice him doing that with Leo but maybe I was staring back at him. I'm a sucker for ponytails on men and he was sporting a long one, pulled tightly back from his face. He was probably in his mid to late forties, strikingly handsome with chocolate brown eyes and jet black hair. His face was lean and there was a gravity to him that I liked.

"First off, Dr. Forgach, let me say how sorry I am about what happened to your daughter."

"Thank you." Leo's response was curt but I knew it was only to cover up the raw place in his psyche.

"Miss Morris, Doctor, please take a seat," said Torvill. He went over to his desk and picked up a copy of Deidre's photograph from the pile on his desk.

"Have a look at this, Ben. Do you recognize her?"

The manager briefly studied the photograph then nodded. "Absolutely. She's a regular. Tuesday nights, always plays blackjack, usually table six."

"I told you he has quite the memory," said Torvill. Like a lot of men with facial hair he had a nervous mannerism of twiddling with it. He did it now, plucking at his moustache for a few moments.

Snake addressed us. "Gamblers are a superstitious lot. Most of our regulars return to the same table unless they've lost money there. They remember a win but don't add up the overall losses. If they make some money, they'll usually try to get the same seat, same dealer."

"Did you see her yesterday?" Leo asked.

"I'm afraid not. I had the night off, so no, I didn't."

"What I suggest is that we go straight to the tapes that were focused on that particular table then," said Torvill. "If Ben is right, and I've no doubt he is, it could save us a lot of time. I'll cue the tapes for you."

There were two of the ubiquitous monitors on a shelf and he inserted one of the tapes into the receiver from the reels he had in a box.

Ben was still holding the photograph. "She was a very pretty girl. I hope you catch the bastard who killed her."

"We will," said Leo.

"We're ready to roll," called out Torvill. "Miss Morris, let me show you how it works. We have two cameras on each table viewing from different angles. Monitor A, on your right, will show one perspective, monitor B the other. You can slow each frame by pressing 'hold' if you need to study something more closely. If you get something, you can print it out. Press 'print.' It's quite simple."

Just like the white rabbit himself he took a large gold watch out of his vest pocket. "I'd better get back to the floor — the customers do like to see me." He touched his right ear. "Tell Ben if you need me and he'll call me."

I hadn't even noticed his earpiece, which was nicely covered by his hair. Whew, the communication system in this place would put CTU to shame. I only hoped Mr. Lee hadn't been taken off to the interrogation room to meet Jack Bauer.

Leo and I took the two chairs in front of the monitor and he pressed the start button. At the bottom of the screen the time clock began running. 7:56. Snake had stationed himself a couple of feet just behind my shoulder. The monitor I was looking at was trained at the dealer, who was a woman. There were seven players at her table and we could see clearly the faces of five of them. The other two had their backs to the camera. The second camera was focused from behind the dealer, and on that monitor, I could see all the faces.

Ben indicated monitor A. "We always keep a camera on the dealers. Believe it or not, it's them we worry about. They're all carefully vetted before we hire them but you'd be surprised how many of them become adept at sleight of hand and try cheating. We catch them eventually, but we've lost a lot of money that way. This woman is one of our stalwarts by the name of Betty Yu. She's Chinese but she's not allowed to speak Chinese to any of the customers. It's all got to be in English. She'd be fired instantly if she even spoke to her own mother." He chuckled. "Especially her mother."

The dealer appeared to have a head cold, and while the players were studying their cards, she seized the chance to wipe her nose. As she was returning the tissue to her sleeve, it dropped to the ground. She stared straight into the camera and raised her hands.

Then she bent down to retrieve the tissue, showed her empty hands again and returned to dealing.

"Good girl," said Ben. "The dealer's hands must be visible at all times. All money has to be put on the table, not into any palm which may be greased."

I wished he'd been a bit more ironic about it but he wasn't.

"There's Deidre," Leo called out and he immediately froze the frame. I might not have caught her. Her hair was pulled back into a ponytail and she had long bangs. She was standing just behind one of the players, her gaze intent on the play of cards. I made a note of the time — 7:57.

"Is there anybody else at the table you recognize?" I asked him.

"No, what about you, Ben?"

Snake pointed at a woman who was seated on the dealer's right. "She's here every single night. She'll be at this table until about nine then she will leave and have a go on the slots. I'm keeping an eye on her. She bets a lot and loses a lot."

The woman was a skinny, bleached blonde with a fifties beehive hairdo. Somebody's grandmother.

"Did Deidre win or lose?"

"She's a good blackjack player and I'd say most times she will be a winner. She's sensible though and she doesn't bet heavily even if she's ahead."

He spoke admiringly. He saw addiction all the time. Ruinous addiction.

"Any other regulars?" Leo asked him.

"That balding guy and the one next to him in the striped T-shirt. They move around all the tables though."

"I'm going to print this off," said Leo.

Ben pressed the button for him and the printer spat out the copy. Leo picked it up and looked at Deidre for a few moments.

"She's got a purse with her. It is navy blue leather. It was a birthday gift."

"Do you want me to backtrack her movements? I can go as far back as the entrance."

"Yes, please."

Ben began to reverse the tape, frame by frame, and we saw that Deidre had gone into the rotunda.

"What's she doing?" Leo asked. "Is she meeting somebody?"

There were cameras in there too and we waited for what felt like an interminable length of time, watching Deidre sitting on one of the benches. Some people came and went but nobody spoke to her. She had her head slightly bent, hands clasped in her lap.

"What's she doing?" Leo repeated.

"We run a very good sound and light show in the rotunda," answered Ben. "It depicts Native heritage."

"Speed it up a bit, will you?" Leo said, full of impatience.

Ben did as he asked and we got as far back as the entrance to the casino. There was a good shot of Deidre coming in. She looked excited and animated. Once again, she made no contact with anybody. I wrote down the time. 7:45 p.m.

"Go back to the blackjack table," said Leo.

Ben did a fast-forward to the blackjack table. The blonde woman threw in her cards, obviously upset, and left the table. Deidre slipped into her place. She put her chips down in front of her and indicated she was in the game. I could see why it was easy for her to play. You didn't need to speak or hear, you watched and signalled when you wanted another card, or you dumped your cards when you quit. The tape moved on for a few more minutes. A round finished and the dealer pushed some chips over to Deidre, who had won the hand. The man on her left tossed in his cards and got out of his chair. He was replaced by another man who had been out of the frame of our camera. In my monitor this man had his back to me, but Leo was watching the B monitor. I heard his sharp intake of breath. He reached forward and stopped the tape.

"Is there any way to enlarge the image?" he asked Ben.

"Who do you want?"

Leo put his finger on the monitor, on the man who was seated next to Deidre, who hadn't paid him any attention as yet.

"Do you know him?" I asked Leo.

"Damn right I do. It's my son. It's Sigmund."

CHAPTER TWENTY-FOUR

For a moment I thought I'd misheard or he'd got it wrong. "I thought you said he hadn't seen Deidre in years?"

"That's right. And when I spoke to him last night he didn't breathe a word about being with her on Tuesday."

"How did he take the news?"

"I don't know. Stunned? Disbelieving? The sort of emotions you'd expect. He asked if we knew what had happened, who'd killed her." He scowled at me. "They were perfectly normal questions, Chris," he snapped. "I never gave it another thought."

"Why would you?" I snapped back, more to jolt him off that track than because I was irritated. He looked ghastly. He turned back to the screen and stared at it with such intensity, I thought he'd push himself bodily into the scene.

Sigmund didn't look much like him. He was taller, a few pounds into chubby, with narrow-framed designer glasses that were too small for his face. He had long sideburns and a quiff, à la Elvis. He'd shoved up the sleeves of his khaki cargo blazer and a beige scarf was tossed with careful insouciance around his neck. Everything screamed "trying too hard."

"Ready to continue?" asked Ben, who hadn't expressed any curiosity about our exchange. Perhaps he'd learned to tune out emotional pain.

"Just a minute." Leo jotted down the time from the screen. 8:19. Ben pressed "play."

The figures on the screen jumped into life. Sigmund put his hand on Deidre's shoulder. She turned and looked up at him. A frown and a shrug to remove his hand. Some words were exchanged. She was talking and signing at the same time but her voice must have been loud because the man seated beside her glanced at her curiously. The dealer scooped up the cards and collected the chips, which disappeared down a small plastic drain beside her. She took more cards from the sleeve, asking the players if they were in for the next round. Deidre tapped the table to indicate she would play on. Sigmund stood awkwardly, arms hanging by his sides, not speaking. The next round went quickly; Deidre showed a queen high but lost to the house. Sigmund said something else to her. It was obvious this was not a friendly conversation. She shook her head. He asked her something which looked from his gesture as if he wanted her to go with him. Hand lifted to mouth. Ah yes, to the bar. Another shake of her head. Whatever she said then clearly upset Sigmund. He spun around and left.

"Stop the tape for a minute," said Leo. "Can we track his movements?"

Ben nodded. "For sure."

"Let's do that first then but come back to Deidre. We've got to get one of those girls to watch this and tell us what they're saying," said Leo.

He could of course ask his son what they'd been talking about, but almost without realizing it, Leo had switched into official mode. Sigmund was now on the witness list.

Ben inserted more tapes and started the first one at the time checkpoint.

"There he is," Leo cried out.

We picked him up on the next frame and then the next. He pushed his way through the crowd and went into the bar. Here, he checked his watch turned around and headed for the exit. He went through the doors at 8:27.

"There aren't any cameras in the parking lot," said Ben. "But we do have them at the entrance. We keep track of the cars coming in and exiting."

Their surveillance was, shall we say, comprehensive, but I

hadn't heard a peep out of civil liberties folks protesting about Big Brother tactics.

"Go back to Deidre, please," said Leo.

Ben did so and we watched the tape for the next two hours. Ben commented periodically on some of the other players that he recognized but nowhere in the tape did we see Deidre talk to anybody or show any reactions to anybody around her. She seemed to have a good night until the end when she lost all her chips. The man two seats down had a flush and cleaned up. Finally, at 10:40, she too checked her watch, looked alarmed, and stood up quickly, indicating to the dealer that she was finished playing.

"She's supposed to be at Memorial Park by eleven. She's cutting it close," said Leo.

She grabbed her coat and purse.

Ben tracked her through the casino, hurrying now, and through the exit at 10:43.

That was that. We knew she'd gone to her car and found she had a flat and then vanished into thin air.

We all sat back. I rotated my shoulders to get the feeling back and Leo massaged his neck.

"I didn't see anybody paying her attention. No covert glances, nothing. What do you think, Chris?"

"From what I've seen, I agree with you. I don't think she met anybody inside the casino."

Other than Sigmund Forgach, but it wasn't necessary to add that. We all knew.

"I think the next step is to speak with my son," said Leo. "He might be able to help us."

And after that? I knew Leo's mind was racing too, sifting, discarding, flinching away from suspicions too horrible to be acknowledged. Why had Sigmund hidden the fact he'd met Deidre on Tuesday night? But what earthly reason might he have for killing her?

Leo looked at me. "I suppose I shouldn't be the one to question him, should I?"

"Uh-uh. We've got to pass all this on to Ed. He'll have to bring Sigmund in for a talk." Leo turned to the manager. "We'll need to keep these tapes."

"I've already got them marked."

"And you do know that as this is a police investigation, you are bound by the rules of confidentiality."

Leo's voice was unnecessarily authoritative but Ben didn't seem to take offence.

"I wish you all the best, Doctor." his voice was soft and sympathetic but I could see Leo bristle. He wasn't used to being the object of pity and he didn't like it.

"Come on," I said. "Let's get back to the office right away. Thank you so much for your help, Mr. Snake."

"I'll take you downstairs."

We went out into the other room. Mr. Torvill was nowhere to be seen. The monitors flickered on, people lost their money and their hopes.

We walked back to the parking lot, not speaking. Deidre's car had been removed by the forensic guys, but we knew where it had been parked. I saw Leo looking around as if some clue would hit him and set his mind to rest. All that happened was the wind gusted and blew a discarded chocolate wrapper onto his foot. He shook it off angrily. I let him into the car, just as my cellphone rang. It was Katherine. I moved away so I could talk.

"How'd it go?"

"Let's say there were some surprising developments but I'd rather tell you when we come in."

"I've just had a call from Ed. Good news. We have a sighting on that camper van."

"Fantastic. Where?"

"Over on Colborne Street. It seems to have been an attempted break-in. The resident is an elderly woman, apparently, but she gave an excellent description of the man who was trying to get in her apartment. It could be Zachary Taylor, from what I've seen on the DVD. She says a blue and white camper van was parked in the parking lot and she saw it drive away."

"Colborne Street is only a couple of blocks from where Deidre lived, isn't it?"

"One west and two south. Ed is over there now but he thought you might want to talk to the woman yourself."

"I'm there."

We disconnected and I went back to the car. I told Leo about the phone call.

"I want to talk to him."

"Not now, Leo. I think it would be best if I got you back to the office and you can follow up on Sigmund."

"What if this Zachary fellow is the one who murdered Dee?"

"If he is, we'll charge him. It won't change matters for you to see him at this point."

He didn't like it but his better judgement prevailed and he nodded agreement.

There was a steady stream of cars leaving the casino and I moved into the lineup to get out. I glanced up as I drove through the gates but the cameras were nothing if not discreet and I wouldn't have noticed them if Ben hadn't told me they were there.

As we headed across the narrows toward Orillia I had another déjà-vu experience. Except that it was midday, it was an exact repeat of our experience of yesterday morning, which felt like years ago. Leo was completely silent, almost asleep. I realized I was getting really hungry. When I was front line, I'd learned to live with very unpredictable meal times but after two years of regular office routine, my stomach was accustomed to eat in the middle of the day. I was contemplating stopping to grab a quick slice of pizza to take with me, bad idea, when Leo said "You don't have to drive all the way back to the Centre. Just go to Colborne Street and I'll take a cab from there."

I was afraid he might be getting sneaky on me and was actually hoping to confront Taylor. What I felt must have showed on my face because he said with a touch of irritation, "Don't worry. I won't do anything. I'm not a complete idiot. Put me down a block before if you want to."

I actually thought that was a good idea and, making the excuse that I was going to turn right on Memorial Drive at Barrie Road, instead of left for the Centre, I let him off. He looked small and vulnerable, his collar turned up against the chilly air as he stood at the side of the road waiting to hail a cab.

CHAPTER TWENTY-FIVE

There was a female constable standing at the door of the building. I showed my ID and she directed me to apartment 305.

"I hope you catch the bastard," she said angrily. "The woman's eighty-two."

There was no answer to that so I hurried off. Katherine had said there was a reported break-in. I hoped it was no worse. At the apartment door, another young constable examined my ID with infuriating carefulness. He was going by the book and going against common sense but this wasn't the time to give him a lecture. "Look at me, not just the ID." He opened the door and I went inside. Ed Chaffey was sitting in an armchair across from two elderly women, one of whom was in the process of pouring tea. Ed was waving his hand, indicating he didn't want any more but she refilled his cup anyway. He looked relieved to see me and stood up, a white napkin sliding off his lap as he did so.

"Chri... Detective Morris, thank you for coming."

He retrieved the napkin and put it on the table near a plate of chocolate biscuits. Both women looked at me expectantly. The one with the teapot beamed.

"Hello. I'm Mrs. Ruth Burgess, Grace's sister. May I offer you a cup of tea?"

I caught a fleeting expression on Ed's face but I was already nodding and she poured very dark tea into a china cup.

"Milk and sugar?"

I didn't know how Mrs. Burgess had spent her adult years but I imagined it was in very high social circles with minor royalty and ambassadors. She was impossible to hurry or deny. I accepted milk and she added a couple of drops to the black brew and handed me the cup. As I took a sip, I caught an under-the-eyelids glance from her sister. She looked furious.

"Maybe she doesn't want tea, Ruth. You always make it too strong anyway."

Ruth's thin lips tightened. "This is a day that calls for very strong tea, Grace."

I took a sip from my cup and almost choked. The brew was so bitter it was virtually undrinkable. Ed grabbed the napkin and dabbed at his mouth.

"Miss Cameron, I'm sorry to have to ask you this, as I know it has been an ordeal, but Detective Morris is from our forensic science department of the OPP and I know she would like to hear from your own lips what happened."

"Forensic science? How interesting," said Ruth before her sister could say a word. "We watch *CSI* all the time. By we, I mean my husband and I. I know Grace doesn't care for it. My favourite is the Miami one, although on occasion I have enjoyed New York."

There was another poisonous glance from her sister. Grace Cameron must have grown up all of her life with Ruth seizing the limelight. Now she had an opportunity for her fifteen minutes of fame and she was having a hard time getting it. I returned my cup to the table and took my notebook out of my bag.

"I'm sorry too that you have to repeat yourself, Miss Cameron, but it would indeed be helpful if you would. As you know we are keen to speak to the young man driving the camper van. You say you saw him...?"

"He tried to break into her apartment," answered Ruth. Grace squirmed a little further away on the couch. I wasn't going to get very far unless I bound and gagged her sister.

"Mrs. Burgess, do you live here with Miss Cameron?"

"Oh dear no. I have my own house near the lake. Grace telephoned me as soon as this happened and I came over directly." She took a sip of her own tea and her hand shook a little, whether from emotion or palsy I didn't know.

"The nice policewoman thought I should have somebody with me," said Grace. She didn't have to speak out loud the subtext. *I wouldn't have called you if I hadn't been told to.*

"How are you feeling now?" I asked her. "Are you up to one more interview?"

"Yes. I've only spoken to two people. This gentleman here and a lady police officer who came after I telephoned emergency. What would you like to know?"

Before I could answer, her sister interjected again. "Can you not look at the other officer's notes? Grace is putting on a brave front but she is eighty-two and last year she had a heart attack. She has to have a pacemaker."

I thought that Grace repeating her story to me was less likely to cause her stress than the decades-old dynamic between her and her sister, which was obviously making her blood pressure soar. Ed Chaffey came to my rescue.

"Mrs. Burgess, I think that Detective Morris needs some privacy. Perhaps you and I could go downstairs for a few minutes."

He held out his hand and Ruth didn't have much choice but to accept. She got to her feet stiffly, picked up a walking stick that I hadn't noticed was leaning against the couch, and with Ed at her side, she shuffled away. I waited until the door had closed behind them.

"Miss Cameron, will you just say in your own words what happened this afternoon."

She had lowered her head during Ed and Ruth's exchange but now she met my eyes. She had probably been very pretty in her youth. Her white hair was still abundant and wavy, her features delicate. I suspected she had made good use of those big blue eyes in her youth.

"Good thing it didn't happen to Ruth; she would have been prostrated. I used to be a nurse. I even went through the war and served overseas. She stayed here and rolled bandages and knitted socks. I saw a lot of ugly things. If I can survive that, I can survive some silly boy trying to get into my apartment."

She stopped and seemed to fall into a reverie but whether it was about her war experiences or what had just happened I couldn't tell. For all her tough-minded words, she seemed frail to me and shaken. I could see a bluish tinge to her lips. She looked at me, and as if I had spoken she said, "You're right. He did give me quite a fright. I was twenty years old when I was in London with bombs falling all around us. It's different when you're young."

I moved the teacup so I could have room for my notebook.

She frowned. "You don't have to drink that muck. As long as I have known her she has never made a good cup of tea. I keep telling her it's too strong but she doesn't listen."

I tried not to make my sigh obvious but she must have seen it. "All right then. Here we go." She consulted a wooden cuckoo clock that hung on the wall over the entrance to the kitchen. The apartment was small but built when it was considered necessary to have high ceilings so it didn't seem cramped. The furniture was well-worn and I could see evidence of cats on the shredded arms of the couch and chair. The perpetrator was nowhere to be seen.

"It must have been about a quarter past twelve. I was sitting here with my feet up listening to the radio. I usually do that in the afternoon. I get tired, although sometimes I couldn't tell you for the life of me what I've been doing that's so tiring. Well never mind that, here I was on the couch..." She actually swung her legs up and put her head back on the pillow so I could see.

"I heard the chain rattling. I always keep the chain on. In my old house, I did have a burglar once. At least I thought it was a burglar, but the police came to the conclusion it was my neighbour who drank too much, and got mixed up. It was a semi-detached house and the two front doors were next to each other. Mr... Dawson or Dawkins, I forget his name. I didn't like him. He was a bachelor, might have been one of those," her voice dropped to a whisper, "... homosexuals. I never saw a woman around ever but I did see a lot of young men. Anyway, where was I?"

"You said where you lived previously, your neighbour might have tried to gain entry to your house."

"That's it. I had my nephew install a chain on the front door and I just got into the habit of keeping it on. So when I moved here ... let's see, that was four years this coming January ... I had a chain put on, no I lie, there was one on already... There's a family that lives on this floor at the end of the hall and they have a boy who's a bit simple. Very sweet boy but childish. I like to bake so I give him cookies all the time, those are mine on the plate, try one, it won't be as bad as the tea, I promise."

"I'm fine thanks."

"You can take some with you then. Now where was I?"

"The boy down the hall."

"Yes. Tommy. He doesn't know to knock and he would walk right in on me. I was in the toilet once. He doesn't mean anything by it. 'Tommy,' I called. 'Tommy, you must knock first,' but he keeps forgetting. I just started to put the chain on so I had some warning."

Her glance moved to the door. "So as I said, I was lying here listening to the radio when I heard the door open and the rattle of the chain. 'Tommy, I told you to knock.' No answer. Usually he says, 'Sorry, Miss Grace,' and he giggles, but there was nothing. The chain rattled again. I could see somebody was there trying to get in. I thought it might be my home care worker, Lou Ann, but she always knocks." Miss Cameron raised her voice. "I yelled, 'Who is it?' but nothing again except the shoving of the door against the chain. I got up and went to see, still half-thinking it must be Tommy. I peered through the crack and there was this young man standing there. I've never seen him before. He was quite tall and he was wearing one of those sweatshirts with hoods which he had pulled up over his head."

"Could you see his face or do you think he was trying to hide himself?"

"Oh yes, I could see his face quite clearly. My eyes aren't what they were but I was close enough. He wasn't coloured or Chinese or anything like that. He was quite fair-skinned, blue eyes. One of those pointy beards, which I detest. Makes the man look like the devil, if you ask me. But that's what he had."

"How would you describe his demeanour? Was he threatening in any way?"

She shook her head. "Not exactly threatening. In fact he looked surprised. I asked him again what he wanted but he didn't answer, just turned around and started to walk off down the hall. Well I wasn't going to open the door or go after him because I didn't like the look of him. I thought it might be wise to call the police because I'd heard on the news this morning about that poor young girl being murdered."

She got up and went over to the window where there was a table. She moved a little stiffly but much more easily than her sister.

"But as I looked down I could see this young man with a hooded sweatshirt come out of the building. Unfortunately, I overlook the parking lot. It's not much of a view, as Ruth is constantly reminding me."

She beckoned to me to join her at the window. "The young man came out and got into a van that was parked near the entrance there, in the visitor's spot."

I looked down onto a small empty parking lot. Bedraggled trees lined each side and another apartment building was behind them.

"Was he running or walking?"

"Walking, but fast."

"Did you see which way he turned out of the driveway?"

"To the right. I realized then that the news report had said the police wanted to know if anybody had seen a blue and white camper van." She looked at me. "That was when I did become afraid thinking a murderer might have been outside my own door. I dialed 911 and the young woman who answered was very kind. She told me to stay exactly where I was until the police arrived. They must have been here in, oh, five minutes at the most. In a moment of panic, I did call Ruth, but that was a mistake. She keeps acting as if it happened to her and not me. But she's always been like that. And that's it. That's all I can tell you."

I closed my notebook. There was no doubt her visitor had been Zachary Taylor. He hadn't replied because he couldn't hear her. But why her? What was he doing?

The clock struck the hour and a wooden cuckoo flew out, its beak opening each time.

"I'll get something to wrap up those cookies for you so you can take them with you," said Grace, and she shuffled into the tiny kitchen which adjoined, emerging with a plastic baggie filled with cookies. "Here you are. I made chocolate chip and peanut butter ones. Tommy likes them."

There was no way I could refuse.

"Miss Cameron, you mentioned you only moved here about four years ago..."

"Yes, that's right. My house was getting too much for me and this is a reasonable rent. I'm on a pension and I don't have money to throw around."

"Do you know who was the tenant before you?"

She stared at me. "Why I suppose so. I sublet for two months, then took over. It was a young woman. She was quite harumscarum and she left the place filthy. If she'd cleaned the stove once in five years you'd never know…"

"Do you know her name?"

"I forget." She pulled open a drawer in the table. "But let me see, I keep everything in here." She took out a pile of papers, dumped them on the table, and started to riffle through them. "Ah, this is it. The original lease." She peered at the paper. "Grace Cameron agrees to sublease… etc., etc., there you go. Her name was Nora Cochrane. That was the young woman. Nora Cochrane."

Was it indeed?

And why was Mr. Zachary Taylor calling on Nora, a woman who claimed never to have met him?

"Do you know a man named Zachary Taylor?" I asked Miss Cameron.

She thought for a moment, looking as if she were going through a Dewey decimal file index in her mind. "No, I don't. I knew a Zachary Bennett in school. You don't mean him, do you?"

"No, this man is young, early twenties."

She gaped at me. "Is that the person who was trying to break into my apartment?"

"I think it might be."

"Why would he do that if I've never even met him?"

"It's possible he was looking for the previous tenant, Nora Cochrane."

Grace made a sort of snuffling noise of disapproval. "I'm not surprised. She was quite a wild young woman in my opinion." She tapped her own nose. "She must have had at least three rings in her nose. Very ugly, if you ask me. Young people today are worse than savages with their rings and tattoos and going about practically naked no matter what the weather."

She pulled out the chair and sat down with a sigh of relief. "I am actually relieved to hear that this man had a purpose for coming here and he wasn't just randomly breaking into seniors' apartments. I've heard stories lately about some pervert peeping through the windows of seniors' residences. And they're old ladies like me. What possible pleasure could it give anybody to see my wrinkles? I don't even like them myself."

I smiled at her, wondering to myself if I could adopt her. I was missing an old aunt or two in my extended family. In fact I didn't have any in Canada and didn't really know all of the ones I did have in the Hebrides.

I touched her shrivelled hand lightly. "Thank you, Miss Cameron, you have been a great help."

She gave me a rather dazzling grin. Dazzling because she had a set of dentures that were ultra-white and shiny. "I'm the one who feels they've been helped. I was getting nervous about the idea this man would come back."

She leaned in toward me so she was only a few inches from my face. "Promise me you won't repeat what I'm going to tell you."

I would have come across as stuffy if I had told her I couldn't be held to a promise where an investigation was concerned so I gave her a nod, hoping she wasn't in fact going to confide in me anything I would have to repeat.

"There was a moment there when I saw this husky fellow outside the door that I was afraid he would push right through the door … I was terrified he might be a rapist… You see, I'm a virgin, Miss Morris. In my day you waited until you were married before you, er, gave yourself to a man. Not like the young people today who get married and their children are the ring bearers."

She grabbed my hand, squeezing it tightly. She was trembling. "You see, I didn't want rape to be my only experience of intercourse."

The enormity of what she was saying was like a blow to the stomach. I squeezed back. "I'm sure you will be quite safe but just to make sure, why don't you go and stay with your sister until we can catch this man?"

"Is he a murderer?"

"I don't know."

She let go. "You're right, I don't think I would sleep tonight, chain or no chain. I don't like staying with Ruth. She is too bossy for words but I think I will. For a little while anyway."

I stood up. "Why don't I go and get her and tell her that's what you'll do?"

I had the feeling that Ruth would be as reluctant as her sister to take her in and a semi-command from the police might overcome her reluctance.

"I think while you're doing that, I'll have a rest on the couch. I'm exhausted. It must be all the excitement." She walked slowly over to the couch and sat down. "It's not fun getting old."

She swung her legs up again and lay back. I picked up the quilt that had fallen to the floor and covered her over. Her eyes were already closed.

"Thank you, my dear. You are most kind. Don't forget your cookies."

I left and went in search of Ed Chaffey. Next stop, a visit to Miss Nora Cochrane.

CHAPTER TWENTY-SIX

W hen we got to the house, a glowering Nora informed us that Joy was being put to bed by both Jessica and Hannah. We stood on the porch again. This time it was me and Ed, who was a lot bigger than Leo but took up less psychic space. Reluctantly, Nora let us into the living room. She was wearing a tight-fitting T-shirt with the logo F@#% OFF. She had a chain-link tattoo around the bicep of each muscular arm.

She fiddled with the ring piercing her eyebrow. "I told you I've never heard of the guy," she said. "Never seen him, never heard of him."

"Why was he trying to get into your old apartment then? The one on Colborne Street?"

"How the hell should I know?" Suddenly she pursed her mouth. "Wait a minute, I almost forgot. One of Deidre's pals crashed at my place once about four years ago. I was... I had entered a rehab clinic. Total waste of time but that's neither here nor there. I had a couple of pals who needed a pad for a few months. They covered my rent, which saved me from having to give up the apartment. Anyway, Marlene phoned me up one day at the rehab centre and said a girl she knew was in need of a place to stay for a couple of weeks and would it be okay with me if she crashed at my apartment. She could pay. Of course I said yes. A bit more money was always welcome. I met her later, and it turned out she was one of Dee's friends."

"Which one?"

"The stumpy one, Hannah.

"What was the name of the friend who knew Hannah?"

"Marlene Robinson, but you won't be able to talk to her. She's gone backpacking in Tibet. As far as I know she doesn't intend to return for a couple of years." Nora picked at the quick of her finger. "She wasn't deaf, dumb maybe but that's another story... So when I got out of rehab, I was struggling a bit. Couldn't find a decent job. They ask for your previous work history and there was a difficult-to-explain gap in mine. One day, Dee comes over to see me. Says she's a friend of Hannah's and asks would I like to move in with her. Said she was knocked up, no dad to be found, and I could have free rent in return for some babysitting when the kid arrives. She must have been at least six months by then." Nora made a gesture with her hands indicating a large belly.

"You were taking a risk, weren't you, to agree to share a house with somebody you've never met before?" Ed asked.

Nora stared at him in astonishment. "This must be what is called the generation gap. People my age do it all the time. Hey, she was offering me a nice house with a garden, no rent, just pay your own food. It was an offer I couldn't refuse. Like I said, my job was just to be the ears while Joy was small and then gradually I did some sitting while Dee was teaching or having a rare night out."

We heard a wail from upstairs.

"Look, I've got to go. Joy's used to me putting her down for her nap. I know the routine. It sounds like those girls need help. Okay?"

She didn't really wait for permission but bolted off up the stairs. Joy's cries stopped almost immediately. Ed and I had no choice but to leave.

"That wasn't very productive, was it? Did you believe her?"

"I did, actually. It certainly makes sense that was the reason Taylor went to the Colborne apartment. He knew Hannah and probably thought she still lived there."

"Let's see if Leo has heard of the Robinson girl just in case she isn't in Tibet. She just might be able to fill in some of the gaps."

"My daughter wants to go to Australia when she graduates from university next year. What can we do? I suppose it's safe enough but it's so damn far and she's planning to be in the outback for a month. All I can hope is that she's got enough common sense she will be safe." Ed shook his head. "I tell you, Christine, having kids has given me grey hairs. You're lucky."

I'd heard this before from people who'd procreated but my childlessness wasn't entirely from choice. I'd never been in a situation where it was a possibility, wrong man, no man, whatever, and when my biological clock rang an alarm, which it did every so often, I ignored it. Now I had the right man but it was late in the game. I didn't want to be taking a child to school and have everybody thinking I was the grandma.

I made a noncommittal noise at Ed. I knew he had two daughters and I thought he was probably a good dad. Lucky girls.

We went out to the street where we'd parked our cars. I'd followed behind him from Grace Cameron's apartment.

He checked his watch. "Shoot, it's almost three already. I've got to get over to the Manticore and buy a book for my mother-in-law. It's her birthday tomorrow and she's coming for dinner. I promised Aileen I'd pick up a gift for her."

"Go. I've got to get back to the Centre."

He eased himself into the car, which was an unmarked grey Chevy, part of the cheap fleet that the officers could use when they didn't want to take the squad car and draw attention to themselves. I was glad that Ed had the sensitivity not to have cruisers showing up in front of Deidre's house every hour. The more anonymity the better for the child at the moment. He drove off and as I headed for my car, I glanced up at Deidre's house. Joy was at the window. She saw me look up and waved excitedly. The next moment, Nora was behind her, drawing her away, although I could see she was putting up a fuss. Then Hannah stepped forward and closed the curtains.

When I got back to the office, I had a quick visit with Katherine. Leo had informed her of the latest development and Sigmund was coming in for an interview at five o'clock. I went into my own cave and started to take care of business that had begun to pile up. I took one quick look at my test case, got as far as the second page, realized I wasn't concentrating, and closed the file. Deep breath, concentrate. I checked my email. There were two requests for my take on some hate mail. One was from the police department in a

Detroit suburb. The sender was a woman I'd met at a conference last year and we'd got along well. She believed in "thinking out of the box," as she called it, and had no hesitation about consulting other police departments even if they were north of the border. They had a nasty case involving two rival unions at the Ford Motor Company. Both were finger pointing and it was crucial she get some grip on who might be lying or lying more than the other fellow. She would fax me the material if I had time?

Arrgh. Normally, I'd have been only too happy to oblige, but I had to put her on the back burner for now. And that reminded me, Gill had sent through some material that I hadn't yet looked at. The second email was from a detective I knew who worked out of North Bay. Some vicious letters were being sent to a local radio DJ. It could be a racial issue, the DJ was a black man, the shock jock type. In my opinion were the letters serious enough to warrant some kind of protection? The third email was from somebody who identified themself only as Sandy and he/she said they had a project for school and would I answer some questions about what it was like being a police profile (sic) on television. What was David Caruso like to work with? I deleted that one, student or no student, and sent off emails to the other two telling them to fax the material.

I had grabbed a sandwich and a coffee from the Stake Out cafeteria downstairs and had just started to unwrap my turkey club when my phone rang.

"Hello to Christine. Gill here. Christine, my sweet, have you had a chance to look at that material I sent you?"

"Er... not yet..."

"There's been, shall we say, a development. The lassie in question made a serious suicide attempt this morning. She's going to be all right but it was touch and go for a wee while. I figure it's connected with this case and the sooner I can get a grasp on what was going on the sooner we can know how to help her."

I groaned to myself. "Gill, I'm sorry, I haven't had a minute. But I'll get on to it today, I promise."

"Sure. We're doing our own questioning but frankly it's going nowhere. Any input from the big city would help."

There was a rather awkward silence. Geez, I hate telephones sometimes. I wanted to be sitting with him in our favourite pub, relaxed and comfortable. I felt guilty that I'd let him down.

"I won't keep you, I know you're busy," he said.

"No, wait. I heard from Joan this morning. She said she and Duncan are planning to get married right after Christmas so they can go on a cruise. She wants me to come to the wedding."

"And will you?"

Gill knew the complexity of my relationship with my mother. He didn't really understand, it as he had old-fashioned attitudes to parents of the loyalty and duty kind no matter what.

"Probably. I could take four or five days max but it would be great to see you earlier rather than later."

"Agreed."

His voice was flat and there was another awkward silence that made me feel wretched. Was he getting fed up with this long distance thing? God, had he met somebody else? I felt an icy flutter of panic in my stomach. Then another beep announced an incoming call.

"Gill, I'll call you back, are you at home?"

"I am but I'm on my way out. Community meeting about the windmills tonight. Let's talk on Sunday."

I got off the phone as fast as I could, not wanting to hear goodbyes that I could interpret as cool. The other caller had hung up, whoever it was.

Feeling decidedly off-kilter, I decided after all to have a look at my test case.

> Five days after ... body was discovered in ... hikers
> stumbled across a set of badly decomposed remains
> in an isolated forest north of ...

I made myself not cheat and riff on the bit of information of isolated forest.

Janice's voice over the intercom woke me up. Good Lord, I'd put my head on my desk for a minute but the clock said I'd been snoozing for half an hour. Ouch. My neck now had a crick in it.

"*Christine Morris to the boardroom.*"

Once again I closed the test case file with nothing accomplished. I grabbed my notebook and hurried out.

CHAPTER TWENTY-SEVEN

"They're in the boardroom and they've already started," Janice told me as I hurried past her.

"Who's conducting the interview?"

"Inspector Chaffey and Katherine. Doctor Forgach is in his office. He wanted to be present but Katherine wouldn't let him. They had quite a row."

Janice was probably wondering what the hell was going on but she didn't ask. She never stepped over the line. Not to worry, she had the uncanny ability to winkle out all the news where her "people" were concerned. She'd find out soon enough why Sigmund Forgach was being questioned by the head honchos.

I gulped back some water from the fountain by her desk and headed for the interview. I had to walk past Leo's office and felt a twinge of relief that his door was closed. Last Christmas, Katherine had given everybody cute signs to hang on our doors to indicate if we were in but not to be disturbed, like they do in hotels. She'd had them custom-made and Leo's was a lion which was glaring from glow-in-the-dark eyes. The sign said "Just Ate. Digesting. Go Away." Mine, by the way, was a border collie in crouched position driving a group of bad guys into a pen. The caption underneath read "Too Busy for Fun. Come Back Later." I liked it.

I tapped on the door of the interview room and waited for permission to enter. I didn't know if they were taping the session or not. Katherine herself opened the door. She looked a little irritated that I was late. Punctuality was high up on the list of good character traits as far as she was concerned.

"Chris, come in... Have you met Sigmund?"

I hadn't. I didn't even know he existed until yesterday.

"This is Christine Morris, one of our profilers," said Katherine.

Sigmund Forgach got to his feet and offered his hand. He was dressed in a formal dark grey suit, white shirt, and tie, unlike his casino clothes, but the same feeling of "trying too hard" still came from him. He greeted me in the tone of voice I thought he saved for difficult customers who needed to be soothed and charmed.

"I feel so terrible about what happened to Deidre. So, so sad. Inspector Chaffey was explaining why you all wanted to talk to me and I was just, er, delivering my statement." He smiled nervously. "It's so, so odd, isn't it, that here I am being interrogated in the very building where my own father is employed."

It was indeed so, so odd as he put it. Ed took over. "I've told Mr. Forgach that we're trying to trace Deidre's movements after she left the casino and as he was somebody we could immediately identify who was with her that night, we thought we'd start there."

Sigmund pushed his glasses up on his nose, a gesture he must have used many times when contemplating the soundness of his clients' loan prospects.

"Right. Well, strange as it may seem, I have had very little to do with my half-sister. In fact, I'd say to be precise, I've had *nothing* to do with her. My parents divorced before she was born, and, er, well, my mother was quite deeply hurt by the divorce and didn't want me to associate with my father's new family. I believe I may have seen her once when she was about four. Father wanted to bring his two families together, old and new, but it didn't seem to work. He and his second wife split up when Deidre was no more than five years old."

"When did you reconnect?" Ed asked.

"Oh, I don't know exactly. A few months ago I received an email from her. She said something like, she was an only child and so was I so perhaps we could get together and develop more of a family connection. She mentioned she had a daughter who would technically be my niece and she said she'd like me to meet her."

"And did you?"

Sigmund shook his head, as if regretfully turning down the request for a loan. "Alas I never did. I was quite busy all summer and the right time never arose."

"Are you saying that yesterday was the first meeting you've had with Deidre since she was a child?"

"Yes, that's right. Oh we did exchange emails as I said, but yes, it was our first meeting."

Ed's eyes met mine. We were both thinking the same thing. There was no way that could be true. Deidre knew him. No introductions had been necessary. None of the usual exclamations of surprise you'd expect. Far from it. Ed let that one ride but let Sig know we'd caught him.

"As you probably know, the casino has closed-circuit cameras everywhere. We have you leaving the casino at about 8:27. Is that correct?"

Again Sig reflected judiciously. "I wasn't paying a lot of attention to the time but that sounds about right. Deidre wanted to continue playing so I left her to it."

"What did you do then?"

He shrugged. "Nothing in particular. I collected my car and drove back to Barrie."

"Did you notice Miss Larsen's car in the lot?"

"No, I didn't."

"Did you pay any attention to the time when you arrived back in Barrie?"

"I'm afraid not, sir. But it is usually no more than a forty-minute drive at most so I assume I was home no later than ten o'clock."

Katherine spoke for the first time. "You share a condominium with your mother, I understand?"

"That's right." His pleasant young manager look slipped. "My mother's health is what might be called fragile. I do hope you don't see any necessity to involve her."

Given the circumstances, it was a rather astounding statement. Like hounds sniffing the wind, I could see all three of us twitch. What the hell was this man concealing?

It was my turn to throw in a question. "Mr. Forgach, given this was your first face-to-face meeting with your half-sister, why did you choose such a busy public place as the casino?"

"It was her idea. She said she went there regularly on Tuesday nights."

"And she informed you of this by email."

"That's right. I had an evening off with no plans so I thought I'd drop over there and surprise her."

What a lie that was.

"Can you describe to us the nature of your meeting with Deidre?" I continued.

He feigned puzzlement. "The nature? I'm not sure what you mean. Our meeting was quite brief. As I said, she was very involved in her game. I said I thought this wasn't a good time, she agreed, and I told her I would be in touch."

"Would you describe your meeting as a friendly one?"

"Yes, of course it was. Most cordial."

"You must have been shocked when Dr. Forgach informed you Deidre had been found murdered."

Sig shifted in the chair and shoved at his glasses again. Beads of perspiration had formed on his forehead. "Of course I was shocked. Terribly, terribly shocked. I hardly knew her, of course, but I couldn't pretend she was entirely a stranger, could I?"

Katherine had her head down and Ed took a drink of coffee from his cup. I could feel what was going through their minds but I didn't know if Sigmund could. Probably, because he jumped in again.

"I hope I don't sound callous but that's the truth of it. We share the same father and that's it. I knew nothing about her life nor she mine."

I smiled at him. "I quite understand that, Mr. Forgach. There was one thing I was wondering about, however. I understand that when your father informed you of your sister's death, you didn't tell him you had in fact met with her the previous night. Why was that?"

This time, he took out a white handkerchief from his pocket, made a show of blowing his nose, and wiped away the sweat at the same time.

"Sorry, I'm just getting over a cold. They're bad at this time of year, aren't they?"

None of us answered. We waited him out. He stowed the handkerchief.

"Please go on. You were saying?"

"I asked you why you hadn't thought to inform your father, Dr. Forgach, that you had met with your sister the same evening that she was killed."

He pursed his lips, his mind was racing so fast it was leaving smoke on the tracks.

"You know, looking back on it, I wonder that myself. I suppose I was so shocked, everything else left my mind. I apologize for that."

"One last question," said Katherine. "While you were at the casino, did you see Deidre with anybody else? Communicating with anybody?"

He shook his head earnestly. "No. Not at all." He chuckled. " As I said, she was so, so focused on her game. I think Elvis Presley himself might have appeared at her side and she wouldn't have noticed."

Ah, that explained the dyed black hair and the sideburns. He was a devotee of the King.

CHAPTER TWENTY-EIGHT

That was about it. We had no reason to charge Sigmund with anything at this stage and I know all three of us were hoping we wouldn't have to. We let him go and with several deferential smiles and soft handshakes, he left.

Ed pushed back his chair. "I've got to get back to the station," he said. "I'm going to leave this in your capable hands. Good luck."

He left and I got up and helped myself to coffee. It was fresh and hot but starting to churn acid in my empty stomach. My neck felt like it was made of wood.

Katherine leaned her elbows on the table. "I'm not looking forward to passing this on to Leo. He's…"

She didn't have to finish her sentence because the man himself came into the room.

"He's what? Don't worry, I'm not going to have hysterics. Tell me what happened."

Katherine hesitated but Leo mowed right on. "Sigmund is one of the last people we know was talking to her before she died. What did he have to say? Just forget he's my son."

Katherine sighed. "Leo, don't be ridiculous. None of us here is a robot and that includes you. How can we ignore the reality that these are your children?"

"Try," he snapped. "I agreed not to sit in on the interview but you owe me the courtesy of telling me what Sig had to say."

Katherine studied her nails for a moment. "Very well. Chris, you take good notes. Why don't you read them back?"

He waved his hand dismissively. "Don't! A summary will be fine."

"He said he hadn't really had any encounters with Deidre since she was a child but in the past few months, they had reconnected by way of emails, initiated by her. She mentioned she always went to the casino on Tuesday night so he thought he'd surprise her and drop in and say hello..."

"Hold on. He said this was their first meeting?"

I nodded.

"That's bullshit," Leo spat out. "You saw the tapes. Were they acting like two people who were meeting face to face for the first time in twenty years?"

"No. Not at all."

"Why is he lying then?"

"I don't know."

"You're sure that's what he said? He hadn't seen her face to face before yesterday?"

Katherine interjected. "That's what he claims, Leo."

"I suggest we bring in Jessica Manolo, Deidre's friend," I said. "She reads lips. We could ask her to look at the tape."

"Good idea," said Katherine. "Let's do that as soon as possible."

There was no window to stare out of so Leo had to make do with an empty notice board with fire drill instructions on it.

Katherine continued. "Sigmund seemed upset about the prospect of our questioning his mother, which we may have to do if we're going to verify his statement. Anything you can tell us about that?"

"Do you have a couple of days?" Leo said, his voice full of bitterness. There was a corridor of space between the table and the wall and he started to pace. Katherine stopped him.

"Please sit down, Leo. Walking up and down like a caged tiger might help you but frankly I find it unsettling."

He gave her a curt nod and took a chair across from us. "Trudy and I met when we were young and stupid. Frankly I was thinking with my dick and not my head. She was a bosomy blonde." He made the universal gesture for well-endowed. "I was a nineteen-

year-old horny virgin, she was … well, I fitted some fantasy
Trudy was carrying from her hundreds of hours watching TV
shows. Up-and-coming medical student, who would eventually
be laying healing hands on the attractively sick, accolades, not
to mention money, raining down on said doctor and his lovely
wife." He stopped but didn't look at either of us. "No bets on
what happened," he continued, his voice maintaining a rather
flat dispassionate tone. The shrink being objective. "We had an
affair, she got pregnant, we got married. One, two, three. Frankly
I wanted to leave her a few months after we'd done the deed but
I thought for the boy's sake I should stick it out. In hindsight, I'm
sure that didn't help him at all. Trudy resented the long hours I
put into my studies. She was, is, not what we'd call an intellectual
or interested in a thought that hasn't first been vetted by Oprah or
whatever guru it was back then. We argued constantly regardless
whether Sig heard us or not. She turned all her attention and
need onto the boy. I … I just buried myself more and more in my
courses. Early on I knew I wanted to be a psychiatrist but she
hated that. It wasn't sexy enough … I suppose I am allowed to get
some coffee?"

The trip to the coffee urn gave him an excuse to move around
and Katherine didn't stop him this time.

"I hung on until I finished my internship then I left her. Sigmund
was eight." He turned around and looked at both Katherine and
me. "You've heard stories like this before; I've heard them dozens
of times. She started, or more accurately continued, drinking, a
habit I'd ignored when I was in the throes of lust. When I left we
loathed each other. She couldn't bear to see Sig liking anybody else,
especially me. Any visits I tried to make were blocked. I didn't try
that hard. I found him an unattractive, whiny kid, a mother's boy if
ever I saw one. We had nothing in common. Over the years I have
met him only sporadically. The last time was about six months
ago. I met him for dinner and neither or us could wait until it was
time to leave… You've met him. He's a phoney. He wants to come
across as cool and with it but he just looks rather pathetic."

I'd had a similar opinion of Sigmund, but coming from his own
father, this judgement sounded harsh indeed. I didn't envy any child
of Leo's. The standards seemed impossibly high.

He picked up on my thoughts as surely as if I'd said them out loud. "I am not proud of my accomplishments in the parental department. I was the classic absent father and I'm sure Sig has taken on the responsibility for that as most children do. It is no doubt part of the reason why he tries so hard to be liked."

There was another awkward silence.

"Shall I go on?" Leo asked.

"Please do," said Katherine, but her eyes flickered to the clock on the wall. Leo saw her do it and I saw him shrink back. He was misreading her: she wasn't indifferent to what he was saying; she just wished she didn't have to hear it. If there was a club for people who were at the far end of the touchy-feely spectrum as far as their private lives were concerned, Leo would be the president and Katherine vice-president.

"I remarried a few years after I wrested, and paid heavily for, a divorce from Trudy. It's true what he said. I brought him and Deidre together once only when she was, hmm, about four, I think. He was very nasty and jealous with her and actually tripped her up when she was running across the yard so that she had a bad fall. I was actually afraid she might have broken her knee." Leo made quotes in the air. "A 'joke,' according to Sig but it wasn't. He wanted to hurt her." He put down his coffee cup. "Whether Dee and he made any attempt to connect with each other over the years I have no idea." His lips were tight. "In spite of what I have said, I do love my son. It grieves me that he has become such a prissy tight-ass and for that his mother and I must take equal blame. She keeps him on an extremely short leash and I didn't try to stop her when I could have... I also loved Deidre and I will carry to my grave the regret that she died without knowing it."

He struggled for control and we waited. Now it was my turn to fiddle with my coffee cup. Katherine took to studying her fingers. Quickly, Leo rubbed away traitorous tears from his cheeks with his finger.

"Leo, I will not insult you by denying that your son is what we in our inimitable police jargon call 'a person of interest.'" Katherine's voice was matching Leo's for flatness. "We will of course pursue the matter of his seeming deception. Is there anything I can do to help you at the moment?"

He managed a wry smile. "You can snap your fingers and say, 'Wake up now, Leo. It's all been a bad dream.' Can you do that for me, Katherine?"

She leaned across the table and briefly covered his hands with hers. "I only wish I could, Leo."

I doubt I had taken in much oxygen for the last several minutes. Katherine picked up her notebook, brisk again, professional.

"Christine, I'll leave it to you to contact the Manolo girl and arrange for her to view the tapes. There isn't a lot we can do now until we start getting back reports from the beat officers. I suggest you and Leo go to your respective homes and get some rest. You look exhausted. We'll meet tomorrow at say one o'clock?"

That was fine and we trekked out. Leo said he'd get a taxi, refused a lift, and we parted.

I was already driving out of the lot when I realized that once again I'd forgotten the report that Gill had faxed me. I promised myself I'd come in early and have a look at it tomorrow.

CHAPTER TWENTY-NINE

Rather than going home first, I drove straight to Paula's house. I wanted to get the latest news, see my godchild, and pay a visit to Mrs. Jackson, who in my mind was my spiritual mother and had been since I was fourteen. I'd talked to her several times on the phone, but I'd only seen her once since Al died last year and I was keen to know how she was doing. She and Al would have been celebrating their fiftieth wedding anniversary this year and I knew she was still feeling his loss keenly. She'd been a stay-at-home mother at a time when there wasn't a lot of choice for women to do much else but I don't think she'd felt unfulfilled or second-class. They'd had four kids, three boys and then Paula. Al became a superintendent of police, respected and liked. He was a great dad, and he and Marion, defying all odds about marrying young, had one of the happiest marriages I knew of.

Even with the two of them as early role models, I can't say my own love life would be considered successful. The longest relationship I'd had lasted seven years. He was an intense, moody guy, a lawyer for personal injury claims. He was keen to make our relationship official and establish a normal family life — house, kids, dog, lawnmower. I was dragging my feet. I loved my work, and the idea of being a parent, given my own childhood, made me nervous. I might have capitulated because I did care for him, but then he got an offer of a partnership with his brother who lived in Los Angeles. I didn't want to uproot, and after much wrangling, he chose the partnership. We'd tried to keep things going but I guess our roots weren't quite as deep as I'd thought because one day he phoned and said he'd met somebody else and was getting married. To be honest, my heartache was short-lived, my pride hurt more than anything else. After that I dated a couple of nice guys, both in the police, but nothing clicked until a couple of years ago when I met Gill on the island of Lewis. Ironically I was once again faced with the problem of a long-distance relationship. God knows how we were going to work it out but for now he was my guy.

I pulled into the driveway and the door opened. Chelsea and Marion were standing in the doorway. Chelsea did a literal dance of delight, on tiptoe, twirling around in excitement. Marion held out her arms. We hugged, bone crushers on both sides. Chelsea was wrapped around my legs. Marion released me and Chelsea grabbed my hand and dragged me into the house.

"I've got a new fish named Fan. He's awesome. Come and see."

She was allergic to cats and Craig wouldn't agree to a dog so she had poured out all her frustrated nurturing instincts or whatever it is that drove some kids to clamour for creatures onto fish. She was the proud owner and caretaker of a large aquarium, which had pride of place in the living room. Duly awestruck, I admired Fan, who was indeed a pretty, colourful fantail, hence the name.

"I made lots of spaghetti," said Marion. "Do you want some?"

"Is the pope Catholic?" I grinned at her. She was proud of her Irish-Catholic ancestry and I liked to tease her about it.

"Sit down. You look tired," she said and went out to the kitchen. Chelsea drew her chair up closer to mine.

"Mommy's in the hospital and Daddy's at his club so Grandma is looking after me. I helped her make the spaghetti."

Marion put a heaping plate of pasta in front of me. I took a taste. "How'd you do it? You're sure you're a mick and not a wop?" I said. Another old joke. Marion made the best pastas I'd ever eaten.

"'Course I'm a mick. Didn't you know we cook in holy water," she said straight-faced. "For a small price the priest lets us drain it off from the baptismal fonts. I think all those tears add a touch of salt."

I burst out laughing. Both she and Al had been practising Roman Catholics but she'd always had a sudden irreverent humour.

"Why do the babies cry, Grandma?" Chelsea asked. She was right in the middle of the why, where, and what stage of growth — mostly delightful, occasional irksome.

"They're not used to some strange man trickling cold water on their heads. You didn't utter a peep when you were baptized though. Just tried to catch hold of Father Crowley's fingers and suck on them."

"I did not," said Chelsea, shocked at this image of herself. As well as the curious stage, she was going through a period of correctness. We were hoping she'd grow out of it eventually.

I polished off the spaghetti with record speed, refused a second helping, accepted the offer of a piece of fresh apple pie for later, and sat back in the chair.

"Grandma said you'd put me to bed," said Chelsea. "We can go on with the story you started last time you babysat me."

"Haven't you finished it yet?"

"Of course I have but you want to know how it ends, don't you?"

"I can't wait."

The meal had increased my tiredness and I couldn't hold back a yawn.

"I don't know how long I'm going to hold out, Chelse. We'd better get the train moving out of the station or you'll be driving it yourself."

She giggled. "No, I can't do that. I'm only a child, I wouldn't be allowed."

"You will be if you pass the exam."

"What exam?'

"Can you run upstairs in fifteen seconds, brush your teeth in thirty seconds, get into your jammies and under the bed covers in another ten?"

"Starting when?"

I checked my watch. "Five seconds. Ready? Five, four, three, two, one. Blast off."

She dashed for the stairs. We heard the bathroom door slam open.

"Is Craig at the hospital?" I asked Marion.

"He said he had a meeting at his club. He's on the board of

directors or something." She paused. We both knew what the other was thinking.

"How is Paula doing?"

"A bit better. They seem to be stabilizing her heartbeat. They might let her out sooner than we thought." She bit her lip. "Then we'll have to hold our breath until she gets the results of the biopsy back."

I grabbed both her hands in mine and shook them. "Try not to worry, Ma. She's a tough one is our Paula."

She smiled. "I know and frankly I'd worry a lot more if you weren't here."

Since I had seen her last, Marion must have dropped a good ten or more pounds. She'd always looked a lot younger than her age. Now she didn't. Usually she wore lipstick, favouring bright colours and sparkly jewellery. Tonight she was wearing a loose-fitting grey cardigan over a pair of brown pants, no jewellery, no makeup. I recognized the sweater.

"Hey, didn't that belong to Al?"

She fingered the sleeve and looked embarrassed. "I didn't have anything warm enough." She stopped. "Truth is, it makes me feel closer to him. I wear it all the time. You don't think I'm going nutty, do you, Chris?"

I got up and came around the table so I could put my arms around her. "Of course I do. And why not, even a bit nutty you're the best woman in the world."

From upstairs, Chelsea yelled at me. "Auntie Chris. Are you still timing me? I'm getting my socks off. How much time have I got?"

"Plenty," I shouted back. "Keep going." I straightened up, giving Marion a chance to wipe her eyes. "I'd better go and see what she's up to."

"She's been really good with me," said Marion. "But I think she's frightened. She told me that one of the children in her kindergarten had a mommy who went into hospital but now God has her in heaven. You know what she said, Chris? Where these children get these things I don't know — she said, 'I hope my mommy will come home first if she has to go to heaven and see God. And I hope he doesn't keep her long.'"

I laughed. "Ah, the daughter of a working mother."

But my mind flashed to little Joy Larsen and how the hell they were going to explain to her that her mommy wasn't ever coming home.

It was close to eleven when I finally left the house. Craig had still not returned. Chelsea had kept me a long time before she succumbed to sleep and then Marion and I had had a visit. It was she who chased me away.

"You, young woman, are falling asleep standing up. Get off to your own bed. I'll be here. I'm planning to stay until next week."

I wished Craig had come back to keep her company but I supposed it was a very important meeting he couldn't snatch himself away from.

When I reached my house, I was almost comatose with fatigue. Tory and Bertie were going to be mad that I hadn't been around for such a long stretch but thank goodness for self-feeders and the fundamental indifference of cat nature. There were no lights showing downstairs, which was rather atypical. Both Gary and Ahmed were night owls.

The two outside entrances to the apartments were side by side, mine on the left. Damn, the porch light was out and I'd replaced the bulb only last week it seemed to me. I gathered up the bits of mail from my box, unlocked the door, and trudged up the stairs to my apartment. There was another door at the top of the stairs and I opened it and switched on the light. The two cats were in their favourite spot on the windowsill and they blinked at me in the light. Then, realizing it was me, owner, dispenser of food, shelter, and warmth, they jumped down and ran over to me, meowing in short bursts to convey their disapproval of my absence. I added some fresh food to their dish and got out of my coat and shucked off my shoes. The message light was flashing on the telephone and I went to check it. Gary's deep voice rolled out at me.

"Hi, Chris. Ahmed and I have gone away for a spell to see if we can work things out. See you then."

I felt a pang of loneliness that I didn't expect. Gary was good company.

I'd dropped the mail on the table and I went to have a quick sort through before getting my own train moving towards bed. There were two bills, a flyer for the opening of a new store, and an unstamped handwritten letter.

I recognized the handwriting immediately. Holding the envelope by the end, I used a knife to slit it open. A single piece of yellow paper.

TOO BAD ABOUT THE DUMMY. GOD'S JUDGEMENT IS MIGHTY. WATCH OUT YOU SINFUL DAUGHTER OF EVE. IF HE SAYS SO YOU ARE NEXT. YOU CANNOT AVOID IT, DON'T EVEN TRY.

CHAPTER THIRTY

That woke me up in a hurry as adrenaline blasted through my blood. There was no frank or stamp on the envelope. Somebody had hand delivered it. Somebody knew where I lived and that same somebody had written hate mail to Deidre. Suddenly I was dreadfully aware that I was alone in the house. I stood still for a moment, antennae quivering. The house was quiet except for the sound of one of the cats scratching in the litter box. The curtains were open and the black windows were mirrors. I could not see out but I could be seen. I took my key chain out of my purse. I'd got into the habit years ago of carrying a small dispenser of pepper spray on the chain. I'd only had to use it once in the last three years and that was to discourage a crack cocaine addict trying to get at his girlfriend who was hiding behind me. The spray, in case you don't know, is actually highly concentrated cayenne pepper and you aim for the face not the enchiladas. The eyes swell shut and breathing is restricted for about twenty to thirty minutes. It will buy you time in nasty situations.

Dispenser in hand, I switched off the light and pressed my back to the wall, waiting until my eyes grew accustomed to the darkness. Something brushed against my legs and my heart thumped.

"Meow."

Thanks a lot, Bertie. You just about gave me a heart attack. The layout of my flat is fairly standard. I was in the living room, the dining area was adjoined to a small kitchen, the door of which was closed. A fire escape led from the kitchen window down to the side yard. To my right from where I was now, a hallway led to the bathroom and the two rear bedrooms. Along the front of the living/dining room was a long porch. When I got the house, I was pleased that we were at the end of a cul de sac. I liked the privacy and the quiet. Now I wished I'd bought something on the highway.

I made myself breath deeply and I started to calm down. I couldn't hear anything, inside or out, but I was damned if I was going to stand here pinned against the wall by some bully boy. I was hot with anger, but I'm glad to say my head was cool as ice, a quality I had acquired somewhere along the way and for which I was grateful. Both the downstairs door and my entrance door had been locked, and although I wasn't paying a lot of attention, I was pretty sure they hadn't been tampered with. If anybody had broken into my flat, they would most likely have come up the fire escape. The front porch was only accessible if you had a ladder. Not out of the question, but again I didn't see any sign that the French doors were broken. When I'd moved in I'd recarpeted the living room with a sturdy practical beige flecked carpet. At the moment, it wasn't showing any trace of footprints or mud, which, given the rain, I would expect if somebody had walked across. I'd left my shoes at the door.

Also in my purse was a set of handcuffs. I often complained about how heavy they were but they were pretty much required even if you were off duty. Cautiously, I slid my hand into the bag and pulled them out, slipping the catch so that they were open.

I held my breath and listened. Nothing. If there was somebody in the flat he was keeping awfully still.

The kitchen was the likely place to start. At least I could determine if anybody had entered via the fire escape. Dispenser held at shoulder height, in front of me, I stepped softly over to the door and pushed it open slowly. No matter what you've seen on television or in the movies, sometimes opening a door slowly is a better move as it doesn't make a noise and startle your antagonist into acting dangerously. Nothing stirred. Now I did move quickly. I stepped inside and flicked on the light, at the same time moving away from the doorway. The kitchen was empty except for Bertie, who stared at me from the countertop. From here the fire escape window looked intact but I walked over to make sure. It was fine.

No muddy marks anywhere. Nobody had come in that way. I let out my breath.

One by one, I examined the bathroom, my bedroom, and the spare room. My adrenaline level was dropping with its resultant slight shakiness. I yawned like a nervous dog. However, I was still livid. It was after midnight but I knew I'd be stupid not to report what had happened. I phoned Ed Chaffey. He answered on the second ring.

"Ed. Christine Morris here. Sorry it's late but I just got in and I've had a love letter from our anon. Same author as Deidre's, I believe."

"Threatening?"

"Yes. It's not stamped so he must have come by my house sometime today to deliver it."

"Jesus. Read it to me."

I did so.

He cussed again. "I don't like that one bit. Can you stay somewhere else for the night?"

"I could but I'm not going to. He's not in here, I can tell you that, and there hasn't been a break-in."

"Damn it, Chris, let's not take any chances. We might be dealing with a psycho."

That thought had crossed my mind. "Can you spare a car?"

"Of course. I'll send one over right away."

"Thanks, Ed."

"Are you going to be okay?"

"Yes, I live with two attack cats."

"Don't do anything until you see the dispatch car."

We hung up. I wasn't sure what he meant by "don't do anything" but in spite of a certain amount of bravado on my part, I was glad to know that the men in blue would be outside. I went back into the kitchen and wedged one of the kitchen chairs underneath the door knob. Then I saw the flashing lights of the police cruiser coming down the road. They stopped in front of the house and an officer got out. I stood at the window and waved. He waved back.

All barricaded in, I finally went to bed, totally exhausted now. I put my pepper spray beside the bed, wedged the chair against the door, and got under the covers. Even the fatigue couldn't keep me completely asleep and I found myself waking up abruptly, all senses on the alert. I was glad when my radio alarm went off. It was now getting light, which felt better. I put on my dressing gown and went through to the living room, followed by two sleepy cats, Tory yowling at me, I presumed in greeting. The cruiser was still outside. I'm sure it had been a very boring shift but I was grateful they were there. I went to make a large Thermos of coffee. At least I could do that for them.

CHAPTER THIRTY-ONE

It was nine o'clock. Me, Leo, Jessica, an OPP constable named Lachlan, and the manager of the casino, Mr. Torvill, were huddled around the screen as eager as if we were all about to tune in to the latest episode of *24*. No, that's not true. Leo and I were eager. Jessica looked apprehensive; Mr. Torvill looked anxious but I think that was habitual. I had chosen not to tell Leo about my love note. One thing at a time. I'd picked up Jessica and met him at the casino. Ben Snake wasn't around but Mr. Torvill gave us his full attention. Jessica was quiet and looked as if she hadn't slept well, which was I'm sure how I looked. We got everybody settled, told her what we wanted, and cued the tape to the place where Sigmund joined Deidre at the table. I switched on the tape recorder I had brought with me.

"He says, 'Hello Dee. How's it going? Sorry I'm late.'" Jessica began.

Already there was a discrepancy with what Sigmund had told us about just dropping in spontaneously to the casino to see her. You don't apologize for being late unless you have a prior appointment.

"She says, 'I didn't think you'd show up.' He says, 'I thought I was a bit ...' Sorry, I didn't get what he said. He ducks his chin; it's hard to read."

"Play it back," said Leo.

The manager did a quick rewind and played the brief scene again. Jessica hesitated. "I'm not sure ... something like, 'ungenerous or ingenuous' ... It's hard to say."

"Go on."

"She says, 'Yes, I was offering you something, not asking to get something."

That fitted with what Sigmund had said about Deidre wanting to be reconnected.

Jessica leaned forward. "He says, 'I know, I'm sorry.' She asks him, 'Have you changed your mind then?' He says, 'Well not exactly but I thought we could go on talking.'" This was the part on the tape where Deidre clearly got pissed off.

"Enough said. No more talk. You're in or you're out."

Sigmund turned away again and Jessica couldn't get the next sentence. "He turned back. 'I told you it wasn't an easy choice.' She replies, 'Yes, it is.'"

The beckoning gesture was next. "He says, 'Would you like to come over to the bar and discuss it further?'"

It was obvious what Deidre's response was.

Jessica gave a rather grim chuckle. "She says, 'No. Go home to your mother.'"

That was it. Sigmund slunk off. The rest we had seen.

I switched off my tape recorder.

"Thank you, Jessica."

"Who is he?" she asked.

Leo looked at her, intent on reading any signals. "Don't you recognize him?"

"No. I've never seen him before."

"His name is Sigmund. Did Deidre ever mention his name?"

Jessica hesitated. "It's not her brother, is it? She did say once she had a half-brother and I remember he had a funny name. Is that him?"

"It is. And you're positive Deidre never said she was meeting him or anything like that?"

"No, she didn't. I always had the impression she didn't like him, or they weren't allowed to talk to each other or some such thing." She had pulled out a tissue and she wiped at her eyes as if she could rub away the images. "It is painful to watch Deedee alive. She loved to play poker."

It had been hard on Leo too. "Thank you. I'm glad to know she had such good friends."

Jessica muttered something about using the washroom and virtually ran from the room. Mr. Torvill followed her, presumably to show her the way and make sure she didn't discover some hidden weakness in their security system to be used against them later. Constable Lachlan withdrew to a position near the door.

Leo slumped in his chair. "What's he covering up, Chris? I don't understand. That wasn't such a big deal conversation that he couldn't have told us."

I didn't have any easy words for him. It was strange all right.

"We'll have to re-interview him. I'll get this to Ed and he can organize it... You said you wanted to see Joy, but are you sure you're up to it?"

"Yes, we should get that over with as soon as possible." He frowned. "I am a bit leery about using Jessica. It might be too much for her. Nora communicates well enough. Let's ask her to do it."

"Good idea. And what about you? You're looking done in yourself. We could wait a bit longer."

He looked as if he were aging before my eyes. "No. You know we can't do that, Chris. The sooner we can fill in the pieces of puzzle the better it will be." He gave me a wry smile. "To tell the truth, the thing I'm not looking forward to is seeing Loretta. I'm glad you'll be there. She is what you might call a formidable woman. God knows why I got talked into marrying her. She scares me shitless."

Jessica came back into the room followed by Mr. Torvill.

"Do you want to continue?" the manager asked.

Leo shook his head. Deidre hadn't spoken to anybody else until she'd left. Now we had to get back to Sigmund and see if we could winkle out some more of the truth. Leo wasn't looking forward to seeing his ex. I wasn't looking forward to questioning a deaf child about whether or not she could point the finger at her mother's murderer.

Nora came to the door. She looked as if she hadn't combed her hair in two days and had slept in her clothes. As soon as she saw who it was, she started ranting, not even stepping out of the doorway to let us in.

"I didn't expect any of this. It isn't my thing, den mother and all that. I've got a low tolerance for kids and I've never pretended otherwise." Even three feet away, the beer fumes from her breath were a knockout. "And frankly I've got an even lower tolerance for control freaks. Dee wasn't like that and we lived just fine, thank you. I'd appreciate it if you'd get her off my back."

"By 'her,' do you mean Loretta?" Leo asked.

"That's the one. She's hardly seen the kid since she was born and she swoops in like a fucking Mary Poppins with fangs. She's making things worse, if you ask me, but of course nobody is asking me. I'm just the dyke who got on the payroll because people felt sorry for her. The charity case who's about to lose her job."

"Nora, you've been drinking," said Leo.

"Now that is very perceptive of you, Doctor Shrink. But you know what? Even a bit totted up, I'm better for that kid than her fucking so-called grandma. She can't communicate with her for piss and she won't let me do it..."

We hadn't even advanced as far as the foyer and Nora would probably have continued her tirade but the door to the kitchen opened and a tall, grey-haired woman came out. Leo had described his ex as formidable and I understood why. She was big-boned, with a tanned complexion that accentuated her keen blue eyes. Her short straight hair and no-nonsense shirt and jeans were all declarations of her politics. Down with Western vanity, up with "tune in to the earth" philosophy, the kind of woman you could easily imagine leading a revolution. But I thought she had a nice face, open and intelligent. Nora stepped back without being asked and Loretta came over to us, taking Leo by the shoulders to give him a peck on the cheek. She was a good eight inches taller and he had to tilt his head so she could reach him. They were stiff and awkward with each other.

She let him go and thrust out her hand to me. "Hello, I'm Loretta Larsen, you are...?"

"Christine Morris. I'm a colleague of Leo's."

We shook hands, hers firm as to be expected.

"Come in. I'm in the kitchen with Joy."

She didn't look at Nora, didn't acknowledge her existence, and the girl was left to trail after us.

Joy was at the kitchen table crayoning on a piece of paper. She had her back to us and didn't move. Loretta went to the light switch and flicked it up and down. Joy turned around. She didn't react for a moment, then she smiled, grunted, and made a sign, then held up her drawing.

"That's lovely, dear," said Loretta. Joy didn't respond and Loretta turned her head so she was facing her. "Lovely," she said slowly, making the word distinct. Nora snorted, went behind her, and made a sign to Joy, who smiled and responded. She made some signs and pointed in my direction.

"She wants you to sit beside her," said Nora.

I did as commanded, aware that both Leo and Loretta weren't happy about me being the chosen one.

"Nora, why don't you make us all some coffee?" said Loretta.

If I could have drawn a balloon coming from Nora's mouth, it would have said, "*Eff off and make your own coffee,*" but she clenched her teeth and stomped over to the sink, where she started to rinse out the coffee pot with much clink and clatter.

"How is she?" Leo asked, indicating his granddaughter.

"She is asking for her mother every five minutes. We have to tell her what's happened. She won't settle down until something definite is said."

Oh God. Selfishly I didn't want to be there when that happened. I couldn't imagine how you can get across that kind of news to a child.

"I want to ask her some questions first," said Leo.

Loretta folded her arms across her full, unfettered breasts. "What sort of questions?"

"We think that Dee had a male visitor sometime in the past two months who may or may not be implicated in her killing. I'd like to ask Joy if she met anybody and what he looked like."

"I suppose Nora will have to be the one to do that."

"I *suppose* I will have to, seeing both of you can communicate dick all in sign language," said Nora.

I felt a light tap on my forearm. Joy was trying to get my attention. She made a sign at me, her fingers outstretched, her eyebrows raised.

"She wants to know where her mommy is," said Nora.

"How do I say 'I don't know'?"

"The way you'd say it to a hearing person."

I grimaced at the child and shook my head, making my expression as friendly as possible. She turned to Nora and made the same sign, "Where's my mommy?" Nora signed back at her, saying at the same time, "Your mommy's late. She'll be here soon."

"Don't tell her that," Loretta burst out. "She'll be waiting for her. She has to be told the truth."

Nora's face turned red with anger. "The truth? You want her to know the truth? That her mother was found in the lake with her scarf wrapped around her neck. The truth that she was murdered in cold blood. Is that what you want me to communicate to her?"

Loretta was prevented from answering by a wail from Joy, who was waving her hands frantically at us. Nora went over to her and scooped her up in her arms. She could protest all she wanted that she wasn't the maternal type but nothing could disguise the love she felt for the little girl.

She rocked her back and forth while Joy continued to wail. Leo got out of his chair and went over to them. He began to stroke the child's hair. "Hush, dear, hush." Loretta remained at the table, her hands clenched in front of her. She looked so unhappy, I wanted to comfort her as well. Finally, Joy stopped crying, lifted her head, and shoved Leo's hand away angrily. She stuck her thumb in her mouth. Her eyelids drooped as if she was on the verge of sleep.

Nora glared at us. "She might not be able to hear but she's sensitive to atmosphere. It scares her when people are angry."

"I might point out, it was not I who was shouting," said Loretta quietly.

I decided to divert any further arguments and went over to the coffee machine. "Nora, why don't you and Joy sit down and I'll finish making the coffee? Shall I get her anything? Milk? Juice?"

"She'd probably like some apple juice. There's some in the fridge."

"I'll get it," said Leo.

He took out a Barney mug and brought it over to Joy. She took it sulkily. She wasn't ready to accept him yet. I put mugs on the table and returned to the counter to watch the coffee drip into the carafe.

"Have you made any progress with the case?" Loretta asked. Her voice was neutral, emotions under control, but she hit some tripwire invisible to me and Leo snapped back at her.

"No! We're just at the beginning."

I didn't blame him for not telling her about Sigmund. What was he going to say? Well, Loretta, my son has suddenly become a prime suspect. He and his ex had long ago stopped expecting sympathy from each other. I was torn between pity at their state and a desire to bang their heads together.

I brought over the coffee pot and filled their mugs. Joy seemed to be actually nodding off in Nora's arms.

"I'd rather not upset her with any questions," she said to Leo. Her voice was softer. "And as for telling her about Deedee, I'd like to bide my time. Find the right moment and all that. If I'm going to be the one to do it, you've got to trust me to do it properly."

She didn't say that with any belligerence, just sadness, and I'm glad to say both Leo and Loretta responded in kind.

"Thank you," he said.

"Her gerbil died a few months ago," continued Nora. "Old age probably but she'd liked to play with it. The three of us had a special ceremony and we buried it in the backyard. Dee was so good. She explained that there was a place called heaven where Digger had gone to where he could run all day long in the sunshine and where he was very happy. She said, all creatures great and small eventually go to heaven and we on earth are very sad for a while because we miss them but they still watch over us and we can send drawings as long as we like and they will know what is going on even if we don't see them." She had to stop. Loretta took out a handkerchief and handed it to her. Nora sniffed hard. "I thought I'd say something like that. You know, Mommy has gone to heaven like Digger did. We can't see her but she is with us in her spirit and we can still send her drawings and tell her what is happening. Do you think that would be all right?"

Leo nodded. "I believe that would be just fine."

Joy snuffled and her hand reached up and touched Nora's chin. She pressed her fingers against it, making a sign.

CHAPTER THIRTY-TWO

The whole profiling team was around the table, including Leo. Katherine was taking it day by day in terms of allowing him to be present at the meetings or not. So far he hadn't been a hindrance; the opposite, in fact. He was quieter than he usually was, and I could see that after the initial wariness, everybody was relaxing around him.

Ray Motomochi, perhaps out of respect, had toned down the sartorial excesses and was sombre in a blue shirt and navy suit. He had the floor and he'd spread the anonymous letters across the table so we could see them.

"All these and the note to Christine were written by the same person. Let's call him Moses. So far we have not been able to lift any distinguishable print. Not even on Christine's billet-doux where there is less contamination from other sources. I have hopes I'll be able to lift a partial or even, God give us luck, a full print. I haven't had the chance to try everything yet so it does seem as if Moses was being careful."

"He must have written the letters with latex gloves on," said Katherine. "You have to leave some trace otherwise."

"I agree. Moses knows what he's doing. The note found in Deidre's car was definitely written by somebody else. Let's for purposes of clarity call that person Roadrunner, as he's in a hurry." Ray was trying to be respectful of Leo but he couldn't totally suppress the habit we all had to introduce as much humour as possible, no matter what.

"The paper of the Moses letters is slightly unusual in that it's yellow lined writer's paper. Easy to get and undistinguished but not everybody's choice. All the letters were written with an ordinary ballpoint pen, black ink. The envelopes are standard; all were clearly franked, except for the recent one, so we have dates; the stamps are the sticker kind." He gave us a little grin. "As we know a good source of DNA material can be a licked envelope but all of these ones have been glued, white school glue you can buy anywhere. Another example that our chappie or chapette is in the know. I've got lots of partials but it was handled by many different people and I doubt if that will help us much. Fingerprints is willing to do the donkey work for us, bless them. They may come up with a match from the files but I rather doubt it."

A brief word here. Computers don't make fingerprint matches. It is a boring, labour-intensive job done by four people who sit around their computers all day long looking at countless variations on swirls and loops. It requires skill and experience and always has to be verified by at least one other member of the team. It's not a job I'd like but it is an essential one. I've heard the Fingerprint Department is legendary for cutting loose after hours and I don't blame them.

Back to the meeting.

"Anything you can tell us about the note we found in Deedee's car?" Leo asked.

"As you can see, lined paper, torn at the side. It comes from a small-sized notebook. The writer used pencil. The problem of course is that it got wet..." He paused awkwardly. Nobody wanted to draw attention to this and leave Leo open to his own recriminations. "The pencil didn't wash out, fortunately, but I couldn't pull any print."

"Thank you, Ray," said Katherine. "Jamie, what's your take on the geographic profile? Let's put Chris in the equation and Grace Cameron as well as Deidre. See what we've got."

Ray quickly collected up his plastics where he'd put all the letters. Jamie had cut himself shaving and there was a bit of toilet paper sticking to his chin that was slightly distracting.

He put down the city map which he'd enlarged and marked.

"Deidre was found here in Memorial Park. Her residence was here on Mary Street. The casino is, of course, way over here.

You can enter the park from two sides, north and south, if you are driving, but it is accessible from any point if you are walking. Houses are well set back from the park and the pier would not have been visible to anybody who was not in the area itself." He wasn't telling us anything new and I shifted restlessly. Lack of sleep was making me cranky.

"Given the apparent connection provided by the letter writer, I have marked Christine's apartment. *G* here stands for Grace Cameron, who is the current resident of an apartment once occupied both by Nora Cochrane and briefly by Hannah Silverstein, who was a close friend of Deidre's. As you can see, except for the casino, all of these locations fall within a very small area. Walking distance of each other. We accept the fact that Miss Larsen knew her attacker well enough to accept a ride from him or her. According to Inspector Chaffey, all of the bus drivers and taxi drivers who were working during our window of time have not made an identification."

"A bus driver wouldn't necessarily notice if he was busy, would he?" said Leo abruptly.

"No, and the process of trying to find witnesses is going on." Jamie sighed. "That's what we desperately need, of course. But let's assume for now she got a ride into town and that her intention was to go to Memorial Park as the note suggests. What we don't know of course is where she was actually, er, killed. There are two possible scenarios. A person as yet unknown but who was *not* her attacker gave her a ride and let her off at the park. From there she may have met with the writer of the note. This person may be her killer but it is very unlikely that she was killed in the park itself. That means this person must have had access to a vehicle which she got into. She was, er, killed somewhere else and her body taken a few hours later to the pier where she was found in the water." There was a tense silence, nobody wanting to imagine Leo's daughter the victim of a torturer, and we all knew only too well that these things happened.

"There was no sign of trauma to the body other than the strangulation," said Katherine with a quick involuntary glance at Leo. "Jamie, you said two scenarios. Spell out the other one for us."

"I think if we take the note found in the car as significant, Deidre would have been in a hurry to get to the Memorial, so let's say, for the purpose of argument, she got a lift with somebody who subsequently attacked her. She might not have arrived at the park at all. Perhaps she was driven somewhere else, subdued, and killed in his car. Then, later on when there is the greatest likelihood of the park being deserted, he drives onto the pier, buys himself some time by filling her pockets with stones, and drops her into the water. This is a relatively short window of opportunity and we can focus our enquiries on a pretty precise time period. She finished playing at 10:40, and we have her exiting the casino at 10:43."

I interjected my information at this point. "The casino has got the exit and entrance CCTV tapes. We can follow up on cars leaving the premises."

"That might help us a lot," said Katherine. "Let's get that information as soon as possible."

David hadn't said anything to this point. He was drinking a glass of some poisonous-looking thick purple fluid. He hadn't offered to share it with anybody, thank goodness. He raised his forefinger to get Katherine's attention. She frowned at him.

"Yes, go ahead."

"With respect, Jamie, you said two scenarios but there is really a third, isn't there? What if she got a ride to the park with an uninvolved person who left her there and went on their own way. She did not meet with Zachary Taylor because she was late. She isn't that far from her house so she sets off to walk home. Along the way, she meets her assailant, who offers her a ride. From what we know of her, she would have to have accepted willingly because she was a strong and fit young woman. She gets into the car; this person somehow and somewhere subdues her... strangles her, keeps the body as we have said, etc., etc."

He was quite right and he gained respect points from me for sure. I knew there was a reason he was on the team other than as a covert apostle for alternative living.

"Good, well put, David," said Katherine.

"If this scenario is the correct one," said Ray, "we are looking for a disorganized killer who happened upon her by chance. Her death may not be in any way connected to the notoriety surrounding her baby. And the letter writer is a completely different person from her killer."

Profilers are not immune in the least from wishful thinking. A case that is neat and tidy is much easier to deal with than one where the possibilities are virtually unlimited. Or so it often seems in the early stages.

Leo spoke. "Whichever way we turn it, I'd say we are dealing with somebody local. Somebody she knew or at least recognized by sight. It was a miserable night. She would have wanted to get home as soon as she could. But come on folks, we're nattering on about scenario this and scenario that. Let's not overcomplicate the story. She got a ride into town, was dropped off, met Zachary Taylor as planned, and he was the one who killed her, as I may remind you, he threatened to do." His tone was truculent. We all understood what he was feeling. He wanted an answer, a face, and I knew he was in a rush to judgement.

"We've got a red alert to find Zachary Taylor." Katherine flicked her thumbnail on her pen, not looking at Leo. "The difficulty here is to keep an open mind."

She said it gently but Leo flushed. He knew it was him she was addressing. Like an invisible wraith, the presence of his son, Sigmund, hovered in the room. Where did he fit into all of this?

Leo's eyes met mine and I grimaced, a "we've all done it" sort of expression. I don't know if that would have calmed him down or not because Janice came into the room.

"Sorry to interrupt but Ed Chaffey just called. He said they've picked up Zachary Taylor's trail."

CHAPTER THIRTY-TWO

Her entrance couldn't have been better timed if we'd all been in some Agatha Christie play. Leo looked as if he was going to jump out of his seat and run right there and then.

"Tell us more, Janice," said Katherine.

"A farmer near Beaverton heard the appeal and phoned in. He said he'd let a man park his camper van in his field. It fits the description we have… unfortunately Taylor isn't there. He has a scooter which he uses to get around on and the farmer says he went out early this morning. Ed's men are going to stake out the place to wait for him to return. If he does."

"Did the farmer give any indication as to whether Taylor knew we were after him or not?" Leo asked.

Janice had brought in a sheet of paper. "The farmer's statement was as follows: 'He seems like a nice enough fellow. He said he was travelling in the area, had some friends to visit, and gave me some money for a few days for use of the field. That was fine with me, nothing in there anyway at this time of year.'" Janice glanced up. "Farmer then says, 'He did seem a bit het up but it was hard to tell as he was deaf as a post so we had to write everything down.' Ed said to tell you that he's on to the 'write everything down' remark and will collect a sample from the farmer as soon as he can, assuming he kept the notes."

"A scooter will give him some mobility," said David, "but he can't move that quickly. If he wants to do a real run for it, I'd guess he'd go to the railway station or the buses."

"Or for that matter, he could rent a car," said Leo impatiently. "They should get somebody down to the depot immediately with his description."

"I'll speak with Ed but I'll bet he's already checking out those options," said Katherine.

Leo went to stand up but Katherine waved him back into the chair. "Hold on. Let's finish the meeting properly. I think Ray had something on the parking ticket."

Ray picked up his notebook. "I haven't got something, so much as I've got nothing. There is no record of a parking ticket being handed to a camper van on Mary Street on the morning our witness mentioned. We've gone four or five days each side of that date but nothing has shown up. No tickets at all were handed out on that street. The department was short-handed apparently so didn't go near some residential streets. Mr. Torres was dreaming."

Katherine frowned. "So we have nothing to put Taylor in the area of Deidre's apartment?"

"None."

"I'll pass that along to Ed. Maybe he can have Mr. Torres re-interviewed. Anything else?"

"Just that Ed expected to have information on the exit and entrance vehicle licence plates later today."

"Fantastic. We'll break for now. Thank you everybody."

I'd brought my lunch upstairs so I could do a bit more work on my test case but I'd barely opened up the CD when there was a knock on the door.

"Come in,"

Leo entered. "Hi, Chris. Sorry to bother you, although that's all I seem to be doing these days. I've got some news I wanted to share."

"Sure. No bother. Have a seat."

I dragged forward my only guest chair. The offices were tiny, as I told you. He didn't sit down but stood near the door as if he might have to make a dash for it at any minute. His alarm monitor was on overdrive.

"I've just been in with Katherine and she told me that they can't find Sigmund."

"What do you mean?"

"Just that. Ed Chaffey phoned the bank where Sig works and they said he'd called in sick. They got hold of Trudy but as far as she knew he had gone to a special seminar on investing that the bank was holding. The bank says there is no such seminar. Of course, she's in a complete state now and is convinced he's been murdered as well. She left a message with Janice that she's coming to Orillia and she'll meet me at my condo in...," he checked his wristwatch, "an hour from now." He stared at me. "My God, Chris, what's he playing at?"

"I don't know, Leo. There might be a perfectly simple explanation. You said his mother is a control freak. Maybe he's gone fishing and doesn't want her to know."

"Fishing? Oh right. I see what you mean. She's got radar like a bat and if you wanted to do anything she didn't approve of, which was a lot of things, you had to get pretty sneaky about it. And I have the sense that my poor son has learned to be very sneaky indeed."

"What's Ed have to say?"

"He's got out an alert to all patrols. He's been gone for several hours though and if he is for whatever reason doing a bunk he could be across the border by now."

He glanced up at my Paddington Station clock that I had on the wall.

"Shoot, I'd better go and get ready to meet Trudy." He gave me a rueful grin. "Of my two wives, I'd deal with Loretta any time. She can be overwhelming if she's got a bee in her bonnet or a cause of some kind to fight for but at least she's straightforward. We like each other, actually; we just shouldn't have got married. Trudy on the other hand is like dealing with a feather pillow with teeth. You think you're grabbing something all soft and squishy and you suddenly find yourself with a bite mark on your hand. A deep one, I might add."

At that moment, my desk phone rang. Leo waved and mouthed, "I'll see you later," and left. I answered the phone. It was Ed Chaffey.

"Chris, we've got Zachary Taylor in custody."

"Fantastic! Where was he?"

"At the post office. I'd alerted the clerk there to let us know if he came in and sure enough he did. I had an officer there within two minutes."

"How is our man?"

"Not sure. He's stone deaf and it's impossible to communicate with him. Apparently McCloskey had to write out that he wanted him to come to the police station to answer some questions. I've been in touch with the social worker at the language centre, a Mrs. Scott, and she has agreed to come and interpret. I was hoping we could have the use of your services as well."

I almost leaped out of my chair. "I'll be over right away. Wouldn't miss it."

The interview room at the station was bare and functional with a table, a telephone, four hard chairs. Ed ushered me in. Mrs. Scott, who had met us in the station lobby, followed behind. A female constable was sitting opposite Zachary Taylor, who actually had his head on the table like a kid in school having nap time. He didn't stir when we came in.

"What's happening, Molly?" asked Ed.

"Nothing, sir. He put his head down and fell asleep about ten minutes ago."

I had a chance to study Taylor. He hadn't removed his red-checked hunting jacket or wool toque and the long fair hair that straggled from beneath it looked unwashed. He was unshaven and there was a strong smell of cigarettes in the room with a top note of sweat and dirty clothes. Except that he looked so young and vulnerable, if you met Zachary Taylor standing on the street, you might expect him to ask for spare change.

"Chris, I'm going to go into the video room with Molly and let you do the interview. We don't want to be accused of intimidating the guy. We'll need you, though, Mrs. Scott. Where to you want to sit?"

"I'll sit beside Miss Morris."

Ed and the constable left. A moment later, Molly's voice blasted over the intercom.

"Hello! Hello! Can you hear me?"

"It isn't us who're deaf," remarked Mrs. Scott.

"Lower the volume a touch, will you?" I replied, talking at the back wall where the video cam was located in an inconspicuous aperture. "Am I coming in clearly?"

"Fine." This was Ed. "We're all set here. Let's get going, shall we?"

Zach kept on sleeping.

"Will do. Mrs. Scott, will you wake him up?"

She reached over and touched Zach's hand. He was awake immediately, staring at the two of us with fear. His eyes were puffy and bloodshot as if he hadn't slept in a long time. However, even looking like he did, there was no mistaking his resemblance to the child he had fathered, little Joy Larsen.

He made an unintelligible sound and Mrs. Scott immediately signed something at him.

He answered in kind.

"He wants to know why you've brought him to the police station."

"Tell him we want to ask him some questions..." I stopped, suddenly realizing I wasn't sure if he knew that Deidre was dead. Unless he was her murderer, of course.

"If you carry on speaking," said Mrs. Scott, "I'll interpret as we go."

"We understand you are a friend of Deidre Larsen."

He made a knocking motion with his clenched hand. "Yes," said Mrs. Scott. "Why do you ask?" He looked alarmed. "Has something happened to her?"

Good acting, psychopathic dissociation, or real concern, I didn't quite know.

"When did you see her last, Zachary?"

"I don't remember exactly, about a month ago, I think. You're scaring me. Please tell me why I'm here and why you are asking these questions."

His gestures were large and frantic and it was odd to hear Mrs. Scott interpreting them in a cool, calm voice. "Has she made a complaint against me?"

"No, why would she?"

"No reason, it's just that..." He dropped his hands and Mrs. Scott stopped speaking.

"It's just that, what?"

"She can get mad about things."

"What sort of things?"

"She didn't like it if I tried to see her uninvited."

"In what way did you try to see her?"

"I went to her old apartment to try to find her. I guess she doesn't live there anymore. She was just subletting anyway. I probably scared the wits out of the poor old lady who's there now. Is that it? Has the old lady made a complaint?"

"No, she hasn't."

Zach's eyes were fixed on Mrs. Scott and he signed rapidly, punctuating his gestures with grunts and half-pronounced words.

"Did Dee make a complaint about that? I just wanted to talk to her and maybe she thinks that's pushing her boundaries. I didn't mean to scare the lady. I wanted to talk to Deedee. I didn't know she'd moved."

"What did you want to talk to her about?"

Zach shifted his gaze and scowled at me.

"Do I have to answer that? It's my business," said Mrs. Scott.

"I cannot force you to answer any questions, this is simply an interview, but it would help us with our enquiries if you would tell us more about your relationship with Deidre."

"What enquiries?"

I groaned to myself. We hadn't charged him with anything and couldn't at the moment. He didn't have to say a thing. In spite of myself, even knowing how deceptive some killers could be, I liked him. There was an intelligence in his eyes, not at all the same as the cunning I've seen in the eyes of psychopaths. Once I was interviewed for one of the Toronto news channels when there was a uproar about yet another vicious murder. "Can you tell who is a murderer?" the interviewer had gasped at me. "If so, how?" "It's all in the mouth," I replied. "Psychopaths seem to have full lips pinched at the side." I was younger then and hadn't learned to pick my words carefully for the media. The interviewer had a field day with that quote. "How very scientific," she said. "I know a lot of people that description would apply to." I'd been teased unmercifully at the station. I should have got them to flash a sign on the screen, *Do not attempt to do this on your own, consult a professional*. However, I stick by what I said. It is in the mouth. And forget all that crap about psychopaths being charming. If you spend much time in their company you can see easily how superficial that charm really is. The icy thermocline is only inches below the surface.

I realized Zach was watching me intently. I had to tell the truth. However, I had the feeling it was not going to be easy.

"Zachary, I'm very sorry to tell you that Deidre Larsen is dead."

Mrs. Scott signed and I saw his face turn white. A strange sound came from his throat, very similar to the one that Joy had made.

"How? What happened?"

"Her body was found in the lake early Wednesday morning."

"Not suicide? She wouldn't do a thing like that."

"No. She was murdered."

He dropped his hands to his lap, put back his head, and howled, a deep primitive cry that pierced to the heart. Mrs. Scott waved, trying to get his attention. Finally he lifted his hand and his fingers frantically shaped a sign I now knew.

"No! No! No!"

CHAPTER THIRTY-FOUR

It wasn't possible to go any further with Zachary Taylor. He was completely distraught, refused to pay attention anymore, and sat with his head in his hands, moaning.

"He probably has questions himself that he wants answering," I said. "Ask him if that's the case."

She did but he didn't seem to take it in and ending up waving her hands away as if they were irritating insects. Ed and the constable came back into the room, and at his request, Mrs. Scott tried to communicate to Zach that we did have to question him again at a later date and he mustn't leave town.

He refused to look at anybody and we decided to leave him alone. Ed made sure there was a constable assigned to keep an eye on him and we left him in the interview room with Mrs. Scott, who was valiantly persisting with her efforts.

Ed closed the door behind us.

"While you're here, why don't you come and meet Tiffany Nowland? She's got some printouts on the licence plates. Do you want a coffee?"

"Machine?"

"No, I wouldn't dare. There's a kitchenette at the end of the hall. There'll probably be a pot of more or less fresh coffee on the burner."

Like hundreds of offices around the country, socializing occurred in the kitchen nook where both officers and civilians, as we call them, were taking a break. I don't know who had ultimate responsibility for keeping the coffee on the go but this pot was good, hot and fresh. The three other constables eyed me curiously but Ed didn't stop for introductions and, coffee in hand, I trotted after him down the hall to the central area, which like ours was divided into cubicles.

Tiffany Nowland was sitting at her computer station, staring at the screen. She was young, a bit on the plump side, and bespectacled in smart narrow trendy glasses. In the current fashion she wore a cardigan over a lacy camisole which revealed just enough cleavage to make the guys distracted. She made me feel a tad old and staid.

Ed introduced us and she thrust out her hand. "Glad to meet you, Ms. Morris. I've heard a lot about you."

That's always an awkward remark to handle. What's the comeback? All good, I hope? From whom? I let it ride and returned her handshake.

Ed tapped my arm. "I'm going to leave you in Tiff's capable hands. I've got some urgent paperwork I must do. I'll be in my office when you're done."

Tiffany reached for a file folder in a lower drawer and I couldn't help but notice his eyes strayed downward as he left.

"I've studied the case notes to date and I have arranged the lists in as logical an order as I could in accordance with the information as I have been g-given it." She had a rapid delivery that made her occasionally stumble over her words. She swivelled in her chair and handed me the first printout from the thick file.

"I've tried to make things easier by making rainbow printouts. Each piece of information is on a different coloured sheet. First, the white sheet. These are times relating to cars only. So, we have our subject, a Deidre Larsen, entering the premises at 7:35. We don't have her exiting but I understand that is because her car had a flat tire and she found some alternative method of leaving. Correct so far?"

She peered at me over the top of her glasses.

"That's the way it's looking at the moment."

"Good. She was clocked exiting the building at 10:43 p.m. I allowed for between six and seven minutes for her to get to her car and discover the flat tire. I've given her another six minutes to have some kind of interface with a person or persons as yet unknown with whom she accepted a ride. It could have been less time than that, so to play it safe, I'm making the departure from the lower end of the lot 10:50 p.m., and from the upper end, say, 11:10 p.m. Now it is possible that she sat in somebody's car for an undetermined length of time and could have left after our 11:10 parameter but I am going on information I received that she was trying to get to Memorial Park by eleven and would have wanted to leave as soon as possible. I am correct about that, am I not?"

"You are correct."

There was something about Miss Nowland, young as she was, which made me speak in complete sentences.

"Obviously, I can pull up a lot more information but I thought it would be easier in the beginning to proceed as logically as we can. There was a concert that night and we're looking at more than three thousand cars so the more we pare it down the better. Are you with me so far?"

I nodded. She reminded me of David but she was nicer.

"Good. Now, if you look at that blue spreadsheet, you can see I've organized it into columns. The first one on the left gives the time of exits from the lot between 10:50 and 11:10. Next column is the make of car, colour, year, and licence number; next the address, name of registrant for all of the said vehicles. The fourth column is the time that the car entered the lot. In brackets, I've put how long they stayed in the casino. I thought that might be helpful. The last column indicates any infractions such as unpaid parking tickets or fines that have been registered to that particular vehicle. I highlighted those in yellow for easier viewing. Of the seventy-five cars that exited during the designated time period, four had infractions, all in the form of unpaid parking tickets, except for one, a Mr. Adams, who is driving with his licence suspended." Another pause for me to catch my breath. Miss Nowland was indeed awesome. "It might not be relevant to our enquiry but I've passed that information on to the duty sergeant."

"That's good thinking."

She handed me a green printout. "Just working with these numbers alone I ran as many permutations and combinations as I could think of. This sheet puts the vehicles in order according to colour; you never know, if we get a sighting on red cars, for instance, this is helpful. I can arrange them in any other order as you require. Year and make of car, that sort of thing."

I nodded in admiration. "Can you pull up any camper vans? Blue and white, older model?"

She swivelled around to her computer, tapped at warp speed. "I've got one here but it's silver, last year's model, and it exited at 9:36. Any good?"

"Probably not. But I'll get back to you if necessary."

She took another printout from her folder. "This sheet lists according to registered address starting with all those local to Orillia. That is to say, all those highlighted in blue are registered locally, brown indicates the surrounding areas within comfortable driving distance, red is other. By that I mean still Ontario but farther away. Black is out of province."

She gave me another sheet, violet in colour. "These are arranged in order of elapsed time in the casino with shortest time first." She beamed at me. "You never know what might be important, do you?"

I could only agree. I did a quick glance down the column. Not surprisingly, Sigmund was at the top. He'd been driving a red 2004 Mazda Miata six-cylinder. Nice car — expensive. He was clocked in at 8:11 and he exited at 8:47. That was quite consistent with his story and what we'd seen on the videotape. The conversation with Deidre hadn't lasted long and he'd gone straight out of the building. The person at the bottom of the list, a Cal Shreyer, had stayed in the casino for sixteen hours!

"This is sheet four, beige. As I understand it, the time of death for our victim may have been as late as 2:00 a.m. Subtract half an hour of driving distance from the casino to Memorial Park, work backwards, and you have exit times from 10:45, which is tight, to 1:30 a.m." She pursed her lips. "This last time would have our victim sitting in a car for at least four hours. Given the public nature of the parking lot, I thought it was not likely that she was killed while she was on casino premises but I suppose we cannot totally rule that out, can we?"

I considered it. The struggle with Deidre could have been short and violent, but as Tiffany said, the risk of being seen was a high one. Nevertheless, we'd have to cast a wide net in our call for witnesses. I said as much.

She continued in her neat precise way. "For simplicity of viewing, I have marked out the lists in the same way as the first sheet but this time in one-hour segments. I kept the pink highlighter for the infractions column as before and as you can see we picked up ten more, making a total of thirteen."

"Are gamblers worse than the general population about not paying fines?" I asked.

She took my joke seriously. "I don't have that statistic to hand. Would you like me to get it?"

"No, no. That's fine."

"Just as a double check, I correlated all vehicle entry times from our furthest parameter at the moment, 1:30 Wednesday morning to 10:00 the previous Tuesday morning, although I can go further back if you want me to." Again she frowned. "There is a discrepancy of six cars. I show them entering but not exiting the casino. Those I have circled in yellow. If we remove our victim's name from the list, we are left with five."

"So? What does that mean?"

For the first time Tiffany's ultra-efficient, "I have a computer for a brain" demeanour cracked and she actually turned pink. "There is a back way. My boyfriend, Simon, works at the casino and we went out that way one time because the lineup was so slow getting out of the main exits. There is a gate and a No Exit sign but you can move aside the gate easily enough. It used to be a service road and leads out onto back dirt roads but sometimes people go out that way on concert nights because it's quicker."

"As Simon did?"

"That's right." She chewed her lip. "I hope you don't have to use his name. He would lose his job. The casino bosses are very strict."

"Do all the employees know about this back way?"

"I doubt it. Just surveillance and security." She shrugged. "But you know how things slip out; it would be impossible to determine who was in the know."

"And you think the five cars unaccounted for might have gone via that exit?"

"There's no other explanation. The camera has a picture of the licence plates even if they're covered with mud. All of the ones in our frame were reading normally." Another sheet, plain white, floated in my direction. "Here are the names of the, shall we call them," she made quotation marks with her fingers, "'missing' cars, in alphabetical order of registrants. The entry times of four of them are consistent with shift times so they are most likely employees. I haven't yet had the opportunity to confirm that with the casino."

"What this means then is that Deidre could have left with somebody by the back exit at any time?"

"Yes, it does mean that. And frankly, I'd be willing to bet on it. She was a regular player and she'd know some employees by sight at least. In this day and age, a girl doesn't accept a ride from a stranger."

I wasn't entirely sure of that. Deidre was in a hurry. Nevertheless Tiffany had a point, especially if this back exit was something of a company secret.

I glanced over the list. A Honda Civic registered to Benjamin Snake had entered the parking lot at 7:00 p.m. I was sure he'd said he wasn't working Tuesday night. I'd better follow that up.

The other name really made me blink. A 1997 Chevrolet Nova, colour beige, was clocked in at 10:41. No exit time.

What gave me one heck of a jolt was that the car was registered in the name of Trudy and Sigmund Forgach!

"Tiffany, is this correct? We have a Sigmund Forgach on the first list as entering at 8:11 and exiting at 8:47."

She checked the sheet. "Yes, that's right. The cameras don't lie. See, it's a different car completely, different licence plate. Would it be his wife? Maybe she was looking for him."

"Uh-uh. He's not married. But you're sure the Chevy didn't exit by the regular gates?"

"Positive. There's no way it could have been missed. No, Sergeant Morris, the car registered to Sigmund Forgach was recorded entering and exiting. The car registered to Trudy and Sigmund Forgach was only clocked in at the entrance."

What the hell did that mean? It was just too much of a coincidence not to be relevant. The timing fit perfectly with Deidre's leaving the casino. She would have had time to accept a ride in the Chevy. But who was driving? Was it the former Mrs. Forgach, or was it Sigmund come back in a different car? If so, why would he? And why hadn't he said anything?

I went back to Tiffany. "Thanks so much for all your hard work."

Her eyebrows shot up. "Oh, it wasn't hard work at all. I just keyed in the data and...," she snapped her fingers, "there you are. The computer does it all for us."

"How on earth did we operate before computers?"

"I don't know," she said solemnly. "It's terrifying to think about."

I headed for the door, the file folder under my arm. I wish she had been able to highlight, perhaps in red, "the most likely murderer in descending order of probability."

CHAPTER THIRTY-FIVE

I drove straight to the casino to check out what Tiffany had told me. I circled the lot twice but for the life of me I couldn't see the secret exit. The area was well organized with large signs to control the traffic flow. One Way Only as you came in, ushering all vehicles into the marked spaces. Along the outer fences were more signs, which said This Way Out. Finally, I parked and went inside.

I asked the OPP constable on duty to phone Ben Snake in the surveillance room and he came down so promptly to meet me, I actually wondered if he'd seen me on the monitor. His smile was flatteringly welcoming.

"Sergeant Morris, what can I do for you? How's the case coming along?"

I'd remained in the lobby, which was filling up with a surge of visitors; more coaches must have arrived. I moved to the wall so I wouldn't get trampled.

"Is there a place we can talk for a minute?"

"Sure. Let this lot go through first."

When the wave had subsided sufficiently for us to be able to move against the tide, he took my elbow lightly and guided me through the doors and off to the left into the atrium. It was designed to resemble a Native village with a central fire. The sound and light show was in progress and the powerful throb of drumming shook the air. I stopped, letting myself feel the vibrations coming up through the floor. I could hear the overlay of voices from the talking heads on the surrounding tree trunks. Deidre wouldn't have been able to hear those words but she could certainly feel the pounding of the drum and I understood why she had taken such pleasure in coming here every week.

"This way," said Ben and he ushered me into the gift shop that opened off from the atrium. The windows were hung with feathered dream catchers and what looked like handmade moccasins and fringed shirts. It was intended for tourists but wasn't cheesy. A man who could have been his twin was sitting behind the counter. He had the same long black hair and dark eyes.

"This is my cousin, Dave Snake," said Ben. He introduced me and Dave gave me a friendly smile.

"I want to borrow your back room for a few minutes," said Ben.

"Help yourself. And while you're in there you can plug in the kettle. I'm ready for some tea."

Ben led the way through a hanging bead curtain that clicked and clacked behind us. The room was mostly for storage and was packed with boxes but there was a small table and a couple of chairs in one corner beside a serviceable fridge. The kettle was on a shelf with a box of tea bags and some coffee makings.

"Tea? Coffee?

"No thanks, I'm fine."

He plopped a tea bag into a mug. "So what's on your mind?"

It might have been my overactive imagination but I thought he wasn't as relaxed as he'd been before. There was tension in his shoulders and he seemed to me to be overly focused on the tea making.

"We've been checking registration numbers for the vehicles exiting the casino grounds at what we think was a crucial time period. There was a discrepancy to the tune of five cars that had been recorded as entering but not leaving."

He raised his eyebrows. "Really?"

"I understand there is another exit from the parking lot but it's in the nature of a secret. Nobody is supposed to use it but on occasion employees do go out that way to beat the rush on concert nights."

"Who told you that?"

I didn't want to get Tiffany's boyfriend into trouble. "Let's just say I heard this on good authority."

Ben was silent for a moment, holding his mug of tea and looking into it as if he were reading the tea leaves.

I took the sheet of paper from my briefcase. "This is the list of names that the missing vehicles are registered to — your name is on the list. Is that your licence plate number?"

He put down his tea and I handed him the paper.

"Yes, that's my car all right."

"Now I am positive you said you weren't working on Tuesday night. Did you come to the casino anyway?"

He didn't answer but turned away from me and sat down heavily in the chair.

"Do you have children?"

"Uh-uh."

"I've got four and they're all still at home, God forbid. My oldest is eighteen. I was at home on Tuesday, like I said, and Aaron asked to borrow the car. He told me he was going over to his girlfriend's house. I never thought twice about it. Now according to what you showing me, somebody brought my car over here."

"Does your son know about the other exit?"

"Sure he does." Ben gave me a wry grin. "Is there a man in the world who doesn't want to impress his teenage son with what a big chief he is? Aaron's come to various concerts with me and the family and I took them home via the back way. I told them it was only for special folks like me and they mustn't tell." He sighed. "I'm going to tan his hide, I don't care how old he is. One for lying to me and two for using the car like that. That rear exit is verboten and I could be in deep shit if the bosses knew I'd used it."

"Why do you think he came here?"

"God knows. The concert was the Irish Tenors, and to say the least, they're not his style. He's a rap man. And he doesn't gamble; I've made sure none of them ever got bitten by that particular bug. So no, I don't know what he was doing here. What time was he clocked in?"

"Just before seven o'clock."

I took out my notebook. "Perhaps I could have a word with him? Where's the best place to reach him?"

"Right now he should be at work. He has a job at the ice cream parlour in Orillia. He won't be too busy on a day like this.

Who wants ice cream in this weather? Are you going to phone or go over?"

"I'll go over."

His eyes met mine. "You don't think he has anything to do with the dead girl, do you?"

I'd like to have said, "oh gosh no," but of course I couldn't. Anybody in that parking lot who couldn't give an account of themselves on Tuesday night was a "person of interest" as far as I was concerned. We badly needed to trace Deidre's movements after she left the building. Young Aaron Snake wasn't the only person on the list, however.

"Do you know these three people?" I asked Ben. "They all clocked in just before seven."

"Cartwright's one of our cashiers. Tom Bruder is a pit boss and Don McBready works in the bar. They'll be easy to verify. They're all working now. If you like I can get them ... maybe this room isn't the best but do you want to talk to them?"

"I'll do it later."

I had to start getting back to the office and I wanted to have a quick chat with young Aaron before I did. I was about to impress on Ben the need for discretion but he beat me to it.

"Don't worry, I won't phone ahead and warn my son you're coming. Whatever the hell he was up to I know it wasn't murder. I'll see him later tonight, but if you want to talk to me some more you can reach me at home. And I won't speak to those other guys either."

"I appreciate that."

Again he flashed me the wry grin. "The Snakes are part of the Bear clan and traditionally we're responsible for security, originally no doubt security of the village or the camping ground, now it's the casino. I don't like the fact that something horrible happened to somebody who was on my turf. You can count on my co-operation ... and I hope you will do likewise. I don't want to be left in the dark."

"Fair enough."

He knew I couldn't discuss the details of the case with him but he wanted to know if he should worry about his son or not. Needless to say, this was all very reminiscent of Leo Forgach.

CHAPTER THIRTY-SIX

In fact, my interview with Aaron Snake didn't take long at all. He was sitting forlornly in the deserted ice cream parlour, waiting for customers. He looked a lot like his dad, tall and big-boned except that his dark hair was cut short and gelled into fashionable spikes. I explained why I wanted to talk to him. He gulped.

"Does my dad have to know?"

"He already knows you took his car, that you said you were going to your girlfriend's but went to the casino. That was you, wasn't it?"

"Yeah. I've met this girl, Nuala, see, and she's crazy about the Irish Tenors. So I took her to the show. Yeah, I know I didn't tell my dad but frankly he gets a bit nosy where my girlfriends are concerned. Not to mention how I spend my money." He threw up his hands in a placatory gesture. "Don't get me wrong, my dad's a great guy, one of the best, and we get along great, but he's what you'd call old school. He'd like me to marry a Native girl eventually and he wants me to get on in the world. I'm not opposed to that." He pointed at the notice board. "I was the one introduced sandwiches so we can get customers in the off-season. They're popular. But I'm not always going to work in a place like this for minimum wage, I can tell you." He grinned at me, showing white even teeth. "But it does for now. I'm learning the business and it gives me pocket money. I live at home, which keeps the costs down, but dad keeps a tight grip, so yeah, I don't tell him absolutely everything. He goes on about how his kids won't leave home but if truth be told, he's the one hanging on, ever since my mom died, which was five years ago. He's even worse with my sisters, if you'd believe. He drives them crazy ... but like I said, he's basically a really good guy. I don't fault him for wanting to look out for us. I just do end runs every now and then."

He admitted that meant literally an end run on Tuesday night. He had gone out of the rear exit right after the concert, at about eleven o'clock, to beat the lineup to go out the normal exits. He'd stayed with Nuala until two in the morning. He'd actually looked a bit shy at that admission, which was a surprise to me. I thought the younger generation was blasé about fessing up to having active sex lives.

I'd got all I needed for now. He hadn't parked anywhere near where we'd found Deidre's Toyota and he hadn't seen her or the car. I believed him but took down the name of his girlfriend. We'd have to confirm his alibi.

"I saw on the television about the girl being killed in the park. She's come in here a few times with her kid. She was cute. She couldn't talk but I could figure out what she wanted."

"Was she ever with anybody else?"

"Yeah. Another woman, sort of tough looking with pink hair. A guy one time. He was deaf too. Fair with a bit of a straggly beard."

"Do you remember when that was?"

He rubbed his finger across his forehead. "I'm bad about time. Days melt together. But it wasn't that long ago, still warm out, people still wanting ice cream. So it would have been about five weeks ago, maybe less. The same guy was here recently though. On Tuesday."

"You're sure it was the same guy?"

"Positive. He came in late. I was just closing up. I couldn't make out what he wanted at first so he was doing a lot of pointing. He wanted a butter pecan with a second scoop of chocolate on top."

Well, that put Zachary Taylor in town on Tuesday evening.

Aaron looked at me. "Do you think I should tell my dad about Nuala?"

"I strongly recommend that you do. Parents get worried if their kids lie to them."

He scowled. "Yeah, I know but it's his own fault. If he cut me a bit of slack, I would tell him things."

I knew that one from the inside out and I sympathized with the lad. But I was on the side of the adults now. "You should sit down and have a good talk. Your dad struck me as a reasonable sort of guy."

Aaron gaped. "He did? If you say so."

I closed up my notebook, ready to leave.

"Hold on." He hurried over to the fridge. "Why don't you have a freebie on me? It's good stuff, I promise you, real cream. What's your fave?"

I couldn't say I was in the mood for ice cream but it seemed churlish to refuse so I left the store licking at a stacked cone of maple walnut ice cream. The chilly wind hit me in the face when I stepped onto the street, making eating ice cream seem ridiculous, but it certainly lived up to Aaron's promise. I thought I'd come back when the temperature was in the thirties.

He seemed a good kid and I hoped he would eventually discover what he wanted to do. I put in the back of my mind a resolution to talk to him at a later date about joining the OPP.

I'd managed to drip ice cream down my jacket by the time I pulled up into the parking lot of the Centre. I wiped it and my sticky fingers as best as I could and headed in. As I passed Janice's desk, she looked up from the phone call she was involved in and held up a finger to indicate I should wait a minute.

She disconnected. "You've had two calls from Scotland. Your mother phoned at three and says to please call her first thing in the morning, our time that is. She has important news."

"Did she say what it was?"

"No, and I didn't ask," said Janice. She'd had experience before with Joan's calls, which could be interminable if she found a sympathetic ear at the other end, and Janice was nothing if not kindly. Joan didn't seem to mind, or notice, the constant interruptions as Janice had to answer other calls.

"Who else?"

"Your friend the policeman. He'd like you to call him today if you can but before midnight his time." She looked up at the clock on the wall. "That gives you one hour. It's going on eleven for them."

"Is Katherine in?"

"No, she's left early." Janice raised her eyebrows. "I think there's another crisis with her mother."

Katherine's mother was in the early stages of Alzeimer's and had become increasingly demanding over the last year. In my view, Katherine deserved sainthood. She never complained, just worked extra hours to make up for the times she had to fly out of the office to see to her mother, who lived with her.

"She asked you to write up your report and leave it on her desk. She'll look at it in the morning."

"Leo isn't here, is he?"

"No. He did phone though and asked if you'd call him as soon as you could."

That was going to be fun!

I traipsed to my office, reversed my sign so I wouldn't be disturbed, and phoned Gill. He answered after the second ring but I could tell I'd woken him up.

"Gill, it's me. Sorry about the hour."

"It's not your fault. I think it has to do with latitude and longitude, doesn't it?"

"Do you want to go back to sleep and call me tomorrow?"

"I was no asleep, lassie. My eyes were closed and my brain had left the room but here in Lewis we men dinna call that sleep, we call it prayer."

He always made me laugh when he put on the heavy accent. His own regular accent was not too marked to make him incomprehensible the way I'd found some of his countrymen.

I heard him sigh, or perhaps he was yawning. "I wanted to tell you a couple of things sooner rather than later."

I almost made a flip remark about his dumping me and marrying somebody else but I'd gone that route and I kept a firm hold on my overblown insecurities.

"You still there, Chris?"

"Still here."

"I just got confirmation: I've got two weeks' leave at Christmas."

"Terrific."

My mind began to race with how this would involve me. We'd been expecting he'd get Christmas and Boxing Day only.

"I spoke to Morag today and she is definitely planning to spend Christmas with her new boyfriend in Tenerife. Isobel wants to stay in Skye and she says it's her mother's turn to be the Christmas Day parent. She's also going skiing right afterward..."

"And that means..."

"It means I can come over to you, if you like. I know you're torn about Joan's wedding and staying put in Canada because of Paula but if you can extricate yourself from your mother, we could have the two weeks together. I've no problem with you having to spend time with Paula if you need to. I'd just be glad to hang around."

I could have wept as I was reminded yet again why I was crazy about the guy. He understood me!

"Gordon Gillies, if you were in this room right now, I'd jump your bones."

He laughed. "We can pretend, if you like."

"No. I want the real thing. That is the best offer I've had all day." But even as I said that, I felt a tug on the complex rope of emotions that attached me to my mother. "I haven't completely decided whether or not I'm coming to the wedding. Joan will be very put out but I must say the thought of having you here and being able to keep an eye on Paula and Chelsea is a powerful inducement to stay in Canada. I have to give Joan a call in the morning. I'll sound her out."

"I can tell you already what she'll say. She's booked the parish hall already."

"You're kidding. She said she'd wouldn't be seen dead in a church even when she's dead."

"I think her views are changing now that she's here. I've seen her going into church for the service."

"She never told me that."

There was an awkward silence. There were lots of things Joan hadn't told me when I was growing up and her habit of playing her cards close to her chest hadn't changed significantly.

"She wants to do this big time is how she expressed it to me," said Gill. "And you being there is very much part of the plan."

I could feel a snap of the old anger. "Well, it might not be part of my plan."

More silence. I said that Gill understood me and it's true but he was sometimes puzzled by my conflicts with my mother. With him she was just as sweet as could be so I can hardly blame him. She saved the knives for me.

"Like I said, Chris. I'm open. I leave the decision up to you. Either way I'd just be happy if we can spend two weeks together."

There was a tone to his voice that made my heart jump. If I could have beamed myself up to the Hebrides at that moment I would have.

"You said there were two things. What's the other one?"

"That case I told you about, the kids and drugs..."

"Shoot. I'm sorry I haven't had a minute to study your report."

"Don't worry about it. The situation has taken a downward turn. The young girl made a serious suicide attempt yesterday. She took an overdose of her mother's painkillers. She's still in a coma and they're not sure she's going to make it. I'd surely like to know what her part in the whole mess has been. You never know, if I can tell her I'm certain she's innocent, it might help her."

"What if she's guilty?"

"My gut feeling is that she isn't but even so I'd like to know with more certainty where I stand."

"I'll look at what you sent."

"Anyway, phone me on the weekend with your decision so I can start booking my tickets if need be."

"Copy that."

He laughed. He was in on the office joke.

We exchanged a few lovey dovey words that I don't need to repeat and we hung up. I picked up his photograph which sat on my desk and planted a big smacker of a kiss. Needless to say it was totally unsatisfying. I wanted to feel warm flesh next to mine, not cold glass.

For the hundredth time I wondered how we were ever going to resolve the distance thing.

I replaced the photograph and keyed in Leo's number.

CHAPTER THIRTY-SEVEN

He answered immediately as if he'd been sitting next to the phone.

"Any word from Sigmund?" I asked.

"Nothing."

"I have some information about the cars entering and exiting the casino."

"Yes?"

I thought I'd give him the good news first. "The tapes confirm Sigmund's statement that he left the casino at 8:47. He was driving a red 2004 Mazda Miata."

"Is that his latest toy? I didn't know."

Now came the bad news. "However, another vehicle was clocked in at 10:41. It's a beige Chevy Nova and it's registered in the names of Trudy and Sigmund Forgach."

"What! What the hell does that mean?"

"Just what it says. We know that was the car, but we don't know who was driving."

"We can settle that right now," said Leo. "Trudy is with me. I'll ask her."

He muffled the receiver with his hand sufficiently to block out what he was saying. Then he said, "Trudy says she does co-own a Chevy Nova but she most certainly did not, repeat, did not go to the casino on Tuesday night. She was at her Daughters of Mary meeting at the church." His voice was grim. "We can only assume that the driver was Sigmund. That he returned and didn't inform us. If he was clocked in at 10:41, he had time to meet Deidre. What time did he exit?"

"We don't know that."

I explained about the back way out. "So we have no way of knowing when he left."

"I see." There was a silence. "It seems even more imperative that we speak to Sigmund."

It certainly did.

We hung up and I decided I'd had enough for the day. Everybody else had gone home. I quickly typed up my report and emailed it to Katherine.

Young Tiffany had looked alarmed at the thought of a computerless world but I was realizing how dependent I had become on my cellphone. Sometimes I looked up and saw other people walking by, cell glued to their ear, or a driver, phone tucked under her chin, trying to negotiate a left turn and I scowled critically. Hey, let she who is without sin throw the first stone. I made a turn onto my street, fiddling with the automatic message list on my phone, just in case Ed had phoned, and almost collided with a man walking his dog. I stopped with a jolt as the man actually scooped up his dog to safety. He glared at me, but just as I was making deprecating, "sorry, my fault" sort of signals, his face changed and he flashed me a big grin and a wave. It was Mr. Torres and Lily. I rolled down my window.

"Sorry, I wasn't paying attention. I do apologize."

"That's all right. No harm done. You must have a lot on your mind. How's the case coming along?"

"It's coming. We're still following up leads."

Lily wriggled in his arms, and he put her down. "I hope you find whoever did it soon. That poor child didn't deserve to die like that."

"Indeed not."

I couldn't really move as he was standing in the road blocking me, but at that moment, a car came up behind and the driver tooted his horn impatiently.

Torres peered around my car. "I should have know it was a young punk. Where can he be going that's so important?"

"Wherever it is, I'd better move before he does a bumper car routine."

Torres stepped out of the way. "You will let me know when you've caught somebody, won't you?"

"Of course."

I knew that people fastened on to a case that they had been involved in. It was "theirs."

With Lily trotting beside him, he headed for the sidewalk and I started up. Within a second, the car behind me surged around and roared off. As far as I could see there were not one but two punks. I recognized them as the teenage sons of the woman a few doors down from me who as far as I knew were under house arrest and not supposed to be anywhere else. I'd better have a word with Ed before the trouble they were heading for escalated.

There were no scary letters in my mailbox and Tory and Bertie were glad to see me, gladder to see the can opener and the cat food. I walked into the living room, drew all the curtains, made sure the kitchen door and window were secure, and after plugging in the kettle, I plonked myself down on the couch to make my phone calls.

First was Paula who answered in a low depressed-sounding voice.

"I'm just going to change my clothes and then I'll be right over."

"No you won't," she said, her voice stronger. "You need a night in. I'm fine. Craig said he's coming."

I wanted to say something sarcastic but bit my tongue.

"And Mom was here this afternoon so I've had plenty of TLC."

"How're you doing?"

"The truth? I'm scared shitless, Chris. It's hard having two problems at once. I don't know which to concentrate on and which I should be more worried about."

I made reassuring noises but tried not to fall into the trap of silencing her with false optimism. If she needed to talk about her fears then I'd listen. In fact, she didn't want to dwell on that and wanted to talk about her mother. Did I think she was all right? She was still too thin and she looked years older.

"She's still grieving, Paulie, she needs a bit more time."

The conversation moved on. "No, Craig hadn't been in yet. He thought it was better if my mother came and he stayed at home with Chelsea and you know how he hates hospitals."

Ah yes, he'd been on the golf course when Chelsea was being born. Even that joyous moment hadn't helped him overcome his fear. I didn't say that of course.

"Is there anything else you want?" I asked. "How about a nice juicy case file to look at?'

That got a laugh and got her distracted from the perpetual enmity between her husband and best friend. I told her more of the details of the case and how things weren't looking too good for Sigmund Forgach.

"Do you think he's a serious possibility?"

"Gut feeling, no, but he's certainly not telling us the whole truth and nothing but the truth, so until I know what that is, he's top of the list."

"Poor Leo. He must be taking it hard."

"He is but he's like King Lear: the suffering seems to be turning him into a more likeable human being."

At that moment, a nurse entered Paula's room to tell her it was time to take her "vitals" and we hung up. I sat and stared at my phone for a few moments. Paula had said she had two problems to deal with. I felt so helpless. Whatever she had to go through if she did have cancer, I would be with her every step of the way, but I wished with every fibre of my being that she would be let off. The racing heart seemed more containable, less dangerous, but it was certainly a worry too.

Suddenly I heard a creak on the landing outside my door and I could feel myself go into high alert. I knew the door was locked, but since the letter, my space had been violated and I was suspicious of everything. The creak came again and this time there was a soft rapping on the door. Mrs. Harley had installed a fish eye in the door and for the first time, I was glad she had. I peered through. Gary Fellows was standing on the other side of the door, his face distorted by the lens. I opened up.

"Chris. I'm so sorry to trouble you this late at night but I wondered if I could sleep with you?"

I burst out laughing and he gave his best Nathan Lane imitation, raising his shoulders and extending his hands. "Whaat?"

"You fickle creature you. What's Ahmed going to think?"

As soon as the words were out of my mouth, I realized I'd said exactly the wrong thing. As I ushered him into the living room, I saw his eyes had teared up. He sat on the couch and Bertie promptly seized the chance to jump in his lap. Gary started to stroke the cat's soft fur. Bertie, the goodwill ambassador.

"Our getaway didn't help at all," said Gary. "In fact, things got worse. He's gone off to his girlfriend's and says he won't be coming back."

He looked so woebegone I sat down beside him and put my arm around his shoulders.

"I'm sorry, Gary."

"I loved him, Chris, more than any other boyfriend I've had. I thought he was happy with me."

"He was, I know he was."

But when I thought back, I realized that the signs had been there ever since Ahmed came back from Egypt. I'd assumed he was still grieving for his father, and his withdrawal from Gary, and me too for that matter, were because of that.

"I was just about to make tea, do you want some?"

He looked sideways at me. "You don't happen to have some of that great Scotch do you?"

"Indeed I do. Do you want Lagavulin or Glenfiddich?"

"Which is the peaty one?'

"Lagavulin."

"A double-double then please. I'd like to drown my sorrows."

"Not on my precious imported you won't. You'll savour one glass and that's it."

It was an ongoing joke between us how little Gary actually drank. The fact he'd even asked for Scotch indicated how upset he was.

"You will join me, won't you? You know what they say about drinking alone?"

"You don't have to share the bottle?"

He managed a grin. "That too."

I went into the kitchen, put aside my oh so healthy herbal tea and poured us each a good slug of the best Hebridean.

The liquor, the laughs, the cat's pseudo devotion worked and Gary relaxed.

"So what happened?" I asked.

"Nothing. And I mean nothing, no sex, no talking, nothing. It was clear he hadn't wanted to go away and he doesn't want to work things through. As far as he is concerned, I was a mistake, a sin if you want to put it that way. He has to make amends to Allah and to his family, of equal power in his mind, and find some nice virgin, marry her, and propagate as soon as possible."

"If he's spending the night with the said girlfriend, isn't he already breaking the commandments?"

"Oh she's not a virgin. Far from it apparently."

"Does she know about, er, does she know about you?"

"No. I've been considering finding out where she lives and showing up demanding I get my boyfriend back."

He took a big, unappreciative gulp of the Scotch which would have caused Gill and the real Scotch drinkers to shudder in horror. This stuff cost $100 a bottle. I sipped on mine.

I felt sorry for Gary, who in my books was one terrific guy, but I also felt sorry for the unknown girlfriend. The villain of the piece was Ahmed but then he was obviously in the grip of other influences. So much for culture clash. There was all too often severe bruising.

Gary put his glass on the coffee table. "Thanks Chris. It's getting late. I'd better let you get to bed."

He paused and his eyes met mine. "I meant it when I came in and asked if I could spend the night with you?"

"What? You don't mean do an Ahmed, do you?"

He grinned at me. "Chris, I've known I was gay since I was four years old. You're a very attractive woman and I love you but I don't want to have sex with you. It's just that, I, well I would feel better if I knew you were in the next room." He patted the couch. "I could sleep here."

"You can use the guest room."

"No, that's all right." He began to do his best Uriah Heep imitation, rubbing his hands and squirming. "I don't want to be any bother. Just think of me as a stray cat you've brought in from the cold. I'll curl up with Bertie and Tory. You won't even notice."

"Suit yourself. Just don't use the litter box, that's all I ask."

He guffawed. "Ah ye're a good-hearted lassie, Christine Morris. If I were straight, I'd ask you to marry me on the spot."

"If you were straight, I'd seriously consider it."

He gave me a flamboyant kiss, first on one cheek, then the other. His chin was unshaven and bristly and he smelled like Scotch.

"Thank you, dear friend," he whispered.

Once again it was pre-dawn when my phone rang.

Groggy, I struggled to grab the receiver, already blaming Joan for an inconsiderate call. I didn't switch on the light so didn't see the call display.

"Hello?"

"Miss Morris, this is Grace Cameron…"

The voice was clear, words precisely enunciated, but for a split second I couldn't remember who she was.

"You were at my apartment yesterday. I returned home after all."

"Yes, yes, of course, I'm sorry, Miss Cameron. I was momentarily in another world."

"Of course and I do apologize for the early hour but I wanted to speak to you particularly because I found you quite a sympathetic person … I have just received a telephone call from my friend who lives in a seniors' building just two blocks from here…"

I heard her intake of breath. "Sorry, I had to use my puffer. My friend's name is Doris Bryant. She is confined to a wheel chair…" Another gasp. There was something coming through the line that made me alarmed. "Before I continue, Miss Morris, I should say that I have given my word to my friend that I would not contact the police. It was with great difficulty that I persuaded her to give me permission to call you…"

What the hell…?

"Doris has told me that she has been the victim of an attack. A man has raped her."

CHAPTER THIRTY-EIGHT

The strong ageless voice suddenly wavered. "Doris is eighty-three years old. She has been in a wheelchair since she had a stroke four years ago but she manages very well. Who would do something like that to an old lady, Miss Morris? What monster would do such a thing?"

"Can you tell me what happened?"

"As I said she had just now telephoned me but she is understandably very upset and it took me a while to make sense of what she was saying. However, perhaps it would be best for you if I related what happened as I now understand it."

"Please do, Miss Cameron." Automatically, I scrambled to get a pen and paper so I could copy down what she said.

"Doris is a light sleeper. She said she got up about two o'clock to answer a call of nature. She can manoeuvre herself quite well into the wheelchair and she went into the bathroom. As she was coming out, she was grabbed from behind and some kind of bag thrown over her head. Her arms were pinned to her sides by what turned out to be her own dressing gown belt. She could put up no resistance. The man told her to be quiet or he would kill her but he also tied something around her mouth, so she could not scream if she had wanted to ... Excuse me, Miss Morris, the excitement has aggravated my asthma, I must use my puffer again." I waited while she did so, hoping she was all right. "I am not completely clear as to what happened next because it was almost impossible for Doris to speak coherently but I gather he removed her undergarments. She was wearing a nightdress but always wears special underpants when she goes to bed. She has no sensation in her legs but she thinks he interfered with her in her private parts. She found ... she found his semen. Then he said he was sorry and he would make sure somebody discovered her before too long. That turned out not to be the case. Nobody came. She eventually wriggled free from the cord and freed her arms. She then took the hood off her head. It was an ordinary bag that she uses for collecting her delicates."

I heard the drag of breath again. "Are you all right, Miss Cameron?"

"Yes. My door is securely locked... Doris said that she got herself into the shower and stayed there for a long time."

I bit my lip. Unfortunately for us, this human reaction to rape was the worst thing to do from a forensics standpoint. Key evidence would be washed away.

"She says that she sat in a sort of daze, not knowing what to do. I had talked to her previously about our encounter, yours and mine, Miss Morris, and said how, er, safe you made me feel. Finally, she called me and asked me to telephone you and ask if you can come to her apartment as soon as you can. At this moment, she cannot face telling the regular police but she believes she owes it to other women to report what happened in case he strikes again."

I could have wept.

"Miss Cameron. I will go and see her immediately but I'm afraid I cannot promise to keep this quiet. I will have to report it. We must catch this man."

"I told her that would probably be the case but she says it must be you first. I think she can only proceed in small stages."

"Where does she live?"

"In the seniors' building at the corner of John Street and McKenzie. It's called Sunshine Lodge."

"I know it."

Grace drew on her puffer. "I was thinking that I had better come with you. She is one of my oldest friends and I believe she will feel better if I am there. She is a widow and has two daughters but neither lives in town."

I hesitated. She was probably right about her friend but she herself was a frail elderly woman. I didn't want to cause her harm in any way. She picked up on my thoughts.

"As I told you previously, Miss Morris, I used to be a nurse and even though it was some time ago, I was good at my work. I was frequently called upon to calm hysteria and nerves."

"All right. Will you call your friend back and say we'll be there in about fifteen minutes? I'll come and get you."

We hung up and a sleepy voice called from the next room.

"Chris, is everything all right?"

I got out of bed and started to get dressed. "I've got to go out, Gary. Help yourself to whatever you need."

I hurried off to the bathroom and when I came out Gary was standing in the hall.

"Bad news, huh?"

I nodded.

"Take care then. Don't worry, I'll look after the pussycats."

I collected my tape recorder and headed out. Gary followed me to the top of the stairs. He had brought up his dressing gown, a rather sedate blue terry cloth, and as he saw me off, I had the sense of how domestic the scene would look to an outsider but with typical roles reversed. Me, a daring police officer off to catch the bad guys, him soft and homey ready to handle the household affairs. I almost laughed at my own thoughts, which was when I realized how deeply troubling the phone call had been.

I found Grace waiting for me outside her apartment building. The needles of rain shone in the lamplight and the chill air was penetrating to the bone. Grace was bundled up in an ankle-length down coat and faux fur hat and she was leaning on a Zimmer frame.

"I was too agitated to wait inside," she said as I jumped out of the car to help her in. She'd forgotten her gloves and her hands were cold. I turned up the heater to high.

"I called Doris back to tell her we were on our way, but she didn't answer. She might have gone back into the bathroom."

As usual, her voice was controlled but I felt her fear. I knew it was rare for a rapist to return immediately to his victim but it did happen. I shoved the accelerator to the floor and we raced down the street. The tires on my car, squealed melodramatically as I roared around the corner, ignoring the stop sign.

The seniors' building was only three blocks away so we were there in two minutes. I pulled to a stop in front of the entrance.

"I've got a key," said Grace. "We have each other's. It saves having to buzz somebody in all the time."

The door was timed to accommodate residents in wheelchairs and it opened with agonizing slowness.

"Doris is on the first floor at the rear," said Grace. "We'll have to take the elevator."

She was doing her best but she couldn't walk quickly.

"Shall I go on ahead?" I asked her but she shook her head vehemently.

"She'll be frightened if I'm not with you."

And she, I realized, would be frightened if I left her alone.

I pressed the elevator button and we waited, me scouting out the place. There were four floors in the building and the elevator must have been at the top and seemed to be stopping at every one of them on the way down.

The hall lights were on low and I could glimpse an open entrance into what was probably the lounge. A door opposite us said Office.

"Stay here a minute, Grace."

First I tried the office door, which appeared to be firmly locked, then I went down to the lounge and flicked on the light. It was empty and there were no hiding places. I shoved open the fire-exit door. There was nobody skulking in the stairwell. I returned to Grace. She was actually sitting on the seat of her Zimmer frame and I could see all colour had drained from her face. She managed a wan smile.

"I think the old dears press every button by mistake and the doors take an hour to open and close which is why it takes so bloody long."

Finally the elevator reached ground level and the doors slowly opened. There was nobody getting out. Grace shuffled in and we crept upward to the first floor. I was on full alert, registering as much information as I could. We'd have to go over it all again with the other police but I knew from experience, these first impressions were important. It might have been residents inadvertently pressing the buttons, or it might not, especially at this hour of the morning. It was certainly a way of delaying the elevator.

Doris's apartment was at the far end of the hall, right next to the stairs. The obligatory fire door was closed. Grace was moving valiantly as fast as she could. The place was utterly quiet and I felt a sudden pang of distress at the impact what had happened might have on the sleeping residents.

Grace knocked softly on the door.

"It's me, Doris. And Detective Morris."

There was no reply and she inserted her key and we stepped inside.

Doris Bryant was in her wheelchair in the centre of the small living room. Her head was slumped forward onto her chest and her face was an ugly livid colour; saliva had trickled from the side of her mouth, which had drooped to a grotesque angle. She was not breathing.

"Oh my god, what's happened to her?" Grace was right behind me, staring in horror at her friend.

I went over to the body and touched the woman's bare arm. Her skin was still warm. She must have died within the last half an hour.

"I believe she's had a stroke," I said.

As far as I was concerned, Mrs. Doris Bryant was now a homicide.

CHAPTER THIRTY-NINE

There was a list of emergency numbers fastened with a cat magnet to Doris's fridge. First I made the 911 call, then I roused the superintendents, Mr. and Mrs. Desjardins. The phone rang for a long time and when Mr. Desjardins finally answered, he didn't seem able to comprehend what I was saying. I repeated myself and then asked him to come to the apartment so he could take care of Grace. She was sitting on one of the kitchen chairs as I'd directed her and she could hear my half of the conversation. She began to gesticulate violently and when I hung up she said, "They drink, that's why he couldn't understand you. I don't want to be with them. I'll sit here."

"Grace, you can't. This is now a crime scene and there will be all kinds of officers swarming all over the place."

"Well, I'm not going to be with those two parasites. Besides, they smoke and their apartment stinks. The woman in the next apartment was a friend of Doris's. I've met her a few times and she impressed me as a steady sort. She was a doctor herself years ago. I'd rather wake her up and be with her until you need me."

If anything Grace had gone even whiter but her voice was still strong. She was gripping her walker tightly but otherwise she herself was steady. No tears, no trembling, just the awful pallor.

"Come on then."

I put myself between the body and Grace as we walked across the living room and she kept her eyes straight ahead.

Unlike the superintendents, who still hadn't appeared, the neighbour, whose name was Edith Cowan, answered quickly. She was a tiny woman who at the moment was wearing a mesh hairnet over iron grey hair and a serviceable navy dressing gown. As Grace had said, it was apparent she was a "steady sort."

I didn't go into details, just explained who I was and said that Mrs. Bryant was dead and could Grace stay with her for a while.

"Of course."

At that moment, the elevator doors opened and disgorged two paramedics, four firefighters, and a uniformed constable.

Grace, who had been so stalwart up to this point, said quietly. "I think I'm going to vomit."

Edith put her arm around Grace's waist. "Let's get you to the bathroom."

She whisked her inside and closed the door, leaving me free to deal with the emergency crew.

I told them I was pretty sure Doris Bryant had died as the result of a stroke but because of other circumstances, I was treating it as a case of equivocal death, which meant the body had to remain where it was until the coroner and the forensics team arrived. Coincidently, the paramedics were the same pair who'd answered the call to come to the pier.

"We probably should check her vitals to make sure," said the girl. She and her partner, although to my eyes looking as if they were barely out of high school, were calm and professional. I suppose old ladies felled by a stroke were much more within the norm than a girl strangled and dumped into the lake.

"Just you then. And you, constable. I can't have a lot of people traipsing through."

They went inside and I had a brief talk with the firefighters, who started to pick up their equipment and head for the elevator. One of them lingered.

"I know Mrs. Bryant. She was a member of our church," he said. "A good soul if ever there was one. She lived in Orillia all her life. She was my mother's teacher." He crossed himself. "May she rest in peace." He hesitated. "I don't suppose you can tell me what happened?"

"I'm afraid I can't at the moment."

He had a kind face and he eyed me sympathetically. "It was nasty, wasn't it?"

"Yes, it was."

The two paramedics came out of the apartment.

"No vitals," said Cathy. She and her partner, whose name I had forgotten, started to fold up their stretcher.

"How's the man with hypothermia?" she asked.

"He's fully recovered, thanks."

From that, anyway.

All of them left except the constable who'd got the emergency call. He was waiting with his notebook in his hand. I briefed him as to what had happened and why I was there. He was a gangly young guy who gave his name as Geoff Purvis. As first on the scene, his job was now to secure the site and then stay with the body until he was told he could leave, and although he didn't complain, I could see the expression on his face. His shift was almost up and he could be here for hours longer.

I went back into the apartment but stayed at the door. No sense in making forensics' job more difficult by the two of us leaving trace elements. At the moment, all I was doing was trying to get an overview. I had more chance to assess the apartment now. Doris must have tried to get out of her wheelchair because her bathrobe was open to her knees. She was naked underneath. I know it wasn't rational but I felt sorry that she was so exposed. I couldn't give her some dignity by covering her up but I understood the impulse that makes people alter clothes or the position of the body when the victim is somebody they have cared for.

"My auntie lives in a seniors' home," said Purvis. "It looks just like this. All her stuff crammed into one room when she used to have a whole house. This lady kept it tidy, though, which is more than I can say for my auntie."

He was right about it being both tidy and crammed. There wasn't a lot of room to manoeuvre the wheelchair and I could see faint lines on the carpet where the chair had started to mark a path. To the bedroom at the rear, bathroom, across the living room to the kitchen. There was a large state-of-the-art plasma TV nestled in a shelving unit along one wall. The senior's delight. I could see several framed photographs on the shelves. Children and grandchildren probably. Doris's life. All victims had a life and sometimes the hardest part of a case was dealing with the impact the death had on those left behind. Unbidden, I felt a wave of anger that actually made me clench my teeth. "A good woman," the firefighter had said. She should have ended her days peacefully, not in this violent shameful way.

"Did you see any signs of how the guy got in?" I asked Purvis.

"None at all. The windows are closed, this door is the only entrance and shows no signs of forced entry. Either it wasn't locked or the bad guy had a key. The bathroom's been used recently, the towels are wet, but she may have done that herself given what you've said."

I nodded. "She took a shower."

We heard the ping of the elevator and out stepped two officers. One was Detective Inspector Ian Franklin, the other a female plainclothes officer who was a few paces behind. I wasn't surprised at that. I'd met Franklin on a case last year and I wasn't happy it was his watch. He was close to retirement, old school, and I thought took undue pride in being "a straight shooter," which meant in his case, a tactless jerk. Rather unexpectedly, he seemed glad to see me, greeting me as if we were old pals. I felt a bit guilty about my uncharitable feelings toward him and warmed up my smile. He didn't introduce the woman but I held out my hand and we shook, like good lads.

"Christine Morris. I'm with the Behavioural Science Centre."

"Detective Constable Susan Bailey," she returned. "I thought you guys never came out in daylight."

She had blonde tips, a firm figure, and there was a twinkle in her eyes that softened the sarcasm and made me think she wasn't as overawed by Franklin as it first appeared.

"So what's the story?" he asked. "You saying this isn't a natural?"

I filled him in on what I knew so far going from Grace's call. He scowled but his only comment was, "My mother-in-law's nearly eighty. I wouldn't want it to happen to even that old biddy. We've got to put this guy away for good."

CHAPTER FORTY

The forensics team was going over everything in the apartment although for now they had to leave Doris's body where it was. Another constable was assigned to keeping watch over the crime scene and Purvis was discharged. Although it was after six by now, it was still dark outside and nobody had yet wandered out into the halls. We'd have to do something about the residents soon. I was anxious that they didn't come out of their rooms to the sight of uniformed officers swarming all over the place. I'd asked Constable Purvis to get hold of the social worker who worked at the residence and she arrived just as Franklin, Bailey, and I stepped out of the interminably slow elevator into the lobby. She was a smart-looking young woman who introduced herself as Barbara Cheevers. She was visibly upset.

"I understand Mrs. Bryant was attacked. I find it inconceivable. She was so … vulnerable. She was quite confined to a wheelchair."

"We've got to talk to all the old dears," said Franklin. "So perhaps you can go along with Sergeant Bailey here and tell them they've got to stay in their rooms until we call for them. We can't have them wandering around. You know them better than we do so you can suggest who shouldn't be left alone, who'd be better off paired up with somebody else, and so on."

Wow. I guess he'd been on a sensitivity training course since I saw him last.

He must have caught the look on my face because he smirked then continued in the same vein.

"If you wouldn't mind, we need a list of next of kin who can be present during the interviews if necessary. We don't want any strokes, heart attacks, panic attacks, or the like, so if you think they require special care, let's get somebody down here right away. Maybe you could go over that with Detective Constable Bailey here before you start waking the old folks up." He beckoned to me and took me out of earshot. "Christine, would you do me a big favour and take over some of the interviews? Bailey can head up the other half. I have a feeling the old folks will feel better if there's a female in the room."

I thought that was a good idea. Franklin was a big guy with too much gut hanging over his belt and a voice he had a hard time bringing down to a non-threatening pitch.

Strictly speaking, my role was that of a civilian but I was involved now and I'd stay as long as I could be useful. The important person was Grace. I'd made notes when she'd first called me, but I needed to get a formal statement from her. I went up to Dr. Cowan's apartment, this time taking the stairs.

She had removed her hairnet and got dressed and she and Grace were having tea. At least I assumed it was tea as there was an elegant china tea service on the side table. Grace had her feet up on a hassock and some colour had returned to her face. I told her what I needed. She was fine with that but Dr. Cowan insisted on freshening up the pot, as she put it. By now, I was suffering from serious caffeine withdrawal but Edith had only tea, which I can't stand to drink in the morning, so I accepted a glass of orange juice. Her apartment was the exact same layout as Doris's but bigger and was definitely less cluttered. Over the artificial fireplace, in pride of place, was a large oil painting in a thick wooden frame. A distinguished-looking man in a dark formal suit stared soberly into the distance. Edith returned.

"That's my husband, Charles. My grandson painted it from a photograph. It makes Charlie look far too serious, which he wasn't at all, but Grant was so proud of it, I didn't have the heart to criticize."

She added the hot water to the teapot, poured out some very dark-looking tea, fussed over Grace, and then took the chair opposite to us. She folded her hands neatly in her lap and I realized she was probably much older than she first appeared. Sitting with a straight spine and quiet in that way suggested a much earlier generation.

Once we were all settled again, I asked Grace to repeat what Doris had said to her. I put my tape recorder discreetly on the coffee table.

"I consider myself released from my promise now that she is dead but I do hope, Miss Morris, that you will give her memory the respect she should have." She paused. "I am sure you yourself would not be indiscreet but many might. She would be appalled if anything of what happened was reported in the newspapers, for instance."

"Doris was a most private woman," chipped in Dr. Cowan.

I wished I could reassure them both but I couldn't do so with any sincerity. I knew from bitter experience how rapacious some media people were for a juicy story.

Grace gave her statement. Dr. Cowan listened quietly and showed no reaction, not from coldness but from years of professional detachment. It helped Grace with the difficult parts and she didn't falter in her narrative.

We took a break while she had some more tea, which she gulped down thirstily.

"Did she tell you any details of this man? His voice? An accent of any kind? A smell perhaps?"

She thought for a moment. "No, nothing. She didn't see him, I know that much, but she did say she smelled disinfectant on his hands."

"We have found no evidence of a break-in. Do either of you know if Mrs. Bryant was in the habit of locking her door at night?"

Dr. Cowan answered at once. "She always locked it. Every so often some derelict has gotten in and they find him passed out on one of the couches in the lounge. All of the residents are warned constantly not to let anybody in that they don't know but they are a trusting lot and think that a person must have a legitimate reason to be here, so in they come."

"When was the last time this happened?"

"You can check with Mrs. Cheevers, the social worker, but I heard that there was an incident just last week. Mrs. Moseley, who is a night owl, went down to the lounge just after midnight. The television is better there. She found some man urinating into the fireplace. "

"I hadn't heard about that," said Grace. "What did she do?"

"Pshaw, you know Henrietta Moseley. She gave him a good talking to and ordered him out."

Dr. Cowan glanced over at me with a wry smile. "Mrs. Moseley's husband was a professional soldier. She says she's seen so much horror in her lifetime, nothing bothers her anymore. She must be close to ninety but she is fearless."

"I've always considered her arrogant myself," said Grace. "And not too intelligent but I suppose that can carry you through a lot of difficult situations."

Grace delivered this rather sharp judgement in a cool sort of voice that made me think she was probably right and simply making an observation.

"Did anybody else see this man?" I asked.

"I believe Henrietta roused Mr. Desjardins, our superintendent. As I heard the story, the poor man was elderly and confused. Not in the least dangerous but the police did come and take him away."

"And this man is the only one who has trespassed into the building?"

Dr. Cowan shook her head. "There have been at least two others that I know of. Mrs. Cheevers came on two young men one afternoon who had got in and were helping themselves to the lunch we used to put out for the residents if somebody had a birthday. They were quite brazen about it and said they thought we were a food bank, which was nonsense."

"Were the police called that time?"

"No. It didn't seem necessary. Mr. Desjardins on this occasion did his job properly and was very stern with them and said if he saw them again he would have them charged."

Grace had been sitting listening to all of this and she suddenly broke out.

"Doris told me that one of the residents claimed a man entered her bedroom and, she said, 'tickled her' all over. You remember her, Edith. Her name was Salmino or Salamander or some such thing."

"You mean Maria Salamonica. But she was suffering from Alzheimer's. I don't know if her complaint can be taken seriously." She halted. "At least, I thought that until now. Oh dear, Miss Morris, do you think it's possible the poor woman was also molested and we didn't believe her?"

I hesitated but unfortunately it wasn't out of the question. "I'll follow up on it. Where is she now?"

"She went to the long-term care unit of Memorial Hospital but I regret to say that she passed away soon afterward."

They were both looking at me and Grace seemed to have shrunk back into her shell.

"And do you know when this is incident is supposed to have happened?"

Grace thought for a moment. "Time melts together; I can't remember. It was after Christmas."

"It was shortly before she was transferred," interjected Edith. "That would make it March or April of this year."

"Did Mrs. Salamonica speak to you about what had happened?" I asked.

"Well yes, she did. She mentioned it more than once. But she was having other delusions. She was certain that her husband who had died many years previously was secretly trying to communicate with her. She became convinced he was being held prisoner by the government because he knew too much about a conspiracy to kill the Queen." Edith's calmness was starting to break down. "She saw me as a confidant, you see. She knew I'd been a physician and I think she had it in her head that she was my patient. She told me several times that she'd heard her husband sending secret messages through the radio." Edith clenched her hands tightly. "When she said a man had come into her room, I'm afraid I didn't take her seriously."

"When you get old, nobody does," said Grace caustically.

Edith flinched. She was already feeling dreadful and the comment didn't help.

I jumped in. "It's completely understandable why you didn't believe her and frankly we don't know if there is credence to what she said. Did anybody else know about it?"

"Everybody in the residence who would listen to her. She went on for days. It was very trying. Then she moved on to something else. The home care girl was stealing from her. That simply wasn't true of course and the girl was very upset about it when she heard." Dr. Cowan pursed her lips. "Believing that everybody is stealing from you is very common in dementia."

"But she said this man had come in once only?"

"Yes. That is to say, she never complained about it again. But good heavens, how could I forget? I can tell you more precisely. I had a dreadful toothache when she cornered me in the lounge that morning. I went to my dentist and had to have a root canal." She got stiffly to her feet. "Let me check my calendar."

She walked slowly into the kitchen. Grace drank some more tea and I could see her hand was shaking.

"Are you all right, Miss Cameron?"

"No, I'm not. I don't walk these days, my eyesight is the pits, and I'm going deaf but God help me, if I lose my marbles, please put me out of my misery."

Edith heard her. "Don't be so silly, Grace. The one nice thing about losing one's marbles, as you put it, is that you don't know they're missing." She returned with a calendar in her hand with a picture of a bear cub on the front. "I was able to see Dr. Stephens on Tuesday, April 30, which means that Maria spoke to me on Monday about something that may or may not have happened on Sunday night, April 28."

I made notes. There was a tap on the door and Edith went to answer it.

I heard Franklin's voice. "Could I have a word with Detective Morris?"

I went out to talk to him, closing the door behind me.

"We've roused all the residents and been able to phone almost all of the family members so we can start interviews fairly soon. In the meantime, the supers have finally surfaced." He grimaced. "I think they're both still half-plastered." He nodded in the direction of the apartment. "How'd it go?"

"Fine. Grace Cameron is an excellent witness. They told me something that may be relevant."

Quickly I filled him about Maria Salamonica's complaint. He frowned. "Doesn't sound credible to me. If the old biddy was doolally, a man tickling her could have just been wishful thinking."

So much for sensitivity.

"It's odd she would say, 'tickling.' Doris told Grace that her assailant stroked her."

He loosened his tie. "Why is it always so frigging hot in these places? I suppose you could be right, God forbid. It could be the same chappie doing his cute number. Disgusting, if you ask me." He licked his lips. "I'd ply my arse for a bottle of beer right now."

"Do you want me to get you a coffee or a glass of water? It isn't daylight yet."

A swift stab to the fat gut but he was impervious. "Don't forget, I've been up all night. It's a nightcap I'm talking about."

I bit my tongue. "I'll say goodbye to them."

I went back into the apartment and Franklin was at my heels.

"Hello, ladies. Detective Sergeant Franklin at your service. I hope Detective Morris has been treating you well."

They both eyed him in astonishment.

"Very well," said Dr. Cowan.

I turned to Grace while Franklin stared around the apartment.

"I think we're done for now, Miss Cameron. Would you like Mrs. Cheevers to get hold of your sister?"

She looked quite wretched but she managed a smile. "Perhaps that would be best. I don't suppose you can spare a strong young officer to take me there, can you?"

Franklin's voice suddenly escaped the leash and he practically bellowed at her. "Of course I can. Don't you worry about a thing, he'll make sure you're all tucked up safe and sound."

I wondered how a frail elderly woman could help but worry when she had faced down a man trying to break into her apartment and heard the anguish of her dear friend's rape, all within two days. I wished we had a platoon of muscular officers to take care of her until the end of her days.

CHAPTER FORTY-ONE

Franklin and I went down to the lounge.

"We'll need to change the locks on the outside doors immediately," he boomed at me. "And try to track down every key that has been issued. I don't want this pervert coming back here."

Statistically, the chances were low that would happen. Typically, rapists and killers prowled, not returning to the same building immediately. But it wasn't unknown and I was all for protecting these residents in any way we could.

"Let's see what the supers have to say," said Franklin.

The couple in question were sitting side by side on the couch in the lobby. They were no spring chickens themselves. He was clad in blue denim overalls and she was wearing what would have been called in the fifties a house dress, flowered, loose, and even from where I was, didn't look too clean.

Franklin introduced both of us. Neither of them moved from the couch but eyed us warily. When the man spoke his voice was surly and aggrieved. I hoped this was merely pseudo-aggression from fear and not evidence of utter callousness.

"The wife and me have got our work to do. I hope you're not going to keep us long."

"As long as it takes," said Franklin with what I'd have to call a wolfish grin.

He held out his arm to indicate they should come into the office and reluctantly they stood up and went in. As they went by me, I was hit by the smell of stale cigarettes and booze with a powerful overlay of garlic.

They'd hardly sat down when Franklin launched into them. I might have felt sorry for them as Franklin was treating them with an abruptness that bordered on rude, but they gave back in kind. Mr. Desjardins did most of the talking and spoke belligerently. He had no idea how many keys were in circulation, could be hundreds. Residents were always losing their keys. Beside that, they handed them out to family members. Yes, there was a master key which opened both the outside doors, front and back, and the individual apartments. He was always being called out because some dippy old lady had forgotten her key. Being a super meant you had no life at all. Always at their beck and call. There were actually two master keys. One never left his side. He pulled out an enormous key ring, which jangled like Marley's ball and chain. The social worker had the other. Mrs. Chester or Chesley or something. When asked if he had checked to see if the building was secure last night, he answered vehemently that of course he had. He always did, eleven on the dot. All was snug as a bug in a rug, he'd swear on his mother's grave. Unfortunate choice of words. His wife popped a piece of raw garlic into her mouth, and realizing I'd noticed she grinned at me. "Keeps away colds," she said. Not to mention people, I thought, and it's a great cover for whisky breath.

Franklin brought up the homeless man Mrs. Moseley had encountered in the lounge and the two young men the super had tossed out of a lunch. "Them," said Desjardins with contempt. "Two Russkies in need of a meal. Or so they says but they left pronto when I read them the riot act. As for the old rubby Mrs M. met up with, his brain was too pickled for him to be a danger to anybody. Even sober he could hardly stand."

Franklin asked them about Mrs. Salamonica.

"Before our time," answered Mrs. Desjardins. "We came here in July of this year."

"Who was the superintendent before you?" I asked.

"Some fellow did it with his boyfriend." Mrs. Desjardins managed to convey her distaste of that relationship. "It's a thankless job and they want blood and won't pay enough to keep a dog alive so there's a big turnover. We took the job but probably shouldn't have because all that vacuuming aggravates his back. But there you go."

"Were you both in each other's presence all night?" Franklin asked. They stared at him blankly, not realizing the implications of the question.

"We was asleep if that's what you mean. We watched some television until about eleven-thirty then we went to bed and didn't stir until we was woken up by this officer."

I was inclined to believe them. Mr. Desjardins didn't fit the description that Doris had given to Grace Cameron. You couldn't pretend that kind of post-binge befuddlement and the man who had molested Doris was not drunk. I did wonder about the disinfectant smell but thought it would not likely be confused with alcohol.

That was about it. Mrs. Desjardins in particular was morbidly curious about what had actually been done to Doris but Franklin was tight-lipped. I forgave him a lot for that.

Finally we dismissed them with strict instructions to bring in a locksmith as soon as possible. Franklin wrinkled his nose in disgust before they had even closed the door.

"Jesus wept, where did they find those two? I wouldn't want a relative of mine living here."

I certainly agreed with him. The one solid piece of information the Desjardins had given us was that it was pathetically easy to gain access to the residence.

Edith Cowan, bless her heart, had sent down more tea and a plate of toast and jam for us. Franklin had ordered in two large pizzas with everything but my stomach still said breakfast and the toast went down nicely.

The next three hours were difficult. Franklin had assigned another young female constable to sit in on the interviews and keep a second set of notes for me. Most of the residents were women and even though I tempered what I said, there was no way to avoid telling them that Doris had been assaulted. She had been well-liked and the shock and sorrow of her death and the circumstances surrounding it were overwhelming to many of the residents. Fortunately, Mrs. Cheevers had worked quickly and efficiently and family members, anxious, hassled, began to arrive. I was glad when several of them decided to whisk away their elderly residents.

We took names and addresses and noted who had keys. Nobody had reported a lost key but once again it was obvious that there were possibly dozens in circulation. I was rapidly ruling out stranger rape. Our bad guy was somewhere in this circle, however wide it might appear.

My last interview was with Mrs. Cheevers. She had actually anticipated the matter of the keys and came with a file folder containing names of residents and next of kin, previous superintendents, home care workers, social workers, anybody who had access to the building as far back as three years ago when she said they'd had new locks installed that were considered safer. This was an invaluable list and I handed it over to Franklin. He riffled through the sheets. He looked miserable but who knows if it was just him thinking about his bottle of cold beer.

"This could be like catching fleas on a black dog. But I'll get some of the guys onto it. Do you want a copy?"

"Sure."

I thought he was hoping I'd cast my eye over it and magically come up with a name. Save him a lot of work.

"You never know, these funny cases might be connected."

"Funny cases?"

"You know, raping old ladies, killing deaf girls."

The coroner hadn't thought Deidre had been sexually assaulted but I didn't feel like going into that with him.

He yawned, hardly bothering to cover his mouth. "You know where to find me if you get any insights. Whose got your other case?"

"Ed Chaffey."

"He's a good man. We're in the same bowling league."

I wondered if I could talk Ed into dropping a bowling ball on Franklin's foot.

I decided to have a look around a bit more before I left. Grace had asked, "Why Doris? Who would want to hurt an old lady?" Unfortunately victims can be any age. There was one notorious case that I'd studied as part of my training. It had occurred in the United States, where a man preyed exclusively on elderly women who all lived in one particular apartment complex. He'd gone undetected for a long time.

I took the ever so slow elevator again to the second floor and just as I exited, I saw a couple of forensics leaving the apartment. They were androgynous in their white bunny suits, which covered everything except for the face. However, one of them pulled back the hood and shook out her long hair. She introduced herself as Sandy Zarowny.

"How's it going?"

She shrugged. "It's hard to say. The victim took a shower and the bathroom is pristine so there's no joy there. We're hoping for something from the wheelchair. Joanne's pulled several good latents and we'll check them out."

The other person, a female, also now hoodless, nodded. "We've put a requisition in to the hospital to hold the clothes. We might be able to get something from them."

"He got in no problem," said the first woman. "There's no scratch on the door jamb. There's a screen on the windows and you couldn't get up there anyway without a ladder. Either he had a key or she let him in."

Doris had told Grace the man appeared behind her as she came out of the bathroom. She hadn't let him in. However, she could have left the door unlocked, in which case his choice of her apartment might be random. He'd entered the first place he found accessible. On the other hand, it is quite possible he had a key and we were back to, "Why Doris?"

I'd been holding the elevator door for them and Sandy looked at it. She sighed.

"I suppose we should dust the panel but it's going to be smothered in prints and it'll be murder to get anything clear."

A forensic's job is not an easy one, that's for sure.

"We were just going out for a smoke," she said. "We'll do it when we come back."

I left them to it and walked down the hall. Doris's apartment was next to the fire exit and the stairs. Had the rapist come that way? I'd guess he had. An elevator was too chancy. There was another apartment directly opposite to Doris's. There was a pine wreath hanging on the door which said Bring on the Snow. A cheery snowman beamed out at the world. Gently, I turned the door handle. It was locked. I was about to knock but decided against it. Franklin was taking care of all of that.

I shoved open the heavy fire door and went into the stairwell. Dust bunnies filled the corners. Somebody had spilled coffee and left the Styrofoam cup on the stairs. So much for the Desjardins's cleaning standards. I continued on down to the ground level. That exit opened directly into the backyard, currently drab and rain soaked in the November gloom. In the summer it must be a pleasant space for the residents to get some sun, but not now.

Unfortunately, all I could see was how private it was, how perfect for an intruder to enter unnoticed. A high wooden fence enclosed the area that was asphalt, and benches were grouped in a semicircle around a stone patio, in the centre of which was a fountain. Mature evergreens stood in each corner, and several iron bird cages hung from the tree branches. Near the gate was a Victorian lamp and tucked into one corner was a large yellow doghouse with the word *Nana* painted over the opening. I looked around and sure enough Peter Pan himself was poised nearby in the shrubbery, a finger to his lips as he prepared to lead a stony Wendy and Michael and Peter to Never-Never Land. I took a peek inside the doghouse but there wasn't anything noteworthy that I could see, just a dry wooden floor.

I walked over to the gate, which wasn't locked, and stepped through into an alleyway that ran parallel to the residence. A high brick wall, that looked as if it was at the end of somebody's garden ran along one side, the residence fence the other. To my left was a ramshackle garage; to the right; was the alley, which ran only a couple of hundred feet past more garages before connecting with a wider one, which I assumed led to the main street. There was one light hanging on the wall near the gate but the glass was smashed. Secluded, dark, it was the perfect entry for a clandestine approach.

I didn't have time to do more than a cursory examination but there were no telltale clues. No monogrammed handkerchiefs, no conveniently bloodstained nail to give DNA. Nothing in the alley except the usual detritus you'd expect to find in a place nobody cared about: sodden newspapers blown up against the garage wall, discarded candy wrappers, a mound of cigarette butts near one of the garage, dog feces. Nevertheless it was an area that the forensics should examine thoroughly. There was no doubt in my mind this was where the rapist had entered. I went back to find the young smokers and tell them.

CHAPTER FORTY-TWO

I'd just got into my car when my cellphone chirruped. It was Ed Chaffey.

"Chris, we've made contact with Sigmund Forgach."

"Way to go! Where was he?"

"At home. He said he had a headache and wasn't answering his phone. I've asked him to come in for an interview. He asked if he could come to the Centre. Hey, I don't care if we see him in the public washroom. Will you do it? I got in touch with Ray Motomochi and he'll assist."

"Fantastic. Does Katherine know?"

"She does and she's informing Dr. Forgach. And by the way, we have some interesting intelligence from the security guard in young Mr. Forgach's building. We thought we'd do a bit of casual checking and according to him, the Mazda was parked early on. He said he saw it just after nine-thirty *but* the Chevy Nova was not in its regular parking space until at least three o'clock in the morning."

"Gotcha."

"The kid's going to be there at one. Call me as soon as you're done with him."

I can't say I was exactly looking forward to this but I was tremendously relieved that at least Sigmund hadn't done a bunk.

Interviews tended to be conducted differently depending on the situation — who was the subject, what we knew about them, and so on. Sometimes the best approach was casual and friendly:

"Would you like a coffee" or "Miserable weather we're having," sort of thing, if we thought it important for the subject to let down their guard. Other times, the most powerful tool was silence or a non-communicative interviewer who let the subject stew.

Neither Ray nor Sigmund was talking when I entered. Ray had got his "inscrutable oriental" face on, as he called it, and Sigmund was looking cowed and miserable. He glanced up anxiously but when he saw it was only me he relaxed. I guessed he'd feared it was his father entering.

"Good afternoon, Sergeant Morris," he said and held out his hand. His palm was so moist I had to resist the impulse to wipe my hand on my jacket. Innocent people are often nervous when they are sitting in a police station being questioned about a serious crime, but I'd yet to see a person pure as the driven snow who was this uneasy. Sigmund was suffering from a bad attack of nerves and 90 percent of the time that meant the interviewee had a guilty conscience about something or other. I was about to open up that pocket of emotional pus.

I sat down across from him. "Mr. Forgach, I guess Sergeant Motomochi filled you in on why we wanted to talk to you?"

I was deliberately adopting a formal stance. Frankly I felt I needed the security of the usual protocol.

"No, not really." Sigmund glanced over at Ray, who was looking down at an open notebook he'd placed on the table. "I assume you are creating an in-depth character analysis or something like that." He gave a small giggle, perhaps realizing what he said sounded like a bank credit check. Even though it was Saturday, he'd chosen to wear his banking clothes, white shirt and dark tie, a smart navy suit with a pinstripe, cut skilfully to hide his slight paunch.

"We were trying to reach you all day yesterday."

I let that sit there for a moment.

He pursed his lips, the thoughts flashing through his mind almost palpable. We must know that he hadn't been at the bank.

"Yes, well as I told Sergeant Chaffey, I didn't check my voice mail until this morning. As soon as I realized you wanted to talk to me, I came straight away."

"I understand that your mother was under the impression you were at a seminar and your bank thought you were home sick. Do you mind telling me where you were?"

Again I could virtually see the rapid sorting out of his words. He was dancing like a drop of oil on a hot griddle, as Al Jackson would say. He gave me a grin that was intended to be disarming but looked furtive.

"I needed a mental health day. Mother is a, er, worrier. If I'd said that she would have made me go to the emergency ward or back to bed so I, er, I thought it was simpler for everybody if I said I was at a seminar."

"What did you do instead?"

"Nothing much. Drove around. Had lunch. Sat in the park."

"Which park was that?"

He rubbed his hands together in what I thought was a Lady Macbeth sort of way. Guilt.

"I didn't really notice. It was just some small park by the lake ... I didn't stay in Barrie. As you can imagine I didn't want to run into anybody I knew, so I, er, I drove over here. That is, in this direction, and stopped at a park off the highway."

"How far would you say you had driven before you went into the park?"

"Oh, er. I wasn't paying much attention. Perhaps half an hour or so."

I knew there was nothing that could be called a park off the highway but I let that pass for now.

"So you said you stayed in the park for a while, enjoying nature." I smiled falsely. "You must certainly be a nature lover as it was a miserable day yesterday. It rained most of the day, didn't it?"

He shrugged. "When you work indoors all day like I do, rain can be refreshing. I had an umbrella and a warm coat. I was all right."

"How long would you say you spent in this park?"

"An hour maybe. It's hard to say."

"But you walked around?"

"Yes, that's right. There was a trail that I followed."

I looked at my notebook. Ray was staring straight ahead. I noticed Sigmund glancing at him uneasily. I could understand why. His silence was unnerving.

"All right, Mr. Forgach. Let me just get my times right. What time do you usually leave for work?"

"Eight o'clock. I am expected to be at my desk at eight-thirty."

"Was that the time you left the house yesterday?"

"No. A bit later than that. Nine o'clock perhaps."

"And you drove for approximately half an hour to the park, where you walked around for about an hour. That takes us up to 10:30 ... then you went for lunch?"

He gave me a sickly grin. "Sounds more like breakfast, doesn't it?"

Sounds like a lie to me, I thought.

"And where did you have this meal?"

"Some diner on the edge of town ... I don't remember the name of it. It was one of those anonymous ma-and-pa places."

"Could you find it again?"

He pretended to think. "You know, strange as this sounds, I don't think I could. I just stopped the car at the first place I saw."

Ray intervened. "If you were coming in from Barrie, you must have been on Highway 11. There's a strip mall just on the edge of town. Was that were you stopped?"

"Er, yes, possibly it was. As I said, I wasn't paying much attention."

"What did you have to eat?"

"Bacon and eggs. There, it was a breakfast, wasn't it?"

My turn. Ray and I in a dance we'd practised before. "What car were you driving?"

"My own car."

"A red Mazda Miata, I understand."

"That's right." He was slumping further down in his chair.

"I understand you have a second car, a Chevy Nova?"

He coughed. "It's my mother's car really."

"Do you drive it?"

"Sometimes."

I hung that one up for now.

Ray now. "How long did you stay in the restaurant, Mr. Forgach?"

"About an hour, more or less."

"Did you talk to anybody?"

"Just the waitress. The place was quite empty." Again the sickly smile. "I'm not surprised, the food was terrible."

"Did you pay cash or by credit card?"

"Cash."

"Do you remember how much the meal cost?"

"Er, no. It was quite cheap really. Five dollars and change."

Me, now. "Did you keep the bill?"

"No, I didn't."

"And what did you do after you left the restaurant?"

"I drove around and then came home."

"But you didn't pick up your messages until this morning?"

"That's right. I felt I wanted a quiet night all to myself, so I didn't check."

Ray actually smiled at him. "That takes discipline. Me, I can't resist for one minute seeing who's called if that red light is flashing."

Sigmund eyed him warily.

I took up the lead again. "Did your mother know you were home?"

"No, she didn't. She goes to bed early and I didn't want to disturb her."

"What time would you say you were back in the house?"

Sigmund Forgach was getting a harried, trapped look. He was trying to be one step ahead of us and he was starting to chase his own tail.

"I'm not sure. It was after ten because my mother was already in bed... Close to midnight, I suppose."

I consulted my notes. "We have you leaving a diner, unnamed, at about eleven-thirty or noon. You arrive home about midnight. That leaves eleven hours unaccounted for. What were you doing in those eleven hours?"

For the first time, he became a tad belligerent.

"Look, I've been pretty accommodating to date, because I know you've got a job to do, let's not forget I'm the son of a crime specialist."

Got that one, Sig.

"However, I don't see the relevance of these questions. What I choose to do with a day off surely has no bearing on what happened to Deidre?"

I waited a moment. "Perhaps you can allow me to be the judge of that. I wonder, Mr. Forgach..."

"Please call me Sig. You're making me feel like a criminal. You know my father. Surely for his sake you can let go of the formality?"

I couldn't do that, of course, not with what was already on the table, but I thought that Sig would relax more if he thought we were applying collegiate rules.

"Sig, as you say, your own father has been with the criminal division for many years. I know you haven't lived together since you were a child but like most people these days, I'm sure you have some knowledge of police procedure. We have found a couple of discrepancies in your statement."

I took out a Jessica's interpretation from my file folder and placed it on the table.

"Previously, you told us that you had not encountered Deidre since you were both children, is that right?"

"We were corresponding by email."

"But you had not met in person?"

He lowered his eyes quickly. "Correct."

"We had a lip reader interpret the conversation between you and Deidre at the casino. It seems quite obvious that you had a previous encounter. She knew who you were, you knew who she was. How would you explain that?"

"Ah… well, we'd exchanged photos. I knew she'd be where she was because she'd told me so. We had a bit of a chat. Quite friendly and above board. I invited her to go for a drink but she was on a winning streak and she wanted to stay at the table. I decided not to wait and left."

"And you drove back to Barrie?"

"Yes."

"How long did that take you?"

"About forty minutes, give or take."

Ray's turn. "You came a long way for a five-minute chat, didn't you?"

He shrugged. "I'm used to it, gives me a chance to run the car on the highway."

I did the notes consultation thing. "Ah yes. Speaking of cars. Sergeant, do you have that file we received from the casino security?" Ray handed it to me. "We have a record here that a Chevy Nova registered in the name of Trudy Forgach was clocked in as entering the casino at 10:41. Was that your mother?"

He guffawed involuntarily. "My mother at the casino? No way."

"But you said it was her car. Who was driving?"

He drummed his fingers on the table. "I was."

"I am correct in saying then that you first arrived at the casino driving your own car, a bright red Mazda Miata, then you drove all the way back to Barrie, got your mother's car, a beige Chevy, turned around and re-entered the casino about an hour and a half later?"

His expression had turned sullen. He was actually pouting. "You have that information in front of you, why are you asking me?"

"I'm just trying to verify it."

"Consider it verified."

Ray stepped in. "Why did you do that, Sig?"

"That's easy. I went home like I said but I felt badly that I'd left Deidre in the lurch, as it were. My own car was feeling a bit sluggish so I decided to take the old reliable."

"Did you see Deidre this second time?"

"No. She had already left."

"How did you know that? We don't show you entering the building at all."

Suddenly, his eyes welled with tears and he said in a little boy voice, "I'd like to speak to my father."

CHAPTER FORTY-THREE

Legally there was no reason why Sigmund couldn't have his father present. We hadn't charged him with anything. I left him where he was and went to phone Leo. I didn't tell him what had transpired so far and he didn't ask. Better it be fresh, a lot can be caught when a subject is asked to repeat their story. He said he'd be right over and I returned to the interview room. Sig had his head in his hands and a more miserable-looking man I'd hardly ever seen.

"He'll be here in about twenty minutes. Can I get you a coffee?"

He looked up at me. "I'd prefer tea if you have it."

"I'll get it," said Ray, and he pushed his chair back quickly. I guess he'd had enough of being inscrutable for now. As soon as the door closed, Sig straightened up, and with a quick unconscious gesture, he smoothed his hair down and patted at his tie. He was preparing for Leo.

"I didn't kill Deidre, no matter what you think."

I didn't answer but said as sympathetically as I could muster, "This must be very difficult for you."

"You don't know the half of it." His tone was petulant. The overly polite nervous nice guy had vanished and I wondered how often and to how many people he showed this other side of himself.

"I'm all ears," I smiled at him. He regarded me warily.

"No, I'm not going to say anything until my father is here." Even saying the word *father* seemed to throw him into yet another mood and I thought for a minute he was going to break into tears.

"Do you get along well with your father, Miss Morris?"

Hmm... That took me off guard. If he only knew.

"My father doesn't live here."

How's that for a non-committal answer.

He didn't seem to notice and said, "Are your parents divorced?"

"No."

Not even married yet.

"My parents divorced when I was a kid, and to be frank with you, it has been like living in a war zone ever since. I can't say I have a relationship with my father... He was too busy helping other people's kids to do much with his own..." Wow, the bile would have curdled milk. He tried to pull back the shreds of his nicey-nicey mask. "I know he's a good man, a very good man who does really important work, but my mother ... er, well, you might say, she has tended to view me as a hostage. She gets very upset, really, really upset, if I have anything to do with him or that other side of the family."

Leo had told us as much earlier. I wasn't sure where this was leading but again I nodded. Better to keep him talking.

"You probably don't understand what it's like, Miss Morris. I would guess that your own home life has been a loving and stable one."

I almost choked on that one but I wasn't about to take him up on it.

"You have that air about you," he said. "I can always tell."

Such utter bullshit. He probably thought it was a line women liked to hear.

"However, as I was saying, it must be hard to understand the situation of someone who hasn't experienced that."

I'd had enough. "I don't think I'd make a very good police officer if I couldn't empathize with people who come from very different backgrounds."

My tone must have made him nervous. "Yes, yes, of course, I didn't mean to imply that you don't do a very good job. I'm sure you do. It's just that..."

He was saved from finally twisting himself into a pretzel by the return of Ray carrying a tray with a Styrofoam cup and a saucer of creamers and sugars.

"Here you go. I didn't know how you take it, so I brought the works."

"Thank you so much, I really appreciate this."

"You have a call waiting, Sergeant." He slipped me a yellow Post-it Note from the reception. "Your mother is on the phone. Says it's urgent."

So much for evidence of a loving stable home. I jumped up without even thinking about it. My usual reflex action to Joan's demands that I thought I'd conquered. Obviously not.

"Did you say she's waiting on the phone?" I asked Ray quietly.

"That's what Andrea said."

Sig was doctoring up his tea, triple-triple by the look of it.

"I have to take a call. I'll be right back."

I headed for my office, scooting past the reception desk. We had a part-time girl on at weekends, a student from the community college. She was talking into her mouthpiece and mouthed at me, "Line one."

Joan had learned some time ago that an easier way to get hold of me was through the office rather than my cellphone where she knew I could see who was calling and respond accordingly. In her opinion, cavalierly.

I grabbed the receiver and closed the door behind me.

"Hello."

"Christine, this is your mother."

"What is it? I'm in the middle of something. I was told this call was urgent."

I made no attempt to soften my tone of voice, too many cries of wolf throughout my life.

"It is. I wouldn't disturb you if it wasn't. I just wanted to let you know that we have decided to postpone the wedding until next spring."

I felt a flood of relief. That let me off the hook. Gill could come here for his two weeks and I wouldn't have to leave Paula.

"That sounds like a good idea. The weather will be better."

"Aye." Joan was reverting more and more to her old dialect the longer she lived in her homeland. "I wanted you to know right away in case you made a booking. You haven't, have you?"

"No. Not to worry."

There was a pause and I knew her well enough to know that the real reason for the call was coming up.

"Duncan didn't want me to be disappointed seeing as how I was looking forward to the cruise so he said, 'Why don't we just go over to Canada and see our daughter? We can spend Christmas with Christine and New Year's with the other kids.'"

Oh no. I didn't say that out loud but I might as well have. She slipped into the "now you've hurt my feelings" reproachful tone that had me jumping out of my skin.

"I thought you'd like that, Chris. We've no spent a Christmas together for years."

Coward that I was, I avoided answering her. "I only get a couple of days off."

"That's all right. We can do some sightseeing on our own. Duncan is very excited to see the country. We'll just fit around your schedule."

Like hell she would. Joan was constitutionally unable to adapt to anybody else's life if it didn't suit her. And what about Gill? Would she insist on him going with them? I'd been looking forward to having him waiting at home for me with a nice home-cooked meal on the stove and my slippers by the fire.

Fortunately I was saved by a knock at the door. Leo stuck his head in. I waved for him to hold on.

"I've got to go now, Joan. I'll call you later when I get home and we can talk more about it."

"Not too late. You know we're six hours ahead of you."

I managed not to explode into a sarcastic rejoinder. "Yes, I am aware of that."

She was really huffy now. "I'll tell your father you sent your love."

"Do that."

She hung up. I didn't slam down the receiver but must have communicated the impulse to Leo.

"Problems?"

"Minor."

And they were in comparison to his.

"What's happening, Chris? I haven't been in yet. How's Sigmund?"

I knew what he needed to know but it was very awkward.

"There are inconsistencies in his statement, Leo. When I pushed him on it, he got very upset and said he wanted to talk to you."

"What do you want me to do?"

"Hear what he has to say, I guess. He hasn't asked for a lawyer and hasn't been charged with anything but..."

"He's lying."

I bit my lip. "It seems that way."

"What's he said so far?"

I told him and he frowned.

"So there are two holes. First off he obviously had made contact with Deidre before he showed up at the casino..."

"That's what it looks like to me. He keeps saying they were in touch by email."

"Bullshit. They'd already met before Tuesday."

"The big problem is that he never said anything about coming back in the Nova."

"Did you ask him about the security guard saying the Chevy wasn't in the garage at three o'clock?'

"Not yet."

"Did he say what he was up to yesterday?"

"His story is very thin. He says he went out for a drive but we've got at least eleven hours unaccounted for."

Leo pinched the bridge of his nose between his fingers, a gesture I'd seen him make many times but I thought this time he was trying to force back tears.

"He's a good kid, Chris. He gets on people's nerves but I don't think he's capable of..."

He didn't finish his sentence. He didn't have to. I reached over and squeezed his arm.

"Come on, let's go and talk to him."

CHAPTER FORTY-FOUR

Sigmund looked up when we entered. "Hello, Dad. We're in a mess, aren't we?"

He was so wan and looked so vulnerable, I half-expected him to climb into Leo's lap. His father, however, was hardly warm and welcoming. He took the chair at the far end of the table and sat down.

"You said you couldn't talk until I was here. Well here I am. What do you have to say for yourself?"

Ray reached for the record button on the tape. "Ready?"

Sig nodded miserably. He couldn't really go back on what he'd said about talking when his father was here. Even though the questioning was still being considered unofficial, we could record the interviews with permission.

"I haven't been quite up front with you all. I did go back home after seeing Deidre. That's absolutely true, but I came back." He ducked his head. "Well you know all that, don't you?"

"Did you see her this second time?" Ray asked.

"Yes, I did. She was actually standing by her car. She had a flat tire. She said she needed to get into town in a hurry. She was meeting some guy at Memorial Park ... so I gave her a ride. I dropped her off just at the top of the park. And that's the truth, I swear."

I took over. "Sig, do you know who she was to meet with?"

He turned to me gratefully. "No. It was hard to communicate with her so we were both pretty silent on the way down. I asked her. I was wondering who was so important but she just wouldn't answer. She got me to let her off and that was that."

"What time was this?"

"By the time we got there it was almost a quarter past eleven."

"Did she meet anybody?"

"Not that I saw. She headed down to the monument and I drove off."

"Did you notice if there was a car parked by the pier?"

"I couldn't see that far."

"It was late, didn't you worry about her?" Leo spoke before I could stop him and his voice would have taken off wallpaper.

"Not really. I mean I know she was deaf and all that but she seemed pretty independent. I just thought she'd meet her fellow and that was it. Besides, if she'd missed him, she wasn't that far from home. She could get a taxi if she had to."

"And that was the last you saw of her?"

He lowered his head. "Yes. I'm sorry, Dad."

I sat back in my chair. If we could believe him, we'd got a tiny piece in the puzzle. We could concentrate the search for witnesses more closely.

Ray's turn now. "After you left Deidre, what did you do?"

Sig fiddled with the crumpled sugar paper. "Nothing really. That is, I went home. It was a work day the next day. I wanted to get to sleep."

"What time did you get to your apartment?" Ray again.

"Gosh, I'm not sure. I wasn't paying attention."

"Ballpark. Midnight? One? Two?"

"Well, let me see, it's a forty- to forty-five-minute drive, so if I left Deidre at eleven-fifteen, I'd be home by midnight."

"Can your mother confirm this?"

"No, I don't think so, she was already in bed. She likes to get to bed early. She always says she needs her beauty sleep."

He gave a quick sideways glance to his father, trying to rope him into an alliance against Trudy. Leo didn't bite. He was staring at a spot on the wall beyond his son.

I continued. "We have a statement from the security guard at your condo, a Mr. Meadows. He is willing to swear that the Chevy wasn't in its parking spot before three o'clock."

"Ah. Well you know what? That's quite right. I was tired and decided to park in the outside lot until morning."

The lie was as transparent as tissue paper.

"We'll follow up on that."

I sat back in my chair. "Why didn't you say at the beginning that you had picked up Deidre?"

Sig twisted the sugar packet into a tight spool. "I didn't think it mattered. I had nothing to do with what happened and I figured you'd find out soon enough who did it then..." he stopped.

"Then what?"

"Nothing. It's just that I was sure you'd find the guilty party. It's what you do, isn't it? Solve crimes?"

Whoa. That poisonous dart flew across the room.

"Good Lord, I can't believe what I'm hearing," Leo exploded. He was so angry he jumped to his feet and his chair went crashing backward in an unintended dramatic gesture. Sig flinched. "Do you realize what you've done? You could be charged with obstruction of justice. Are you a complete idiot? You must have known this was crucial information for the investigation." Leo was red in the face. "Why? What's the real reason? You were about to say, 'You'd find out soon enough and then...' Then WHAT?"

Sig looked as if he were about to sink under the table. "Then Mom wouldn't need to know."

I flashed a warning glance at Leo which I don't know if he even saw.

"Are you afraid of your mother, Sig?" I asked.

"Not afraid exactly, afraid of upsetting her. Her nerves are terrible and well..."

His voice tailed off but I got the picture. She made his life miserable. Leo was staring at his son in disbelief but he was the one who'd described Trudy as a marshmallow with sharp teeth.

Leo righted his chair and sat down again. I turned to Sig and smiled reassuringly at him.

"Can you say more about that, Sig? You didn't want your mother to know that you'd had any contact at all with your sister, is that what you mean?"

He nodded gratefully. "That's right. She would have freaked if she'd known. She saw it as betrayal of the worst kind."

"But in fact you met with Deidre before you saw her at the casino, didn't you?"

"Yes. Sorry. You're right. She sent me an email about a month ago. Out of the blue. I mean I was stunned. She said she had a daughter now and she'd like her to know her own blood. She invited me to come to the house and I could meet her. So I did. I was curious myself as to what the fuss was all about."

"That was on Monday?"

"That's right. I mean she is a cute kid but given the state of the nation with my mother I didn't know what I could do. The kid's deaf too so I don't know what we'd accomplish. Deidre was disappointed, naturally. That's why I said I'd think about it and she said she was always at the casino on Tuesday nights if I changed my mind."

He took up another sugar packet and started to twist it tight.

I thought of Joy and how easy it was to communicate with her. He would be missing out on a lot.

"Why didn't you say you'd seen Dee only the night before when I called to tell you she was dead?"

Leo's voice had gone ice cold. Again I intervened. "Was it the same reason as you just gave? You were afraid your mother would know?"

"Yes." He gave a smile that was tinged with shame. "I'm totally embarrassed to admit how much of my life is governed by my fear of my mother's reaction but I'm afraid it is."

I liked him a lot better for the honesty but he'd gone back to staring at the clock on the wall.

"Do you want to revise your description of your day yesterday?"

He sighed and his eyes flickered over to Leo. It wasn't only his mother he was afraid of, poor guy.

"Will my mother have to know what I say?"

"Not necessarily."

"She's a mite possessive of me, as I've said. Understandable in the circumstances. Single mother and all that." He wasn't so afraid he couldn't send another dart in Leo's direction. And I saw it landed and hurt. Sig drew in his breath, and like a diver on the edge of a very cold pool, he held his nose and jumped in. Or should I say a very hot pool?

"Because of our circumstances, my mother has tended to be overprotective and I, er, haven't really had, shall we say, much to do with the opposite sex. The ladies," he added for my benefit in case I was offended by the term *opposite sex*. "However, I am in every respect a man with, begging your pardon, Miss Morris, with normal appetites and needs…"

"For Christ's sake, get to the point, Sigmund," interrupted Leo.

Sig's mouth tightened into a hurt pout. "I am getting to the point. This is the point. I do have a lady friend but mother doesn't know about it. I was with my friend yesterday."

"Does she have a name or do you make her wear a bag over her head?"

That was cruel and Sig flushed painfully. "Her name is Natasha."

"Surname?"

Sig looked as if he hoped the floor would open up and swallow him. "I don't know what it is, I'm afraid. She's Russian and, well, her last name is difficult to pronounce."

"How long have you known her?"

"About six months. I told mother I was taking a course at the college so I have a legitimate reason to be away one evening a week. I also visited her on Tuesday night after I let off Deidre."

"We'll need to speak to her," I said. "Given the circumstances, we'll need to verify your whereabouts."

"Of course."

"What is her address?"

Again Sig squirmed in a fit of embarrassment. "To tell the truth, we don't meet at her home and I don't know where she lives."

Suddenly Leo slapped his hand on the table. "My god, manly needs and appetites indeed. What is she, a stripper?"

Sig nodded miserably. "She works at the Atherley Arms strip bar. I meet her there. She's a very nice person."

"I'm sure she is," said Leo, conveying just the opposite. He leaned forward and glared at poor Sigmund. "Is that it then? Do we now have the whole sorry story or is there something else you haven't yet said?"

"No, that's it. I was with Natasha all day and went with her to the strip club in the evening. I got home about 3:00 a.m. I also went to see her on Tuesday night after I left Deidre."

"So you didn't tell us the truth about coming straight home? Mr. Meadows was right about the Chevy not being in the parking space."

"Er ... yes." Suddenly he buried his head in his hands. "I'm sorry I've let you down, Dad. I just get so scared sometimes. What with you and Mom, I can't do anything right..."

I felt really bad for the guy and Ray was shifting uncomfortably in his seat. Leo was transfixed and as far as I could see was completely unmoved by his son's distress. In fact his expression was one of contempt. He stood up. I thought for a minute he was going to go over and comfort Sigmund but he didn't. He headed straight for the door.

"I don't think you need me anymore. I'll be in my office."

Sig howled in an anguish that was genuine even if it was totally self-centred. I reached over to the box of tissues in the middle of the table, pulled one out, and stuffed it into his hand.

CHAPTER FORTY-FIVE

Sigmund must have cried for half an hour non-stop. I felt as if he was crying out tears that he'd buried all of his life. He kept repeating over and over, "I'm sorry, I'm so sorry." He wasn't noisy but the anguish was palpable and heart-rending. After about ten minutes of it, Ray slipped away. No sense in two of us staring at the poor guy. I just kept feeding Sig tissues. He was a wet crier and was using up a lot of them. Finally, he slowed down. He'd rubbed his eyes swollen and red and mucus was trailing down his nose to his mouth.

"He'll never forgive me, will he?"

I knew he meant Leo of course and he was probably right.

"If only I'd driven her down to the dock and waited with her. But she didn't seem to want me to, I swear she didn't. It all seemed sort of hush-hush."

I could at least reassure him on that count given what I now knew about her appointment with Zachary Taylor and the probable reason for it.

He heard me out but it didn't really soothe him. He was hell-bent on self-flagellation and nothing would deter him.

Finally, I gripped his fist in mine hard and made him meet my eyes.

"Sigmund, one of the hardest parts of being a police officer is the 'if only.' 'If only I hadn't locked the door on her when she broke her curfew.' 'If only I followed my instincts and not let her go to that supposed photo shoot.' I could fill a book with 'if only's' but all it does is rub the wound raw. Parents, spouses, friends. Most people who have been touched by violent crime reproach themselves. But we're not God. Sure sometimes people are careless, callous even, but mostly they're not, they're just ordinary people going about their lives. The one responsible is the one who does the killing, does the rape, or commits the assault." I must have been speaking with some intensity because I got his attention. "Sure, if you had taken Deidre down to the pier and waited, you might have prevented a murder, but we don't know for sure. And we will never know."

He had an expression on his face that I'd seen on Chelsea's when I tried to reassure her that the things in her life that were spinning out of control weren't hers to worry about. That was for grown-ups. He managed a smile. "Thanks. You're talking to me as if you think I'm innocent and I appreciate that. I was afraid that even my own father suspected me."

He was correct on both counts. When the whole sorry story had come tumbling out I had believed him. Besides, his alibi was going to be very easy to check. He withdrew his hand so he could get yet another tissue and wipe his nose. I waited while he mopped up.

Not unusual in situations like this, he looked exhausted.

"Is there anybody you'd like to be with? You've gone through quite an ordeal. Your mother is here. She's at your father's condo."

"Oh God no. I couldn't bear to see either of them at the moment." He glanced at me with a duck of his head. "To tell you the truth, I'd like to go and see Natasha. Oh not professionally or anything like that but she doesn't work until evenings and she's really good company. She's a good person really. She's only dancing for the money. When she's saved enough she's going to take a computer course. I like hanging out with her. And I think she likes me."

Hey, a Russian exotic dancer and a bank manager, why not? Stranger combinations have succeeded before now.

He rubbed his neck and rotated his stiff shoulders. "On the other hand, I'd better not go today. Two days in a row might be a bit much. I should go and see my mother. She'll be wondering."

"We can have a car take you there."

He shook his head nervously. "I don't think so. Showing up in a police car wouldn't be cool. I'll be all right to drive myself. Do you think Dad will tell her what I've been doing?"

"I don't know. It's your business and it's up to you how much you want to reveal."

He stared at me, trying to assess my sincerity.

"I suppose you have a point... Do you need to talk to me again?"

"We might. For now don't leave town, or rather don't go anywhere without letting me know."

"Oh, I won't." He started to gather the tissue balls together so he could dispose of them. "I haven't even had time to ask when the funeral will be for Deidre. Do you know?"

"No, I don't."

"I think I'll go to it. Mom will have a hissy fit but it's the least I can do, don't you think?"

I would have liked to have suggested he get counselling but I didn't. I just hoped he'd find his own way there someday.

Leo had his snarling lion sign facing out but I ignored it, tapped, and went in. He was sitting in front of his computer but it didn't take a shrink to see that what he was looking at was the story of his life and it was reading failure. He didn't bark at me for coming in but said, "I've made a right cock-up of things, haven't I, Chris?"

There wasn't any answer to that question that would make him feel better. It was true. On the other hand we're all only human, even psychiatrists. I tried to say as much.

"Sigmund is a grown man, Leo. He is responsible for his own life now."

Frankly, I was fishing for something that wouldn't exacerbate the situation. He scowled.

"Come off it, Chris. I'm in the game. You know what I'd say if you presented me with this case and I didn't know who it was?"

"I don't know if it's helpful to go that route, Leo. You do know him. This isn't a stranger."

I might as well have saved my breath.

"I'd say, this man has a serious problem with self-image. He is insecure, passive aggressive, and sexually immature. The absence of a positive father image and an overly controlling mother has stunted his emotional growth. He is unable to maintain a normal sexual relationship and resorts to prostitutes or women on the margins of society for sexual gratification."

"Leo..."

Nothing doing.

"At an early age, he was forced into a secret life from fear of his mother's reactions. Typically with a man like this there is a huge amount of rage buried under the surface, directed mostly at women who substitute for the mother he hates."

"Leo, cut it out! I don't think Sigmund killed Deidre. Do you hear me? I don't think it was your son."

It was like dumping a bucket of cold water over him. He actually shuddered but at least his eyes cleared and the darkness shifted.

"You don't? It seemed to me there was a lot of indication that he might have done just that, God forbid."

"Let's say I have an intuition, but more usefully, he gave us an alibi that is very easy to check."

"The Natasha girl?"

I nodded. "I was going to pass this information on to Ed and have him talk to her right away."

Leo looked at me, his eyes wide. "Could you go yourself? You know how these immigrants are. If she sees a police uniform, she might freeze or deny everything. You're very easy to talk to, Chris. You're a woman. She might open up to you. Besides, you know exactly how to describe Sigmund..." He gave a brief smile. "She might have more than one man competing for her favours. Please, Chris. For me."

"I'm not front line anymore as you know. It's Ed's patch."

"He's not territorial like a lot of them. He'll welcome it."

What he was suggesting wasn't standard procedure but it did happen sometimes and I had to agree that in this instance, it made a lot of sense. I'd have to get a detective constable to go with me and I'd liked Susan Bailey. I'd see if she was available.

"I'll give him a call. But in the meantime, Leo, I suggest you go and talk to your son. He's completely wasted and eating his arse with guilt, pardon the expression. You said you were a cock-up as a father. This might be the opportunity to put some of that to right."

Yes, I know I was coming across as a bit self-righteous, but I felt that in the last couple of days, a sudden and intense bonding had taken place between me and the good doctor and I could talk to him the way I'd talk to Paula or Al for that matter. You can dish out a lot of unpalatable truths when you care about somebody. Thank God they'd both done it to me on occasion.

He winced. He was accustomed to being the one who gave out the home truths but he took it well.

"Is he still in the interview room?"

"Yes. He says he should see his mother. Maybe you could help him out. I'm not sure she'd be the best person for him at the moment... He is pretty cut up, Leo."

For a moment, Leo looked as if he was going to change his mind, and suddenly I saw something I'd missed because he'd covered it up so well with rudeness and bad temper. The man was terrified of intimacy. No wonder he'd been an absent father and no wonder he'd gravitated to a line of work where you never had a sustained relationship with your clients. Often he never even met them.

I stood up. "I'll get on to Ed right away."

"Would you mind calling me later to let me know what happened?"

I nodded reassuringly. "How are you going to deal with Trudy?"

He shrugged. "I'll think of something. All I know is I'm not going to let her within six feet of Sigmund tonight."

"Sounds good to me."

He came over to the door and held it open for me. As I went through, he patted me on the shoulder.

"Thanks, Chris. I do appreciate what you've done."

In the hall, he went north and I went south to my own office.

The red light was flashing on my telephone. I had two messages. The first was from Barbara Cheevers.

"Miss Morris. Will you please call me at your earliest convenience? I can be reached at home. I've written up my own report on Sunshine Lodge. Filled in the gaps, you might say. We weren't always able to keep a super on the premises. When people left there was sometimes a gap while we looked for somebody else. During those periods, we had to use a temp agency. They are called Reliable Cleaning Services. I thought you might like to get in touch with them."

Way to go, Barbara. Thinking like a detective. I jotted down the number.

The second call was from Paula.

"Chris. Sorry to do this, I know you must be up to your eyebrows in work, but I need to talk to you." I could hear her gulp hard. "I was released today. I'm feeling much better. Craig said he'd come and get me, which is why I didn't call you until now." Another gulp. My heart sank. I had a feeling I knew what was coming next. I was right. "He hasn't shown up, Chris. I'm sitting in the waiting room. I tried to reach Mom but I think she's taken Chelsea out for the afternoon. She didn't think I was coming home today. Neither did I, but they said I was stabilized so I could be discharged if I wanted to and of course, I jumped at the chance. He should have been here an hour ago... Could you possibly come and get me? I'm supposed to have somebody with me, and frankly, I'm feeling a bit fragile. You can call my cellphone and I'll keep checking it. Thanks, Chris." There was another long pause with sniffy noises. Then she said so quietly I hardly heard her, "I think this is the last straw. I'm so angry with him I could knock his head off." There was a beep warning that the message time on the tape was almost finished. "I'm going to leave him, Chris, I've made up my mind."

Shit. I'd wanted her to leave the jerk for years but this was such a bad time to be making a decision like that. I checked my call display. The call had come in half an hour ago. I picked up my cell and punched in her number. She answered.

"Chris, I was just about to call you. I'm home. I took a taxi. Nice guy. He brought me into the house, even offered to make me a cup of tea."

"Where's Craig?"

"Well, that's a good question. Some of his things have gone and he, er, he left a note. Shall I read it to you?"

"Go ahead."

"Dearest Paula. I know I am going to look like the worst coward in the world but I have to get away for a few days. You know how I am with sick women. It drives me batty. Your mother is here so I know Chelsea will be fine and you are on the mend. Probably not having me around will even help you get better faster. I'm sure your friends will agree with that. I won't be long, I promise. Just a few days at the most and I will phone as soon as I land somewhere. Take care darling, I love you even if I have funny way of showing it."

I exploded. "Funny way of showing it! What a prick."

Her voice on the other end was tight. "I know I said it was the last straw and I would leave him but he's sort of taken the wind out of my sails."

"Good riddance, I say. Hang onto that resolve, Paula mine. You'd had it with him. Coward indeed."

I knew I shouldn't be going on in this way; it tended to send Paula to his defence. This was no exception.

"He did have a rotten time when his mother died."

"Paula. A lot of people have had rotten times when they were children and they get over it. They don't abandon their wives when they are in the middle of a crisis. For God's sake, when are you going to face the truth about this guy? He's a self-involved flake who doesn't give a shit about anybody except himself!"

I was practically shouting down the phone but I heard the quiet sob at the other end and I stopped myself. "God, I'm sorry Paula. I'm sorry. The last thing you need is a diatribe from me. Look, I'll come over as soon as I possibly can. There's something I've got to do here and I'll call you. Are you going to be all right? Shall I see if Brenda can drop in?"

Brenda was a neighbour who Paula was friendly with.

"They've gone on a cruise to the Caribbean. Don't worry. I'll be all right. It's good to be in my own home. Mom and Chelse should be back in a couple of hours. I'll just have a rest."

"Try not to worry. I'll be there as soon as I can."

"All right. See ya."

We hung up.

Staring at my desk, I saw the photo of me and Paula when we were sixteen. Chelsea minutes old, all red scrunched-up face. And the wedding photo. Craig and Paula looking like the perfect couple. She had pulled in the growing bulge that was Chelsea and as long as she didn't stand sideways, you wouldn't notice. Tenderly, I touched the photo. Al had looked so handsome in his tuxedo and Marion, a bit plumper then, had glowed. Her happiness at being a grandmother had out balanced some good old-fashioned Catholic principles about wedding first, then baby. I was maid of honour, looking rather skinny in the blue silk dress that Paula insisted on. Goes with your eyes was the usual remark. What the heck had I done with that dress, anyway? Oh right. I'd had it cut down to cocktail length but I never seemed to go anywhere that dressy and a few years had rearranged my waistline. Eventually I'd given it to a Goodwill charity store.

The phone rang.

"Miss Morris, Susan Bailey here. I've got the all clear from Sergeant Chaffey. Shall I pick you up out front in, say, ten minutes?"

"I'll be there."

For a minute, I considered letting Susan interview the Russian bombshell by herself. It would save some time and I could go over to see Paula. Damn. I had promised Leo I would be the one to go. I grabbed my raincoat and hurried out.

CHAPTER FORTY-SIX

Susan was driving one of the OPP's generic American cars that we got such a good discount on. The heater wasn't working properly and the way it moved suggested the cylinder capacity of a motorcycle. Typical. The inside smelled as if somebody had sneaked an illegal cigarette. I glanced at her, wondering if she was the culprit. No smoking in police cars under any circumstances. Gone were the days that still existed in my time on the active force when the cars were so thick with smoke you couldn't see into the back seat. I was a non-smoker but it never occurred to me or anybody else to complain. Smoking was the norm and you just accepted it. She glanced over at me apologetically.

"Sorry about the cigarette smell. It's the mechanic. He's a chain smoker and his clothes reek. He was working on the clutch this morning and I can always tell. He must have transferred some of the stink to the car." She wound down the window. "I'll blow in some air for a bit."

Take your choice. Wet, cold air blasting you in the face or a warm odorous car. No contest. I knew I'd become inured to the cigarette smell within minutes. I told her so.

"Yes, ma'am."

"Oh please, don't call me ma'am. You make me feel ancient. Sergeant is fine with me and in private we could even try Christine, if you like."

She grinned.

Police protocol was fluid these days but still retained some formalities concerning rank.

I filled her in as to our task and told her about Sigmund's escapade with the exotic dancer.

"Let's hope he's telling the truth. It'll be terrible for Doctor Forgach if he isn't."

It would indeed and I hoped I was right in my intuitions.

The Atherley Arms was about twenty-five minutes away. I left her to negotiate getting there.

"I just have to make a call," I said to Susan.

"Another case?"

"Uh-huh. A nasty one."

I keyed in the Reliable Cleaning Services number and a chipper young voice answered. I introduced myself and explained that I needed a list of their employees starting from May 2002. There was a silence at the other end of the line, then she said, "How do I know you're who you say you are? Cleaners are worth their weight in gold, you know. Anybody could impersonate a police officer and steal our list from us."

She had a point. "Look, I'll give you a number to call where you can confirm who I am. Do you have another line? You can call while I wait."

"No, I don't. We're a small company. Give me the number and I'll call you right back. Your name again?"

I told her, gave her the number of headquarters, and disconnected.

Susan put on her indicator to make the turn.

"Let me make one more call," I said and keyed in Barbara Cheevers's number. A mechanical prompt answered. "The party you are trying to reach is not available. Please leave a message at the tone or try your call again."

Damn.

Susan pulled up into a parking space. The Atherley Arms had a neon sign across the roof, a bosomy girl bent over to touch her toes and peered over her shoulder in jerky repetitions. There were some clumsy paintings on either side of the door, both of semi-nude girls looking coy. Tuesday night was lady's night, half price for escort. Gorgeous girls, exotic dancers. Pole dancing and lap dancing. There were only two other cars parked in the lot. Perhaps a bit early for erotic arousal.

"Let's go," I said to Susan and we got out of the car.

At the same time the door opened and a chunky dark-haired man emerged, buttoning up his raincoat. He saw us and an expression of uneasiness flashed across his face. We were obviously not his usual clientele.

"Can I help you, ladies?"

"Are you the manager?"

"That's right. I'm Clive."

I took out my ID card to show him and introduced myself.

"We'd like to have a word with one of your employees. She goes by the name of Natasha."

He frowned. "She don't work here anymore."

"Since when?"

"Since this morning... What you want her for?"

"We just want to ask some questions concerning an investigation we're conducting."

"Drug squad?"

"No, actually. Is that why she was fired?"

"No. I don't allow drugs here. It causes too much problems. My girls are clean. No, she didn't get along with the other girls, so I had to let her go." He shrugged. "You know how it is with these Russkies, they'll do anything the men want and I draw the line. No screwing, pardon the language. No kissing or fondling. They're paying for a dance and that's it. Lookee, lookee is all they get. The girls complained that Natasha would go all the way, so of course she got more customers. Too much trouble. I didn't want to lose my best girls and I keep my place in bounds. I know the law."

"Where can we find her?"

He fished in his pocket and took out a notebook. Flipped the pages.

"She lives on Ogden street. Number 67. Just go back along the Atherley Road heading toward the town and turn left at the first street then left again."

"Thanks. By the way, do you know anybody by the name of Sigmund Forgach? He's a regular customer."

"Never heard of him."

"Medium height, kind of plump. Wears sideburns. A sort of Elvis look-alike. He says he was here on Tuesday night."

Clive shrugged. "I keep the lights low on purpose. Keeps it cozy. I didn't see nobody like that."

"He sometimes drives a red sports car or a beige Nova."

"No, sorry. I don't ever see who comes in what. They could walk here for all I care. I'm busy inside." He made a point of consulting his watch. "Is that it? I've got a dentist's appointment and I'm gonna be late."

"One more thing… you said you fired Natasha this morning?"

"That's right. She came in and I gave her the heave-ho at once. No point in delaying it, was there?"

"Was she bothered by that?"

"Yeah. But she knew it was coming. She'll get a job. She's a good-looking girl. Okay then? I gotta go. My tooth is killing me."

I released him and he headed for one of the two other cars that were in the lot. Susan hadn't said anything, just stood by and observed.

We walked back to our car. "I have to tell you, Chris, I don't get this stripper business. Why pay to see a girl's nude body? These days, you can get it for free. Just walk downtown in the summer, even here. They don't leave anything to the imagination I can tell you."

We had a chuckle together about male foibles.

Natasha had located herself within walking distance of the strip club and number 67 was one of the most decrepit buildings not yet condemned that I had ever seen. There were blankets and sheets covering the windows, any paint on the door and frames had long been burned off by the elements and the front yard looked like a local "bring your own garbage" dump. A fridge without a door was tipped on its side and as we approached some creature that was using it for a home darted away. I didn't see what it was and didn't want to know.

I'd asked Susan to wait in the car. I didn't want to scare off our subject. Cautiously, I walked up the rotting stairs to the front door. There was a list of at least seven names, all handwritten, tacked to the mailbox. Natasha was in the basement. In pencil beside her name was written Side Door. I signalled to Susan and she got out of the car while I went down the short flight of stairs to the door and knocked hard.

Music was blaring from the other side of the door, a hard-beat aerobic style. I wasn't sure she was going to hear anything above the din. I thumped as hard as I could, thought I heard somebody shout, "Just a minute," and finally the door opened a crack and a young woman peered through the chain.

"Yes?"

I showed my ID. "We're police officers. I wonder if we could have a word with you?"

She didn't budge. "What about?" She hadn't lowered the music at all and it was hard to hear her.

"Can we come in? I'd rather not explain standing out here."

Not to mention having to compete with some track way over the legal decibel limit.

She thrust a skinny bare arm through the gap in the door like a tough-minded Gretel trying to put off the witch. "ID. Gimme your ID."

I handed it over and she studied it carefully, looking at the photograph then at me then back at the photograph. I felt as if I was going being checked out by a particularly obsessive customs official. Yes, I did pack my bags myself. I've always wanted to know if anybody answered no to that question.

"Hers!" she pointed at Susan, who promptly stepped forward, and Natasha did the same scrutiny on her, not opening the door any wider than it already was. I wondered if this was peculiar to Russian girls or to her specifically.

Satisfied, she stepped back, slipped the chain off and opened the door so we could come in. The music was deafening and the room reeked of sweat and reefers. There appeared to be only one room and a small one at that. Natasha was dressed in skimpy workout clothes, her hair pulled back tight with a pink scrunchy. She was anything but voluptuous, with thin arms and legs, no bosom to speak of, and wide hips. I guess some exotic dancers rely on other charms to attract the guys, beauty of movement perhaps.

With obvious reluctance, she went over to a boom box, which was perched on top of a minuscule fridge, and lowered the music.

I'd have preferred it if she'd turned the whole thing off but that was too much to ask. She picked up a tea towel and wiped her face. She'd been working hard, I'll give her that. She didn't invite us to sit down so I took the initiative.

"Do you mind if I move these clothes?"

There was only one chair and a two-seater couch in the room which I assumed pulled out into a bed. An old-fashioned wardrobe dominated one corner but either Natasha had a lot of clothes or she hadn't got around to putting them away yet. Jeans and tops, tights and underwear were scattered everywhere.

"Help yourself." She went over to the tiny sink and poured herself a glass of water.

I took the chair and Susan the couch.

"So why you want talk to me?"

Her accent was actually slight, just a *v* instead of *w*.

"We're investigating a serious crime and we're verifying statements."

She was continuing to towel off with a casualness that reflected her profession. Armpits, inside her tights to get at her rear end and crotch, but she halted when I said that.

"You've come about Siggy's sister, haven't you?"

"If you're referring to Deidre Larsen, yes, we have. Mr. Forgach told you what has happened, did he?"

"Oh yes, he was very disturbed. Tragic event."

"Can you tell us when you were together?"

She stared at me. "Why?"

"As I said we need to verify statements."

"You not suspect Siggy?"

"It's not a question of suspecting anybody. This is standard police procedure."

I admit I was fudging. These days of tight budget, it's standard procedure only if we do suspect somebody but I could sense Natasha had, shall we say, an aversion to police authority.

"What you want to know?"

"As I said, when you were last together?"

"Yesterday. He came here in the morning. I didn't have to work until six so he stayed with me for the day."

"When did he leave?"

She shrugged. "Not until after midnight. He came with me to see the show."

She gulped back some more water. "Did that prick at the Arms tell you I was fired?"

"Yes, he did."

"I went to pick up wages and, bam, he gave me the can. Said I didn't get along with other girls, which is bullshit. They are jealous because I steal their customers. They so timid these Canadian girls." She went into a falsetto. "Oh no, I'm a good girl. I can show you my pussy but I won't, no I simply won't let you touch." She mimicked a hand slap. "No, no, naughty man. Lookie, no touchie."

"But you do let them touch do you?" Susan asked. She looked tense.

Natasha shrugged. "What's the difference? All of it is lies, one big fucking fake. I don't care what they do as long as they pay for it."

I figured she must be twenty-five years old if that. I've encountered many prostitutes before and I know what a hard bunch they can be and also what troubles they've often got to deal with. This girl bothered me. She was talking tough and perhaps she was. Perhaps I was being fooled by her athletic build and wholesome appearance. I probably wasn't the first person to wonder what the hell she was doing on the game. She must have sensed some of what I was feeling because she said, "I'm getting out as soon as I have enough money. I want to be a manicurist, get a job in a rich ladies' spa. Do French polish instead of... never mind. I'm going to school next year. In the meantime, I live in rat hole like this, give men whatever they ask for, and then ... boom, I'm gone. New life, new place."

I wondered where Sigmund fitted into her plans.

"My name not really Natasha. That is stage name. My name is Irina Petrova. I'm glad nobody knows it. When I start my new life, nobody will know."

"Will Sigmund Forgach be part of your new life?"

"Of course. He is my fiancé. We will be married one of these days." She grinned and was transformed from scrappy street kid to mischievous school girl. "His mother will have what you call a conniption, don't you think? She expects he will be at her beck and call until she dies but now he has met me, and boom, out goes the mother, in comes the wife."

Susan met my eyes and I saw the cynicism in them, which was probably reflecting mine. Hollywood aside, a stripper who goes the limit for money and an uptight bank manager with a controlling mother had a slim chance at lasting happiness, although in this case I'd like to be proven wrong. Natasha/Irina was so unabashedly herself she was appealing.

I came back to the issue at hand.

"Miss Petrova, may I just go over what you have said? Sigmund Forgach was with you continually from ten o'clock yesterday morning until midnight."

Another cheeky grin. "Well he did go take a leak once or twice so he wasn't with me then but otherwise, yes, constantly. He sat in the front row at the Arms where I could see him and when I wasn't dancing we were in the back room. That asshole, Clive, makes sure no customer sits too long without paying for a private dance or two."

Now was the time to slip in the crucial time. "Other than yesterday, did you spend time together last week?"

"Yes. He came to the club on Tuesday night. I danced for him then as well. He likes it. It makes sure nobody else is getting me. I'm happy with that."

"What time were you together?"

"It was a weeknight so he was there just after eleven o'clock and stayed until well after two, maybe later."

"You're sure about the times, are you?"

Again she flashed the impish grin. "You are wondering if I am simply, what you call it, corroborating his alibi. But it is truth. You can ask that prick, Clive. He will tell you the same and probably if you ask the other girls they will say so. They always have their eye open for customers so they would have tried to get him to buy a dance. You can ask them."

"I will. What names do they go by?"

"There were only three of us on that night. Belle, the one with the ginormous tits, not real; the blonde, not real, is named Starr; and the other, the short stubby one with no ass, is Lulu. In the dressing room they're Sharon and Louise but I don't know their surnames. Mr. Asshole will know."

I stood up. "Thanks for your help."

"You're welcome. I hope you find your murderer. He should be hung, the bastard."

Much more friendly now, she opened the door for us. I followed Susan up the steps and out into the wonderful fresh air.

"Well, I guess that puts our prime suspect in the clear, doesn't it?" said Susan.

"I'd say so. The coroner was pretty sure Deidre died around two o'clock. We should follow up with the dancing girls just to make sure."

"I'll give that relationship six months, max," said Susan.

Before I could put in my own two cents, my cellphone rang. It was Leo.

"Chris, get over here as fast as you can. Joy's vanished."

CHAPTER FORTY-SEVEN

For one crazy second I thought he was being poetic, then I realized he was referring to his granddaughter. He was speaking in a monotone, and you'd have to know him to detect the immense pressure underneath the words.

"I would appreciate it if you would come here immediately, Chris. I'm at Deedee's house. There is no doubt Joy has been abducted. I have telephoned the police and they are on their way. Where are you now?"

"In Atherley."

"Did you find the girl?"

"Yes."

"Does she confirm his alibi?"

"Yes."

"Thank God for that. Do you believe her?"

"I do."

"Sigmund and I are here together so there are no worries on that score, but I'd better not tie up my phone, Chris. I'll explain everything when you get here."

We clicked off and I saw that both Susan and Irina were eyeing me curiously. My shock must have shown on my face.

"I have an emergency to deal with but I think we've pretty much finished here. Thank you, Irina."

"No problem." She gave me a worried look. "Your emergency doesn't have to do with Siggie, does it?"

"No."

"Good. He's my one-way ticket out of here."

Nothing hidden about this young woman.

Susan and I left on the double. I doubted Leo would have used the word *abducted* unless he was sure but I had an irrational hope that he was wrong. That Joy had wandered off or Nora had taken her somewhere.

I filled Susan in and she drove fast to the house.

There were two police cars in front of the house, lights flashing, and a couple of people were standing on the street watching to see what was going on. A constable was manning the door and he let us in.

Ed Chaffey, a uniformed constable, Leo, Sigmund, and Loretta were all jammed together in the living room. Nora was sitting alone on the couch, nobody beside her. Nobody seemed to be talking. Ed got up as soon as he saw me and came out into the narrow hallway. He spoke quietly.

"Glad you're here, Chris. The nanny has given us her story and we are treating this as an abduction. I've had a cursory look at the child's bedroom but I'd like you to see it yourself. I've sent constables to speak to the neighbours and we're ready to put out an Amber Alert." He rubbed his hands over his face. He looked exhausted. "Child abduction is one of my nightmares. I don't know if it has anything to do with the murder of the kid's mother but I guess we'll have to assume there is a connection until proven otherwise."

I felt sick. There were indications that Deidre's death was a hate crime and it wasn't too big a step to encompass the child. Ed was virtually whispering.

"We need to rein in Dr. Forgach. He's not helping the situation any. He and the nanny are at total loggerheads. It's ridiculous. Can you cool him out, Chris?"

"I don't know. I'll try."

He ushered me into the room. Nobody had moved, as if they were actors waiting for the director to start the rehearsal. Nora was slouched over, hugging her knees. Loretta was perched on the edge of her chair. Sigmund was sitting next to her. He looked as if he would like to have become invisible. He also had a guilty hangdog expression on his face but I decided that was his habitual state of mind. Leo was standing by the window.

"We were waiting until you arrived, Sergeant Morris. Allow me to apprise you of the situation as we understand it."

He spoke as if he were addressing a rather dim-witted jury. His formality was incongruous after what we'd been through but perhaps it gave him something to hold onto.

"Ms. Larsen had gone out to do some shopping at about one forty-five this afternoon. Nora, Ms. Cochrane, decided she needed some cigarettes … or so she has told us. She had put Joy down for a nap at approximately two o'clock. Is that correct, Nora?"

She nodded sullenly. "Give or take a minute."

"She says that she latched Joy's bedroom door before she left. When she returned…"

Nora burst out. "I keep telling you. I was only gone for ten fucking minutes."

Leo ignored her. "When she returned she did not go directly to check on the child but remained in the living room…"

"Why shouldn't I? How was I to know something had happened? I thought she was still asleep."

"At which point, Ms. Larsen returned. Nora did not tell her she had left the house and at Ms. Larsen's enquiry simply said that Joy was taking a nap."

Unable to contain herself, Loretta jumped in. "It didn't occur to me to check on her. I was unloading the groceries."

"Did you notice the time when you got back to the house?" I asked.

"I think it was about a quarter to three."

"When did you realize Joy was missing?"

I'd addressed both of them but it was Loretta who answered.

"I made myself a cup of herbal tea and Nora was in the living room watching television. I realized it was almost three-thirty and Joy should be waking up by now. I said that to Nora, who said, quote, unquote, 'Why don't you go get her if you're that concerned? It'll make a nice change.'" Loretta bit her lip. "I went upstairs. The door was slightly ajar which I thought was odd…"

"You mean you thought I'd been sloppy," burst out Nora. "Say it, woman. You're just like him over there, you think I'm a total fuck-up. Admit it!"

Leo turned red and I could see he was just about to boil over. I managed to catch his eye, warning him not to lose it. I went and sat beside Nora.

"Look, everybody is upset but I'm going to ask you to have some self-control. We need to establish a timeline. It is most important. I'd appreciate it if you would let me do that."

She scowled and held on tight to her knees but subsided. Loretta drew in her breath sharply, ready to kill but having the self-discipline to keep to the facts.

"As I was saying, I went upstairs. Joy's door was open and the bed was empty. I thought she might have woken up and gone to the bathroom, which she can do by herself, or gone down the hall to her mother's room. I started to call..."

Nora had to put in her two cents' worth and I could have smacked her. "She keeps forgetting she's deaf as a post. You have to stamp on the floor or flick the lights if you want her attention."

Loretta refused to rise to the bait. "It's true, I did forget for a moment. It was so instinctive to call for her. Nora heard me and asked what the problem was. She was focused on her show and didn't want to be interrupted. I presume it was worth it."

Loretta had a scalpel and Nora's hammer was no match for it.

"She did not at this point tell me that she had left the child unattended..."

Nora suddenly screamed at her. "I was only gone for ten minutes and I locked her in. How many times have I got to repeat myself?"

"As many as is necessary," said Leo, and I don't think I've ever heard a voice as icy. I could understand but it wasn't helping the situation. Nora was escalating by the minute, fear driving her over the edge.

"What did you do next?" I addressed the question to Loretta.

"We searched the house. Then Nora admitted she had left the house earlier. We went outside but of course there was no sign of her. Nora went to the neighbours on one side and I went on the other."

"How long did that take you?"

"Perhaps another half an hour. Nobody had seen her, and given what Nora had said, I thought we had better contact the police."

"In other words, Joy has not been seen for about two and a half hours?"

Nora burst into sobs, her tough exterior melting like the wicked witch of the west.

"I swear I locked her in. I would never allow any harm to come to her, I swear it. I loved that kid."

I put my arm around her shoulders. "I believe you, Nora. That's why we're treating this as an abduction."

"You mean she's been kidnapped?"

"Yes, I'm afraid so."

"By who?"

"I wish I had an answer to that, but I don't."

I met Ed's eyes. I knew what I saw there was reflected in my own. The percentage of child abductions that ended happily was very small. Leo knew that too. Back to Nora.

"Are you positive you latched Joy's door when you left?"

She hesitated. "Yes, well, at least I think I did. I wasn't paying much attention really so it's easy to think you've done something when you haven't. But yes, I'm pretty sure that's what I did. Then I ran up to the corner store for some cigarettes. It's just a block up and round the corner. It must have taken me ten or twelve minutes at the most."

"Did you lock the front door?"

"It locks automatically."

"Nora, you said that the variety store is around the corner. Does that mean you were out of sight of the house for most of your ten-minute period?"

"Yeah."

"Did you notice any cars parked on the street?"

"Not really. I wasn't looking for anything, was I?"

"Have you ever done that before? Shut Joy in her room and gone for cigarettes?"

She got tense again. "A couple of times. Just in emergencies."

I wasn't sure a nicotine fix qualified as an emergency but then I wasn't a smoker.

"What did you do when you got back to the house?"

"I didn't do anything."

"But you'd run out because you were desperate for a smoke. Did you go outside?"

"No."

"So you didn't have a cigarette after all?"

Our eyes locked at this point. Nora's pupils were dilated. "The urge had passed."

"What did you do then?"

"Like I said, nothing. I came in and went to the bathroom." She tried for a little defiance. "Do you want to know if I did a piss or a shit?"

"Only if you think it's necessary to the enquiry."

Leo spoke, still in a monotone. "It would seem that we are looking at a very narrow window of time when she could have been taken. If Miss Cochrane is to be believed, she returned at about twelve minutes past two. Joy must have been taken almost as soon as she left the house."

"They'd have to be fucking quick about it," said Nora.

Abductors often were appallingly quick.

"Her clothes have gone," said Loretta. "And her favourite toy, Harold the dinosaur."

"It's Horace, not Harold," said Nora.

"We'll need a description of the clothes," said Ed.

Sigmund was so quiet I'd almost forgotten about him. He was looking at his father in action with a sort of horrified fascination.

Ed shifted in his chair and frowned at Nora, who glared back. "So Joy was most likely taken when you were on your way to the store and it suggests somebody who was familiar with the house and possibly saw you leave."

She snorted. "Chancy, wasn't it? I didn't even know I was out of smokes myself til I came downstairs."

Many criminals are opportunists on the lookout for a victim and some horrible destiny comes into play. Wrong place, wrong time. In spite of Nora's remark, this case didn't fit that mode at all. First, there was the question of entry, which had to be with a key and a knowledge of the child's bedroom; secondly, as she said, she could quite easily have not left the house. Was the abductor lying in wait, ready to strike whenever they could? There must have been a vehicle involved. Joy's abduction was not done on impulse. It had been planned.

CHAPTER FORTY-EIGHT

Katherine had called for an emergency meeting and the team, including Ed, was gathered in the boardroom. Once again, Janice, bless her, had thought of bodily needs and sent out for pizzas. She'd also ordered salads for those who were health conscious, which right now meant only David.

Katherine gave us a moment to get the pizza from the box.

"Chris, can you let us in on your thinking?"

I'd made notes and I consulted them. Not that I really needed to; everything was burned in my mind.

"I think we can rule out a stranger. The abductor had to know the layout of the house and the current situation. I'd say somebody was watching the house and saw Loretta leave and then Nora shortly afterward. Joy is deaf but she has a good pair of lungs, and even though Deidre's house is detached, the houses are close together. I think if she had been yelling top volume, somebody would have heard her and nobody did. There were people at home on either side."

"The window of opportunity seems incredibly small," said Ray.

"It is. One of the constables did a quick time check of a walk from the house to the convenience store and back. Twelve minutes. Nora was probably minimizing the time she was absent but it wouldn't have been much more than that if she did what she said she did."

"She wasn't coming clean about everything, I'm sure of it," said Leo.

"Do you think there's a likelihood that she is implicated?" Katherine asked.

"I'd say not. And if she is, she'd have to have an accomplice. What was your take, Ed?"

"I agree with you. She's not the most endearing of people, but yes, I believed her. She seemed too upset to be faking."

"Leo?"

"I would find it hard to believe that she would do this. It simply rebounds on her anyway."

I went on. "The proprietor of the convenience store confirms that she came in when she said she did. They have an ongoing joke about her stopping smoking. He offered to sell her one cigarette to get her through the 'craving moment,' as he called it."

Ray snorted. He was still struggling to stay off cigarettes.

"Did he confirm the time?" Katherine asked.

"He's sure it was just after two and that she was in and out very quickly."

David raised a finger to indicate he had a question. "I don't disagree that the abductor might have been watching the house but that too is risky. If he, can we use 'he' for now, it's easier, or do I have to be PC?"

Katherine nodded brusquely and David continued. "Let's say he drives up to the house but has some other method of entry on his mind, say a home invasion, as it were. He sees the two women leave. He thinks this is his lucky day and immediately goes into the house, up to the kid's room, gets her out of bed. She may or may not know him. He could have subdued her if she protested, and he carries her into the car. What? Seven minutes maximum."

"He had to get her dressed," I said. "That would add some time. Her clothes are missing and a raincoat and boots, which were in the hall closet."

"If he had a car, he wouldn't need to dress her, he could collect the clothes and carry her out as she was. Most hall closets hold outdoor things so that doesn't prove a hell of a lot." David had a rather irritating "point scored" tone to his voice but he was right.

"Neither Loretta nor Nora noticed a car parked outside the house," said Ed.

"If you're not looking, you often don't see."

Again David was right about that. The unreliability of witness testimony was notorious.

"Christine and I were talking about the big question on the way over," said Ed. "Motive. What the hell's the motive? There's been no ransom demand."

"It's early days," said David. "We know that kidnappers sometimes wait before making contact with the victim's family."

He was playing devil's advocate but it was necessary to have somebody do that. Nobody wanted to get into tunnel vision. That had led to too many a tragic wild goose chase.

"I tried to get in touch immediately with the close friends, Jessica Manolo and Hannah Silverstein, but didn't get any answer."

"We sent a constable to the house but there was nobody home," said Ed.

"Is that suspicious, do you think?" Katherine asked.

"I don't know. Either or both of them fit our profile of person in the loop, but they don't have a car and as far as I know no reason to take Joy."

"Is it within the realm of possibility that the whole thing is a variation of David's thesis?" Jamie asked. "Not a home invasion as such, but say one or both of these girls came over to visit, found that nobody was home and Joy had been left alone. They enter the house, get her, and take her back to their place just to make a point that she isn't being looked after properly."

Katherine took off her glasses and polished the lens. "If that is the case, they are unusually insensitive and callous young women with no regard for the anguish they've caused. It's been four hours since Joy was last seen."

In my brief meetings with Jessica and Hannah, neither one had struck me as like that but who knows? The nicest people can do uncharacteristic things if they feel strongly about something.

Suddenly Ed grabbed at his pocket. "Excuse me," he said. We all had our cellphones turned to silent ring and he'd just got a call. I was just about to go back to the question of the letters when he gave a yelp of pleasure.

"That was the station. I think we've got a positive ID on Joy. One of the neighbours on Mary Street, six or seven houses down from Deidre, says she looked out of the window and saw, get this, a woman walking with a child along the street. She was vague about the time, but thinks it was just after she'd listened to the news on the radio at two o'clock. She's not vague about what she saw. A little girl about three years of age in a bright yellow raincoat and matching boots."

"Yes!" That was from me, I couldn't help it. The missing raincoat and boots were yellow.

"She noticed, she said, because the child splashed through some puddles and obviously wanted to do it again but the woman, who she assumed was the child's mother, hurried her along. Bingo!"

Leo was looking at the table. I thought he was afraid to risk meeting anybody's eyes. The rest of us were beaming at each other even though we were well aware this was only the beginning. It didn't necessarily mean that Joy wouldn't come to harm.

"Did the woman give any ID on the so-called mother?" he asked.

"She describes her as quite short, stocky, and she was wearing a dark-coloured raincoat with a hood which she had up."

"Hannah Silverstein," I burst out. "When I first saw her she was wearing a dark plaid raincoat with a hood. Joy would certainly go with her happily."

Katherine sat back in her chair. "She's our first priority then. But before we break up..." she paused. "Chris, in your opinion, what level of threat do you think we're dealing with?"

I tried to distance myself from the image of the smiling, round-cheeked face of the child who'd waved Horace's paw at me.

"Given what we know of the relationship between the suspect and the child's mother, I'd say we are dealing with low threat."

"Unless, of course, Silverstein was connected with my daughter's murder," said Leo. "We don't even know yet who wrote those hate letters or where they fit in."

He was voicing our worst fears, that there was some psycho on the loose who thought they were acting on behalf of a vengeful God. I flashed back to the letter I'd received and how disturbing the sense of a deranged mind had been. But Hannah Silverstein? I didn't think so.

"I'm going over to the girl's apartment right now," said Ed. "Chris, I'd like you to come with me. You know them."

I was only too happy to go. It would keep Leo from shooting

off on his own, which I suspected he would do. I saw his expression when Ed spoke. I seemed to be the only person he trusted to investigate the case. So be it.

CHAPTER FORTY-NINE

The apartment building was a fifties-style walk-up in yellow brick with a flat front and symmetrical square windows. The two girls lived on the third floor. The blinds were down but there was a crack of light showing through, so somebody was at home. Ed pressed the bell, and through the old-fashioned stained glass vent above the door, I saw a light flashing on and off. Things went dark and he pressed again. More flashes.

"We're not leaving until we get some answers," said Ed. His face was grim and I knew how much all of us were affected by what was going on.

We heard footsteps and the door opened. Jessica Manolo looked at us in surprise.

"Yes?"

I faced her squarely so she could read my lips. "Is Hannah at home?"

Either the hall was too dark or she didn't want to answer.

"Pardon me?"

"May we come in, Jessica?"

"Pardon?"

"We'd like to come in," I made some gesture to illustrate what I meant and she nodded, stepped back, and waved us in. I felt almost like a dog going into a strange place. All senses were on the alert, including my smell trying to pick up any evidence of Joy. All I got was a rather delicious aroma of baking chicken.

"I was making dinner," said Jessica. "A moment please."

She headed down the hall, leaving us to follow. The living room was to the left and the kitchen opened off it. The place was rather untidy, not unduly so for two young women, but a cursory glance around showed no sign that a child had been here. No chairs moved or cushions on the floor for childproofing. Jessica took a pot off the stove and returned to the living room. On the way, she retrieved two hearing aids from a dish on the table and began to twist them into her ears.

She smiled at us. "That's better."

"Jessica, we would particularly like to speak to Hannah."

It must have been obvious that we were here on a serious matter and she started to look alarmed.

"She's not here. She has gone to visit her parents in Toronto for the weekend."

"When did she leave?"

"I was at the library so I'm not sure but she usually takes the afternoon train. But please tell me what is wrong?"

I looked at her closely but I didn't think she was dissembling. "Little Joy has disappeared. Somebody abducted her from her room about two o'clock this afternoon."

"What do you mean abducted?"

"Unfortunately Nora had left the house unattended believing that Joy was asleep. She says she was gone for only a short period of time and did not immediately check on her. Ms. Larsen was also out. Neither person checked on Joy until about three-thirty, when Ms. Larsen found the door was open and Joy was gone."

"Oh that stupid girl," Jessica snapped. "We kept telling Deidre that she wasn't the right person to have as a nanny but she insisted that Joy loved her. She said Nora had a heart of gold and not to be fooled by her tough manners. That's bullshit. What did she say she left the house for? Drugs, I bet. Stupid wicked girl. She is a drug addict to boot." Jessica's hands fluttered as if they had to talk. "But I don't understand ... what does this have to do with Hannah?"

Ed answered this one. "We have a witness who saw a young woman fitting Hannah's description walking with a child who was mostly likely Joy."

"It can't have been her. She has gone to visit her parents. She said nothing about taking Joy with her."

"What time was it when you last saw Hannah?" I asked.

"About noon. I went over to the library. But it's all some silly misunderstanding. Hannah must have decided to take Joy with her at the last minute..."

"Without informing anybody?"

"Perhaps she left a note and nobody saw it yet."

"There is no sign of any note."

Jessica was looking more and more distressed.

"I wonder if you would mind checking Miss Silverstein's things," said Ed. "Let's confirm that she did indeed intend to go away for the weekend."

"Come this way." Jessica hurried down the long narrow hall. There were several posters on the walls advertising long-gone rock concerts. Somebody was a Madonna fan.

"Forgive the mess," said Jessica, and as we followed her into the bedroom, she quickly pulled the duvet over one of the twin beds. The other bed was neatly made.

She opened the closet door. "This half belongs to Hannah. She has more clothes than I do." She riffled quickly through the coat hangers, several of which were empty. Then she rummaged underneath where the boots and shoes were. Finally she turned back to us. "For some reason she has taken more of her clothes with her than she would normally do and she has borrowed my wheelie suitcase, which is bigger than hers. She must be intending to stay more than the weekend. How odd. I know she is booked into work on Tuesday."

"Is there anything else missing?"

Jessica looked around the room. "She's taken her laptop."

"I think the best thing to do is get in touch with her parents and see if they have heard from her. Do you have their phone number?"

"Come this way. We will have to use the TTY machine. Mr. and Mrs. Silverstein are deaf too."

Jessica hurried down the hall back to the living room and went over to a desk by the window on which was what looked like a small combination keyboard and telephone.

"Not as modern as text messages but it is what they are used to. Shall I contact them right now?"

"Yes, please. Will you just ask if Hannah is with them or if they have heard from her. It might be early for her to be there as yet but if she is, I'd like to communicate with her directly."

Jessica sat down and typed quickly, the text moving across the display window. I moved closer so I could read over her shoulder. She finished with the letters *SK*.

"That just means I've finished the message," she explained up at me. "We'll have to wait a minute for them to answer."

I saw Ed walking casually around the room.

"Do you mind if I use your bathroom?"

I knew what he was up to and Jessica probably did too but she didn't look worried as if she had something to hide.

"Down the hall to your left."

The Silversteins answered promptly and the message began to appear in the display window.

"*Jessica. How lovely to hear from you. No, Hannah is not here. We have not heard from her for a few days. We were not expecting her for a couple of weeks. Is something wrong?*"

Jessica looked up at me. "What shall I tell them?"

I didn't know how to reassure them without a long explanation.

"They know about Deidre's death, don't they?"

"Yes, they do. They had visited us many times. They were very distressed."

"Tell them then that as part of the ongoing investigation the police would like to speak to Hannah as soon as possible and if she does get in touch with them, they must tell her to contact the police department at once. She can text me. Here's my number."

Jessica typed the message. A reply came almost immediately and even in the print I felt the helplessness of the couple on the other end.

"*We will do as you ask but we don't understand. What is the urgency?*"

"Say it is necessary to our enquiries to speak to Hannah."

We'd also have to send along an officer to the house but I thought if I wrote that it would alarm them even more. Jessica finished her message. "*Okay*" appeared in the screen.

She switched off.

"Jessica, does Hannah have other friends that she might be staying with?"

"Well, yes. There are some but why would she tell me she was going to Toronto if it wasn't true?"

Why indeed?

"We will need a list of the names, addresses, and phone or emails of everybody in your circle of friends. And will you please indicate which of them, if any, have a vehicle and which are hearing and which aren't."

"Most of them are deaf. If you are going to see them in person, you will need an interpreter."

"Will you do it? We mustn't waste time. If Hannah doesn't have Joy then somebody else does. And we are pretty sure it is somebody the child knows well."

"Shall I start by emailing everybody?"

"All right."

Only those who had no nefarious reason would answer honestly but we might get some information out of it. She went over to the computer that was on the table and booted it up. Immediately, she swivelled around to look at us.

"I have an email from Hannah."

"Open it," said Ed.

She did. We had both moved to stand behind her and I read,

> *Hey Jess. I've decided not to go to TO after all. I need a break from everything. Time in the sun for some R and R. I've let Mrs. Scott know I'll be off next week. I'll be in touch. Don't fret, Jess the best. I'll be back.*
>
> *Love and hugs, Hannah.*

"Does she have a wireless laptop?"

"Yes, she does. She just got one."

So she could be anywhere with a wireless connection.

"Write back, will you, Jessica, and tell her she must get in touch with the nearest police station. Tell her that Joy has disappeared and if she doesn't have her we must find out who does."

Of course she had the child but we had to go through the motions.

There was no need for both of us to hang around, so Ed left me to keep an eye on Jessica and went back to the station so he could get the Amber Alert mobilized.

"Call me as soon as you've done. I'll have a car pick you up."

I stayed with Jessica for the next couple of hours. Her friends were prompt and she'd heard back from all but three either by text message or email. Of the three who didn't answer, one was reached on the TTY, the other she thought was out of town, and the third was Zachary Taylor. I felt like the strobe light was going off in my head.

"Do you know that there is a strong probability that Zachary is Joy's father?" I asked her.

She nodded, shamefaced. "Dee would never admit it, but we all thought that's who it was. I hate to say this about the dead but Dee used him. He's a sweet goofy guy who had the hugest crush on her. She wanted a child but didn't want to be involved long-term with a man. Don't get me wrong, she wasn't a lesbo like that stupid Nora, but she liked to be independent. So she chose a sperm donor. He needed to be congenitally deaf, with a high likelihood of passing it on, but otherwise with good genes, eyes, and so on. Zach fitted the bill perfectly. She got pregnant and promptly dumped him. He was heartbroken."

"Did she confide in you that she was planning another such pregnancy?"

"She made a few noises about it. Said Joy needed a companion. From the looks of it, she crooked her little finger and Zach came running."

"Jessica, you know Hannah. Do you think it's possible that she is with Zachary and that they have taken Joy with them?"

"My God, they'd never harm the girl. Hannah loved her."

"I'm not saying that. None of you seem to care for Nora. Maybe they're teaching her a lesson, punishing her."

Jessica's face was full of hurt. She had been left out of her best friend's life. She sighed. "I will tell you this, Hannah has been in love with Zach Taylor ever since our university days. She would do anything for him."

Which could include kidnapping his child.

She put her fingers to her mouth, realizing something. "Hannah had a text message sometime this morning. She seemed quite agitated by it but when I asked who it was from, she blew me off and wouldn't say. I'll bet it was him."

"What time was this?"

"Quite early, we'd just got up. Maybe nine o'clock."

"And it was after this she told you she was going to visit her parents?"

"That's right. I was surprised I must say. I wanted her to stay with me but she was adamant."

I stood up. "That's probably as much as we can do for now. Thanks so much for your help."

She shifted on her chair. "This is one sad thing after another, isn't it?"

I phoned Ed as promised and within five minutes all the table lamps started to flash. He had pressed the doorbell. I said goodbye to Jessica, who was sitting forlornly on the couch. As she said, it was one sad thing after another. No matter what their motive, Hannah Silverstein and Zachary Taylor had got themselves into a very serious situation.

"You look as tired as I feel," Ed said as I followed him out to the cruiser. "There've been no new sightings but we've got everybody on the alert for the camper van. He's left the farmer's field where he was before. I'm guessing he's tucked away somewhere. He must know we're looking for them and they'll hide out a while." He held open the car door for me. "I thought Jessica was telling the truth, didn't you Chris?"

I nodded. "She looked betrayed when she realized Hannah had lied to her. Yes, I believe it played exactly as she told it." I told him about the morning text message to Hannah.

"Taylor?"

"I'd bet on it."

"So what's Hannah up to?"

"There's no love lost between the two deaf girls and the nanny, that's for sure. I'm still leaning on the side of punishment."

"I'll put every available officer on to checking on the list of friends' addresses and we'll use the radio and television. The Sunday paper can print it too." He tried to stifle back a yawn. "Lord, I'm tired. I'd better get off home. Aileen won't recognize me if I'm away much longer."

I must say, I felt a twinge of envy. I had the sense that Ed had a good marriage, often quite a feat among police officers. Long unpredictable hours and lots of emotional stress that most guys and a lot of women didn't talk about. I did however wish there was a nice patient somebody waiting for me to get home. But hey, Tory and Bertie were good listeners.

"I'd better get back to Leo and Loretta. They'll be waiting to hear."

Ed turned onto my street. "I liked her. Too bad about the son. Almost makes you feel sorry for the old doc. But my guess is he would be one difficult dude to live with."

It shows how far I'd come that I almost leaped in to defend Leo.

CHAPTER FIFTY

The house was in darkness downstairs and frankly I was glad when Ed insisted on coming up to my apartment and making sure nobody was hiding in the closet. I might joke about having an attack cat on the loose but the most help Bertie or Tory would provide was if one of them tripped the bad guy in an attempt to wrap themselves around his legs. Which they did to me as soon as I opened the door. I talked Ed out of stationing a patrol car outside and he left, assuring me he was as close as a call away. Sweet guy. It was ten o'clock by now and I was both exhausted and adrenalized, a bad combination that usually meant I wouldn't be falling asleep any time soon. I put some cereal in a bowl, picked up Bertie, and went into the living room to see if some late-night TV would calm me down. Before that, however, I owed it to Nora to bring her up to speed. Ed had agreed to get in touch with Leo for which I was thankful.

The phone rang several times before she answered. She sounded breathless.

"Sorry. I was in the john. Any word? Have you found her?"

I decided, given all the uncertainty of who was complicitous with whom, to withhold some of what we now knew.

"Not yet. Nora, I've been going over this sequence of events over and over in my mind..."

"Me too," she interrupted.

"The problem is the chancy nature of the whole thing. How would somebody know you were going to leave the house when you did? You said yourself it was a spontaneous decision."

There was dead silence at the other end of the phone, then she said in a tight voice, "Yeah."

"Yeah what? You told somebody?"

"Yeah... "

I held on to my patience with difficulty. She finally went on. "Don't get this all wrong, but yeah, when I think about it there is somebody who knew."

Another silence and I could hear a deep prolonged intake of breath. She was toking up.

"Go on."

"Don't rush me. This isn't easy for me to tell you... Fact is, I've been stressed out of my mind ever since Dee's death, so I called this fellow I know to see if he could sell me some weed. I needed to relax big time. He called me back just after Joy went down and said he'd meet me on the corner in two minutes. So I nipped out like I said, got cigs and the weed, came back and went for a smoke in the shed. I can see the kid's window from there and I knew I'd hear her if she was crying or anything. You've heard the pair of lungs she's got on her."

"Could you see anybody in the room?"

"No. Not unless they were standing right in the window. But I swear to you, I'd have heard. That kid can bellow when she wants to... I'm sorry I didn't tell you before. I've already got a form for possession and I didn't want to go there again."

"I'll need the name of your dealer."

"Yeah, yeah. He's a creep anyway."

She gave me the name — Eric Jones — somebody, as they say, known to the police. I'd be glad to nail him. I had one more question before we hung up.

"Nora, you said a couple of times that you were hired. That's not the same as pitching in for free rent. Which is it?"

"Does it matter?"

"I don't know, I'm just curious."

"*He* hired me. The doc."

"Dr. Forgach?"

"Yeah. Dee wouldn't have anything to do with him and he wanted to know what was happening. I was what you might call the mole." She laughed. "Can't you just see us meeting in underground parking garages so I could give him my report?"

"Is that what you did?'

"Naw, course not. I phoned him every so often. Not that there was anything to report, just domestic stuff, like you know, Joy had a cold, Dee had a new class at the institute. That sort of thing."

"Did you know that Sigmund came to see her on Monday night?"

"No, that's my night to go to my support group. But you know I'd had a suspicion she'd got somebody coming over. She primped up a bit and got Joy's hair washed and cut. So it was the bro, was it?"

"It was."

We hung up. I put Bertie down. I felt slightly queasy that I'd outed Leo. It seemed a sad way to have to know what was happening in the lives of somebody you cared about.

Back to the abduction.

Was this all one huge coincidence? Did Hannah just have incredible luck or had she known Jonesy was going to call Nora out of the house? What would she have done if that hadn't happened? Knocked Nora over the head? Pretended she was taking Joy for a walk? I was inclined to believe she had a connection with the dealer and had set him up to phone Nora. Good. We could lean on the slimy bastard with threats of accessory to unlawful confinement charges. I picked up the phone and called Ed. Aileen answered and didn't sound too pleased to have to bring him to the phone as he was having a late dinner. But hey, that was the policeman's lot. And the lot of the policeman's wife.

I told him the latest bit of news and he said he'd have a cruiser over to visit Jonesy right away. If there was anything else to tell me he'd call, otherwise, he suggested I get off to bed. Given our suspects, he still thought Joy would be unharmed and I agreed with him. I would just like to be absolutely sure we weren't barking up the wrong tree and that Hannah Silverstein wasn't just off doing what she said she was going do. Getting some R and R. Then the horror was, who had Joy?

I put that thought away as best I could. I munched on my granola, not the best meal in the world but the only thing to eat before bed. One more call. I had to see what was happening with Paula. I phoned and Mrs. Jackson answered.

"Chris, she's gone to bed. She said to tell you if you called that she was doing fine and do you want to come over for breakfast tomorrow?"

"Yes, I do, and is she? Doing fine, I mean?"

Mrs. J. sighed. "It could be worse. I think she's got so much to worry about that in a funny way, Craig's buggering off like this has gone on the back burner. But not on mine it hasn't. I intend to give that man a piece of my mind when he deigns to come back."

"Hey, you've got to stand in line."

"I mean, how could he do this to her, Chris?"

I had no answer and it was a plea I'd heard from heartbroken parents before. Those situations were far worse of course but it boiled down to the same thing, one human being who was incapable of empathizing with any other person. Which made me think of Joy. If Hannah and Zach had taken her, for whatever reason, they were revealing a serious level of callousness.

"How are you holding up?" I asked her.

"All right. It cheers me up to have time with Chelsea and the boys have been wonderful. They call me almost every hour on the hour."

Paula's brothers were all into their fifties by now but Marion always called them the boys.

"How's the case coming along? You sound exhausted."

How did she detect that? I'd made a point of putting on a chipper voice. I told her what had been happening since we last talked.

"I know what you mean about them being callous, Chris, but at least that poor little child will have somebody to communicate with her. Maybe that's why they've taken her. She's one of their own."

I held that idea to my chest for comfort. We chatted a bit more, then hung up.

I got the cats and crawled into bed.

Before I even got over to Paula's Sunday morning, there was a series of phone calls.

The first was from Leo.

"I know I'm supposed to be bonding with Sigmund and repairing the past, but I tell you, Chris, I've had it with the yin-yang. I don't know how I spawned somebody whose values, interests, and appetites are the antithesis to mine."

I risked a joke. "You mean he hates opera?"

That actually got a laugh out of him. "He loathes it. I wouldn't mind that so much but he's trying to pretend he doesn't. It's horrible. He's got no spine."

"You're probably scaring him to death. Pretend he's a patient, be nice."

"My patients are all psychopaths. Surely you're not saying my own flesh and blood is psychopathic?"

Now he was having a joke. We did an update. I had to tell him about Nora and the dealer. He was less upset than I'd thought he'd be.

"I suspected as much. So in other words, the window of opportunity has expanded somewhat?"

"Yes. I'd say we can tack on at least another twenty-five minutes before she actually went inside the house."

"I suppose all we can do now is wait?"

"I'm afraid so."

He invited me over for dinner, which I refused, saying I was spending the day with Paula, and I went back to finishing my shower. Not to be. Next call was from Katherine. Meeting tomorrow at nine. How was I? And so on.

I'd barely dried off when there was another call. Jessica reported no further word from Hannah, and all the circle of friends were pleading ignorance of her whereabouts.

Next was Ed reporting on the encounter with Jonesy. "He claims that Nora called him asking for weed and said she wanted it right away. He called back and arranged the drop like she said. The only problem is that Nora swears she didn't call him at two o'clock. She says it was much earlier, maybe as early as one. Back to him and he said he makes a point of not recognizing voices. And yeah it might have been some other bitch but he gets a lot of calls, don't he?"

"Good witness."

"He's going down with this one, Chris. I'll make sure he does."

"So it looks like we're dealing with somebody who knew Jones and knew Nora's connection with him. Which in my books brings us back to Hannah. Deidre might have told her."

"That's still our most likely scenario, and her partner is Zachary Taylor, who now cannot be found."

"A camper is a good place to hide a child. It'd be a bit cramped but they can keep her inside most of the time."

"We've warned all border crossings and the highway patrol guys but it's my gut feeling they haven't gone too far. It's easier to hide if they're not on the move."

"Any progress on Deidre's case?"

"None. We're doing door to door but so far everybody was sealed up tight on Tuesday night, watching the *Sopranos*. Bad guys are fascinating if you don't have to deal with them all day. Then they are the boring ignorant heartless pieces of shite we know them to be."

"Copy that."

CHAPTER FIFTY-ONE

I finally got hold of Barbara Cheevers. She sounded harried and I could hear a baby wailing in the background.

"Er, would you hold for a moment?"

While I waited I walked over to the window. It had stopped raining and a thin sickly sun was struggling with heavy overcast. Looked like a losing battle to me.

Barbara returned. "So sorry. She's teething. Miss Morris, I wonder if it would be possible to meet you in person? I have some papers that would be easier to explain if you could see them. Frankly, I think I need a breath of fresh air, not to mention a coffee. My husband says he is willing to hold the fort for a short while. Would you be free in, say, ten minutes to meet me at the Tim Hortons on West Street?"

I hesitated. I didn't want to deprive the poor woman of her mental health break but I was expected to be at Paula's by now.

"Can you give me some idea what this is about?"

The baby noises were if anything worse. Mrs. Cheevers didn't seem to have anywhere else to go. I repeated what I'd said.

"You wanted to know if we had had any complaints from residents about, er, inappropriate behaviour. Well, I spoke to Avril Bentley who is now the supervisor for all the retirement homes in the city and she said there were a couple that I thought you might like to know about..." Her next words were drowned out. "Will you hold on for a moment?"

When she came back to the phone I said. "Ten minutes at Tim Hortons."

I phoned Paula's as I was on the move. She sounded very stressed out.

"Come as soon as you can."

As promised, I reached the Tim Hortons in ten minutes but Barbara Cheevers must have run out of the house and not stopped until she was sitting down at a table. She even had a coffee and a doughnut in front of her. When I entered she waved at me and I slid into the molded plastic chair across from her.

"Do you want to get a coffee?" she asked. She had the hollow-eyed look of a sleep-deprived mother and she was in mufti, a tatty sweater and jeans.

"I wouldn't mind. Be right back."

Tim's was, bless its Canadian socks, busy, as people lined up anxious to get their gloom-chasing fix of caffeine and sugar. I joined the lineup, which was moving fast as relentlessly cheerful women, all of them well into middle age, took orders. I got my large black coffee and a coconut-sprinkled donut that I couldn't resist. As I headed back to join Barbara, a well-turned-out woman entered the café. It had started to rain as expected and she was shaking out her umbrella. She smiled at me.

"Good morning, Miss Morris."

For a moment I didn't recognize her out of context and also she was wearing a smart coat and a red hat. It was Mrs. Scott. She was with a man, also well-turned-out. I presumed this was her husband and they were on their way to church. I returned her greeting and continued on my way. I had just sat down when my cell buzzed. Leo's name showed on the call display. I sighed. I wasn't in the mood to play family counsellor; I wanted to talk to Barbara Cheevers and get on over to Paula.

I barely had time for a greeting when he said, "Chris, they've located the camper van. You were right; they didn't go far. Would you believe they are in the trailer park on the other side of the narrows?"

"And Joy? Is she with them?"

"We don't know yet. Ed has moved his officers to the vicinity but he's being absolutely careful. We don't know if this is a dangerous situation or not. Nobody has approached them yet. Ed is on his way, and given the circumstances, I'm going too. I'm actually waiting outside right now to be picked up." He paused and I knew what was coming next. "Chris. Will you come? At the very least you can keep me from killing those two bastards. But you've got some relationship with both the guy and the girl. If we need anybody to talk to them, you can."

"Of course I'll come but we'll need an interpreter or we're dead in the water."

"Shit, of course. We'd better roust out the Manolo girl."

"Leo, just a minute, I have another possibility. I'll call you back." I held up my finger to Barbara, who was looking at me with curiosity, and went over to Mrs. Scott, who had just been served.

"Mrs. Scott, may I have a word with you?"

Rather startled, she nodded and I led her over to a corner of the room where we could speak in privacy. I told her as succinctly as I could what we suspected had happened and that I needed her help.

"Of course I'll come. Let me just tell my husband."

While she did that, I clicked back to Leo. "I'll be there right away. I've got Mrs. Scott, I'll explain later."

Barbara Cheevers was waiting patiently at the table.

"I'm so sorry but I've got an emergency to deal with, I'll have to get back to you."

She reached down into her briefcase, which was the only vestige of her workday world she had about her. "Take these with you. I think they're clear enough. I'll be at my office tomorrow, all being well." She gave a wry grin. "Teeth take precedence."

I grabbed the folder and hurried over to Mrs. Scott and we went out to my car.

"I cannot believe Hannah would do anything to harm that child," she said. "She's her godmother and I know she doted on her. Why would she abduct her?"

"We don't know with complete certainty that she has, but everything points in that direction. We believe she is with Zachary Taylor. The police have located his camper van on the other side of the narrows. Needless to say we are treating the situation with extreme caution."

Henley Trailer Park was off the main road that led to Casino Rama, where even on a Sunday morning there was a steady stream of hopefuls heading in that direction. As I approached the turnoff, I saw a cruiser ahead of me. It slowed down to make the turn and I could see Leo was in the front seat. He must have noticed me in the side mirror because he swivelled around and gave a curt wave.

I'd only been to the trailer park once before when we'd been called in to look at a possible arson case. Several trailers had been set alight. All the occupants were attending a dance at the community centre, so nobody had been hurt, but the result was devastating. It turned out the arsonist was a ten-year-old boy with major mental health problems. He said later he liked to see the flames eating up the trailers and he liked even more to see the firefighters putting out the blaze. He was in a correctional facility for juveniles now and I shuddered to think he'd be out in the near future.

What I remembered about the place was that there was a long road in with twists and turns. We soon came up to a bend and there were five or six cruisers parked to the side and one blocking the road. Ed, bless him, had had the forethought to have all the flashers turned off. Our suspects might not be able to hear us but they might pick up flashing lights reflecting off the rain.

I pulled up, asked Mrs. Scott to stay in the car, and got out. Ed was leaning against his cruiser, talking to Leo. He smiled at me and I thought there was relief in his eyes.

"Chris. I was just saying to Dr. Forgach that we have to be careful. We don't know what we're dealing with and the last thing we need is to scare anybody into doing something dangerous."

"And I was saying," said Leo impatiently, "this is my own grandchild we're talking about. Both you and I don't think the threat level is high. I want to just walk up to the door and talk to them, or whatever passes for communication with these damn people. You can keep your officers on the ready but I just don't think we'll need the cavalry. Tell him, Chris."

I spoke to Ed. "Have there been any sightings?"

"No, but we can hear the generator running and there are lights on in the trailer so somebody's home. Come, I'll show you. Dr. Forgach, I understand your concern but I would prefer you to remain here for the moment."

Ed was not a loud-voiced guy like Franklin but when he meant business there was no mistaking it. Besides, Leo was still a professional and he knew he could be a liability. He gave a nod.

I followed Ed down the track. Years ago, somebody had built a stone fence around the property that later became the trailer park, and although it was crumbling in places, there were still long intact stretches. The road went through the open gateway and dipped down through fields to the waterfront. On both sides were stands of thick evergreens that afforded an excellent cover.

"This way," said Ed. He was speaking softly. We assumed our subjects wouldn't hear us but you never knew who was with them. We stepped through tangled weeds that were choking a gap in the wall. I was glad I'd put on my winter boots, as the ground was soaked. Ed moved cautiously up to the rise of the hill and stopped. He handed me a pair of binoculars.

"Down there."

The lot was deserted; November isn't a favourite time for RVs and Henley's had nothing to offer except space. But there nestled in the corner close to the treeline was a blue and white camper van. I looked through the binoculars, and as I did so, the rear door opened and Zachary himself climbed out. He lifted his arms and I saw Joy jump from the step so he could give her a big swing to the ground. Hannah was behind her and she came down as well. I felt such a flood of relief at seeing them, my legs actually felt shaky. Zachary took Joy by one hand and Hannah by the other and they started to walk away from the camper. Joy was wearing her canary yellow raincoat and matching boots. I realized they were headed for a playground at the far end of the lot. A happy family if ever I saw one.

"What do you recommend?" Ed asked.

"I think Leo is right. But I don't think it should be him who talks to them. I'll go."

"Chris, are you sure?"

"No ... but let's put it this way. We're not going to communicate with them by loudspeaker and we certainly don't want to frighten the child. Mrs. Scott is a civilian so we can't involve her yet. But Joy and I did all right before. Let's hope the magic works now."

I took out my notebook and quickly scribbled out, "Let's talk. Mrs. Scott is here and she will help us sort this out."

Ed squeezed my arm. "Go girl."

I started to push my way through the evergreens so I could get back to the path. Zachary must have spotted the movement because he turned, signed something to Hannah who also turned. Then he snatched up Joy, and like startled deer, they began to run back toward the camper.

Ed called over to me. "Shit, Chris, what now?"

"Same scenario. Don't move yet."

I reached the path that made walking much easier and began moving at what I hoped looked like a brisk non-threatening pace toward the camper. Zach bundled Joy inside with Hannah close behind.

He followed them but in a moment he was out again, and this time he was carrying a rifle.

CHAPTER FIFTY-TWO

I halted and waved my hand in what I hoped would be construed as a friendly greeting. Behind me in the woods, I heard Ed shout, "Hold it." I didn't turn and look at him but I assumed he had come out from his cover. It was often a tough call to show police power. Sometimes it worked and intimidated the bad guys, sometimes it had the opposite effect and panicked them. In this case I thought the latter was going to swing into play. Although Zach hadn't raised the rifle, his body was tense and on the alert. I could see his quick glance behind me. He stepped back. I started talking, it made me feel better even if he couldn't hear me.

"Zachary. I've just come to see how Joy is doing. We were worried about her. Nobody knew where she was."

I made a gesture of child, pointed at the camper, and acted out worried. It might not be ASL but it seemed to work. He flapped his free hand in a clear "go away" signal.

Again I heard Ed shout from somewhere behind me. "Christine, we've got him covered. If he raises that fucking rifle we're taking him out."

I didn't turn but shouted back. "Not yet. I don't want the child caught in this."

Zach must have got the gist of what I was saying because his eyes darted over my head to where I guessed a formidable row of officers were lined up. He took yet another step back so that he was now at the foot of the steps to the camper. I saw him shift his weight so he was more prepared for action.

What action that was I never knew because the door opened and Hannah emerged with Joy in her arms. She grabbed Zachary's arm, forcing him to face her, and made some fast gestures in the universal language of, "Are you out of your mind?" Joy was making some happy chirrups and pointing at me. She struggled to get to the ground and Hannah put her down, whereupon the child ran over to me, a huge smile on her face. She didn't see some crazy guy with a rifle and a situation that was potentially extremely dangerous. She saw somebody she knew and had had fun with. She grabbed my hand and tugged me in the direction of the camper. I let her until I was close enough to the two adults that Hannah at least could read my lips.

"We were worried," I said again. "Nobody knew where Joy was."

"She is with her father where she belongs," said Hannah in her harsh voice.

"Will you come and talk to us? Mrs. Scott is here."

Hannah made signs at Zachary. He replied with some excited gesticulating.

"He wants to know why you have brought the police. She is his child. He has a right to bring her here."

I wasn't about to discuss the legalities of non-authorized custody with a rifle as a persuader.

"You must ask Zach to drop his rifle. I would like to take Joy and we can all have a talk."

"Where?"

"Well there's not much room in your camper and it's cold out here. Why don't we go to the OHHA centre and discuss this?"

She translated this for Zachary, who was still looking mutinous. Finally Hannah placed her hand on his arm in a pleading gesture and he gave a reluctant nod. His eyes were glistening, the pupils dilated. This guy was pumped up, testosterone or synthetic, I didn't know and didn't care. He was scary.

"Hannah, please tell him to toss the gun away from him. I don't feel comfortable with him holding it and above all we don't want Joy to be frightened."

She had to know what I was getting at because she was looking pretty frightened herself. I sure hoped she had some influence over him. She signed to Zach. He didn't do what I'd asked but took a couple of paces away to a tree stump and put the gun on top of it. Then he walked back to us. I was holding my breath. *Dear God, Ed, don't do anything precipitous.* Hannah tapped his arm to get his attention and made more signs. He shrugged and stuffed his hands in his pockets. Then he gave me a grin that in other circumstances I would have called mischievous, made a sign with his right hand and a striking motion against his left. I recognized it from the DVD. His finger was pointed in my direction. The K handshape, to kill. Hannah was already turning away from him and didn't see what he did.

"Let me get my purse," Hannah said to me.

I hoped to hell she meant what she said and there wasn't another gun in the camper.

"I'll go on ahead with Joy, then. There's a police car parked just down the lane. We can go in that."

Joy was still holding on to my hand but I wasn't sure if she would come with me. I gave her my biggest smile. "Do you want to race me?" I asked and made running movements with my fingers. She grinned with delight and immediately set off down the path. I followed her.

Ed, with his revolver drawn, was on the edge of the clearing. Still trotting, I shouted. "They've agreed to talk. Can you hide the cruisers, just one or two will be enough. I don't want to scare them off."

It felt strange, acting as casually as I could, trotting fast, and at the same time, shouting anxious messages at a fully armed police contingent.

Ed yelled back. "Copy that."

Joy slowed down, more interested in my catching her than in winning the race. I grabbed her by the waist and swung her around. This gave me a chance to see what was happening behind me. Hannah was out of the camper and walking down the path, Zach, rifle-less, was a few paces behind her. I spun Joy around again and saw Hannah reach for his hand. I picked up Joy and held her against my chest so she didn't see the police officers, who were crouched behind the wall, jump up and seize Hannah and Zachary and force them to the ground so they could be handcuffed.

I continued on, carrying her to a waiting cruiser. Mrs. Scott's anxious face was at the window. I put Joy on the seat.

"Tell her I'll be right back. We're going for a ride."

I closed the door and walked back to the fence.

Ed, grim-faced, was standing over a handcuffed Zachary Taylor who was actually bellowing, half-formed words mixed in with sheer animal sounds that communicated even more. Another officer had Hannah by the arm. She was crying. Her hands were behind her back and she was trying to sniff back the mucus running from her nose and the unwiped tears. I felt sorry for her, but I was thoroughly pissed off. You don't participate in a situation with an armed man pulling a gun on a police officer and not expect to be taken down. I stood in front of her so she could see what I was saying.

"We are going down to the police station. We will have an interpreter. Do you understand?"

She nodded yes.

"Is the child all right?" Ed asked me.

"She seems fine. Mrs. Scott is with her. I think she should be taken home until we get this sorted."

We were all moving out of the muddy field now. Zachary, still yelling, was being put into one of the cruisers flanked by two constables. Hannah was being led to another one.

"Let's go in my car," said Ed, and he put his arm around my shoulders. It felt really good.

"You gave me a bit of a scare out there, Chris. I have to tell you, my blood pressure must have shot up when that lad appeared with a rifle."

I grinned at him. "Your blood pressure! You weren't the one looking down the barrel."

He gave me a big squeeze. "You done good, kid."

"Ed Chaffey. That's the nicest thing I've heard since I was ten."

CHAPTER FIFTY-THREE

The next two hours were filled with the usual police business of writing endless reports, followed by a long interview with both Zachary and Hannah. Mrs. Scott delivered Joy to her home then returned so she could interpret for us. It wasn't difficult to guess what Zachary was telling her. Joy was his child and he wasn't happy with the way she was being treated. She should be with him. Hannah had agreed with this, he said. Nora was worse than useless. It had been so easy to lure her out of the house, she was a pothead and should never be looking after Joy. Zach had waited outside the house until Loretta left, then he texted a dealer he knew and said Nora wanted dope right away. By coincidence she had already contacted the guy so she wasn't suspicious when he called and said he could come right then. They knew she'd done that before; Dee had caught her once and told Hannah about it. Hannah waited until Nora left the house and went in and got Joy. Zach was around the corner in the camper.

"Didn't you think people would worry about her?" I asked through Mrs. Scott.

"I was going to leave a note," said Hannah, "but in all the rush I forgot. When we realized the police were involved, we were scared and decided to hide out for a while until we could decide what to do. She was far better off with us and was having a good time."

"Why the gun when Sergeant Morris approached the camper?" Ed asked Zach.

"I don't know. It wasn't loaded. I wanted to scare her away. We didn't need anybody else. We were doing fine the three of us."

"That was a stupid and dangerous thing to do," said Ed. He was angry and didn't hide it. "You could have got yourself killed. Not to mention the child being in danger."

Zachary suddenly looked sullen, and to my astonishment, he closed his eyes. He had switched off. That was that. We got more information from Hannah but the picture was now clear. What she did add though was a stunner. She said Zachary had gone to her apartment on Tuesday night. One thing had led to another and he'd stayed with her until the wee hours of the morning. No, she hadn't told us that because she was embarrassed. What kind of girl sleeps with her best friend's ex-boyfriend? He hadn't mentioned a date with Dee but she would swear an oath that he had been at her place by quarter past eleven and stayed late. It never occurred to her that he was a suspect in Dee's murder. Why did people always think the worst of deaf people?

That was essentially it. If she were to be believed, Zachary had an alibi for the crucial times of Dee's death.

Finally we wrapped it up. Ed was charging both of them and they were being held over until tomorrow, when the court would set bail or not. We got back to Jessica and she in turn contacted Hannah's parents who said they would come immediately. I left it in Ed's hands.

My mind was swirling round and round. It appeared that two of our prime suspects, Sigmund Forgach and Zachary Taylor, were now off the list. That was good on the one hand, but on the other, I felt sick at how chancy it all was. Deidre had been late getting to the appointment with Zach, who had not waited as he'd threatened. Sigmund had let her off at the park and not waited either. After that she'd encountered somebody else who had picked her up, taken her somewhere, and killed her. Here I was on surer ground. The odds were high that this was somebody she knew at least well enough to accept a ride from. Yes, I know it was all happening in small-town Ontario where people never locked their doors and there was no serious crime, but it was getting late and she wasn't a fool. Don't get into a car with somebody you don't know.

Ray had been on the right track at our earlier meeting. We'd been too focused on Deidre's murder as if it were a celebrity issue, taking the position that her high profile had been what made her a target. This was reinforced by the strange letters she'd received. However, I was becoming more and more convinced this was a random and disorganized act. If it hadn't been her, it might have been some other woman. So who was on the prowl and what was his territory? If I put Deidre in the picture, both where she lived and where she had been found were in a small area. And that area included Doris Bryant's apartment. Franklin's words kept echoing in my head. "Funny cases." Were the two crimes connected? I'd have to get to Ray and see if we could do a geographic profile. ViCLAS could pull up any other assaults reported in the city in the last year. Where the heck had I left Mrs. Cheevers's report? It might come in very handy now.

I'd called ahead to Paula to say I was delayed. Mrs. Jackson opened the door but Chelsea was right behind her. I scooped her up and held her so tightly in my arms she yelped.

"Auntie Chris, where've you been? We've been waiting all day long. Since I got up. Mommy isn't well and she's lying down but I've been playing with Grandma all the time."

"And you can tell I've run out of ideas," said Marion with a grin.

"No, we've been having lots of fun," said Chelsea loyally. But Mrs. Jackson looked worn out, and I could see a very energetic six-year-old had taken its toll.

"Paula's in the living room having a rest."

Over Chelsea's head Marion frowned. I gathered Paula hadn't had a good day.

"Anything happen with that other business?" I asked.

"Not a thing."

Chelsea looked up at us. "I know what you're talking about."

I tweaked her nose. "You do, do you, Miss Clever Clogs?"

"Daddy has gone away for a holiday because his nerves were shredded."

I gaped at her. "Is that what he said?"

"Yes. He's been so busy, he said he needs a rest too. Mommy is getting her rest but she had to go to the hospital. He doesn't have to do that." She paused. "I think he could have rested here just as well, don't you, Auntie Chris? There's a couch downstairs he could use."

"True. Anyway, let's go see your mother."

She skipped ahead of me, calling out, "Mommy, Auntie Chris is here. I think she's had a hard day. Her nerves look shredded."

I looked at Marion and we both burst out laughing. "I guess that's the word of the week, is it?'

"Seems that way, thanks to my son-in-law. It'll be more than his nerves that are shredded if I get hold of him."

I went into the living room. Paula was stretched out on the couch and she looked so wretched and ill, I felt a rush of fear. However, she pushed herself into a sitting position when she saw me and waved a mock fist in the air.

"What kept you? No, no, let me guess, you were working, even though today is Sunday and most folks can get the day off. Or are you in it for the overtime?"

This was a running joke at the office. Profilers don't get overtime. Our hours are Monday to Friday, nine to five. What you do over and above is up to you, just don't turn in a requisition. I think if we added up and charged for accumulated extra hours, the province would go broke.

I gave her a hug. She seemed to me even thinner and fragile although she'd only been in the hospital a couple of days. She had dark circles under her eyes and her lips were cracked and dry.

"Do you want to see the drawings Grandma and I made?" Chelsea asked.

"Of course I do, what do you think I am, a Philistine? Go get them."

She raced off. "I'm going to put the kettle on," said Marion. "And I saved the pancake batter. I can whip you up some pancakes in minutes. Do you want coffee?"

"You bet."

She went out to the kitchen, tactful as ever. I seized the opportunity.

"Any word from Craig?"

"He sent an email. Probably didn't want Mom to answer the phone. He said he'll be away a week maybe less but he has to get away. His nerves are..."

I stopped her. "Let me guess, his nerves are shredded."

She gave me a wan smile. "Chelsea told you that, did she?"

"The word came up more than once."

"Chris, how could he do this? I feel like I've been living in a dream and I just woke up. He is a self-centred bastard and I couldn't see it. I know nobody liked him but I kept kidding myself that he was different with me, that I was the only one who understood him. And he adores Chelsea, that counted for a lot."

I didn't think this was the time to point out that a man who adores his child doesn't just take off on her when her mother is ill.

She looked away. "He's been seeing somebody. I got into his cellphone — yes, I know, but being a detective comes in handy sometimes. There are at least a dozen calls. Easy to trace. There're all to a Miss Waneta Bloom, great name eh? She works at the golf club. I called there this morning and they said she's off on sick leave for a week."

"I guess her nerves are shredded."

She laughed but tears filled her eyes. Chelsea came bouncing down the stairs with a bundle of papers in her hand.

She immediately started to spread them on the floor. I thought she'd noticed that her mother was crying but chose to ignore it.

So that was about it. I ate Marion's delicious pancakes with more gusto than I really felt, played with Chelsea a long round of Snap, put her to bed with a story, then spent the rest of the evening with Mrs. Jackson and Paula. I told them what had happened, not holding back on the scene in the field. It was a good distraction for both of them.

"Surely they'd know people would be distraught at Joy's disappearance," said Paula. On all of our minds was the horror of anything like that happening to Chelsea.

Finally, Mrs. Jackson asked if I'd stay the night and I agreed. I phoned Gary to ask him to look in on Bertie and Tory. Paula found me some PJs and a toothbrush and at about ten o'clock we all went to bed. At Paula's request I shared the king-sized bed with her but it wasn't like it used to be when we were teenagers. There was no giggling together, no sharing of secrets. She took a sleeping pill and fell asleep quickly. In spite of my fatigue, I stayed awake for almost an hour longer, re-experiencing over and over the image of a large young man filled with anger aiming a long-barrelled rifle right at my heart.

CHAPTER FIFTY-THREE

Paula woke up early. She had been moaning in her sleep, which in turn woke me up so we lay talking for quite a long time. Some of it was rehashing the situation with Craig, but some of it was serious reflection about what would happen if she did have cancer and if that meant a death sentence and what would happen to Chelsea in that case.

We must have been talking for almost an hour and daylight was just happening.

"I don't have to ask you to take care of her, I know you will," said Paula.

I grabbed her hand and squeezed it hard.

"Chelsea will be getting up soon, I'd better look lively... Thanks Chris. When we were teenagers did you ever imagine we'd end up as two old broads lying in bed together sharing deep thoughts about the meaning of life?"

"Hey, who are you calling an old broad? I'm three months younger than you. Call yourself an old broad if you like but don't include me."

"Can you hold your pee for eight hours the way you used to?"

"You have to be kidding?"

"Old broad! Have you noticed some of your eyebrows are migrating to your chin?"

"On occasion."

"Old broad! What's the best definition of a really old broad?"

"I'm almost afraid to ask. What is it?"

"If a man asks to see her tits, she lifts her skirt."

I dumped a pillow on her head and got out of bed.

"Speaking of holding your pee, I've got to get to the bathroom."

"Another characteristic of an old broad, you build your trips according to how many bathroom stops there are along the way."

We did old broad jokes right down to the kitchen, sharing them with Mrs. Jackson who had one of her own.

"Old broads know if they can't be a good role model to the younger generation, they can at least be a dire warning."

Chelsea soon joined us and we had to stop as everything needed explaining. But we actually had fun and when I left I was happy to see some colour in Paula's face and a sparkle in her eyes.

The office meeting was scheduled for nine-thirty so I raced back to my apartment long enough to change my clothes and give Bertie and Tory a couple of rubs they were mad about. I brought the papers with me that Barbara Cheevers had handed to me in Tim Hortons, which seemed a lifetime away.

As usual, Janice greeted me with a cheery, "Coffee's freshly made."

"No calls for now, Janice, unless they are urgent."

"Does that include, 'this is her mother and it's urgent' calls?"

"Bless you, Janice, I leave that to your judgement, but it especially includes those kind."

"What if your friend phones? Shall I just talk to him myself? I don't mind a bit. He sounds like Sean Connery."

"Keep your hands off, that call should most definitely come through."

I poured a cup, carried it to my office, and turned my "busy" sign around.

Barbara had photocopied all the records from Sunshine Lodge as far back as the changing of the locks three years ago and she had added some notes of her own.

> January 14, 2001: Locks changed on outer doors
> and each individual apartment. *(Before that we*

had open access to the building which the residents preferred but when we had what seemed to be a rash of petty thefts, the city decided for security reasons to change its policies. Each resident was given a key to the outer door and a separate key to their apartment. The superintendents had a master key for both the outer doors, front and back, and the apartments. The superintendents at this time were Mr. and Mrs. John Nicholls. They had been with the city in the Sunshine Lodge for twenty years. In March 2001 they retired and went to live in Florida.)

On the page was a list of complaints that had been made to the superintendents. Nothing that stood out, a litany you might expect.

Mrs. Sweeney, apt. 201, says her toilet keeps over-flowing. Plunged it out. She keeps putting paper towels down.

February 17, 2001: A call from Mrs. McGinnis that her husband was breathing funny. On checking, I found Mr. McGinnis in the middle of an apparent heart attack. Called 911 and he was removed to hospital.

March 1, 2001: Miss Burman found in the hallway. She had had a stroke. Removed to hospital. Two malfunctioning televisions were replaced and a new stove installed in apartment 333.

March 2001 to March 2002: New superintendents Mrs. Pereira and son.

Either the new supers had had a trouble-free year or they hadn't bothered to keep a record of the light bulb changes and TV fixing. However Barbara had attached, on a separate sheet, a report from the social worker, a Miss Avril Bentley. The report was handwritten on yellow lined paper. I got a bit of a jolt from that.

February 22, 2002: I received a complaint from Mrs. Pereira that one of the residents was harassing her son by making inappropriate remarks and touching inappropriately. I was unable to determine exactly what constituted these actions except that Mrs. P. said the resident was "acting sexy." Miss Cohen, the woman accused, is an elderly woman. I questioned her as delicately as I could but she denied doing anything amiss and she was very upset at the suggestion. All I can say about her is that she is in the habit of wandering down to the common room in her nightclothes. However, Mrs. Pereira is still upset about the incident and has tendered her resignation.

April 2002 to December 2002: Unable to find a suitable replacement. We are using Reliable Cleaning Services.

That grabbed my attention. This must be the woman that Grace had mentioned.

Miss Bentley wrote:

I spoke to Mrs. Salamonica as best I could but she is very confused. I also reported it to her son who is her guardian. He saw no reason to involve the police as his mother is having delusions on a regular basis and should be placed in a long-term facility as soon as possible.

May 15: Done.

January 2003 to June 2004 Norman Evans:
Norman resigned in May citing personal reasons. He has returned to Nova Scotia. His long-time partner apparently has died from AIDS.

April 29, 2004: Mrs. Maria Salamonica has complained to me that a man entered her apartment and "tickled her all over."

July 2004: Mr. and Mrs. L. Desjardins hired. Some doubt about their suitability but beggars can't be choosers.

So there was one complaint of sexual harassment, no, that's not right, two, if you include the super and her son, but I couldn't conceive of an old lady with Alzheimer's continuing on to a life of crime.

There was a phone number on the sheet and I keyed in Avril Bentley's number.

She answered right away. Her voice was lightly accented, British.

I explained who I was and why I was calling.

"Oh my yes, I remember Mrs. Salamonica. It was most distressing. Poor woman was in the grip of Alzheimer's and her family were in complete denial. She would say the most outrageous and inappropriate things and they would just laugh at her."

"Can you give me an example?"

"Hmm. Let me see. There was one time when we were having a do in the common room, somebody's birthday, I believe it was, Mrs. Salamonica suddenly called out, 'Hands up all those here who are getting laid on a regular basis...'" Miss Bentley gave an embarrassed chuckle. "I mean to say, the average age in the room must have been eighty. And such a vulgar term. Heaven knows where she heard it."

This was an old broad indeed.

"That was the last straw as far as her son was concerned," continued Miss Bentley. "He had her put in a long-term facility the same week."

"Do you think there was any credence to her story about a man coming into her apartment?"

"None at all. I've seen it happen so many times now. Some people with Alzheimer's lose control of their libidos, shall we say. They will, er, touch themselves, constantly and in public. It can be quite embarrassing. Maria was like that."

"Was she upset when she made her report to you?"

"She was but then she was prone to cry about everything. The news on television, the state of Africa, you name it... I assure you, Sergeant Morris, if I had thought for one moment that what she said was true I would have been on the blower immediately to you people."

"May I ask how strict a control you kept on the keys?"

She made tut-tutting sounds. "We are as careful as we can be but with elderly residents it's very difficult. They give out a spare key to family members who forget to return them if the resident moves on. And we can't possibly afford to change the locks every time a resident loses a key or if they move on."

I could see her point. I went back to Barbara's report. "Could I just ask you about one other case? In February 2002 the super, Mrs. Pereira, lodged a complaint about one of the residents who she said was harassing her son and quote, making inappropriate remarks and touching inappropriately, unquote. What was all that about?"

More tutting sounds on the other end of the phone. "In my opinion, Mrs. Pereira completely overreacted. The resident, Miss Cohen was her name I believe, was a sweet rather dotty old lady who was deaf as a post. To make sure people were talking straight at her, she'd turn them around. She was always very gentle about it but she liked to get up close so she could hear better, I believe. Mrs. P. said she had her son around the waist, which she might have done, but it wouldn't have been lechery like it was with poor old Maria."

"And inappropriate remarks? What about them?"

"I couldn't make head nor tail of that from Mrs. Pereira. She is Portugese and has a heavy accent. But as far as I can tell, Miss Cohen had said something like 'I love you sweetie,' when he'd done something nice for her."

"Was the boy bothered by that?"

"What boy?"

"The superintendent's son."

She laughed heartily. "Oh no, he wasn't a boy. He was an adult. Must be in his late forties, early fifties. No, it didn't bother him. I think he liked the attention he got from the old ladies. But his mother had such a grip on him. I doubt he could take a pee, excuse my language, without her permission."

"Do you remember the man's name?"

"I'm sorry, I don't."

"Miss Bentley, I understand you are now the supervisor for all of the city lodges."

"That's right. I've been here since last year."

"Have there been any complaints from residents in any of the other lodges that were to do with sexual harassments, assaults, or anything like that?"

"No... if there were I would call the police as I said. We are required by law to do that."

"So there was nothing?"

"Not in my time, except..." Another pause. "There was one incident but it wasn't a formal complaint or anything like that, and it didn't involve a resident as such, but there was what you might call an incident at the Atrium Lodge last October. The granddaughter of one of the residents stayed over in the lodge. She has Down's syndrome but is quite high functioning. She told her grandmother that a man had come into her room and asked her to do naughty things. The girl lives in Huronia Residence and apparently she says this at least once a week."

"So it might have been a case of crying wolf once too often."

"I doubt that." Miss Bentley sounded quite huffy, as if I were impugning her reputation. "It was all a fabrication, all her imagination."

I tried a different tack. "At the time this last incident happened, was there a lock on the front door?"

"Yes. All of the lodges were changed over at the same time. Do for one, you have to do for all."

"And did the superintendent confirm that the door was securely locked?"

"Yes, of course... no, wait a minute, that was when Arthur Bennington was the super and he had a sudden appendectomy. He had complications and was off for a month."

"So there wasn't anybody checking on security?"

"Dear me, of course there was. In cases like this we always get in a temporary super."

"The temps come from Reliable Cleaning Services, I understand."

"That's right. But Sergeant, please don't make a mountain out of a molehill. We, I, take the best care of our residents. These cases you have dragged up are isolated incidents. I discount Mrs. Pereira. Nothing happened."

"Something did happen to Doris Bryant. That was not a figment of her imagination."

Dead silence. "I am very sorry about that."

I heard a beep on the line. "I have another call. I'm afraid I have to go."

"I don't mind waiting."

"Very well. Never mind, I'll leave it."

"You said, 'in my time,' earlier. Was there a complaint concerning sexual assault at another time?"

"I understand there was but I don't know much about it. I can't be expected to look over every single previous report, can I? The social worker in charge was Elaine Mortimer, who is an experienced woman. It would have been settled before I took over."

"Can I have a copy of the report you're referring to?"

"I suppose I can dig it up."

"Please do. One other question. I see you use yellow notepaper for your report."

"Yes, I do. I don't type and I didn't expect to be raked over the coals for it."

"Oh, it's nothing like that. I just wondered if your notepaper is accessible to others. Did you ever miss any?"

"The answer to that is no. I keep it in my drawer and I suppose somebody could steal some if they were so inclined but it's not exactly vellum, is it?"

Quite right. And at best it was only a slender connection to the anonymous letters sent to Deidre. But then spiderwebs look slender and are virtually indestructible.

We hung up. It was part of my job to make mountains out of molehills, then you can knock them down again if you have to. I'd rather have four unnecessary mountains than one overlooked molehill.

My suspicious friend at Reliable Cleaning Services had faxed Barbara a list of their employees. Each column recorded the name of the temp, where they were sent, and for how long.

I laid it alongside of Barbara's report. At Sunshine Lodge, the one complaint, fanciful or not, from Mrs. Salamonica had occurred when the lodge was using temps. The incident with the girl with Down's syndrome at Atrium Lodge was also at a time when Reliable Cleaning Services was supplying supers.

Bingo.

I reached for the phone and punched in Miss Bentley's number. This time she sounded decidedly frosty. She obviously now considered me a confirmed impugner.

"Miss Bentley, you said you couldn't remember the name of Mrs. Pereira's son. The one who was supposedly being harassed by a resident. Do you have it written down anywhere?"

"No, I don't. He had a different last name, as I recall. Something to do with a stepfather he didn't get along with. He kept his own father's name."

"Does the name Sylvio Torres sound familiar?"

"Why yes, that's it. I was thinking Sylvester, but no, that's it. Sylvio. What is happening, Sergeant? They haven't reopened the complaint surely."

"No, they haven't, but I'm going to."

I got off the phone, grabbed my papers, and raced out of my office. Time for a team meeting.

CHAPTER FIFTY-FOUR

W hile the team was assembling, I made a couple of phone calls. One to Elaine Mortimer, the social worker Miss Bentley mentioned, the other to the Huronia Institute. The team had assembled quickly except for Leo, who excused himself and decided to stay with Joy and Loretta at the house. He said things were going as well as could be expected. He'd even learned a few signs by now. I didn't tell him at this point what I'd discovered.

I'd got everybody copies of Barbara Cheevers's report and the list from Reliable Cleaning Services and we were going over it.

"Torres and his mother, whose name is Belva Pereira, were the supers at the Sunshine Lodge for one year, 2001 to 2002. This means that Torres could easily have copied the master key and gained access to the building whenever he wanted to. As we know, there was no sign of forced entry into Doris Bryant's apartment. He also made sure she couldn't see him. Doris was a resident when Mrs. Pereira was superintendent."

I told them what Avril had reported about Mrs. Pereira's complaint. "It seemed completely innocuous but his mother resigned and kicked up a fuss. I'd say she was revealing a high level of protectiveness."

David, who always liked to be shown as eager and attentive, pointed to the Reliable list. "I see he was hired out again at the end of April 2002 for a week. He was sent to Leisure World on West Street. And a resident there lodged a complaint on June 10, Chris has given us that report separately. The resident said a man entered her apartment and tickled her. There is no reference to his being masked or of her face being covered."

I took up the thread. "The woman is eighty-nine and suffers from macular degeneration so her eyesight is very poor and it was dark. She couldn't give a description of the man except, get this, that she kept referring to him as a farmer. Nobody made sense of that, but I'm guessing she may have meant he was wearing overalls, and I saw Torres in a pair of blue overalls when I was at his apartment."

"Has that come up anywhere else?" asked Ray.

"No. Doris never saw him because he blindfolded her. But she told Grace he smelled of disinfectant. Cleaning fluid, maybe? She also used the word *stroked*, by the way. She said he stroked her legs."

Nobody likes hearing stories like this no matter how experienced we are and there was a brief silence around the table. I let everybody have a breather to absorb what I was saying, then I continued.

"There was one more complaint from yet another lodge, the Atrium. This did not involve a resident as such, but was concerning her granddaughter, who is a Down's syndrome woman. She says a man came into her bedroom and asked her to show her bum-bum but she was scared and she shouted for her grannie. Grandma is hard of hearing and it took a while to wake her up and by then the man, if there was one, had fled. Now ladies and gentleman, if you look at the Reliable list, you can see that our Mr. Torres was hired out to the Atrium while their super was off sick. He was there one month earlier."

"Did the Down's woman say anything about him being masked?"

"No, she said he looked like one of her teachers, whatever that means. The woman has a long history of being seductive and then saying some man asked her to expose herself. The case was not taken to the police for this reason but the institute does have it on record along with nine other incidents this particular girl reported."

"Is that it for the lodges?"

"Yes, but Deidre went with somebody she knew. Torres lives two blocks away; he walks his dog. Why would she suspect him if he offered her a ride home? He was also walking Lily at the end of my street after I found that note in my mailbox. He gets around, that man does. And ... one more thing. There is a doghouse outside in Doris's backyard. Having the dog gives him a reason to be out on the streets at all hours but he could leave her in the kennel when he goes inside to do his prowling."

"I've just thought of something else," said Ed. "Remember he told us that he saw an officer writing out a ticket for Taylor's camper van? We have been unable to find any record of a parking ticket being issued so I assume he made it up. I'm wondering what he was trying to conceal."

"Where he was. I saw Deidre's bed; it's pretty narrow. It's fairly certain that Taylor visited her a few weeks ago. She wanted another sperm donor. He's a tall guy and I sort of doubt he would have stayed the night with the two of them in that bed. What if he left the house in the wee hours and Mr. Torres saw him? Sylvio wouldn't want to admit he was on the streets at that hour, so he made up a story about the ticket. Directed us toward Taylor quite nicely."

"Clever sod, isn't he?" said Jamie.

"And ruthless. My guess is that Deidre was only one of various people he was keeping an eye on. I am convinced he targets the vulnerable and or the disabled."

"But Deidre was a strong young woman," protested David.

"She was, but in his eyes she was disabled. He might have thought she'd be weaker than she was. And perhaps he hates what he'd see as deformity, but at the same time he is excited by it."

"Do you think he wrote the letters?" David asked.

"I'd bet a month's wages on it. It's just too much of a coincidence that Miss Bentley was using yellow paper when he had a temp job in the building. Maybe he liked the look of it, professional and all that."

"We'll get a search warrant," said Katherine. "Does he have a vehicle?"

"Yes, he owns a 1999 green Ford van."

Ed laced his hands behind his head. "It's time to have a talk with Mr. Torres. And a look into that van of his. Do you want to come, Chris?"

"I wouldn't miss it."

We were there within ten minutes. Mrs. Pereira was as dour as ever in her black dress and tightly drawn grey hair. She regarded us with thinly disguised hostility, not anxiety, which I thought would be a more normal response.

"He no here. What you want?"

"We'd like to talk to him."

"What about?"

Mrs. Pereira was the kind of woman who projected such sour energy, it was hard not to respond in kind. Whatever had happened in her life had turned her as bitter as absinthe. Ed was the one who was speaking to her but she didn't look at him, addressing her answers to me. She struck me as one of those women who are on the edge of madness most of their lives. Not certifiable but mad nonetheless: for whom the world is a place of danger, where people can never be trusted, and the only way to handle it is to keep your own den as small and tightly controlled as possible. She was a woman it would be easy to hate and I wondered if that was what happened to her son. A hatred he then acted out on other, more vulnerable women.

I forced myself to smile. "Is Sylvio out walking Lily?"

"Yes. Why should he no walk her?"

"Where does he usually go?"

"I don't know. He walk dog, not me. She his dog."

"Thank you, Mrs. Pereira." Ed handed her his card, which she handled as if it had been dropped in shit. He nodded at me and we went outside.

"Whew, nasty old bat, isn't she? What shall we do? Wait until he gets back?"

"I suppose that's all we can do but frankly I'd like to find him right now before he finds somebody else."

"So far he's only worked at night, Chris."

"True, but he's accelerating. If we assume he's the one who killed Deidre and molested Doris, that's only two days apart."

"I'll put out an all car alert."

"Good idea. Let's have a look out back and see if he's taken his van. If not, we can impound it."

We went around to the parking lot at the rear of the building. The spot that said Reserved For Superintendent was empty.

"Shit, Ed. I might be getting as paranoid as Mrs. Pereira but I'm getting more queasy by the minute."

"Me too. It must be catching. Well, there's nothing to stop you and I doing a bit of prowling ourselves. Orillia isn't that big a place and so far we've no reason to think he knows he's under suspicion."

CHAPTER FIFTY-FIVE

We drove around the streets for the next hour and darkness fell. The alert was out but so far nobody had sighted the man or his van. First off, I'd phoned Avril Bentley and told her to warn every residence on her list to call the police immediately if anyone answering Torres's description was seen in the vicinity. And make sure all supers knew this was serious and to be extra-vigilant. I put the fear of God up her proper British behind.

"Do you want to go to Tim Hortons for a coffee?" Ed asked me.

"Sure. Who knows, Torres might be sitting in there having a donut and make our life easier."

He wasn't but it helped both of us to take a break. Ed treated me to another coconut-sprinkled donut. We sipped our coffees quietly for a few moments.

"Ed, let's think the unthinkable. Our man is out there on the prowl and we don't know where he's going to strike next. Let's assume he's following the same MO. He targets vulnerable women and he has used his line of work to get into the buildings and to alleviate suspicion, which means he is probably in his coveralls. Not to mention trailing around with a cute little dog. Remember Ted Bundy was superb at allaying suspicion. A supposedly broken arm, and if I remember correctly, he also used a dog once."

I fished in my briefcase and took out the precious list from Reliable Cleaning Services. "He's targeted two buildings where he was working previously as a temp. Let's see." I scanned the list. "He worked for a couple of days over on John Street at a home for the mentally handicapped. That was in September." I stuffed the last piece of donut into my mouth. "Let's go and check it out. There are five other places that house seniors. Some of them have underground parking, which may be where he's put his van and why we can't find it."

Activity was better than sitting around worrying, and although I didn't hold out much hope I could feel my pulse beating faster.

Our first two stops yielded us nothing. I was beginning to wonder if Torres had done a flit on us. We checked back constantly with the officer who was stationed outside the apartment building but he hadn't shown up there.

Finally, we pulled up in front of the Oak Tree Residence. A discreet sign on the front lawn announced what it was but the house itself was one of the grand old mansions left over from a time when Orillia was a town of rich merchants who wanted the world to know how successful they were. At a guess it would house about twenty people. Not the best place for somebody to move around unnoticed the way Torres had been able to in the more institutional seniors' residences.

"Let's check out the back first," I said to Ed.

We left the car and walked around the building, which at the moment was ablaze with light. I could see into most of the rooms where it seemed the residents, some of them in wheelchairs, were sitting in front of television sets. Some were alone, others with a minder beside them. In a large dining room downstairs, two women in white aprons were setting the tables for dinner.

At the rear of the building was a small paved yard and in the far corner was an overhang of evergreens, which created a deep pool of shadow. The single light on the building didn't extend this far but I could just make out the shape of a van, colour indistinguishable in the gloom. I touched Ed's arm and whispered.

"We've got him. That's his van."

"Do you think he's in there? I can't see a damn thing."

Even as he said that, I detected a slight movement from the front seat.

"He's there all right."

Ed pulled out his cellphone. "I'll get back up."

Torres must have noticed us because I heard the car engine growl into life. It was an old enough model that the lights didn't come on automatically and all I saw was a dark shape suddenly hurtling toward us. There wasn't really anywhere to go. The house was on one side of us, the fence on the other. Ed leaped one way and I the other and the van raced past, missing us by inches. I could see Torres, and sitting up beside him, gazing curiously out of the window, was his dog, Lily. The van made the turn onto the driveway, with tires squealing like some Hollywood chase scene.

He would have got away but he'd misjudged his speed and the sharpness of the turn. The van swayed, stood up on two tires, and skidded into the side of the house. Torres threw open the door and jumped out. Ed and I were both scrambling; an adrenaline rush leaves you exhausted within minutes but we both ran like hell toward him. Neither of us was armed but Ed has a good voice and he bellowed.

"Stop. We're police. Stop right now."

Torres turned around stumbled and then sat down ignominiously in the driveway, his hands raised.

"Don't hurt me. Please don't hurt me."

Panting, Ed stood over him.

"One move from you, you fucker, and I'll kick your balls in."

Under oath, I would never admit I heard that, but in truth he said it for me. Within minutes we heard the wail of cruisers and uniformed officers poured out of their cars. Torres was safely handcuffed, read his rights, and taken off to one of the cars. As he walked away, Ed called out. "Officer Johnson, will you tell the prisoner to zip up his fly. It's come undone."

So that's what he was doing. I'd suspected as much.

EPILOGUE

We were able to get a search warrant immediately and I accompanied Ed and the forensic officers to Torres's apartment. Mrs. Pereira was hysterical and even though we had taken the precaution of bringing along her parish priest, she did everything she could to physically prevent us entering Torres's room. Finally, Ed was forced to have her restrained and removed temporarily from the premises. Torres didn't own a computer but I wasn't the least surprised to find dozens of porn magazines stashed under his bed. I've yet to see a case of rape where the rapist hadn't fed on a steady diet of pornography. He'd also made copies of all his "correspondence," which was extensive. They were in fact neatly pasted into a scrapbook. He was proud of them. Deidre was only one of the recipients. The other letters were to people in the news who in some way had drawn his ire, mostly by breaking some moral code. The note he'd put in my mailbox was something of an anomaly, but I'd bet he got off on thinking he was inducing fear. The room was small and stuffy but the feeling of breathing in foul air was more psychological than physical.

Finally, Ed, me, a legal aid lawyer who couldn't hide her dislike for her client, and Torres all came together in the interview room at the police station. Torres made our job easy. After a brief denial — "I was just walking Lily" — he collapsed and made a complete confession. I wish I could say it was because he was seized by conscience but I can't. He was full of the rationalizations and self-centredness that was so characteristic of men like him. He told us he made a habit of parking somewhere outside of places where he might be able to see handicapped people or elderly people. And yes, he admitted he did masturbate in his van while he watched. Yes, he had taken it further on several occasions, taking advantage of his job as super to gain access to the buildings. He swore he didn't intend to hurt anybody, and according to him, he was gentle with all the women. There were several more that we didn't know about, including two young residents at the Huronia Institute, both of whom were confined to wheelchairs. They hadn't reported him.

I asked him about the sexual assault on Doris Bryant and he answered eagerly. After all he'd had nobody to share his experience with before this. Although he wept every so often, I thought it was pity for himself only. Rather like Sigmund Forgach, he was initially concerned about his mother and what she would say.

"Will she have to be told what the charges are?" he asked.

I stifled back a sarcastic retort. "We could just pretend you haven't paid Lily's dog licence, if you like."

All of this outpouring had taken about two hours. We took a break, then returned. Torres's counsel met my eyes as we went in. She was too professional to say anything but it was clear from her expression what her feelings were. She would have been only too happy to get a different brief.

He was across from me, his arms on the table, hands clasped as if in prayer.

"Why don't you tell us in your own words what happened on Tuesday night?"

His eyes welled up with tears and mucus ran from his nose. He wiped it away with the back of his hand. "I didn't intend to hurt her. I was just driving around when I saw her walking away from the park. It was a miserable night so I thought she'd appreciate a lift. To tell the truth, I didn't notice it was Deidre at first. I just thought ... I just thought she was another young girl who should have been at home. She recognized me and Lily and got in no problem. It was then that I realized who she was. She was the one who had deliberately made her child deaf to suit her whim."

At this point, Torres looked angry. He became lost in his thoughts for a few minutes. I didn't hurry him. Then he went on.

"I drove her in the direction of the Narrows away from the town centre. I don't know why exactly, I thought I'd try to talk to her. Get her to see how wrong she'd been. It was impossible. She didn't understand what I was saying and when she saw we weren't going to her house, she became alarmed and wanted me to let her out ... I had to hold her in the car or she would have jumped out. She struggled and she actually hit me ... I don't really remember what happened after that. All I wanted to do was talk to her and she was fighting like a wildcat ... Her scarf got sort of caught in the seat belt and she started to choke ... Before I could do anything to stop it, she died. Right before my eyes..."

A long pause now. Given what I'd seen of the scarf, so tight it was biting into Deidre's neck, I didn't believe him for a minute that the strangulation was an accident.

"What happened then?" I prompted him.

"I panicked, I suppose. I thought if I put her in the lake I'd be able to get far away from the scene. Maybe it would look like suicide. So I drove back to the park, filled her pockets with stones, and put her in the water. Then I went home."

"You came back in the morning?"

"I couldn't help myself. I wanted to know what was happening. I didn't expect to see you there and her father. Poor man, she's brought him a lot of grief." He looked at me from underneath his eyelids. "I tried to help, didn't I? "

His tone was "I was a good boy, wasn't I?"

I didn't answer.

That was it. He was charged and remanded over until magistrate's court the following day.

The following week was hectic. I told Leo about Torres's confession and he looked stricken. "A few more minutes and he might have missed her." Then he rubbed at his arms as if they were covered in mire. "And to think I actually had that man's coat on my body."

I took Chelsea to visit Joy and she was wonderful with her. We went to a park and they ran around and played on the slide till their noses were getting red with the cold. Nora had told Joy as best as she could about her mother's death. She herself had agreed to stay on at the house for the foreseeable future and I thought Joy was as settled as she could be. Loretta had to fly out to the east coast but Leo was visiting every day and getting to know his grandchild.

Ahmed moved out.

Paula's biopsy came back positive and we're getting ready to deal with the onslaught of chemotherapy treatment.

On Friday, Gill phoned me just as I was reading over the statements of the kids involved in the drug bust.

"Give me your opinion first then I'll tell you what has happened."

"Is this a trick question? Is my reputation on the line?"

"Yes."

"Here goes then. I think that the girl, Janet, is telling the truth about what happened, as are the other two lads. But I'd say Angus definitely has something to hide. He's the one I'd lean on."

"Angus, huh?"

"Oh come on Gill, out with it. Am I right or not?"

He laughed. "Absolutely right. On all counts. And you did that with your coloured pencils?"

"Cut it out."

"Right then. What has happened is that Angus Neil had made a clean breast of it. He was devastated about what happened to Janet, who is recovering nicely by the way. He confessed he has been dealing in cannabis for some time. He has a job at the grocery store and every two weeks, a boat comes in from the mainland. He unloads the groceries and transports them to the shop. Get this. In a box of Cadbury Tray chocolate that is marked for him, he will find his weed, all ground up and ready to go. It's in a false bottom apparently. He just declares the box to be damaged and nobody questions it. Then he had a system worked out with the other boys to put their dope in a hollow tree on the school playing field. They put in their money then later on pick up the dope.

"Angus also said he was the one trying to seduce Janet and she didn't want to."

"Wow, you didn't need me at all, did you? Never mind about my intensive study of statement analysis. All we need is a kid with a conscience."

"I suppose so."

"I'm definitely thinking of relocating to the Hebrides."

"Sounds good to me."

Unfortunately, Gill was called away at that point and we had to hang up. I sat staring at the phone for a while longer. It was a pipe dream but I let myself fantasize about a place where people lived by their principles, had an almost non-existent crime rate, magnificent landscapes, the sea, not enough daylight, Inspector Gordon Gillies...